COLLECTED
WORKS

ADVENTURES INTO THE
UNKNOWN!

VOLUME TWO

August/September 1949 to
April/May 1950
Issues 6 - 10

Foreword
Peter Crowther

Collected Works
ADVENTURES INTO THE UNKNOWN
Volume Two

FIRST EDITION
MAY 2012

Bookshop ISBN 978-1-84863-329-2
Slipcase ISBN 978-1-84863-330-8

Published by
PS Artbooks Ltd.
www.psartbooks.co.uk

A subsidary of PS Publishing Ltd.
www.pspublishing.co.uk
award-winning, UK-based, independent publisher of SF, fantasy, horror, crime & more...

Copyright © PS Artbooks 2012

Originally published in magazine form by ACG Best Syndicated Features, Inc.

Foreword © Peter Crowther 2012

Printed in China

design communique

E. Nelson Bridwell:
A Foreword of sorts to the second volume
of ACG's Adventures into the Unknown

Let's talk about Nelson Bridwell. (I'll tell you why we should do in just a few minutes.)

Edward Nelson Bridwell (1931–1987) was a writer for **Mad** magazine and various comic books published by DC. One of the writers for the **Batman** comic strip and **Super Friends**, he also wrote **The Inferior Five**, among other comics, plus—according to his entry in Wikipedia—he was noted for possessing an encyclopedic knowledge of various comics-related trivia, as well as of **The Bible** and Shakespeare's plays.

Bridwell's early childhood interest in mythology and folklore stayed with him throughout his professional life and permeated much of his work. He credited his fame to his third grade teacher, Ryan Samuel, for interesting him in comics. Bridwell "was one of the first 'comics fans' hired in the industry after the long, bleak 1950's," Although his first published work consisted of text pages in comics published by ACG in the late 1940s, he had since he "was still a kid" created various characters who would later evolve into those used in comics such as *The Inferior Five*.

In 1962, while still residing in Oklahoma City, Bridwell submitted to the **Magazine of Fantasy & Science Fiction** his first idea for a Feghoot adventure, a specific type of shaggy dog story that ends in a humorous and unexpected play on words. His story was promptly accepted by the feature's pseudonymous author, Grendel Briarton (Reginald Bretnor) and shortly followed by yet another submission from Bridwell which was also accepted ("Dr. Jacqueline Missed

The Magazine of Fantasy and Science Fiction from May and July 1962, each containing one of Brldwell's shaggy dog shorts.

Her Hide" and "Nude Rally Tea Pact", respectively). Besides **F&SF**, both stories would appear in the various Feghoot anthologies to follow.

After writing a few stories for **Mad** and for **Katy Keene**, Bridwell began working for DC Comics in 1964 as an assistant (to editor Mort Weisinger) on the **Superman** titles, eventually becoming an editor himself (**Lois Lane**, and later **Superman Family**). As it happens, our very own Roy Thomas was Nelson's (temporary, as it turned out) replacement in late June of 1965.

Nelson's time with DC was not without its downside (watch out for a more detailed article in a future issue of **Alter Ego**), though Weisinger's tutelage provided some valuable lessons and Bridwell used them to help the company produce three 1970s anthologies — **Superman from the Thirties to the Seventies** (1971), **Batman from the Thities to the Seventies** (1971), and **Shazam from the Forties to the Seventies** (1977) — and he wrote for the comic book series based on one of the best rated TV shows on Saturday morning, **Super Friends**. In addition, he ably put together many of Weisinger's influential **Superman Annuals** and other DC reprint comics— including the regularly-published version of **Secret Origins**— which is doubtless what led to the hardcover books.

Concurrent with his duties for DC, Bridwell was submitting material as a freelancer to **Mad**, some of which was illustrated by Joe Orlando, who would later be suggested by Bridwell as artist for **The Inferior Five**.

Recalling an early interest in comic book continuity, Bridwell remembered getting a bit perturbed at times when he was a kid by having things that didn't fit, particularly over the wide range of Martian races in evidence in many of DC's titles. Bridwell was also an early advocate of the theory that the Marvel and DC characters exist in the same universe, pushing for early inter-company crossovers such as **Superman vs. the Amazing Spider-Man**.

Bridwell's love and knowledge of old comics led to his becoming editor on numerous reprint books, including digests, giant-size comics, and hardcover anthologies. He also worked as assistant editor to Julius Schwartz, keeping track of continuity between the numerous **Superman** titles published. Part of his job was to manage the letter columns for all the Superman titles, and in response to constant reader questions, Bridwell standardized the Kryptonian language and alphabet. Dubbed Kryptonese, Bridwell established the 118-character alphabet, which was used by DC until John Byrne's 1986 reboot of the Superman universe.

In Alan Moore's **Watchmen** series, Moore named Captain Metropolis 'Nelson Gardner' as a tribute to Bridwell and Gardner Fox (the latter responsible for what were, in my opinion, hundreds of the very best stories for DC).

Not a bad lifetime achievement, but all great journeys start with but a single step. Nelson's came in late 1949 when he wrote a fan letter to **Adventures Into The Unknown**'s 'Let's Talk It Over' letters column and having it appear in issue #8 (you can read it on page 138). That faltering first step led in issue # 9 to Nelson's one-page text tale 'The Gray One' appearing as **AITU**'s third-prize contest-winning story (page 200). Reading it now, of course, it's kind of difficult to replicate the emotional slam! these text-pages—when they were well-written —delivered, and this one is a fine example of their occasional success.

Nelson Bridwell

Mort Weisinger & DC proofreader Gerda Gattel (1975)

Katy Keene - Pin-up Parade #20

Superman Annual #1 Advert

Showcase Inferior Five #62

Julius Schwartz

Aler Ego #61

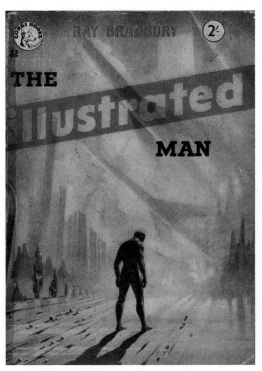

The Illustrated Man

I guess reading these things as a kid, which I did with great gusto, packs a huge amount of inspiration: they certainly inspired me to try my own power-punch-ending shorties . . . grimace-making examples of which litter my English Language school exercise books from the late 1950s and early 1960s. These same exercise books contain several red-penned notes from my Leeds Grammar School English tutor (Alan Jones, a chubby and almost Dickensian man whose florid countenance led to his being referred to as 'Plum') telling me time and again that a short story is NOT an essay. "Please do as instructed."

But Plum must have seen something in the 11- or 12-year-old Peter Crowther, because at one of the school's occasional end-of-day book sales, he called me across to him in a booming voice, waving a paperback majesterially, his black gown fluttering like Batman's cape. "Crowther," he announced, "you like space stories, do you not?" When I nodded, with a sheepish "Yes, sir," he thrust the book towards me and deposited it in my hand. "Then you should read this." He turned quickly, paid the requisite few pennies to the boy manning the stall, and marched off.

The book was **The Illustrated Man** by Ray Bradbury, and it started me on a rollercoaster love affair with Bradbury's work that continues to this day, with my being invited to provide an Afterword for Gauntlet's re-issue of **Something Wicked This Way Comes** and, latterly, with PS editions of many of his finest books.

So if you're a kid—*you*, the person reading this piece before flicking through all the wonderful gore-filled four-color adventures the book contains—spare a moment to read the text pages. They're often clunky, frequently unexciting and occasionally downright dire . . . but that's fine. It's fine because you'll say to yourself, I could have done better myself! In which case, go do it. And while you're doing it, spare a kindly thought for Nelson Bridwell and his long-ago teacher, Ryan Samuel, for ACG mainstay Richard Hughes and even for dear Plum Jones, a now surely ancient retired (if, indeed, he's still with us at all) British schoolmaster . . . not to mention other stalwarts whose own journeys started in the letter columns (Paul Gambaccini, Paul Levitz, Roy Thomas and many more).

Ah, it's a good life, you know . . .

See you in the funny pages!

Peter Crowther

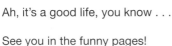

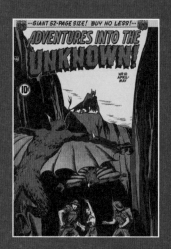

Adventures into the Unknown
August/September 1949 - Issue #6

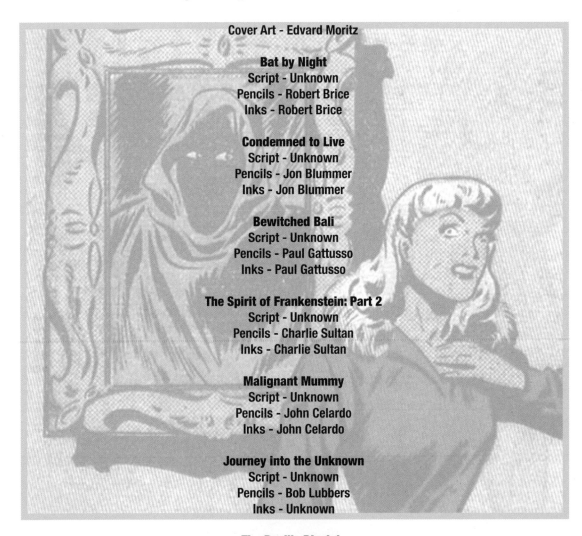

Cover Art - Edvard Moritz

Bat by Night
Script - Unknown
Pencils - Robert Brice
Inks - Robert Brice

Condemned to Live
Script - Unknown
Pencils - Jon Blummer
Inks - Jon Blummer

Bewitched Bali
Script - Unknown
Pencils - Paul Gattusso
Inks - Paul Gattusso

The Spirit of Frankenstein: Part 2
Script - Unknown
Pencils - Charlie Sultan
Inks - Charlie Sultan

Malignant Mummy
Script - Unknown
Pencils - John Celardo
Inks - John Celardo

Journey into the Unknown
Script - Unknown
Pencils - Bob Lubbers
Inks - Unknown

The Devil's Disciple
Script - Unknown
Pencils - R. S. Pious
Inks - R. S. Pious

Now YOU CAN HAVE
DARING *Newest Look* BEAUTY
WITH ALL-IN-ONE
TRIOLETTE

It's All These
{ 1-uplift bra
2-waist nipper
3-garter belt

For That Thrilling NEW LOOK

Put your figure in *style*! Look feminine, curvaceous—*instantly*—with new marvelous TRIOLETTE. It's taken New York by storm ...it's all the rage with smart girls...because it rounds you enticingly in the *right* places with never a bulge in the wrong ones! Lightly but cleverly boned—to pull in your waist, give fullness to hips, lift bust to alluring firm contours. No matter *what* shape bosom you have! Magical, you'll agree...and this one little garment does it all! In luxury rayon satin—with revealing lace inserts at bust, dainty net edging at top and bottom. Comfortable! Lastex insert, adjustable hook-and-eye back fastening, 4 adjustable garters. Bra straps included, adjustable, easy to attach. New TRIOLETTE costs little more then bra alone! We know you'll be thrilled—your money back if not 100% pleased with your glamorous "New Look" figure. A cup, 32 to 36. B cup, (larger) 32 to 38. Blue white or nude.

Have **Tiny Waist —Full Bosom FIGURE**

$595
• BLUE
• WHITE
• NUDE

BE SMARTLY STRAPLESS OR WEAR STRAPS ALSO INCLUDED

Costs so little

➤ *MAIL COUPON NOW!*

SEND ON 10-DAY APPROVAL

**WILCO CO., Dept. 605-H
45 East 17th St., New York**
Rush your new TRIOLETTE for $5.95. CUP_____ SIZE_____
☐ Send C.O.D. I will pay postage. ☐ I enclose $5.95. You pay postage

1st Color Choice	2nd Color Choice

Name_____
Address_____
City, Zone, State_____
I understand if not delighted with TRIOLETTE I can return in 10 days for full purchase price refund.

ADVENTURES INTO THE UNKNOWN, published bi-monthly and copyright, 1949, by B. & I. Publishing Co., Inc., 45 West 45th Street, New York 19, N. Y. Richard E. Hughes, Editor; Frederick H. Iger, Business Manager. Subscription (12 issues), $1.20; single copies $.10; foreign postage extra. Reentered as second-class matter December 2, 1948 at the Post Office at New York, N. Y., under the Act of March 3, 1879. No. 6, August-September, 1949. Printed in U. S. A.

BAT By Night

One of the countless legends which throng from the *UNKNOWN* is that of the *VAMPIRE*--an unearthly creature which preys upon mortals! True, it is only a superstition, whispered when midnight falls-- but let's fancy, for a moment, that such things *COULD* exist! Our story takes us to Europe-- where a thrilling tale unfolds---

THE SORBONNE, PARIS. PROFESSOR GOLLET, RENOWNED AUTHORITY ON THE *UNKNOWN*, ADDRESSES HIS CLASS --

--AND THIS REMOTE, WILD SECTOR, AMIDST THE GLOOMY PEAKS OF THE PYRENEES, HOLDS ANCIENT WONDERS YOU YOUNGSTERS HAVE NEVER DREAMED OF!

THE SUBJECT HELD A STRANGE INTEREST FOR ONE PUPIL, YOUNG GEORGE TELLIER --

I HEAR YOU'RE LEAVING US, GEORGE, AND I'M SORRY! ANYTHING WRONG?

NOT REALLY! IT'S JUST THAT I'VE INHERITED AN OLD CASTLE -- IN THE *PYRENEES*, STRANGELY ENOUGH -- AND I'VE GOT TO GO THERE TO TAKE OVER! IT'S CALLED THE *CHATEAU OF BYRN* -- EVER HEARD OF IT?

HAVE I! IT'S A FASCINATING OLD PLACE -- IN A REGION KNOWN FOR ITS SUPER-NATURAL PHENOMENA! YOU'RE A LUCKY CHAP!

MAYBE -- BUT I'LL BE LONESOME THERE! SAY, IF IT'S *THAT* INTERESTING TO YOU, HOW'S ABOUT COMING ALONG FOR A *VISIT*?

WHAT WONDER IS THIS, THAT COULD SURVIVE A 500-FOOT DROP? WHAT DO *YOU* THINK, READER?

SHE'S -- BEAUTIFUL! BUT THOSE NAILS -- SO STRANGELY LONG ---

LET'S NOT LOSE ANY TIME! WE MUST GET HER TO THE CHATEAU!

YES -- IT WOULD BE TRAGIC IF SHE DIED *NOW!* -- WONDER WHO SHE IS? I'VE NEVER SEEN HER IN THESE PARTS!

HOURS LATER -- AS THE UNKNOWN VISITOR REGAINS CONSCIOUSNESS ---

YOU -- YOU SAVED MY LIFE, AND I'M THANKFUL! I'M THE BARONESS -- JEANNE CALLEAU --

AND I'M GEORGE TELLIER! I NOTICED A CALLEAU CASTLE ON THE MAP SOME DISTANCE AWAY -- YOU MUST BE FROM *THERE!*

AH, MADAMOISELLE, IT WAS OUR HAPPINESS -- RESCUING SUCH A *BEAUTIFUL* YOUNG LADY!

NEVER MIND THOSE PERSONAL REMARKS NOW, BRIOT! BETTER SEE WHAT'S KEEPING THE DOCTOR!

BUT MR. TELLIER -- THERE'S NO WOMAN IN THE WORLD WHO DOESN'T LOVE TO HEAR THAT SHE'S BEAUTIFUL!

AND AFTER THE DOCTOR'S EXAMINATION ---

IT'S THE STRANGEST CASE IN MY CAREER! NEITHER EXTERNAL NOR INTERNAL INJURIES -- AND AFTER A FALL LIKE *THAT!*

NEVERTHELESS, THERE MUST BE SOME SHOCK -- AND I INSIST ON HER STAYING HERE UNTIL SHE'S COMPLETELY RECOVERED!

THEN CAME HAPPY DAYS, DURING WHICH GEORGE FELT HIMSELF DRAWN CLOSER AND CLOSER TOWARDS JEANNE! FINALLY, HER STRENGTH ENTIRELY REGAINED --

YOU'VE BEEN WONDERFUL TO ME -- BUT NOW IT'S TIME FOR ME TO GO BACK HOME! I'LL RIDE BACK TONIGHT! FATHER PROBABLY THINKS I'VE BEEN VISITING A GIRL FRIEND --

I HATE TO SEE YOU GO! I'LL HAVE *TWO* HORSES SADDLED, AND RIDE WITH YOU!

ER -- MAYBE YOU'D BETTER NOT, GEORGE! YOU SEE, I -- WELL, MY FATHER'S NEVER BEEN VERY FRIENDLY WITH YOUR FAMILY! -- YOU UNDERSTAND, DON'T YOU?

THAT'S TOO BAD ... BUT I'M NOT GOING TO LET YOU RIDE THROUGH THESE DARK MOUNTAINS ALONE! ONE OF MY SERVANTS MUST ACCOMPANY YOU -- I INSIST!

AND SO JEANNE DEPARTED, ACCOMPANIED BY A SERVANT! BUT, AN HOUR LATER ---

JEANNE -- YOU'RE BACK! WHY ARE YOU LOOKING LIKE THAT -- WHAT'S WRONG?

SOMETHING -- TERRIBLE HAS HAPPENED! YOUR SERVANT -- HE'S BEEN KILLED!

I -- I CAN HARDLY FIND WORDS FOR IT -- BUT JUST AS WE APPROACHED CALLEAU CASTLE -- A MONSTROUS BAT CAME FLYING TOWARD US!...

"OH, HE TRIED TO PROTECT ME -- HE TRIED -- BUT IT WAS NO USE! THE THING WAS UPON HIM IN A MOMENT! LIKE A COWARD, I TURNED AND RAN, BUT BY THAT TIME -- IT WAS ALL UP WITH HIM!"

MOMENTS LATER ---

IT'S A RIDICULOUS STORY, PROFESSOR ... OBVIOUSLY, SHE MUST STILL BE SUFFERING FROM SHOCK FROM THAT FALL! SHE'S ASLEEP NOW -- I GAVE HER A SEDATIVE!

MAYBE -- MAYBE HER STORY ISN'T RIDICULOUS, GEORGE! I'D SUGGEST YOU SEND OUT A PARTY TO CHECK ON WHAT REALLY HAPPENED TO THAT SERVANT OF YOURS!

THE PARTY WAS SENT OUT -- AND IT RETURNED, PALE AND HORROR-STRICKEN!

WE -- WE FOUND HIM, SIR! HE WAS -- DEAD! IT -- IT WAS AS IF SOME WILD BEAST --

SHAKEN BY HER EXPERIENCE, JEANNE STAYED ON AT THE CHATEAU OF BYRN, AND GEORGE'S FEELING FOR HER GREW UNTIL --

I -- I'VE GOT TO TELL YOU, JEANNE -- YOU'RE THE GIRL I'VE BEEN WAITING FOR! I CAN'T DO WITHOUT YOU, DARLING!

AND I -- LOVE YOU TOO --

BUT THERE'S ONE THING I MUST TELL YOU, GEORGE! COULD YOU DO SOMETHING ABOUT BRIOT, YOUR MAJOR-DOMO? HE SEEMS IN LOVE WITH ME, TOO, AND HIS JEALOUSY IS BEGINNING TO BOTHER ME!

YOU MEAN HE'S DARED TO -- DON'T WORRY, DEAR! I'LL SEE THAT HE DOESN'T TROUBLE YOU ANY FURTHER!

BUT BRIOT SHOWED AN UNEXPECTED REBELLION!

MAYBE I DO WORK FOR YOU, M'SIEU, BUT I'M STILL A MAN -- AND I LOVE HER! IT'S YOU THAT'S JEALOUS -- BECAUSE YOU KNOW JEANNE CARES FOR ME!

FOR THE LAST TIME, BRIOT, I'M WARNING YOU -- LEAVE THAT GIRL ALONE OR YOU'RE FIRED!

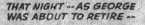

THAT NIGHT -- AS GEORGE WAS ABOUT TO RETIRE --

WHAT THE --! AM I AWAKE, OR IS THIS A BAD DREAM? THAT LOOKS LIKE JEANNE -- IN BRIOT'S ARMS!

NO, IT COULDN'T BE -- IT COULDN'T BE! IT MUST BE SOME OTHER GIRL! BETTER TAKE THIS GUN ALONG, THOUGH -- BRIOT CAN BE DANGEROUS!

ON THE TERRACE BELOW -- AN AWFUL DISCOVERY!

HOLY SMOKE! IT'S BRIOT -- DEAD -- WITH THE MARKS OF A WILD BEAST ON HIM!

5

NEXT MOMENT, A LOOMING SHADOW -- THE BEATING OF GREAT WINGS --

IT -- IT'S A GIGANTIC BAT!

BANG!

BANG!

WHAT IS IT? THOSE SHOTS -- WHAT HAPPENED, GEORGE?

YOU -- YOU WON'T BELIEVE THIS, PROFESSOR GOLLET -- BUT A GIANT BAT HAS DONE FOR BRIOT! I -- I THINK I MAY HAVE WOUNDED THE CREATURE!

HMMMM ... YOU MAY HAVE AT THAT, BUT ONLY SLIGHTLY! HERE'S A PIECE OF ONE OF ITS TALONS THAT YOU SHOT OFF!

TOO BAD! I WAS HOPING I'D DONE MORE DAMAGE! WE -- WE MUST GET THAT CREATURE, BEFORE ---

YOU'RE RIGHT! TELL ME, DID YOU NOTICE IN WHAT DIRECTION IT HEADED!

WELL, LET'S SEE -- GREAT HEAVENS -- IT FLUTTERED TOWARD JEANNE'S ROOM! -- THAT SCREAM! IT MUST HAVE HER NOW!

OH-HHH! HELP!

DON'T STAND THERE AS IF YOU'RE PARALYZED, MAN -- COME ON! THERE MAY BE A CHANCE OF SAVING HER YET!

6

JEANNE -- THANK GOSH YOU'RE STILL ALIVE! THAT BAT -- DID IT --?

I WOKE UP TO FIND IT HOVERING OVER ME! IT -- IT WAS TERRIBLE!

I--I'LL NEVER FORGET THE SIZE OF IT..ITS FEROCITY! IT LUNGED AT ME, AND IT WAS THEN I SCREAMED! I TRIED TO FIGHT AGAINST IT, BUT ITS STRENGTH WAS AWFUL! IF IT HADN'T HEARD YOUR FOOTSTEPS AND HEADED OUT THE WINDOW. I'D HAVE BEEN ---

THERE, THERE -- DON'T CRY, JEANNE DARLING! NOTHING'S GOING TO HAPPEN TO YOU AS LONG AS I'M WITH YOU!

I'VE SEEN ONE THING -- AND I'M BEGINNING TO GET A CLUE TO THIS WHOLE MYSTERIOUS AFFAIR!

HOPE SHE GETS SOME SLEEP NOW -- I MUST HAVE BEEN CRAZY TO THINK THAT IT WAS SHE I SAW WITH BRIOT! -- YOU SAY YOU WANT US TO GO SOME-WHERE NOW, PROFESSOR? WHERE?

TO CALLEAU CASTLE! I THINK I'VE GOT AN IMPORTANT LEAD THAT MAY HELP US TRACK DOWN THAT VAMPIRE!

OVER THE MILES THROUGH THE EERIE, MOONLIT MOUNTAINS-- TO THE SITE ON THE MAP MARKED "CALLEAU CASTLE"! AND THERE -- A STUNNING SURPRISE!

HOLY SMOKE IS THAT THE CASTLE? BUT -- BUT IT'S NOTHING BUT AN ANCIENT RUIN!

UH -- HUH -- UNINHABITED FOR CENTURIES! THAT'S WHAT I WAS AFRAID OF!

BUT THAT'S IMPOSSIBLE! THIS CAN'T BE ANYBODY'S HOME -- LET ALONE JEANNE'S!

RIGHT! BEGINNING TO GET THE IDEA?

7

AS GEORGE DEPARTS, MYSTIFIED---

LOOK--COMING OUT OF THE CASTLE! IT--IT'S A SWARM OF BATS!

YES--BATS BY NIGHT! AND I'M NOT SURPRISED, EITHER!

OH, COME, PROFESSOR -- YOU AND YOUR AIRS OF STRANGE KNOWLEDGE! THERE MUST BE SOME PERFECTLY NATURAL EXPLANATION FOR ALL THIS! I DON'T KNOW WHY JEANNE DIDN'T TELL ME ABOUT THE CONDITION OF THIS PLACE, BUT SHE MUST HAVE HER REASONS FOR IT!

I'M AFRAID SHE HAS, MY BOY-- GOOD REASONS!

IT WAS THE FIRST ARGUMENT BETWEEN GEORGE AND HIS OLD TEACHER --

PLEASE DON'T QUESTION JEANNE IN ANY WAY, PROFESSOR! I LOVE HER AND WE'RE GOING TO BE MARRIED! I WON'T HEAR OF ANY SUSPICION OF ANY KIND AGAINST HER, AND THAT'S THAT!

WHY, IT'S RIDICULOUS TO THINK THAT JEANNE KNOWS ANYTHING ABOUT ALL THIS! SHE'S JUST A LOVELY GIRL-- THE GIRL I LOVE!

WELL -- I HOPE YOU WON'T LEARN DIFFERENT TO YOUR SORROW!

SLEEP WAS FAR FROM GEORGE AS THE STRANGE AND TERRIBLE EVENTS HE HAD PASSED THROUGH CROWDED HIS MIND! THEN SUDDENLY--THE CREAKING OF A DOOR--

JEANNE! WHAT ON EARTH ---

I -- I OVERHEARD YOUR CONVERSATION WITH PROFESSOR GOLLET IN THE CORRIDOR OUTSIDE MY ROOM -- AND IT'S BEEN TORTURING ME!

OH GEORGE I COULDN'T STAND IT IF YOU THOUGHT THAT --

UH-HUH! IT'S ENOUGH THAT I HAD TO LISTEN TO GOLLET, WITHOUT ANY MORE SUCH NONSENSE FROM YOU! REMEMBER, DARLING -- I LOVE YOU!

8

HERE'S -- THE MIRROR ROOM -- BUT WHAT CAN HAPPEN *HERE*? HOW CAN *THAT* STOP THE CREATURE?

JUST WAIT -- *AND SEE!*

THE GLINTING MIRRORS REFLECT THE BAT A THOUSANDFOLD! FOR A MOMENT IT PAUSES, HOVERING UNCERTAINLY, AND THEN --

EEEEEEEE!

ONCE AGAIN A SUBTLE CHANGE -- AND WHAT HAD A MOMENT AGO BEEN A BAT IS NOW --

SHE'S -- *DEAD!*

YES ... MY STUDIES OF THE SUPERNATURAL TAUGHT ME THAT THERE'S ONLY *ONE* THING A VAMPIRE CAN'T WITHSTAND -- *MIRRORS!*

YOU'VE SAVED ME FROM A TERRIBLE FATE, PROFESSOR GOLLET! BUT JEANNE ---

TRY NOT TO THINK ABOUT HER, MY BOY! SHE CAME OUT OF THE *UNKNOWN* -- AND TO THE *UNKNOWN* SHE HAS RETURNED!

The End 10

22

CONDEMNED-- to LIVE!

Many are the strange tales which come to us from out of **THE UNKNOWN**-- but none stranger than the weird story of **Juan Delbourgo!**

For here was a man who spanned the centuries-- who walked the earth for 400 years!

Countless the evil-doers who have been sentenced to death, but here's one who was --

"CONDEMNED-- TO LIVE!"

THE OFFICE OF PROFESSOR KENDALL, DIRECTOR OF THE OCCULT INSTITUTE --

THERE OUGHT TO BE A STORY OUT OF THE FORTY YEARS YOU'VE BEEN DIRECTOR OF A PLACE LIKE THIS! HAS ANYTHING **REALLY** STRANGE EVER HAPPENED TO YOU HERE -- ANYTHING THAT WOULD MAKE A GOOD NEWSPAPER YARN?

WELL, THERE'VE BEEN MANY THINGS-- BUT OUT OF ALL OF THEM, THERE'S ONLY **ONE** WHICH I CAN NEVER FORGET! PRETTY UNBELIEVABLE, TOO, BUT SINCE YOU ASKED FOR IT- **HERE GOES!**

"IT ALL BEGAN TWENTY YEARS AGO, IN THIS VERY SPOT! I WAS WORKING LATE, AND THE INSTITUTE WAS LOCKED FOR THE NIGHT, WHEN SUDDENLY ---"

WHO ARE **YOU** -- AND HOW'D YOU GET IN HERE WITH ALL THE DOORS LOCKED?

THE NAME'S **JUAN DELBOURGO**, PROFESSOR KENDALL! AND I'VE GOT WAYS OF GETTING INTO PLACES -- **STRANGE WAYS!**

"THERE WAS SOMETHING ABOUT HIM -- SOMETHING IN HIS DARK AND AGELESS EYES -- WHICH WAS ODD AND DISTURBING! AS A COLD FEAR CLUTCHED AT MY HEART--"

YOU -- YOU'VE GOT NO BUSINESS HERE! *GET OUT!*

YOU DEAL WITH PSYCHIC PHENOMENA, SIR -- YOU MIGHT *WANT* TO SEE ME! YOU SEE, I'M A *DEAD MAN!*

YOU'RE -- *CRAZY!* I -- I WON'T LISTEN TO ANOTHER WORD!

YOU FORCE ME TO TAKE EXTREME MEASURES TO PROVE MY POINT! THIS OLD PISTOL, FOR INSTANCE---

LOOK OUT-- THAT THING'S *LOADED!* DON'T---

BANG!

NO HEART BEAT OR PULSE! HE'S-- *DEAD!*

OPERATOR, GET ME THE POLICE DEPAR--- *WHAT?*

BETTER NOT BE IN SUCH A HURRY TO CALL THE POLICE, PROFESSOR -- I DIDN'T KILL MYSELF! YOU SEE -- *YOU CAN'T KILL A DEAD MAN!*

THERE -- THERE'S GOT TO BE A *SCIENTIFIC* EXPLANATION! I'VE GOT IT -- THE PISTOL MUST HAVE CONTAINED JUST POWDER, AND NO BULLET!

STILL HARD TO CONVINCE, EH? *THIS* SHOULD DO IT-- THE BLADE'S STILL KEEN!

YOU -- YOU'RE NOT GOING TO HARM ME -- JUST BECAUSE I WON'T BELIEVE AN IMPOSSIBLE STORY?

HARDLY! I'M JUST GOING TO SHOW YOU THAT THE *IMPOSSIBLE* IS *TRUE!*

2

②

GREAT HEAVENS! YOU'VE DRAWN IT THROUGH YOUR FLESH -- AND -- AND YOU'RE NOT BLEEDING!

"THEN IT WAS THAT CONVICTION CAME-- AND WITH IT, TERROR! SOMETHING INSIDE ME SNAPPED -- I HAD TO GET AWAY FROM THIS MONSTROUS THING! I FLED TO MY CAR --- "

THANK GOODNESS I'VE MANAGED TO ESCAPE! I'VE GOT TO -- PUT DISTANCE BETWEEN US!

"AS THE CAR RACED ALONG THE LONELY ROAD TOWARDS MY MOUNTAIN HOME --- "

THE WIND'S BEGINNING TO CLEAR MY BRAIN! -- IT COULDN'T HAVE HAPPENED! I'VE BEEN OVERWORKING -- I MUST HAVE IMAGINED ALL THIS!

IMAGINED, PROFESSOR? I WONDER!

DELBOURGO!

"YES, IT WAS DELBOURGO -- AND I COULD SEE NOW THAT THIS WAS NO HUMAN! IN PANIC, I TROD ON THE GAS, TRYING TO SHAKE HIM OFF -- BUT TO NO AVAIL! THEN -- IT HAPPENED!"

LOOK OUT!

CRASH!

DON'T BE AFRAID! I'VE GOT YOU -- AND YOU'RE SAFE!

"I MUST HAVE FAINTED THEN! THE NEXT THING I KNEW, I WAS AT HOME, IN MY OWN STUDY!"

WELL? DO YOU BELIEVE NOW?

YES, DELBOURGO -- I BELIEVE!

3

I'VE DELVED INTO THE *UNKNOWN* FOR YEARS-- AND I WON'T FLEE FROM IT BECAUSE IT'S HAPPENING TO *ME!* I KNOW NOW THAT YOU'RE NOT MORTAL-- BUT YOU SEEM SO VITAL, SO YOUNG!

YOUNG? YOU CAN JUDGE FOR YOURSELF -- AFTER I TELL YOU THAT I WAS BORN IN MADRID IN *1549!*

BUT-- THAT'S *IMPOSSIBLE!* IT WOULD MAKE YOU *400 YEARS OLD!*

IS IT ANY MORE IMPOSSIBLE THAN THE FACT THAT I'M A *DEAD MAN* -- AND YET WALK AND TALK LIKE YOU DO? LET ME TELL YOU MY STORY, PROFESSOR KENDALL!

"I WAS A WEALTHY, WILFUL YOUNG GRANDEE WHO FELL INTO EVIL COMPANY -- WENT FROM BAD TO WORSE! I WAS NO STRANGER TO MURDER -- "

THIS MAKES ALMOST FIFTY PEOPLE THE BLACK-HEARTED DEVIL HAS SLAIN!

"FINALLY I WAS SUMMONED BY THE ONLY MAN I'D EVER CARED FOR -- THE GOOD PADRÉ, FATHER RAMON! MUDDLED BY STRONG DRINK, I WAS ONLY ANGERED BY HIS WORDS!"

YOU MUST BETTER YOUR WAYS, MY SON! YOUR VERY SOUL IS IN DANGER!

NOBODY TALKS TO *ME* LIKE THAT! MEN *FEAR* ME -- *AND YOU MUST, TOO!*

"IMPRISONED AND AWAITING EXECUTION, I RECEIVED A SPECTRAL VISITOR FROM THE GREAT BEYOND-- *THE GHOST OF FATHER RAMON!*"

YOU! -- FORGIVE ME FOR WHAT I'VE DONE! I'M GOING TO PERISH FOR IT -- LET THAT BE MY PUNISHMENT!

IT IS NOT ENOUGH FOR YOUR BLACK-HEARTED SINS! DEATH WILL BRING YOU NO RELIEF FROM THE CRIMES THAT HANG HEAVY ON YOUR CONSCIENCE!

"BUT NEXT MORNING -- "

GO -- AWAY! WANT TO -- SLEEP --

THERE'S LITTLE SLEEP LEFT FOR *YOU* IN THIS WORLD! *WE CHARGE YOU WITH THE MURDER OF FATHER RAMON!*

INSTEAD, YOU MUST WALK THE EARTH THROUGH ETERNITY, KNOWING NEITHER REST NOR PEACE -- UNTIL HATRED IS BANISHED BY *SOMEONE WHO LOVES YOU FOR YOURSELF ALONE!* YOU ARE CONDEMNED-- TO LIVE!

④

THERE'S -- SOMETHING *BEYOND* YOUR STORY THAT YOU'RE NOT TELLING ME! THE CURSED *UNDEAD* MUST ALWAYS COMMIT *NEW* ACTS OF VIOLENCE! HAVE .YOU PICKED *ME* TO ADD TO YOUR BLACK LIST?

PERHAPS --- BECAUSE THE TIME DRAWS NEAR FOR ME TO SEEK ANOTHER VICTIM TO ADD TO MY GUILT! BUT YOU STILL HAVE *ONE CHANCE TO ESCAPE!*

I SELECTED *YOU*, PROFESSOR KENDALL, BECAUSE OF YOUR GREAT KNOWLEDGE OF THE *UNKNOWN* AND ITS RESTLESS SPIRITS! AND EITHER YOU SET YOUR KNOWLEDGE TO WORK, LIFT THE CURSE FROM ME AND SET MY WANDERINGS AT REST, *OR --!*

"FACED WITH A DESPERATE CHOICE, I CALLED ON ALL OF MY OCCULT EXPERIENCE! SPELLS, INCAN- TATIONS, ANCIENT SYMBOLS -- *ALL FAILED!*"

IT -- IT'S NO USE! I'VE TRIED MY BEST, BUT NOTHING WILL PLACE YOUR SPIRIT AT REST!

THEN YOU'LL *PAY THE PENALTY-- WITH YOUR LIFE!*

WHY, DADDY-- WHAT'S GOING *ON* HERE?

OH -- I DIDN'T KNOW YOU HAD A VISITOR! I'LL LEAVE ---

YES, ALICE, YOU'D-- BETTER! THIS IS NO PLACE FOR *YOU!*

PLEASE, PROFESSOR! AREN'T YOU GOING TO *INTRODUCE* US?

YOU -- YOU DON'T KNOW WHAT IT *MEANS* FOR ME TO MEET SOMEONE LIKE *YOU*, MISS KENDALL!

THAT LOOK IN HIS EYE -- I DON'T TRUST IT! I'D BETTER MAKE SURE THAT SHE DOESN'T SEE HIM AGAIN!

"I KNEW THAT HE HAD SPARED ME BECAUSE OF ALICE -- BUT THAT MEANT THAT *SHE* WAS IN DANGER! SO I SENT HER AWAY FOR A MONTH'S VACATION --"

HAVEN'T SEEN HIDE NOR HAIR OF DELBOURGO DURING THE WHOLE TIME ALICE HAS BEEN AWAY! GUESS HE'S GONE OUT OF MY LIFE FOR GOOD, SO THERE'S NOTHING TO WORRY ABOUT ANY LONGER!

TELEGRAM, SIR!

TELEGRAM

X6423 · MV- 2:25-9-30
PROFESSOR OTIS KENDALL
SEVEN KEYS LODGE
ARNVILLE, N.Y.

RETURNING TOMORROW WITH WONDERFUL SURPRISE FOR YOU. ALL MY LOVE.
ALICE

IT'LL BE GOOD TO SEE HER! WONDER WHAT THAT *"SURPRISE"* IS!

⑤

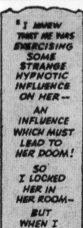

"MEANWHILE --"

JUAN -- I'M HERE!

I WAS EXPECTING YOU, ALICE .. I *KNEW* YOU'D COME! CLOSE THE DOOR -- WE'VE GOT MUCH TO TALK OVER, YOU AND I!

I -- I HAD HIGH HOPES FOR YOU, MY DEAR! BUT IF YOU'VE LISTENED TO YOUR FATHER, THERE'S SOMETHING *ELSE* IN STORE FOR YOU!

BUT -- JUAN! IF I'D LISTENED TO HIM, I WOULDN'T BE HERE NOW, WOULD I?

YOU -- YOU'VE GOTTEN TO MEAN SO MUCH TO ME THAT I THOUGHT I'D *DIE* IF I WERE SEPARATED FROM YOU A MOMENT LONGER!

THEN -- THEN THERE *IS* HOPE FOR ME! LISTEN! -- YOU'VE GOT BUT ONE CHANCE TO LIVE, AND I'VE GOT ONE CHANCE TO FIND PEACE! *YOU'VE GOT TO HEAR MY STORY!*

"WITH THE TALE COMPLETED --- "

-- AND SO, RATHER THAN THE YOUNG MAN YOU THINK ME, I'M A BEING CENTURIES OLD-- *A DEAD MAN, WITH ANCIENT CRIMES BLACK UPON ME!* I'VE LAID MY SOUL BARE TO YOU -- CAN YOU TELL ME YOU LOVE ME *NOW?*

OH-HH!

THAT LOOK IN YOUR EYES -- THE WAY YOU RECOILED, AS IF FROM SOMETHING SHAMEFUL -- IT'S ALL THE ANSWER I NEED! AND THE CURSE IS UPON ME AGAIN -- ONCE MORE I'VE GOT TO --

NO! IF I WAS SHOCKED, IT WAS JUST BY THE TERRIBLE PUNISHMENT YOU'VE UNDERGONE --A PUNISHMENT THAT EVEN YOUR PENITENCE COULDN'T WIPE AWAY!

LOVE CAN BE GREATER THAN LIFE ITSELF, JUAN, FOR WHETHER YOU'RE LIVING MAN OR GHOST-- *I STILL LOVE YOU!*

THE -- THE WORDS I'VE BEEN HUNGERING TO HEAR THROUGHOUT THE CENTURIES! AT LAST-- SOMEONE LOVES ME -- *FOR MYSELF ALONE!* HATRED IS BANISHED --*AND WITH IT, THE CURSE!*

7

STRANGE SPIRITS
~ BEWITCHED BALI! ~

AT MIDNIGHT ON THE ISLAND OF BALI, PHANTOMS ARE SAID TO GATHER IN THE CEMETERIES TO BE JUDGED BY **DURGA** --- GODDESS OF THE DEAD!

THE EVIL SOULS, ACCORDING TO SUPERSTITION, ARE CHANGED INTO DEMONS! ONE OF THESE IS THE **BUTA** --- WHO BRINGS DISASTER AT SUNDOWN!

BE MERCIFUL DURGA! LET OUR SOULS BE AT REST!

DURGA REMEMBERS THOSE WHO HAVE SINNED --- AND THEY ARE DOOMED!

HAA-HAA-HAAAAA!

OUR ENTIRE CROP IS BURNING! WITHOUT THE GRAIN --- WE'LL STARVE!

EVEN MORE FEARFUL, NATIVES BELIEVE, ARE THE **LEYAKS** --- WHOSE FLICKERING LIGHTS APPEAR AT GLOOMY CROSSROADS!

NATIVES CLAIM THE **LEYAKS** ARE GHOULS --- AND ANYONE THEY MEET DISAPPEARS FOREVER!

I --- I THOUGHT THEY WERE FIREFLIES! BUT WHAT IS THAT STRANGE CHUCKLING SOUND --- ALL AROUND ME?

YAK-YAK!

YAAAK-YAK!

YAK

YAA-HAAA! YOU VENTURED INTO THE DARKNESS ALONE --- AND NOW YOU WILL BE ONE OF US --- A VAMPIRE!

THE LEYAK IS CASTING A SPELL! I CAN'T MOVE!

BUT THE MOST TERRIBLE IMAGINARY DEMON OF ALL IS **RANGDA** --- "QUEEN OF THE EVIL ONES" --- WHOSE CURSE BRINGS DOWN EARTHQUAKES AND EPIDEMICS!

SMALL WONDER THAT ONCE A YEAR, THE BALINESE HOLD A NOISY FESTIVAL --- HOPING TO FRIGHTEN OFF THE DEMONS WHOM THEY BELIEVE PLAGUE THEIR ISLAND!

RUN! THE EARTH IS SWALLOWING OUR VILLAGE!

BRRR-OOOM!

THE EVIL SPIRITS FEAR NOISE --- AND I WILL KILL THEM WITH MY MAGIC SWORD!

BOOM! BOOM!

BLAM!

SUPERSTITIONS ALL!

The SANDS of the DESERT

THERE'S a great future for oil field engineers in Arabia—but I'm never going back. Not after what happened that day in the sandy, burning wastes of the wild desert, far from the last outposts of civilization. There were three of us—Benson, Collins and myself—and we were engaged in a preliminary surveying tour, having heard that this unknown territory had a rich oil potential. But there was something frightening about the desolate loneliness that confronted us—an air of brooding mystery as if we had invaded a territory forbidden to all mortals. Benson laughed that I was getting desert-happy. As for him—*he* wasn't leaving Arabia until he had gotten hold of some of this easy money!

Suddenly our attention was distracted by an amazing sight. There, in the midst of all this unexplored emptiness, was an odd spectacle—an ancient stone building with a strange dome, standing alone in the sand. Around it there hung an eerie atmosphere of unknown danger that warned me off—but my companions insisted on a closer look. We reached the old heap, peered through the openwork brass doors. What we saw made us blink. Gold furniture—gold vases—everything gold, and studded with gems as big as marbles! Benson and Collins didn't say anything—they just clawed at the door and pushed.

It didn't occur to me then that there's just one kind of door in Arabia that's never locked—and as for the others, they were too busy trying to roll out a big gold vase to notice what I saw. I could have sworn he hadn't been there a moment ago—an ancient Arab with strangely-glinting eyes, whose timeworn face bore a cruel crescent scar. There was something about him, some strange presence which chilled

me to the core. I tried to tell Collins and Benson to forget the gold and leave this place, but they didn't even listen. So I walked back to the car just as Collins pushed the old man aside. *He* wasn't going to pass up a fortune just because of an old Arab!

From inside, the Arab wailed something that sounded like, "*Afreet! Afreet!*" "You *bet* you're afraid!" grunted Benson—but that isn't what the Arab meant at all. I don't know what came first—the roar, or the slamming blows that sent me flying thirty feet. When I got up, the air was full of hissing sand, and an immense brown thing towered over the building. It caught Collins and Benson as they rushed out, swept them up and hurled them against the masonry. That sometimes happens in sandstorms—but *this* wasn't just sand. It was a giant, a monstrous thing with a head and staring eyes! The eyes turned into shafts of sunlight, and then the huge figure collapsed, and tons of sand swirled down over the bodies of Benson and Collins.

During the week it took to dig them out, I learned what "afreet" means. An afreet, according to the Arabs, is an evil giant that can be summoned only by a great magician when danger threatened him or any of his property I asked the laborer who told me this whether there were many such magicians kicking around nowadays. "A few," he grunted as he uncovered Benson's body, "but none as great as Atmar, who was buried here 3,000 years ago! *Atmar—he of the glinting eyes and crescent scar!*"

They never lock tombs in Arabia—and the sands of the desert cover many ancient mysteries.

SPIRIT of FRANKENSTEIN

THAT CREATURE STILL FRIGHTENS ME, DAN! HOW CAN YOU BE SURE IT ISN'T READY TO BREAK LOOSE AGAIN?

I'VE TAUGHT IT A SIMPLE TRICK, MARCIA... AND AS LONG AS IT RESPONDS I CAN BE PRETTY SURE IT'S UNDER CONTROL! *SHAKE HANDS, ROBOT!*

CAN MODERN SCIENCE CREATE A MECHANICAL BEING THAT WALKS...TALKS...ALMOST SEEMS TO *THINK*? THAT WAS DR. DAN WARREN'S PURPOSE WHEN HE BUILT A ROBOT IN THE *SPIRIT OF FRANKENSTEIN ITSELF!* BUT LIKE FRANKENSTEIN'S MONSTER, IT RAN AMOK, GUIDED BY THE EVIL BRAIN OF A DEAD MAN! IT'S UNDER CONTROL NOW, BUT... *FOR HOW LONG?*

THE DULL, UNMASTERED BRAIN STIRS...AND SLOWLY... THE MASSIVE HAND RISES!

UHHHH...

ALL RIGHT, ROBOT...*AS YOU WERE!* WISH I COULD *COMPLETELY* TRUST THIS THING, MARCIA...BUT I DON'T LIKE THAT FAINT, SULLEN GLEAM IN ITS EYES!

I MANAGED TO DESTROY PROFESSOR PARDWAY'S GHOST IN MY CYCLOTRON...BUT THE ROBOT *STILL* HAS PARDWAY'S BRAIN! ANY KIND OF EVIL INFLUENCE, ACTING ON A MIND LIKE *THAT*, WILL MAKE THE ROBOT RIP LOOSE...AND I'VE GOT A HUNCH IT'S *WAITING* FOR JUST SUCH A CHANCE!

BUT SUPPOSE PARD-WAY'S EVIL SPIRIT *WASN'T* DESTROYED, DAN? I WISH WE *KNEW* ...BEFORE SOMETHING HAPPENS!

THE GHOST *COULD* BE LURKING AROUND THE LABORATORY... INVISIBLE...BUT I DON'T THINK SO! BESIDES...THERE'S NO WAY TO CHECK UP ON IT!

BUT THERE *IS*, DAN! REMEMBER READING ABOUT DR. DAGGETT... THE FAMOUS PSYCHIC INVESTI-GATOR? HE'S FREED HUNDREDS OF HOUSES FROM THE GHOSTS THAT HAUNTED THEM...AND *HE'D* KNOW IF PARDWAY'S SPIRIT WAS STILL ACTIVE!

I'LL PHONE DR. DAGGETT TO DROP AROUND...AND SEE IF HE CAN DETECT A PHANTOM *HERE!*

1

...THERE'S JUST A HINT OF REBELLION IN THE ROBOT, DR. DAGGETT...AND I'D LIKE YOU TO DETERMINE WHETHER THERE'S A SUPERNATURAL INFLUENCE AT WORK IN THE LABORATORY!

I'LL BE GLAD TO HELP, DR. WARREN! BUT SINCE I HAVEN'T GOT A CAR...I'LL HAVE TO WAIT HERE AT RAVEN ROCK UNTIL THE EIGHT O'CLOCK TRAIN!

EIGHT O'CLOCK...BLAZES...I CLEAN FORGOT I'M SUPPOSED TO SPEAK AT THAT SCIENCE FORUM TONIGHT!

THAT'S STILL TWO HOURS OFF, DAN! YOU'LL HAVE PLENTY OF TIME IF I DRIVE OUT TO RAVEN ROCK AND PICK UP DR. DAGGETT...AND YOU'LL BE FREE TO WIND UP YOUR LAB WORK!

BUT DAN WORKS FITFULLY AFTER MARCIA LEAVES...HIS THOUGHTS CLOUDED BY A MOUNTING UNEASINESS!

A SCIENTIST ISN'T SUPPOSED TO SENSE THINGS...BUT THERE'S SOMETHING IN THOSE GLINTING EYES I HAVEN'T FELT BEFORE ...AND IT'S MORE THAN BROODING DEFIANCE!

YES...MORE! THOSE HEAVY, CLOD-LIKE FEATURES HOLD A SECRET--AN AWARENESS OF WHAT IS TO COME!

A HALF-HOUR LATER...AS MARCIA REACHES RAVEN ROCK...

THERE'S REALLY NO REASON TO THINK DR. DAGGETT'S HOUSE IS SPOOKY...EXCEPT FOR THAT FOG! STRANGE I DIDN'T NOTICE IT DOWN BELOW!

YES, THERE'S FOG HERE...STRANGE, SWIRLING FOG! WHAT DOES IT HIDE?

I KNOW THAT IF THERE'S ONE PLACE GHOSTS WOULD STAY AWAY FROM, IT'S DR. DAGGETT'S HOME...BUT I'M NOT GOING TO WAIT TO KNOCK!

CRRREAK!

BRR-R! I NEVER DID LIKE EYES STARING FROM PAINTINGS...THEY SEEM TO FOLLOW YOU! AND WHAT PAINTINGS! THEY'RE GHOSTLY...

2

SLOWLY AND SILENTLY, MARCIA TIPTOES DOWN THE CORRIDOR...AND SLOWLY...SILENTLY...THE SHINING EYES ROLL...AND WATCH!

THEN, CUTTING THROUGH THE SILENCE...A VOICE!

DIDN'T I *PROMISE* YOU YOUR POWERS WOULD BE GIVEN FREE REIN? IT'S THERE...WAITING FOR YOU ...*IN DAN WARREN'S LABORATORY!*

STRANGE! I WONDER WHAT HE CAN MEAN?

HE MUST BE TALKING ABOUT DAN'S ROBOT... BUT TO WHOM? *WHO'S IN THERE WITH DR. DAGGETT?*

YOU CAN CONTROL THE THING...GIVING IT A WILL AND A PURPOSE IT'S LACKED UNTIL NOW... *AND TURNING IT LOOSE AS ONLY YOU KNOW HOW!*

THAT'S WHAT HE'S TALKING TO...A ROOM FULL OF HORRIBLE PAINTINGS...JUST LIKE THE ONES IN THE CORRIDOR BACK THERE!

SUDDENLY...

OHH-H!

SHADES OF SHEOL! WHO ARE YOU...AND WHAT BROUGHT YOU HERE?

I'M MARCIA HOLMES! I CAME TO DRIVE YOU TO DAN WARREN'S LABORATORY...BUT I CERTAINLY WISH I *HADN'T!*

IF...IF YOU COULD ONLY *EXPLAIN*... THAT AWFUL FOG OUTSIDE...THESE PAINTINGS...THE THINGS YOU SAID...

DON'T YOU *KNOW?* THOSE PHANTOMS I LURED FROM SCORES OF HAUNTED HOUSES ...CAN'T YOU GUESS THEY'RE *HERE?*

HERE IS NO MERE INVESTIGATOR OF GHOSTS! HERE, INSTEAD, IS A MAN WHO BENDS SPIRITS TO HIS OWN WILL!

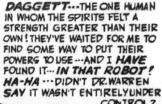

DAGGETT...THE ONE HUMAN IN WHOM THE SPIRITS FELT A STRENGTH GREATER THAN THEIR OWN! THEY'VE WAITED FOR ME TO FIND SOME WAY TO PUT THEIR POWERS TO USE...AND I *HAVE* FOUND IT... *IN THAT ROBOT!* HA-HA ...DIDN'T DR.WARREN *SAY* IT WASN'T ENTIRELY UNDER CONTROL?

ONCE MY PHANTOMS TRANSFER THEIR POWER TO THE ROBOT, IT WILL OBEY *ME*... *AND I'LL HAVE HUMANITY AT MY FEET!*

THOSE THINGS DON'T REALLY EXIST...THEY *CAN'T!*

YOU'VE SEEN THE ROBOT PLODDING AROUND WARREN'S LABORATORY... YOU KNOW *THAT* ISN'T HUMAN... AND YET YOU HOPE TO SHRUG OFF THINGS LIKE *THESE!* COME FORTH...SHOW HER!

Then...AS IF SUMMONED BY THEIR MASTER...SWIRLING IN A WAVE FROM THE GAPING FRAMES...

CREATURES FROM OUT OF *THE UNKNOWN*, ALL OF THEM... *AND THEY'RE MINE TO COMMAND!*

WARREN WON'T SEE THEM...BUT THEY'RE ON THEIR WAY...READY TO GIVE THE ROBOT A POWER NO LIVING THING CAN CHECK! AND IF HE *DOES* FIND A WAY TO WARD THEM OFF...HE'LL THINK TWICE ABOUT USING IT... WITH *HER* HERE!

Minutes LATER... I CAN'T GUESS WHAT'S KEEPING MARCIA AND DR. DAGGETT...BUT I'M LATE *NOW* FOR THAT SCIENCE FORUM! I'LL GIVE THE ROBOT A QUICK CHECKUP BEFORE I LEAVE!

THE ROBOT IS *MY* RESPONSIBILITY...BUT IF THERE'S ANYWHERE I CAN FIND HELP, IT'S *HERE*! THIS IS A TEST...A TEST TO PROVE WHETHER WE CAN KEEP OUR GRIP ON THE THINGS WE CREATE...OR HAVE THOSE THINGS TAKEN OVER BY THE EVIL POWERS THAT *CAN* CONTROL THEM!

PERHAPS PROFESSOR MARSDEN'S NEW SERUM MAY HELP! IT AFFECTS CERTAIN AREAS OF THE BRAIN...DULLING VIOLENT IMPULSES, AND STIMULATING THE REGION GOVERNING CONSCIENCE!

THERE'S A SLIM CHANCE THAT AN EXTRA HEAVY INJECTION MAY HELP, WARREN...BUT IT'S A GAMBLE! IT'S POSSIBLE THE SERUM MAY MAKE THE ROBOT *MORE DANGEROUS* THAN EVER!

I'LL TAKE THAT CHANCE, PROFESSOR MARSDEN! AN INJECTION IS THE LAST RESORT...*IF I CAN GET CLOSE ENOUGH TO THE ROBOT!*

As Dan Rushes From The Auditorium...

THEY'VE PROBABLY GOT A LINE ON THE ROBOT! AND IF IT'S CORNERED...I'LL HAVE TO ACT BEFORE IT'S GOADED INTO A MURDEROUS FURY!

WOOO-OOOO!

Half-Way Across Town...Police Searchlights Are Trained On A Narrow Alley!

EASY, NOW...WE'LL FIRE TOGETHER...AND KEEP BLASTING AWAY UNTIL IT DROPS!

WAIT! FOR THE LOVE OF PETE ...*DON'T FIRE!*

I DIDN'T RECOGNIZE YOU FOR A MOMENT, DR. WARREN! SORRY...BUT WE'VE GOT OUR ORDERS TO DESTROY THAT THING!

THERE ISN'T A BULLET MADE THAT CAN PIERCE THE THREE-INCH ARMOR PLATE SHIELDING ITS NERVOUS SYSTEM! GUNFIRE WILL MAKE IT RUN HOG-WILD...AND RUIN MY CHANCE TO USE *THIS!*

But The Creature At Bay Is No Longer A Mere Robot! It Waits With A Craftiness That Is Half-Human...And Half Rooted In Nameless Evil!

TRYING TO LURE ME INTO SHAKING HANDS AGAIN, EH? I'LL OUT-WIT IT...BY PRETEND-ING I'VE FALLEN FOR THE TRICK!

HUUUUH!

WANT TO SHAKE HANDS, ROBOT?

Then...With A Desperate Lunge...

YAARRRGH!

GARRRGH!

THE WALL! DR. WARREN ...LOOK OUT!

CRASH!

DEA END

THAT DOES IT! HE MUST BE SMASHED FLAT AS A DIME!

I CAN FEEL THE ENTIRE MOUND MOVING! GREAT GUNS...THERE'S A HAND SHOVING CLEAR!

Then...WITH A SINGLE SURGING RUSH...

YAARRRGH!

SLOWLY THE THUDDING FOOTSTEPS FADE ...AND THE ROBOT VANISHES INTO THE NIGHT!

A BULLDOZER COULDN'T HAVE DONE IT! WHAT WAS THAT STUFF YOU INJECTED ANYWAY?

A SERUM... I THOUGHT IT WOULD WORK ON THE ROBOT'S BRAIN ...BUT THERE'S NO USE LOOKING FOR A CONSCIENCE IN A THING THAT'S GRIPPED BY EVIL!

EVIL...IT CAN'T BE JUST ONE GHOST...NOT EVEN PARDWAY'S ...BUT SUPPOSE IT'S SEVERAL? HERE I'VE BEEN WONDERING WHAT'S BEEN KEEPING MARCIA ...AND IT NEVER OCCURRED TO ME THAT DAGGETT MAY BE BEHIND THIS!

DAN SETS OUT FOR RAVEN ROCK... LITTLE KNOWING THAT THE ROBOT IS FOLLOWING THE SPIRITS THAT HAVE DOMINATED IT...TOWARD THE SAME DESTINATION!

CRRAK!

CRRUNCH!

8

SOON AFTERWARD...

I'VE SEEN THAT FACE IN NEWS PHOTOGRAPHS! HAAA···IT'S DR. WARREN ···THE ONE MAN WHO MIGHT THREATEN MY CONTROL OF THE ROBOT! *VERY CONVENIENT...*

WE'LL SKIP THE USUAL COURTESIES, DAGGETT! *WHERE'S MARCIA?*

YOU SEEM UPSET, DR. WARREN! IS THAT *ALL* YOU EXPECT TO FIND HERE···*JUST THE GIRL?*

SUDDENLY···A WOMAN'S SCREAM!

MARCIA! SHE'S IN THERE!

HELP! HELP!

IN THE NEXT INSTANT, DAN HOLDS MARCIA···AND A GRISLY TRAP HOLDS THEM BOTH!

SLAM!

FOUR OF THEM···THINGS NO HUMAN POWER CAN STEM···*AND THEY'RE COMING CLOSER!*

THEN···AS DR. DAGGETT AWAITS ···HE HEARS···

FOOTSTEPS··· WHAT A SURPRISE TO HAVE IT TURN UP *NOW*···JUST IN TIME TO HELP *DESTROY* ITS MAKER!

CLUMP... CLUMP... CLUMP...

YES, DR. DAGGETT···*WHAT A SURPRISE!*

YUUUGH!

WHAM!

YUUGH... YARRRGH!

OH···DAN! I'LL FACE ANYTHING ···ANYTHING BUT *THAT!*

CRASH!

41

AS THE PHANTOMS TURN TOWARD AN EXPECTED ALLY...

THE SERUM WORKED! THE ROBOT'S PROTECTING US, MARCIA!

GARRRGH!

BLAM!

WITH A RELENTLESS FURY NOT EVEN THE CREATURES OF TERROR CAN WITHSTAND...

A MOMENT LATER...

YOU MASTERED THE ROBOT ONCE! COME FORTH... MAKE IT OBEY!

DAN! HE'S SUMMONING HIS FIENDS... THE VERY ONES THAT MADE THE ROBOT REBEL!

SOMETHING TELLS ME HE'S JUST A SECOND TOO LATE, MARCIA!

POW!

I'LL TAKE CARE OF THE ROBOT... BUT I WANT YOU SAFELY IN THE CAR BEFORE ANYTHING ELSE HAPPENS!

THERE IT IS NOW... COMING OUT!

STANDING STARKLY IN THE MOONLIGHT...THE ROBOT TURNS ITS FULL STRENGTH AGAINST THE STRONGHOLD OF EVIL!

CRRUNCH!

THIS TIME YOU NEEDN'T WONDER ABOUT THE HANDSHAKE, DAN... WE KNOW IT'S UNDER CONTROL!

STRICTLY FROM SERUM, MARCIA! THERE'S NO TELLING HOW LONG THE EFFECT WILL LAST... AND WHILE I HOPE IT'S PERMANENT... I'VE GOT A FEELING IT'S LIKE CUDDLING UP TO A STACK OF TNT!

HEAR THOSE THUMPING FOOTSTEPS? YOU'LL FIND WHAT'S BEHIND THEM... IN THE NEXT ISSUE!

10.

TRUE GHOSTS OF HISTORY

"The Case of The Malignant Mummy"

TRUE GHOSTS? It sounds strange, because there's no SCIENTIFIC evidence that spirits exist! But history records many strange and unexplained facts — and none stranger than this eerie tale!

DURING THE EARLY PART OF THE 20TH CENTURY, A BRITISH ARCHEOLOGICAL EXPEDITION SEARCHING THE ANCIENT EGYPTIAN RUINS AT THEBES FOUND —

WHAT A FIND! THE MUMMY OF AN EGYPTIAN PRINCESS 3500 YEARS OLD — A PRIESTESS OF THE TEMPLE OF AMMON-RA!

YES -- BUT THIS INSCRIPTION IS SOMETHING YOU WON'T LIKE AS MUCH!

IT -- IT'S A WARNING TO ANYONE WHO DARES DISTURB THESE REMAINS! IT SAYS TRAGEDY WILL BEFALL WHOEVER COMES IN CONTACT WITH THE MUMMY!

A CURSE, EH? DON'T TELL ME YOU PUT ANY STOCK IN THAT STUFF! HA-HA!

SEVERAL DAYS LATER ---

GUESS I'LL TRY A LITTLE TARGET PRACTICE! -- BY THE WAY, HOW'S THE MUMMY'S CURSE GETTING ALONG?

LAUGH IF YOU WANT TO -- BUT I FEEL STRANGELY UNEASY ABOUT THE WHOLE THING!

POW!

GREAT HEAVENS!

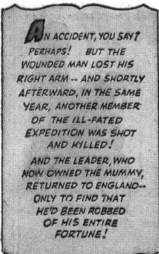

AN ACCIDENT, YOU SAY? PERHAPS! BUT THE WOUNDED MAN LOST HIS RIGHT ARM -- AND SHORTLY AFTERWARD, IN THE SAME YEAR, ANOTHER MEMBER OF THE ILL-FATED EXPEDITION WAS SHOT AND KILLED!

AND THE LEADER, WHO NOW OWNED THE MUMMY, RETURNED TO ENGLAND-- ONLY TO FIND THAT HE'D BEEN ROBBED OF HIS ENTIRE FORTUNE!

UPON ITS ARRIVAL IN LONDON, THE MUMMY WAS FIRST BROUGHT TO A PHOTOGRAPHIC STUDIO --

I'D LIKE SOME PICTURES FOR EXHIBITION PURPOSES! ER -- THERE'S SUPPOSED TO BE A *CURSE* ON THIS THING! HOPE I'M NOT *SCARING* YOU!

NOT AT ALL, SIR! AFTER ALL, TAKING PICTURES IS MY BUSINESS!

BUT ONLY A SINGLE HOUR LATER --

LISTEN -- IT SOUNDS AS IF SOME- ONE'S *CRAZY* IN THERE! WE -- WE'D BETTER CALL A CONSTABLE!

THE CAMERA -- IT SAW *THE TRUTH!* THAT FACE-- *THAT FACE!*

WONDER IF *THIS* IS THE PICTURE HE'S BABBLING ABOUT-- *OH, MY HEAVENS!*

ONLY THE PHOTOGRAPHER HAD TAKEN THIS PICTURE, AND NO LIVING SOUL HAD TAMPERED WITH HIS EQUIPMENT! BUT THAT PICTURE SHOWED NOT THE SHRIVELED FEATURES OF A LONG-DEAD MUMMY... *BUT A LIVING BEING OF MALIGNANT EVIL!*

A MESSENGER'S BROUGHT THE REPORT THAT THE PHOTOGRAPHER JUST DIED, SIR -- *OF AN ILLNESS NO PHYSICIAN COULD DIAGNOSE!*

THAT SETTLES IT! I DIDN'T WANT TO BELIEVE THE STORIES ABOUT THAT MUMMY BEFORE, BUT NOW I'VE GOT NO ALTERNATIVE! I'VE GOT TO GET RID OF ITS EVIL INFLUENCE -- MAYBE THE *BRITISH MUSEUM* WILL BE WILLING TO ACCEPT IT!

AH! L-22-542-- THE NEW MUMMY! JUDGING FROM THE STORIES *I'VE* HEARD, YOU SHOULD BE AFRAID TO EVEN DELIVER IT!

WHAT -- A BIG, STRONG CHAP LIKE ME? I'D LIKE TO SEE THE MUMMY THAT'D SCARE *ME!*

SERVICE ENTRANCE MUSEUM

②

BUT WITHIN A WEEK -- THE MAN WHO HAD DELIVERED THE EVIL MUMMY WAS DEAD!

OMINOUS STORIES OF THE MUMMIFIED PRINCESS-PRIESTESS SOON SPREAD THROUGHOUT ENGLAND!

THIS IS THE ARM I TOUCHED THE MUMMY CASE WITH! BROKE IT NEXT DAY!

I WALKED AS WELL AS ANYBODY -- TILL I SAW THAT AWFUL THING!

IT WAS THE DAY AFTER I SAW IT THAT MY HOUSE BURNED DOWN!

AND AT THE MUSEUM ---

SORRY, SIR, BUT THE MEN THREATEN TO STRIKE IF THE MUMMY'S KEPT ON EXHIBIT! THEY'RE SCARED OF IT -- AND SO AM I!

BUT CURIOSITY-SEEKERS STILL WANT TO SEE IT! -- ALL RIGHT! I'LL WITHDRAW IT, BUT KEEP THIS QUIET!

AND SO THE ORIGINAL PRINCESS WAS HIDDEN, AND IN HER PLACE WAS SUBSTITUTED A CLEVER IMITATION! BUT THE DECEPTION WAS SOON DISCOVERED BY AN AMERICAN ARCHEOLOGIST---

THIS ISN'T THE SAME MUMMY THEY HAD ON DISPLAY LAST WEEK -- IT'S A FAKE! WONDER WHERE THE REAL ONE IS -- AND WHETHER I COULD GET HOLD OF IT!

CONTACTING THE MUSEUM AUTHORITIES, THE AMERICAN OFFERED TO TAKE THE REAL MUMMY TO THE UNITED STATES!

HIS OFFER WAS ACCEPTED PROMPTLY -- WHY?

TO DISPOSE OF THE CURSE -- END ITS REIGN OF TERROR!

LET'S CONSULT THE RECORD FOR WHAT HAPPENED NEXT!

ON APRIL 15TH, 1912, ABOARD A SHIP BOUND FOR AMERICA, CAME THE FINAL AND STRONGEST MANIFESTATION OF THE MUMMY'S CURSE!

AND SO, AT THE BOTTOM OF THE OCEAN, LIES A GREAT SHIP -- AND A 3500-YEAR-OLD MUMMY WHOSE EVIL CAREER IS FOREVER ENDED!

THE SHIP WHOSE SINKING MARKED THE MUMMY'S GREATEST MALEVOLENCE WAS THE TITANIC!

DID THIS ANCIENT EGYPTIAN CURSE REALLY SPAN THE CENTURIES? WHAT DO YOU THINK?

EDITOR — LET'S TALK IT OVER!

Gather 'round, all you ADVENTURES INTO THE UNKNOWN fans—and let's chat!

This is a big moment for us—the moment when we can announce the first results of our great reader contest! These have been hectic days in the editorial sanctum, with the postman groaning under the weight of thousands of entries. Frankly, we never dreamed of the extent of our readers' personal adventures into the *Unknown*, nor how fascinating these adventures could be. It made our job of selecting the best a difficult one. As a matter of fact, we received so many great stories that we wished that it was within our power to award a thousand prizes. But since that couldn't be, we plunged resolutely into our task—and came up with a lalapaloosa in our Grand Prize Contest Winner! You'll find it presented as a complete and captivating picture story in this issue—"*Journey Into The Unknown*," by Lynneal H. Diamond, of Mallary, New York. Congratulations, Mr. Diamond, on one of the most gripping and challenging yarns ever! By this time you've received your first prize winner's check—and we hope you like the way we've portrayed your fine story in picture form!

We hope you'll enjoy "*Journey Into The Unknown*" as much as we did, readers. There's more enjoyment ahead—because in our next issue, we're going to announce our second and third prize winners and present their stories under their own names. Don't miss this succeeding issue—who knows, you may find *your* name there!

Okay—let's talk of other things now. It's nice being able to sit down with you folks and let our hair down. Putting out a magazine like this is fun. It's swell to deal with a fascinating subject like the *Unknown*, and to publish the tense and gripping stories of the Supernatural that all of us seem to enjoy so much. We've really gone to town in this issue—and we'd like to know your reactions. Why not write us, telling which of our tales you liked best, and what you'd like us to feature in future issues? Remember, we're always anxious to hear from you!

We've heard from many of our readers—like to know what they're saying? Here goes with a couple!

"I have every issue of 'ADVENTURES INTO THE UNKNOWN' that you have published so far, and I think that they are all super. I believe that it is the best organized and best drawn book on the stands. My favorite kind of stories are the 'age-old specter' type, such as 'The Living Ghost' in your first issue and 'Out of the Unknown' in your second. I would like to see more of 'The Living Ghost' in your future issues. Next to these, I enjoy reading the 'curse' stories such as 'The Castle of Otranto' and 'The Old Tower's Secret,' and ones like 'The Vampire Prowls,' 'Do Such Things exist,' 'The Affair of Room 1313' and 'The Women Wore Black.' I would like to see this magazine published every month, but I am happy that is is bimonthly instead of quarterly as it was going to be. Enclosed please find my $1.20 for a 12-issue subscription."

R. L. Flanagan
Graeagle, Cal.

"I am 13 years old and have been reading comics since I was six. In all that time, I have never come across a comic that I have enjoyed so much as 'ADVENTURES INTO THE UNKNOWN.' The stories are wonderful and are especially well-drawn. I have read each issue as much as eight times. Enclosed is my $1.20 for a 12-issue subscription. Keep on with your *super* comic! Oh, by the way, while I was watching 'Child's World' on television (they were discussing the topic of comics) several participants picked your magazine as their favorite. Personally, I think *everybody* likes your comic.

HIP-HIP-HOORAY FOR 'ADVENTURES INTO THE UNKNOWN'!"

David Harfeld
2302 Ocala Ave.
Baltimore, Md.

Well—it's been nice talking to you, folks! So long—*see you in the next issue!*

Notice to all readers! We have received many letters telling us of difficulties in obtaining our issues. If your newsdealer doesn't have "ADVENTURES INTO THE UNKNOWN," please send us *his* name and address, and we'll try to see that he has it for you in the future.

48

The MOSS MAN

THERE it was in the paper—the article announcing the discovery of bactolyte, the new germ-killer derived from moss. Hodgins scanned it eagerly, and felt a hot rage boiling up within him. For the newspaper attributed the discovery entirely to Alvin McReady, carrying only a slight mention of the fact that one Hoggins—even the name was misspelled—had served as the great man's assistant! It had always been that way for the last twenty years, Hodgins felt — he had shared equally in the work, and McReady had usurped the credit! During all this time, Hodgins had said nothing—merely brooded. And when a man, even a scientist, broods for twenty years, a deadly solution is sometimes decided in seconds.

Unpremeditated, it all happened in a blaze of fiery anger. No one saw Hodgins swing the shovel—least of all McReady, who was stooping to examine the last clump of moss he would ever see. It was done, and there was no time for useless regrets. Better for Hodgins to hide the evidence of his crime, and quickly! The spot was ideal for his purpose, a hidden hollow about a hundred feet from the laboratory which the two men had shared for so long. There—it was done, and the hole he had dug was filled in. Hastily, Hodgins threw a few clumps of moss over the raw earth, knowing that it would help to hide the signs of digging. It was funny, in a way—McReady, the great expert on moss, and now it marked his tomb!

It was a morbid fascination that drew Hodgins back to the scene of his crime next day. Curious, the way that patch of moss he had laid seemed to have moved —at least six feet nearer the laboratory! And he was positive that it hadn't possessed that strange shape before, with that roughly shaped protuberance at one end almost suggesting a human head. Strange, the way moss could grow It called for scientific study, and Hodgins determined to return next day for further observations.

The following morning found the odd patch of moss ten feet nearer the laboratory. It seemed to have grown strange, bristly tufts at the round end, the *head* end—almost like hair. And as the days passed, he noted a peculiar growth—appendages that seemed almost like arms and legs. And always—that steady, relentless creeping towards the laboratory! As a man, Hodgins was terrified, but as a scientist, fascinated. Here was a phenomenon he could study and report on alone, without McReady to usurp the credit. He spent hours with a turf fork, getting the thing up intact and trundling it in a wheelbarrow to McReady's quarters. Now that he kept the door closed, it was dark and dank in there—a good growing place for moss. Especially if that's where the moss wanted to be, and there was no longer any doubt of *that*.

Yes, the moss grew. Hodgins could *hear* it growing—what else could explain those sounds of stealthy motion behind the closed door? And later there were *other* noises, sounding almost like panting breath. It was at this point that Hodgins started laughing at himself. It was ridiculous for him, a scientist, to entertain the strange fears that crowded his mind. It was a new type of moss, that was all—a fast-growing, oddly-shaped specimen that would make him famous as its discoverer. Then why did his heart beat faster as the sounds from the closed room grew in intensity? Why was he trembling at that clumping noise, like muffled footsteps coming nearer, *nearer?*

That creak—it was the door opening. And the last thing that Hodgins ever saw was a monstrous green thing on the threshold—a green thing in the weird shape of a man, arms outstretched to grasp him.

HERE SHE COMES!

SHE'S LUCKY TO ESCAPE THAT BLAZE ALIVE!

AND NEXT... I'VE HOOKED A *TROUT!* GOLLY, IF I CAN ONLY REEL HIM IN···*OOF*···THE *PADDLE!* IF *THAT* GETS AWAY, I'LL *REALLY* BE···

···SUNK!

H-E-L-P!

I CAN'T HOLD ON MUCH LONGER! THE CURRENT'S TOO STRONG!··· *MY FINGERS*···THEY'RE *SLIPPING!*

IN THE NICK OF TIME···RESCUE!

IF YOU HADN'T COME TO MY AID WHEN YOU DID···OH, I CAN'T BEAR TO EVEN *THINK* ABOUT IT! BUT I DO WANT TO THANK YOU, MR.···

WAYNE MORSE··· AND SKIP THE GRATITUDE! ANY MAN IN MY PLACE WOULD HAVE DONE THE SAME THING! *I'M* JUST THE LUCKY GUY WHO HAPPENED TO BE AROUND!

5.

IT'S JUST AS WELL YOU FOUND OUT, JUDY! I KNOW NOW I NEVER REALLY LOVED YOU! I'M GOING TO MARRY HESTER *TONIGHT!*

WAYNE, HOW CAN YOU HURT ME SO? OH, I *WISH I'D NEVER BEEN BORN!*

"NEVER BEEN BORN!" THE DEVIL *SAID* HE'D MAKE ME WISH THAT! ...THEN ...IT WAS *NO DREAM!* HE *DID* APPEAR ...AND I TALKED TO HIM! SOMETHING'S HAPPENING TO ME... SOMETHING *HORRIBLE I CAN'T CONTROL!* ...THE DIARY...I MUST SEE *THAT OLD DIARY* AGAIN...

STRANGE! ...WHY, HER HEART WAS BROKEN JUST AS MINE WAS ...IN ALMOST THE SAME CIRCUMSTANCES ...AND ON THE VERY SAME DAY, *JUNE 1!* ...IT'S AS IF SOMEONE *PLANNED IT* THAT WAY! ...BUT SHE VOWED REVENGE, WHILE I...

I'LL BE REVENGED, TOO ...JUST AS SHE WANTED TO BE ...EVEN IF I MUST SELL MY SOUL TO THE DEVIL!

EEEEEEE!

I...FEEL SO NUMB ...HELPLESS ...SOME STRANGE EVIL SEEMS TO POSSESS ME...

THE DEVIL'S DISCIPLES

WHO SIGNS THIS BOOK SHALL BE BOUND TO ME AND DO MY WORK FOR ETERNITY!

June 1, 1949
Judy Orl

THE CAT DISAPPEARS ...AND IN ITS PLACE...

7.

YOU! THE CAT WAS YOU...!

CERTAINLY, MY DEAR... I OFTEN ASSUME THAT GUISE! BUT NOW THAT YOU'VE SIGNED THE BOOK OF WITCHES, I CAN BE MYSELF!... YOU'VE ASKED FOR REVENGE... AND YOU SHALL HAVE IT! TONIGHT... AT NINE O'CLOCK... HE WHO BETRAYED YOU WILL DIE!

AND YOU WILL BECOME ONE OF MY DISCIPLES! PREPARE YOURSELF!

NO! WAIT! DON'T DISAPPEAR AGAIN!

THE DEVIL'S DISCIPLE... DOOMED TO DO HIS AWFUL WORK ON EARTH! OH, WHATEVER POSSESSED ME TO SEEK REVENGE? IF WAYNE DIES, I'LL... WHAT'S THIS? IT DROPPED FROM THE DIARY...

A PORTRAIT OF HESTER PRINCE! BUT HER FACE...! IF-- IF HER NAME WASN'T ON THE PICTURE, I'D SWEAR IT WAS HESTER PRENTISS!... HOW COULD TWO PEOPLE BORN ALMOST THREE CENTURIES APART LOOK SO MUCH ALIKE? OR DOES ONLY ONE EXIST? -- OF COURSE! THE DEVIL SCHEMED IT FROM THE FIRST!... I MUST WARN WAYNE BEFORE IT IS TOO LATE!

MR. MORSE JUST LEFT WITH MISS PRENTISS! THEY SAID THEY WERE DRIVING TO ELMVILLE TO BE MARRIED!

THIS SHORTCUT SHOULD ENABLE ME TO HEAD THEM OFF! OH, IF ONLY I'M IN TIME!

WHEW... THAT WAS CLOSE! IF LIGHTNING HADN'T FLASHED, I'D NEVER HAVE NOTICED THE BRIDGE HAD COLLAPSED!... IT'S NEARLY NINE O'CLOCK! THIS MUST BE THE PLACE WHERE WAYNE IS TO DIE!

8.

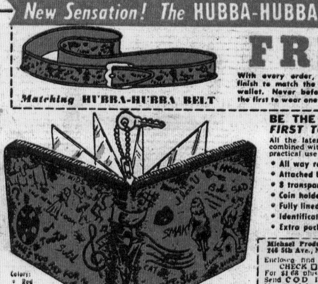

61

62

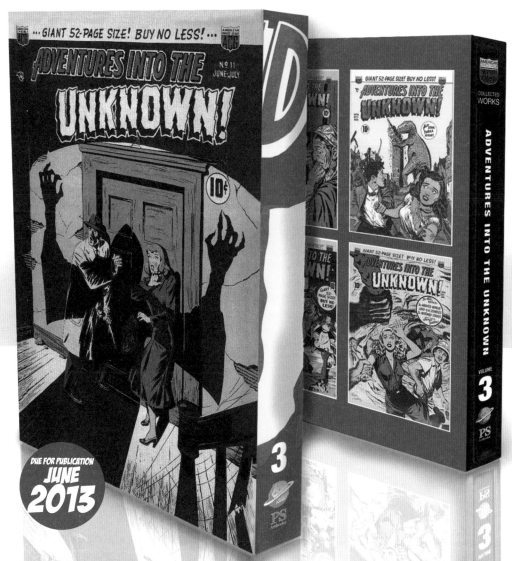

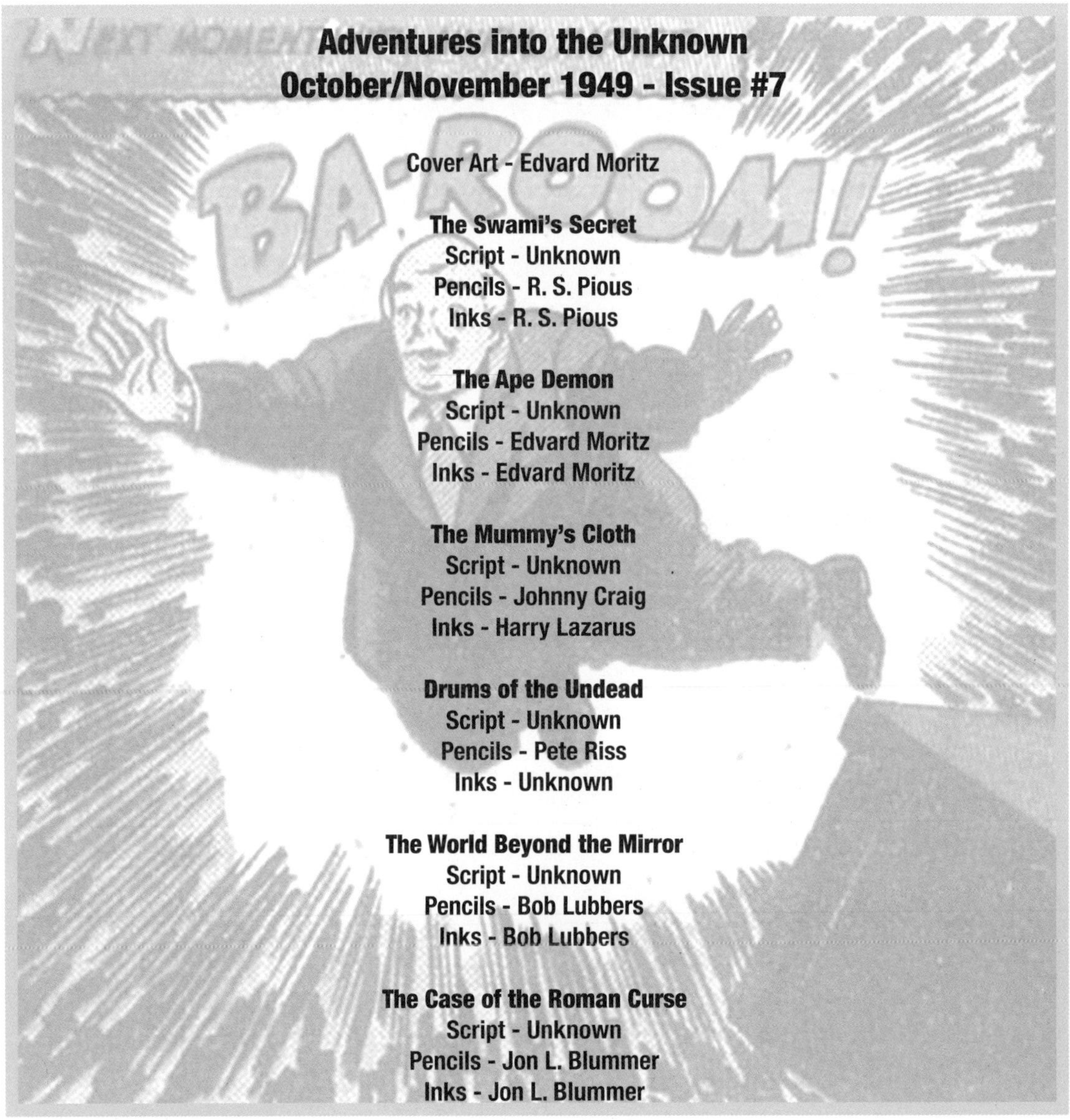

Adventures into the Unknown
October/November 1949 - Issue #7

Cover Art - Edvard Moritz

The Swami's Secret
Script - Unknown
Pencils - R. S. Pious
Inks - R. S. Pious

The Ape Demon
Script - Unknown
Pencils - Edvard Moritz
Inks - Edvard Moritz

The Mummy's Cloth
Script - Unknown
Pencils - Johnny Craig
Inks - Harry Lazarus

Drums of the Undead
Script - Unknown
Pencils - Pete Riss
Inks - Unknown

The World Beyond the Mirror
Script - Unknown
Pencils - Bob Lubbers
Inks - Bob Lubbers

The Case of the Roman Curse
Script - Unknown
Pencils - Jon L. Blummer
Inks - Jon L. Blummer

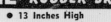

ADVENTURES INTO THE UNKNOWN, published bi-monthly and copyright, 1949, by B. & I. Publishing Co., Inc., 45 West 45th Street, New York 19, N. Y. Richard E. Hughes, Editor; Frederick H. Iger, Business Manager. Subscription (12 issues), $1.20; single copies $.10; foreign postage extra. Reentered as second-class matter December 2, 1948 at the Post Office at New York, N. Y., under the Act of March 3, 1879. No. 7, October-November, 1949. Printed in U. S. A.

THE SWAMI'S SECRET

Since the long-past age when wizards crouched in their musty dens, spiritualists have tried to lure phantoms through the hushed portals of the *UNKNOWN*!

How could this be done? *That* was the Swami's secret -- a secret that promised untold power-- but it was a dread power no human can control!

I'VE ALWAYS *WANTED* TO VISIT A SPIRITUALIST-- BUT NOW THAT I'VE GOT AN APPOINTMENT WITH *SWAMI HESHUG* -- I HATE TO THINK OF WHAT *MIGHT* HAPPEN!

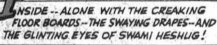

INSIDE -- ALONE WITH THE CREAKING FLOOR BOARDS -- THE SWAYING DRAPES -- AND THE GLINTING EYES OF SWAMI HESHUG!

I'VE HEARD ABOUT YOUR AMAZING POWERS FROM FRIENDS, SWAMI -- AND I THOUGHT YOU MIGHT BE ABLE TO SUMMON THE SPIRIT OF MY UNCLE! HE DIED SIX YEARS AGO!

AH, YOUNG LADY -- HE HAS BEEN *WAITING* FOR THIS MOMENT! PLEASE STAND BESIDE THE CRYSTAL BALL -- AND AFTER I HAVE GONE INTO A TRANCE -- *YOUR UNCLE'S GHOST WILL RISE!*

THEN -- AS THE SWAMI'S VOICE DRONES INTO THE GLOOM ⇒

I AM SURROUNDED BY SPIRITS... ONE OF THEM *RECOGNIZES* A FAMILIAR FACE... IT IS CROSSING OVER -- INTO THIS ROOM!

OH, HEAVENS -- I'VE SEEN *ENOUGH!*

SUDDENLY -- BOTH GLOOM AND TRANCE DISSOLVE IN A FLASH OF LIGHT!

IMPS OF TOPHET-- WHAT'S THAT?

NICE GOING, TRUDY! I THINK I'VE GOT THE PICTURE WE'RE AFTER!

CLICK!

PICTURE! HOW DARE YOU SUBJECT MY SPIRITS TO PUBLIC GAZE!

GAUZE WOULD BE MORE LIKE IT! THERE'S *YARDS* OF THE STUFF!

SEE THIS PEDAL? IT SENDS HOT AIR RISING FROM THE FURNACE TO THE CRYSTAL BALL — UNDER ENOUGH PRESSURE TO PUSH THE GAUZE THROUGH THAT SMALL HOLE! JUST GOES TO PROVE HOW MUCH YOU CAN ACCOMPLISH WITH *HOT AIR* — HEY, SWAMI?

WHO ARE YOU? WHAT DOES THIS ALL MEAN?

WE'RE BILL CARLTON AND TRUDY ROLAND OF THE *"GRAPHIC"* — AND IT MEANS WE'RE EXPOSING THE *SPIRITUALISM* RACKET YOU'VE BEEN WORKING FOR FIFTEEN YEARS! YOU'VE PREYED ON THOUSANDS OF PEOPLE, SWAMI — AND WE'RE GOING TO SHOW YOU UP — JUST AS WE WOULD ANY *OTHER* CRIMINAL!

YOU THINK I'M A FRAUD, HAH — BECAUSE I HAVEN'T REVEALED WHAT THE *SUPERNATURAL* IS *REALLY* LIKE? PUBLISH ONE WORD AGAINST ME, AND I'LL *PROVE* WHAT I CAN DO — AND YOU'LL REGRET IT FOR THE REST OF YOUR LIVES! NOW — *GET OUT!*

THE WORDS ECHO IN TRUDY'S MIND — LIKE A CHILL PROPHECY —

I HATE TO SAY THIS, BILL — BUT THERE'S SOMETHING ABOUT HIM — SOMETHING IN HIS VOICE — THAT I WOULDN'T CARE TO DREAM ABOUT!

THAT CARNIVAL CHARACTER IN A RUN-DOWN TURBAN? DON'T LET HIM BLUFF YOU, TRUDY!

THAT NIGHT, THE STORY APPEARS — BUT ANOTHER ONE OCCUPIES THE *HEADLINES!*

5¢ EVENING GRAPHIC

"CAT" HARRIS GOES DEFIANTLY TO ELECTRIC CHAIR!

Killer Dies Vowing He Will Find Some Way To Get Even!

"GRAPHIC" TEAM EXPOSES SPIRIT-RAISING!

Swami Uses Crude Gimmick!

WHAT LUCK! THEY *WOULD* EXECUTE A VICIOUS KILLER LIKE HARRIS JUST IN TIME TO TAKE THE HEADLINE AWAY FROM *OUR* STORY!

TOUGH BREAK, BILL — BUT THAT HARRIS STORY IS THE KIND OUR READERS WANT! HE'S BIG NEWS — RIGHT DOWN TO HIS EXECUTION AND BURIAL!

WE WANT A FOLLOW-UP ON "CAT" HARRIS--SOMETHING THAT WILL DRAMATICALLY SYMBOLIZE A KILLER'S END --A PHOTOGRAPH OF HIS GRAVE! IT'S FOR THE MORNING EDITION, BILL -- SO YOU'LL HAVE TO DRIVE OUT TO THE CEMETERY TONIGHT!

WOW! I'VE HAD SOME GRIM ASSIGNMENTS LATELY-- BUT PROWLING AROUND A CEMETERY AT NIGHT CERTAINLY TOPS 'EM!

JUST TO KEEP UP THE OLD TEAM SPIRIT--I'LL GO ALONG WITH YOU!

MEANWHILE--WHAT OF THE SWAMI'S THREAT? SO FAR-- HE HAS MERELY GLANCED AT THE PAPER --

SO THEY DID EXPOSE ME, HAH? THOSE MEDDLING REPORTERS HAVE RUINED A PROFITABLE CAREER-- AND, BY BEELZEBUB-- THEY'LL PAY!

AND THEN --

WHAT'S THIS IN THE HEADLINE? THEY'VE EXECUTED "CAT" HARRIS -- AND THAT MEANS HIS SPIRIT HAS BEEN RELEASED-- CHARGED WITH THE SAME VICIOUSNESS THAT MADE HARRIS A RUTHLESS KILLER!

YES, THE HATE-RIDDEN GHOST OF "CAT" HARRIS WON'T BE AT REST UNTIL IT TAKES ITS REVENGE-- AND THAT'S EXACTLY WHAT I WANT MYSELF! HERE'S SOMETHING I'VE BEEN SAVING FOR JUST THIS MOMENT -- THE SECRET METHOD USED BY THE ANCIENTS TO RAISE EVIL SPIRITS!

HERE'S THE VERY FORMULA SET DOWN BY CORNELIUS AGRIPPA--OVER FIVE HUNDRED YEARS AGO! FIRST -- EXACT AMOUNTS OF CORIANDER, HENBANE, AND HEMLOCK --NEITHER TOO MUCH NOR TOO LITTLE -- MUST BE KEPT SMOLDERING ON A FIRE --

THEN, AS THE SMOKE THICKENS, I WILL GO INTO A TRANCE -- AND CONDUCT THE SPIRIT OF "CAT" HARRIS TO MY RETREAT! IT WILL OBEY ME--AS LONG AS THE MAGIC HERBS GIVE OFF THEIR FUMES!

69

SOON AFTERWARD -- WITH THE MOON BROODING OVER THE CEMETERY LIKE A GHOSTLY EYE --

HOPE WE WON'T HAVE TO SEARCH FOR HARRIS'S GRAVE, BILL -- IT MIGHT TAKE *HOURS!*

PERK UP, HONEY -- THE POLICE GAVE ME THE PRECISE SPOT!

AT THE FRESHLY-TURNED MOUND --

I KNOW THERE'S NOTHING REALLY SPOOKY ABOUT A CEMETERY -- BUT SOMEHOW, I CAN'T CONVINCE MY *NERVES!*

THAT'S A *FINE* WAY TO TALK -- RIGHT AFTER HELPING ME DEBUNK SWAMI HESHUG!

SUDDENLY --

FEEL THAT, TRUDY? THE GROUND SEEMS TO BE *SHAKING!*

BILL -- LOOK! THERE'S SOME KIND OF TERRIBLE GLOW COMING FROM THE EARTH!

AND THEN -- BARELY SEEN IN THE DRIFTING MOONLIGHT--

BILL!

EASY... I SEE IT!

I DON'T LIKE THE WAY IT'S STALKING US -- BUT I WANT MORE PICTURES OF THAT THING! KEEP CLEAR, TRUDY!

AS THE STRANGE SHAPE HOVERS SILENTLY CLOSER--

BILL -- LOOK OUT! DON'T LET IT GET YOU!

CRASH!

UNEXPECTEDLY--

FUNNY! HERE I AM, HELPLESS-- AND *THAT THING IS VANISHING!*

4

NOW THE GRAVEYARD HOLDS NOTHING BUT SHADOWED TOMBSTONES -- AND AN ODD FEAR!

I'D LIKE TO THINK IT WAS A TERRIBLE HALLUCINATION, TRUDY-- BUT THAT SHRUBBERY I FELL INTO IS HAZEL -- ONE OF THE FEW THINGS THAT CAN CHECK AN EVIL SPIRIT!

WE DID SEE HARRIS'S GHOST, BILL -- BUT THERE WAS SOMETHING ELSE THERE, TOO! SOMETHING INVISIBLE-- AND SINISTER!

WHY DID I FEEL SOMETHING EVIL -- WHEN I COULDN'T SEE IT? WAS IT ALL IMAGINATION, BILL?

THERE'S ONE WAY TO FIND OUT! I'LL DEVELOP THE FILM AS SOON AS WE GET BACK TO THE "GRAPHIC"!

AN HOUR LATER -- IN THE DARKROOM--

BRACE YOURSELF, TRUDY -- AND TAKE A LOOK!

GOOD HEAVENS! I DID SENSE SOMETHING BESIDES HARRIS-- BUT IT CAN'T BE HIM!

BUT IT IS! HOVERING DARKLY ABOVE THE GRAVE -- AS IF SUMMONING WHAT LIES BELOW ---

SWAMI HESHUG!

IT'S UNBELIEVABLE -- BUT REMEMBER THE SWAMI'S THREAT? SOMEHOW, HE'S MANAGED TO RAISE "CAT" HARRIS'S SPIRIT-- AND THEY'LL MAKE A DEADLY TEAM!

IT STILL SOUNDS LIKE A CRAZY DREAM! PEOPLE JUST DON'T SEE GHOSTS NOWADAYS!

CALM DOWN, LADY -- AND LOWER YOUR WINDOW BLINDS! IT WAS PROBABLY JUST A PIECE OF NEWSPAPER BLOWING DOWN THE STREET -- OR MAYBE SOMEONE'S IDEA OF A JOKE!

I'M BEGINNING TO WONDER WHETHER THAT STORY ON SPIRITUALISM HASN'T DONE MORE HARM THAN GOOD! THAT'S THE FOURTH PHONE CALL I GOT ABOUT SOMETHING CREEPY PROWLING DOWN BROOKHAVEN ROAD!

BROOKHAVEN ROAD! THAT'S THE WAY TO SWAMI HESHUG'S HOUSE!

PLEASE, BILL--TAKE THAT PICTURE TO THE POLICE-- BEFORE SOMETHING TERRIBLE HAPPENS!

THAT WOULDN'T HELP! EVEN IF I *COULD* CONVINCE THE POLICE THAT THE PHOTO ISN'T A TRICK SHOT COOKED UP FOR A GAG-- *THEY* HAVEN'T ANY MORE CONTROL OVER THE *SUPERNATURAL* THAN YOU OR I! NOPE-- I EXPOSED SWAMI HESHUG IN THE FIRST PLACE -- AND I'M GOING TO SEE THIS THROUGH -- NO MATTER *WHAT* HAPPENS!

ALL RIGHT--WE'LL *BOTH* SEE IT THROUGH! ONLY I'D FEEL A LOT BETTER ABOUT TACKLING THE SWAMI IF WE HAD A SPRIG OF THAT *HAZEL!*

WE *HAVE!* I HAD A HUNCH, BACK AT THE CEMETERY, THAT IT MIGHT COME IN HANDY!

A HALF-HOUR LATER --ITS GABLES RISING AGAINST THE MIDNIGHT SKY LIKE A CLUTCHING HAND--

WE'D BETTER SNEAK UP QUIETLY, TRUDY -- WITHOUT GIVING THE SWAMI A CHANCE TO STAGE ANY SURPRISES!

BUT, IN THE SWAMI'S LABORATORY--

IT'S TIME TO ADD ANOTHER BIT OF HEMLOCK --AND I'VE GOT TO BE INFERNALLY CAREFUL ABOUT BURNING THESE HERBS IN THE RIGHT PROPORTION! I NOTICE THE GHOST IS GETTING RESTLESS -- BUT MAYBE IT'S A *WARNING!*

SO *THAT'S* THE REASON! NOT IN MY WILDEST HOPES DID I EXPECT *THOSE* TWO TO COME *HERE!* WHAT A CHANCE FOR MY REVENGE ON THEM!

I WON'T TURN HARRIS LOOSE ON THEM *YET*--. NOT UNTIL THE MECHANICAL FEATURES I USE FOR MY FAKE SEANCES HAVE PROVIDED A LITTLE HAIR-RAISING ATMOSPHERE!

A MOMENT LATER--

HUG THE WALL WHILE I TRY TO FORCE THIS WINDOW -- SO YOU WON'T BE SPOTTED FROM ABOVE!

BUT HOW DO YOU KNOW THE DANGER'S *ABOVE*, BILL? SUPPOSE IT'S *DOWN* HERE -- *NEAR US?*

THEN...AS TRUDY LEANS AGAINST THE DARK MASONRY...

T-RRIP!

TRUDY! I THOUGHT I HEARD HER MOVING -- BUT SHE'S DISAPPEARED!

SHE COULDN'T HAVE WALKED OUT OF SIGHT IN JUST A FEW SECONDS! THE SWAMI'S GOT HER -- AND I'M TAKING THE QUICKEST WAY IN!

CRASH!

CATCHING ON THE JAGGED GLASS, THE HAZEL TWIG DROPS FROM BILL'S POCKET -- THE ONE THING THAT CAN STAVE OFF THE LURKING EVIL IN THE SWAMI'S LAIR!

AHEAD -- NOTHING BUT A STAIRWAY RISING ENDLESSLY INTO THE GLOOM -- AND A DISTANT HUM!

NO USE WONDERING WHAT MAKES THAT STRANGE WHIRRING NOISE -- OR WHERE THESE STAIRS LEAD! I'M GOING UP!

R-RRRRRR!

MINUTES PASS -- AND STILL --

I WOULDN'T BE SO TERRIFIED -- EVEN WITH THAT THING STARING AT ME -- IF I ONLY KNEW BILL WERE SAFE!

I DON'T GET THIS! I KEEP CLIMBING -- AND THERE'S NOTHING AHEAD BUT STEPS!

MEANWHILE --

WONDERING ABOUT OUR YOUNG FRIEND, HAH? HE'S TRYING TO GET UP THE CELLAR STAIRWAY -- AND HE'LL KEEP TRYING UNTIL HE DROPS -- BECAUSE IT'S AN ESCALATOR THAT DESCENDS AS FAST AS HE CLIMBS!

7

GOADED INTO AN ANGER GREATER THAN FEAR--

I'M NOT GOING TO STAND HERE -- AND LET YOU TORTURE BILL WITH YOUR HORRIBLE SCHEMES!

YOU THINK *THAT'S* ALL HAH? *JUST WAIT!*

IN THE NEXT INSTANT--

OOOPS! I'LL BE JIGGERED! THESE STEPS HAVE BEEN MOVING *DOWN* --AND THEY'VE SUDDENLY STOPPED!

IT'S EASY ENOUGH TO THROW A SWITCH -- BUT NOW--*LET'S SEE WHAT YOU CAN DO AGAINST THE SPIRIT OF "CAT" HARRIS!*

HERE'S WHERE THE SWAMI LEARNS ABOUT HAZEL TWIGS! GREAT GUNS-- *I'VE LOST IT!*

AS THE PHANTOM HOVERS CLOSER--

OH, BILL-- *DARLING!*

NOW THAT YOU'RE TOGETHER, YOU'VE CERTAINLY GOT THE MATERIAL FOR A GRIPPING NEW ARTICLE ON *GHOSTS*--IF YOU *LIVE LONG ENOUGH* TO WRITE IT!

JUST IN CASE WE *CAN'T* STOP THE PHANTOM -- I MIGHT AS WELL TAKE CARE OF *YOU* WHILE I HAVE THE CHANCE!

POW!

CRASH!

SHADES OF SHEOL -- MY ENTIRE SUPPLY OF MAGIC HERBS IS BURNING! THERE'S NO TELLING NOW *WHAT* THE GHOST WILL-- WHAT'S *THAT?*

YARRGH!

LIKE THE SHADOW OF DOOM REARING THROUGH THE MURK--

STOP! IT'S GROWN LARGER-- FIERCER -- AND IT'S TURNING ON *ME!*

ARGHH!

8

STALKED BY THE BEING HE PLANNED TO ENSLAVE!

I'VE GOT TO FIND A WEAPON-- *ANYTHING!* MAYBE IF I THREATEN IT--BRANDISH THIS PAPER KNIFE--IT WILL THINK I'M STILL MASTER!

THE SWAMI LUNGES FORWARD--TRIPS-- AND--

YAAAGH!

WAM!

BILL--LOOK! THE GHOST IS FADING OFF INTO A THIN MIST!

THAT'S STRANGE-- AFTER THE SWAMI SAID HE COULDN'T CONTROL IT! WONDER WHAT HAPPENED TO *HIM!*

HE'S *DEAD*, TRUDY-- BUT *THAT* DOESN'T EXPLAIN WHY HARRIS'S SPIRIT VANISHED!

MAYBE I'LL FIND THE ANSWER IN THIS OLD MANUSCRIPT! IT'S ALL ABOUT GHOSTS!

HERE'S *ONE* WAY TO DISPOSE OF EVIL SPIRITS, BILL -- BY KILLING THE WIZARD WHO SUMMONED THEM WITH A SILVER BULLET!

OR ANY *OTHER* SILVER OBJECT-- *INCLUDING A PAPER KNIFE!* THE SWAMI FELL ON IT--*AND IT PIERCED HIS HEART!*

WITH DAWN STREAKING THE SKY BEYOND THE GRIM AND SILENT HOUSE --

OH, CREEPERS! HERE IT IS MORNING--AND WE'VE FORGOTTEN TO GET ANOTHER PICTURE OF "CAT" HARRIS'S GRAVE FOR THE FIRST EDITION!

WHAT A FIX! IT'S A SURE BET WE CAN'T TURN IN *THIS* PHOTOGRAPH FOR PUBLICATION!

AND THERE, IN THE GREY HALF-LIGHT, COMES A FINAL SURPRISE!

WE *BOTH* SAW THE FRIGHTFUL THING THAT CAME OUT OF THE DEVELOPING TRAY, BILL -- BUT THE PICTURE'S *CHANGED!*

GUESS WE CAN BE *SURE* "CAT" HARRIS'S SPIRIT IS AT REST-- *BECAUSE THERE'S NOTHING HERE BUT THE BARE, FRESHLY- TURNED EARTH OF A KILLER'S GRAVE!*

The END

"GHOST MOTHER" by MRS. J. YAKAYIMA

I WOULD have laughed, once, if you asked me whether I believed in ghosts. Now, I'm not so sure. The reason dates back to Okinawa, during the fiery days of the second world war. The Americans were routing the Japanese in a bitterly-fought engagement, and the island was a virtual inferno. Shells shrieked through the air, bombs fell from the sky in a frenzied nightmare of rending horror. It was a life-or-death ordeal for the military, as well as for the native Okinawans, of whom I am one. I'll never forget it—never forget how we fled from the barrage.

I remember running with my wife—like the others, trying to find any shelter. It was a pitch-black night, rent by flaring explosions which dimly illuminated the grotesque heaps of bodies which lay sprawled everywhere, victims of the scourge we were attempting to escape. It was then, in a moment of sudden silence, that we heard it—a weak and childish crying that seemed oddly terrifying in itself. There couldn't be a child here—not in the midst of this carnage! But there was—a thin and miserable lad of about five or six who came falteringly towards us through the eerie gloom. I ran toward him, clutched him to me comfortingly. "What is it, sonnie?" I asked. "Lose your mother?"

A heartbroken sob was enough answer for me, and his choked syllables soon supplied the rest of the tragic story. For the child's mother was dead—killed by shrapnel as she fled for safety with her small son. And now he was alone, unprotected amid this horrible strife! Mutely, he pressed a tattered photograph into my hand. Obviously, it was his mother—a slight and wistful-looking woman with dark and haunting eyes, a faint scar like a half-moon cutting across her left cheek. I tried to cheer the lad by telling him he could come with us, share our food—that we would care for him and protect him from harm. And so it was that my wife and myself continued our search for shelter amid the raging battle, but this time with the helpless child of a dead woman!

There was little rest that night. It seemed as if the heavens themselves had opened, raining blazing bombs upon us. From spot to spot we fled, the three of us, driven by a relentless hail of fire. We sought protection finally in a deep crater, and there fell into a sleep of utter exhaustion. It must have been hours later that I awoke with a sudden start and a feeling of strange unease. I didn't know what had aroused me, but then I saw her there—a woman whose features were barely distinguishable in the gloom. She was beckoning to me frantically, signalling for me to awake the others and follow her. I don't know why I obeyed her, but there was something about her—some strange presence—that brooked no denial. As I woke my wife and the child, the moon passed from behind a cloud, throwing an eerie radiance about this new visitor. She was a slight and wistful-looking woman with dark and haunting eyes, a faint scar like a half-moon cutting across her left cheek. I gasped, remembering the photograph, and it was at this moment that the lad caught sight of her. "Mother! Mother! You've come back!" he screamed, and threw himself frantically into her arms. I stood there dazed, rooted to the spot, cold chills chasing each other up and down my spine—and then collected myself.

Now she had detached herself from her son's grasp, and once more was soundlessly beckoning to us. There was a mute appeal about her summons that couldn't be denied. We quit the crater in which we had sought shelter, followed her questioningly across the pitted field. We must have been a hundred feet from the crater when it happened. The air was rent by the demoniac shriek of a falling bomb. There was a tremendous concussion as we hurled ourselves to the ground. When we arose, fearfully, it was to a terrible sight. The crater in which but a moment ago we had slept was vanished—blown to smithereens! Shaken, I turned to thank the woman, but there was no one there. *She had vanished into thin air!*

AND SO THE PARTY SETS OUT··· HEADING INTO THE STRANGELY QUIET, MIST-SHROUDED JUNGLE!

WEIRD, ISN'T IT? IT'S SO STILL THAT I'VE GOT A FEELING OF BEING *WATCHED!*

CERTAINLY *IS* PECULIAR, JEAN! WE'RE DEEP IN THE TROPICAL FOREST ···AND WE HAVEN'T COME ACROSS A SINGLE ANIMAL OR BIRD! THERE'S NOTHING···NOTHING BUT *SILENCE!*

BUT MAYBE THAT SILENCE HAS A SHAPE···THE HIDEOUS FORM CROUCHED HIGH IN A NEARBY TREE!

FOR THE REST OF HER LIFE, JEAN WILL REMEMBER THIS INSTANT···WHEN SHE CASUALLY STOPPED···AND RAISED HER COMPACT!

WHAT'S THE MATTER, JEAN ···SOMETHING ON YOUR FACE?

JUST A COBWEB!

OHHH! LINK!

GARRRGH!

THE HANUMAN APE! BLAZES, LINK··· WE'LL NEVER BE ABLE TO GET HIM DOWN FROM *THERE!*

JUST A BEAST AT BAY? BUT THE OLD HEADMAN HAD TREMBLED···WHEN HE CALLED IT THE *BLACK HORROR!*

I'D HATE TO CLIMB UP AFTER HIM, DR. VANCE ···BUT THERE'S ANOTHER WAY! WE'LL BRING UP A CAGE···AND THEN SPREAD THE NETS DIRECTLY UNDER THE BRANCH HE'S PERCHED ON!

AND SO···

CR-RRAK!

GARRRGH!

HERE HE COMES!

CAREFUL, DR. VANCE! DON'T TAKE ANY CHANCES!

THE VICIOUS DEVIL··· HE NICKED ME ON THE WRIST! NICE TRY, YOU BRUTE··· *BUT YOU'RE NOT ESCAPING!*

2

WHAT A SPECIMEN, LINK! I NEVER DREAMED SUCH A THING *EXISTED*!

THAT BITE YOU GOT IS JUST A SCRATCH···BUT SOMEHOW, I DON'T *LIKE* IT! WHERE'S THE FIRST-AID KIT, JEAN?

I FEEL AS LINK DOES! THE NATIVES *DID* SAY THAT THE APE'S BITE MEANS *DEATH*, DR. VANCE!

I'LL PIT SCIENCE AGAINST SUPER-STITION, JEAN···AND GIVE MYSELF ANTI-RABIES AND ANTI-TETANUS SHOTS! AFTER THAT, I'LL LEAVE THE WORRYING TO YOU TWO··· AND TAKE A STROLL IN THE JUNGLE!

HALF-BURIED IN THE SILENT GREEN DEPTHS···

CRIMPERS, A RUINED TEMPLE ···AND A *BIG* ONE!

IMAGINE THE NATIVES *FEARING* THIS REGION ···WHEN IT WAS ONCE A CENTER OF CIVILIZATION!

SOON AFTERWARD···

DR. VANCE CAN LAUGH··· BUT I STILL FEEL THE NATIVES ARE RIGHT ABOUT LEAVING THE APE *HERE*···WHERE IT BELONGS! THERE'S SOMETHING ABOUT IT THAT *SCARES* ME, LINK!

LISTEN! DR. VANCE IS CALLING US!

BUT THIS CIVILIZATION WAS ROOTED IN TERROR··· SOMETHING THAT LINK IS GOING TO LEARN!

HERE'S THE MAIN ENTRANCE ARCH! FUNNY I SHOULD *WANT* TO GO IN···AND YET FEEL IT'S BEST I *DON'T*!

TERROR···TERROR RISING IN GRIM RANKS FROM THE DANK FOLIAGE!

STATUES···CARVED AGES AGO··· *EXACTLY LIKE THAT THING WE'VE GOT IN THE CAGE!*

"ONLY THE POWER OF OUR GREAT GOD SIVA HAS KEPT HANUMAN IN THE JUNGLE!" THAT'S WHAT THE OLD HEADMAN TOLD US ... AND I'M GETTING A QUEER NOTION THAT *HE KNOWS WHAT HE'S TALKING ABOUT!*

LINK ... WHERE ARE YOU?

COMING, JEAN!

WHAT WITH DR. VANCE HAVING BEEN BITTEN BY THE APE ... AND JEAN UNEASY ABOUT IT ... I'M NOT GOING TO SAY ANYTHING ABOUT *THIS!* NO USE TELLING THEM THERE'S SOMETHING *BEHIND* THE NATIVES' TERROR!

A WEEK LATER ... ON A SHIP BOUND FOR THE STATES ...

NOW THAT WE'VE GOT THE APE IN A STURDY STEEL CAGE DOWN IN THE HOLD, LINK ... I FEEL A BIT EASIER ABOUT THOSE WEIRD JUNGLE LEGENDS!

I'M SURE THERE'S NOTHING IN THAT YARN ABOUT THE APE'S BITE BEING DEADLY ... BUT JUST THE SAME ... I DON'T LIKE THE WAY DR. VANCE HAS BEEN *ACTING* SINCE WE SAILED YESTERDAY!

HE HASN'T LEFT HIS CABIN ONCE! HE SEEMS TO BE TROUBLED BY SOMETHING ... BUT IT ISN'T LIKE DR. VANCE TO BROOD OVER A NATIVE MYTH!

IT IS FOOLISH TO MOCK THE MYTHS OF INDIA, MY FRIEND!

WHAT? WHO ARE YOU?

MY NAME DOES NOT MATTER! IT WOULD MEAN LITTLE TO THOSE WHO DO NOT REALIZE THE TERROR THEY HAVE RELEASED FROM THE JUNGLE!

YOU MEAN ... THE HANUMAN APE?

TAKE THIS AS A TALISMAN ... AND PRAY THAT IT HAS NOT COME TOO LATE!

I HATE TO SOUND SILLY, LINK ... BUT PLEASE LET'S SEE HOW DR. VANCE IS!

I WAS JUST GOING TO SUGGEST IT! LET'S GO TO HIS CABIN ... *NOW!*

A MOMENT LATER...

THERE CAN'T BE ANYTHING SERIOUSLY WRONG WITH DR. VANCE! HE'S *LAUGHING!*

HA HA HA HA!

ABOUT *WHAT?* I NEVER HEARD HIM LAUGH SO... SO *STRANGELY,* LINK!

Then...IN RASPING ACCENTS BEARING A TOUCH OF FRENZY...

HAAA! I'LL GIVE YOU A WHOLE BOAT-LOAD OF SLAVES MASTER! THEY'LL OBEY YOU ...AS I DO!

LINK... WHAT'S WRONG? WHAT'S *HAPPENED* TO HIM?

I...I *HATE* TO GUESS!

DR. VANCE!

YOU'RE HARDLY RECOGNIZABLE! AND WHAT'S ALL THIS WILD TALK ABOUT *SLAVES?*

HAAA... *YOU'LL* FIND OUT! YOU'LL BE THE *FIRST* TO FIND OUT...I PROMISE YOU!

AND AS THE CACKLING FIGURE GLIDES OUT...

DID YOU GASP, JEAN?

HE'S *HERE*... DR. VANCE IS LYING ON THE BED... *DEAD!*

THAT HORRIBLE, EVIL THING WE SAW...IT WAS... DR. VANCE'S GHOST!

THE DOOR'S LOCKED...*FROM THE OUTSIDE!*

BUT *WHY,* LINK? WHY WOULD SOME-ONE AS HARM-LESS AS DR. VANCE CHANGE INTO A THING LIKE *THAT?*

JEAN, I SHRUGGED OFF THOSE WARNINGS FROM THE NATIVES... EVEN AFTER I FOUND THAT RUINED TEMPLE CROWDED WITH STATUES OF THE HANUMAN APE! BUT THERE WAS SOMETHING ELSE...*EVEN MORE TERRIBLE!*

IN A MOMENT OF CONVULSIVE ANGUISH---A FINAL SHUDDER---AND THE APE STANDS RIGID IN THE GLOOM!

LOOK AT IT! IT'S TURNED INTO STONE--- A STONE STATUE!

JUST LIKE THE ONES I FOUND AT THE RUINED TEMPLE, JEAN! NOW---WATCH WHAT'S HAPPENING TO THE GHOST OF DR. VANCE!

DRIFTING LIKE SMOKE BEFORE THE WIND---ITS HARSH VOICE FADING IN A DYING WHISPER---

MASTER! MASTER!

WE'VE BROKEN THE HANUMAN APE'S EVIL POWER---AND DR. VANCE'S SPIRIT IS RELEASED! I'M GLAD ABOUT THAT MUCH---BUT LET'S GET UP TO THE CABIN AND SEE WHAT THE DOCTOR LEARNED!

WE'RE DR. VANCE'S ASSISTANTS! WOULD YOU SAY THERE WAS ANYTHING ---MYSTERIOUS--- ABOUT HIS DEATH?

IT'S HARD TO SAY! IT COULD BE SOMETHING UNKNOWN---OR IT COULD BE JUNGLE FEVER--- THE SEVERE KIND, THAT CAN KILL IN A MATTER OF HOURS!

FINE LITTLE ANTIQUE YOU'VE GOT THERE! BUT I SUPPOSE YOU KNOW IT'S AN ANCIENT FIGURE OF THE GREAT GOD SIVA!

SIVA---THE ONE POWER THAT KEPT THE APE FROM LEAVING THE JUNGLE! BUT SPEAKING OF STATUES, DOCTOR--- THERE'S ANOTHER ONE I WANT YOU TO SEE--- DOWN IN THE HOLD!

A MOMENT LATER---

YOU SEEM TO KNOW A LOT ABOUT HINDU LEGENDS! CAN YOU TELL US ANYTHING ABOUT THIS HANUMAN APE STATUE?

FRANKLY, I'VE NEVER HEARD OF A HANUMAN APE! THIS THING MAY LOOK APELIKE ---BUT IT REPRESENTS HANUMAN---THE DEMON BEHIND ALL EVIL!

YOU WERE LUCKY TO FIND SUCH A FINE SPECIMEN---THESE DEMON STATUES ARE ALMOST UNKNOWN! FOR SOME REASON---THE NATIVES HAVE BEEN SMASHING IMAGES OF HANUMAN FOR OVER THREE THOUSAND YEARS!

YES---THEY KNOW! ---I'VE GOT A STRANGE REQUEST TO MAKE, DOCTOR! I WANT A DECK CREW TO RAISE THIS THING OUT OF THE HOLD WITH A CARGO WINCH---AND DUMP IT INTO THE SEA!

Later

I'M GLAD YOU UNLOCKED DR. VANCE'S CABIN FOR US, STEWARD ---BUT WHAT MADE YOU TURN UP?

WELL, SIR---I THOUGHT I'D GO AND TELL DR. VANCE THAT YOU AND THE YOUNG LADY WERE ACTING A BIT QUEER! GAVE ME QUITE A TURN TO SEE YOU BOTH SITTING HERE ---TALKING TO AN EMPTY CHAIR!

AS THE APE DEMON PLUNGES INTO THE GREEN DEPTHS THAT WILL CLOSE UPON IT FOREVER

LINK---WE DID GET THE FIGURINE OF SIVA FROM SOMEONE---BUT THE STEWARD DIDN'T SEE HIM!

MAYBE IT'S SOMETHING THAT MUST BE BELIEVED BEFORE IT CAN BE SEEN, DARLING---SOMETHING THAT KEEPS THE FORCES OF TERROR CHECKED---THE POWER OF THE GREAT GOD SIVA!

The MUMMY'S CLOTH

TIME: THE PRESENT. PLACE: THE VALLEY OF THE NILE, EGYPT. A PARTY FROM THE INTERNATIONAL ARCHAEOLOGICAL SOCIETY HAS JUST UNCOVERED THE TOMB OF SESOSTRIS, PHARAOH OF THE TWELFTH DYNASTY...UNWITTINGLY BLAZING THE PATH FOR ONE OF THE MOST GRIPPING ADVENTURES EVER TO HAVE EMERGED FROM OUT OF THE GREAT UNKNOWN!

WHAT A FIND...EH, DICK? ONE OF THE FEW TOMBS THAT HAS NEVER BEEN RAIDED BY ROBBERS! BIGGEST COLLECTION OF HISTORICAL DATA THAT'S EVER BEEN DUG UP, TOO!

LET'S OPEN THE SARCOPHAGUS, DOC...I'M ANXIOUS TO HAVE A LOOK AT THAT OLD BOY IN PERSON!

HEY...WHAT'S THIS? I'M A LITTLE RUSTY ON MY HIEROGLYPHICS, BUT...HMMM... "HE THAT TOUCHES AUGHT THAT TOUCHES ME SHALL SUFFER THE VENGEANCE OF THE UNKNOWN!"

OLD SESOSTRIS WAS PROBABLY JUST TRYING TO SCARE OFF GRAVE-ROBBERS, I GUESS! FORGET IT ...AND LET'S GET THAT LID OFF!

WOW! LOOK AT HIM! ...THIS OLD BOY IS ONE OF THE MOST REMARKABLE SPECIMENS I'VE EVER SEEN! HE'S PERFECTLY PRESERVED...THE EMBALMING BANDAGES LOOK AS IF THEY HAD JUST BEEN PUT ON!

THIS WILL BE A FEATHER IN OUR CAP, SIR! EVERY OTHER MUMMY DISCOVERED HAS BEEN IN SOME STATE OF DISINTEGRATION...BUT THIS ONE IS ABSOLUTELY PERFECT!

WELL... I DON'T THINK WE'LL HAVE TO WORRY ABOUT THAT VENGEANCE THE OLD MUMMY PROMISED US! WE'RE THE LAST ONES THAT WOULD WANT TO TOUCH OR DISTURB ANYTHING ON HIM!

HA-HA! THAT'S RIGHT, DOCTOR... WE WON'T TOUCH ANYTHING THAT TOUCHES HIM! ...WE'D BETTER GET ON OUTSIDE AND SEE THAT OUR THINGS ARE BEING PACKED FOR SHIPMENT!

YOU, THERE! GET GOING... WE WANT TO GET THIS STUFF OUT OF HERE!

BUT, SAHIB, THE STRAP ON MY SANDAL HAS BROKEN!

WELL, FIX IT AND GET STARTED, OR YOU'RE OUT OF A JOB! WE CAN'T AFFORD IDLE MEN!

YES, SAHIB! IMMEDIATELY, SAHIB!

IF ONLY I HAD A PIECE OF STRING OR... HA! A PIECE OF CLOTH FROM THIS ANCIENT CORPSE WILL DO! HE NO LONGER NEEDS IT!

A FEW MINUTES LATER...

AND SO A SMALL PORTION OF THE CLOTH WHICH HAD SWATHED THE ANCIENT MUMMY FOUND A NEW USE... IN THE SANDAL OF A SIMPLE WORKER! WOULD THE AGE-OLD PROPHECY HOLD TRUE? LET US SEE! BRIEF MOMENTS LATER...

DOCTOR WINBER! WE'VE JUST DISCOVERED THAT THE MUMMY'S BEEN TAMPERED WITH! PART OF THE EMBALMING CLOTH HAS BEEN REMOVED!

WHAT!! SO HELP ME, IF I FIND THE SCOUNDREL RESPONSIBLE...

I MUST LEAVE! IF THE SAHIBS DISCOVER IT WAS ME, I WILL NEVER HAVE WORK WITH THEM AGAIN!

2.

LATER THAT NIGHT, IN THE LABORER'S HOME... WHAT STRANGE, AGE-OLD SECRET IS THIS?

HELP! HELP! AH-HH!

QUICK, CAPTAIN! WE'VE GOT TO DO SOMETHING! SOME POOR DEVIL MAY BE TRAPPED IN THERE!

THE FIRE DIED DOWN AS STRANGELY AS IT STARTED, SIR... *BUT I'M AFRAID THIS POOR BLOKE IS FINISHED!*

FUNNY THING! THE WHOLE INTERIOR OF THIS ROOM GUTTED, BURNED TO A CRISP.. *EXCEPT FOR THIS OLD PIECE OF CLOTH!*

THE...CLOTH! THAT'S WHAT CAUSED IT! IT... TRIED TO KILL ME! TAKE IT AWAY!

RELAX, MATEY! SURE! YOU'RE GOING TO A HOSPITAL... BUT WE'LL TAKE THE CLOTH WITH US IF IT'LL MAKE YOU FEEL BETTER!

A STRANGE HAPPENING...AND STRANGER WERE TO COME!

SHE'S COMIN' DOWN IN BLOODY SHEETS, CAPTAIN! I CAN'T SEE A FOOT PAST THE BOW!

MIGHTY UNUSUAL! I'VE NEVER HIT A SQUALL IN THESE WATERS AT THIS TIME OF YEAR IN ALL MY YEARS AT SEA!

DERELICT DEAD AHEAD, SIR! B-BETTER TAKE THE WHEEL, QUICK!

MY HAND! I CAN'T GET MY HAND FREE! SOMETHING SEEMS TO BE HOLDING IT FAST IN MY POCKET!

A FEW MINUTES LATER..

THE FOR'ARD HOLD IS FLOODED AND WE'RE DOWN HARD BY THE BOW, CAPTAIN, BUT THE BULKHEAD IS HOLDING AND WE'LL MAKE IT OKAY!

I TELL YOU, MARTY, THIS OLD *CLOTH* IS THE CAUSE OF IT ALL! IT GRIPPED MY WRIST LIKE A VISE! I'M BEGINNING TO THINK THAT POOR NATIVE WAS RIGHT! IT WAS THE CLOTH THAT CAUSED THAT FIRE... *IT WAS THE CLOTH THAT CAUSED THIS TERRIBLE COLLISION!*

SEVERAL DAYS LATER, IN THE OFFICES OF THE STEAMSHIP COMPANY...

SO HELP ME, MR. WAVERLY, THE STORY I'VE TOLD YOU ABOUT THAT CLOTH IS THE *TRUTH!* IT CAUSED THE...

BALDERDASH! DO YOU EXPECT ME TO BELIEVE SUCH *TOMMY-ROT?* CAPTAIN, OUR SHIP WAS DAMAGED BECAUSE OF YOUR GROSS NEGLIGENCE... NOW *GET OUT! YOU'RE THROUGH!*

HUH! DID THE MAN THINK ME A *FOOL?*... I'LL JUST KEEP THIS CLOTH AS A SOUVENIR OF THE MOST PREPOSTEROUS EXCUSE FOR NEGLIGENCE I'VE EVER *HEARD!*

A SHORT TIME LATER, WHEN MR. WAVERLY ARRIVES HOME...

YOUR DINNER IS WAITING, SIR!

THANKS, ALFRED, AND SEE THAT I'M NOT DISTURBED, WILL YOU? *UNDER NO CIRCUMSTANCES* ANSWER ANY CALLS AT THE DOOR!

NOW WHAT COULD HAVE MADE ME SAY *THAT?* ...NERVES, PROBABLY...THAT CAPTAIN UPSET ME!

MEANWHILE, JUST OUTSIDE THE WAVERLY HOME, TWO BOBBIES HAVE MADE A HORRIFYING DISCOVERY!

IT'S ONE OF THOSE BLINKIN' DELAYED-ACTION BOMBS THE JERRIES DROPPED! HOW THE REMOVAL CREWG EVER MISSED IT I'LL NEVER KNOW ···BUT IT COULD GO OFF *ANY* TIME!

I'LL WARN OLD WAVERLY AND HIS HOUSEHOLD TO GET OUT OR THEY'LL BE BLOWN SKY HIGH!

WHAT THE ···THEY DON'T SEEM TO HEAR ME! I'LL HAVE TO TRY PHONING THEM!

KNOCK!
KNOCK!

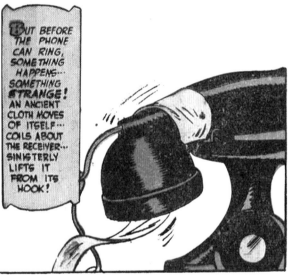

BUT BEFORE THE PHONE CAN RING, SOMETHING HAPPENS···SOMETHING *STRANGE!* AN ANCIENT CLOTH MOVES OF ITSELF···COILS ABOUT THE RECEIVER···SINISTERLY LIFTS IT FROM ITS HOOK!

I MUST GET OUT A FEW LETTERS AND··· *THAT CLOTH!* IT···IT'S WRAPPED AROUND THE PHONE AS IF IT HAD PULLED IT OFF THE···

NEXT MOMENT WITH AWFUL IMPACT···

BA-ROOM!

A FEW MINUTES LATER···

THANK HEAVENS YOU'RE ALIVE, MR. WAVERLY··· BUT YOUR HOUSE IS WRECKED! WE TRIED TO WARN YOU, BUT YOUR PHONE MUST HAVE BEEN OFF THE HOOK!

THE PHONE! *THAT CLOTH WAS WRAPPED AROUND IT!* THEN IT *DID* PULL IT OFF!

5.

WHAT WAS THAT, SIR? WHAT DID YOU SAY ABOUT A CLOTH?

EH?···ER···NOTHING, OFFICER! IF YOU'LL CALL ME A CAB, I'LL GO ON IN TO MY APARTMENT IN LONDON!

SEVERAL HOURS LATER, IN LONDON···

COULD I BE GOING MAD, OR WAS IT JUST MY IMAGINATION? BUT THEN WHY DID I GIVE THAT STRANGE ORDER NOT TO ANSWER THE DOOR? AND I SAW THAT CLOTH ON THE PHONE···

AND THEN THERE WAS THE CAPTAIN'S STORY OF THE NATIVE'S FIRE···AND THE ACCIDENT TO THE SHIP···BUT WHY? WHY? WHY SHOULD A MERE PIECE OF CLOTH CAUSE IT ALL? IF THERE WAS ONLY SOMEONE I COULD TALK TO THAT WOULDN'T THINK ME MAD ···DOCTOR WINBER! MY BEST FRIEND···I'LL CALL HIM!

NO, NO! NOT AT ALL, OLD FELLOW! IF IT'S THAT IMPORTANT, I'LL BE RIGHT OVER!

SEVERAL HOURS LATER·· WAVERLY HAS FINALLY FINISHED TELLING HIS STORY TO HIS FRIEND, DOCTOR WINBER···

···THAT'S IT, TOM! I KNOW THIS IS THE TWENTIETH CENTURY, AND THAT YOU'RE A HARD-BITTEN MAN OF SCIENCE, BUT I'M NEITHER INSANE NOR···

I KNOW THAT, GEORGE! NOW THE CLOTH···MAY I SEE IT?

GOOD HEAVENS! CAN IT BE POSSIBLE THAT··· GEORGE, IF MY SUSPICIONS ARE CORRECT, I THINK I HAVE THE ANSWER TO THIS MYSTERIOUS MATTER!

TIMELESS IS THE NIGHT

THE doctor's waiting room was crowded. But in the office, the old doctor stood idle by the window, looking out, his gaze turned to the weather-beaten shingle on the gatepost . . . *Michael Everett, M.D.* Just below was another, gleaming new . . . *Michael Everett III, M.D.* The young man seated by the desk was a carbon copy of his grandfather. His glance was fond, his voice confident as he spoke.

"Believe me, I've learned one fact! There's *nothing* that medical science can't do . . . can't *explain!*"

The old doctor turned away from the window, "Nothing that science *can't* explain?" he asked. His voice was the voice of a wise man facing a lifetime of memories. "How long ago it was . . . and how short a time it seems . . . that I too was proud, confident of the powers of science! I was new in town, and full of my medical knowledge. I couldn't sleep nights waiting for my first call. I knew it would come, and it did—at night, of course!

"When my doorbell rang that night, I leaped from my bed to answer. At the door there was no one. *Not a soul!* But on the threshold I found a note. And fifteen minutes later, I found myself in the hall of a large house on Silver Hill. My patient was rich, and beautiful. Her hair was blacker than coal against the satin coverlet of her bed. Her face —whiter than milk! Her lungs were laboring, but thank Heaven there was still time to head off pneumonia. Pitifully, the girl cried out. 'Doctor, save me! I don't want to die!' As gently as I could, I comforted her and wrote out my prescription.

"'You'll be fine . . . fine!' I promised confidently. 'Science knows just the way to save your life! Send one of the servants for this medicine. I'll stop in to see you first thing in the morning.'

"Next day, I came back to Silver Hill. I was whistling as I turned the corner to the house. Strange . . . the corner was overgrown with a tangle of weeds! And the house — suddenly I stopped, shocked breathless.

"In the light of day, the house was grey, broken, crumbling. An old ruin, in the space of a single night! A hand tapped my shoulder. I turned quickly.

"The old man had come up from the street. 'Who be ye, and what're ye after, son?' he asked. 'This place has been deserted fer *ten years!*'

"My voice grew loud and wild. 'What do you mean? Hear me, old fool, I was in there myself *last night!*'

"The old man's reply was like the cackle of a parrot. 'There ain't been anyone livin' there fer ten years. Come on in an' see fer yerself!'

"Inside, the richness was gone. Grime, soot remained. And one thing more . . . *the smell of death!* I remembered the way to the girl's room. It was deserted. The bed was broken, empty with the emptiness of years . . . *ten years!*

"Behind me, the old man babbled, 'Ain't no one been livin' here *since the purty young mistress died!*'

"All at once, I was down on my knees on the floor, bending over a scrap of clean, white paper. I couldn't pick it up. I couldn't look at it . . . and yet I couldn't bear to tear my eyes away! I was shaking uncontrollably. My voice was a shout for help.

"'Here, old one . . . here! This is the prescription I wrote for my patient last night . . ., *in my own handwriting!*'"

The old doctor turned back to the window. In the chair by the office desk, the younger Doctor Michael Everett was silent.

DRUMS of the UNDEAD

AN ANCIENT SUPERSTITION, OLD AS THE JUNGLE GODS THEMSELVES, CLAIMS THAT SOULS CAN BE ENSNARED BY THE POWER OF *VOODOO*...PROWLING AS *ZOMBIES* THROUGH AN ETERNAL NIGHT! THEIR SIGNAL IS A *DRUM*...A VOODOO *DRUM*...THE HALF-HEARD, HALF-FELT THROB THAT SUMMONS *THE UNDEAD!*

GLAD YOU DROPPED IN, SHEILA! I'M ILLUSTRATING A STORY ON HAITI...AND WITHOUT BACK-GROUND MATERIAL...I'M STUCK!

HOW ABOUT DIGGING UP YOUR *OWN* BACKGROUND MATERIAL? IT JUST MEANS TAKING A CAMERA TO THE MUSEUM!

I'VE HEARD THAT HAITI IS THE HOME OF *VOODOO!* WHAT'S IT ALL ABOUT, BILL?

NOT MANY PEOPLE KNOW! ALL *I'M* SURE OF IS THAT IT'S A GOOD THING TO STAY AWAY FROM!

OH, MURDER...I DIDN'T REALIZE IT'S PAST CLOSING TIME! THERE'S SOMETHING STRANGE ABOUT MUSEUMS THIS TIME OF DAY... SORT OF *CREEPY,* BILL!

WASN'T THIS *YOUR* IDEA? WE'RE GOING INSIDE ...I'VE GOT AN AFTER-HOURS PASS!

AND SO...THROUGH THE SHADOWED CORRIDORS --- STIRRING WITH ECHOES...

THAT'S THE STUFF I WANT...THINGS THAT ALMOST MURMUR ABOUT MYSTER-IOUS MIDNIGHT RITUALS!

BILL...STOP! YOU'RE MAKING ME IMAGINE THINGS ...OR *IS* IT IMAGI-NATION?

CARIBBEAN EXHIBIT

I'M DR. WENROD ··· THE CURATOR! DID I HEAR A DISTURBANCE?

QUAINT WAY OF PUTTING IT! I TOOK A FALL ··· TRYING TO STOP A GIRL WHO MADE OFF WITH ONE OF YOUR *DRUMS!*

H'M ··· THERE *IS* A DRUM MISSING ··· A *VOODOO* DRUM ··· THE ONLY ONE OF ITS KIND EVER TO LEAVE HAITI! A *GIRL,* YOU SAID?

I MANAGED TO GET HER *PICTURE!* MIGHT HAVE GOT *HER,* TOO ··· IF THAT WALL-EYED FIGURE HADN'T BEEN PLACED SO CLOSE TO THE DOOR!

FIGURE? BUT THERE'S NOTHING ANYWHERE *NEAR* THAT DOORWAY!

THERE *WAS,* DOCTOR ··· WE BOTH SAW IT! A TALL THING ··· SCAREY ··· WITH A MARK LIKE A *U* UPSIDE DOWN ON ITS FOREHEAD!

I'VE BEEN FOOLED BY SHADOWS MYSELF! BUT THIS *PICTURE* ··· CAN YOU HAVE IT DEVELOPED FOR ME BY TOMORROW? IT SHOULD BE HELPFUL TO THE POLICE!

I DON'T KNOW WHETHER WE SHOULD GET MIXED UP IN THIS, BILL! DR. WENROD SEEMED UPSET ··· MORE UPSET THAN HE CARED TO SHOW!

THERE ARE CERTAINLY MORE ANGLES THAN I HAVE TIME FOR ··· WITH A DEADLINE ON THOSE DRAWINGS! IF YOU HAVE A FREE MINUTE IN THE MORNING ··· HOW ABOUT GETTING THE FILM DEVELOPED?

LATE THAT NIGHT ··· AS BILL BENDS OVER HIS DRAWING-BOARD ···

STRANGE SENSATION! WHY SHOULD MY PULSE THUD LIKE THAT JUST BECAUSE I'M DRAWING ··· A *DRUM?*

BUT THE THROB BEATS LOUDER ··· LOUDER THAN ANY PULSE ··· EVEN A PULSE QUICKENED BY FEAR!

ALL RIGHT ··· I *HEAR* IT! BUT I'LL BE SWITCHED IF I CAN SCARE MYSELF INTO THINKING I *SEE* SOMETHING, TOO!

BOOM BOOM BOOM

YOU CAN'T FORGET IT, CAN YOU? IT BEATS ··· BEATS ··· LIKE THE PANT OF MIDNIGHT ··· AND YOU WONDER! YOU WONDER ···

WHO'S THERE? *WHO ARE YOU?*

THE GIRL IN THE *MUSEUM!* WHAT'S ALL THIS *ABOUT,* ANYWAY?

THE *PHOTOGRAPH!* I WILL NOT THREATEN OR FRIGHTEN YOU... I *PLEAD* ...GIVE ME THE FILM!

IF YOU COULD ONLY UNDERSTAND WHAT THE DRUM MEANS TO ME... YOU WOULD KNOW WHY I HURRIED TO THE MUSEUM WHEN I ARRIVED FROM HAITI TODAY! YOU WOULD NOT ASK QUESTIONS... *OR TAKE PICTURES!*

JUST A DRUM... A QUAINT LITTLE DRUM ...NOT WORTH A PICTURE... NOT WORTH YOUR *PEACE OF MIND!*

BUT WORTH A TWO THOUSAND MILE TRIP FROM HAITI, EH? YOU CAN SWITCH OFF THE ACT, SISTER... *I'M NOT LISTENING!*

YOU WOULDN'T GET THE FILM EVEN IF I HAD IT... BUT AS A MATTER OF FACT, I GAVE IT TO SHEILA! THE PICTURE WILL BE IN TOMORROW'S TABLOIDS... IF YOU'RE INTERESTED!

THEN IT IS DECIDED! YOU CANNOT GUESS MY POWER... YOU CANNOT SENSE YOUR DANGER... *BUT YOU WILL FIND OUT!*

WHAT A CASE... MUTTERING ABOUT *POWER, DANGER!* CARIBBEAN CRUISE SHIPS DOCK ONLY ON SATURDAYS... SO SHE MUST HAVE COME IN ON A *PLANE!* LET'S SEE... SOUTHERN AIRLINES MAKES A DIRECT RUN FROM HAITI...

THERE WAS ONLY ONE WOMAN ANSWERING YOUR DESCRIPTION ON TODAY'S PLANE! SHE'S LISTED AS *ERZULIE BOCOR* ...NO AGE... NO ADDRESS... NO DESTINATION!

GREAT! THANKS A LOT!

NERTS ON WORK ...*THIS* I'VE GOT TO TELL SHEILA ABOUT!

NATURALLY, THERE *WOULDN'T* BE LIGHTS IN SHEILA'S HOUSE... IT'S LATE! NOTHING TO GET SO JUMPY ABOUT!

*N*OTHING? THEN WHY BE TENSE WITH A COLD FEAR... AND WHY THAT STRANGE THUDDING OF A *DRUM?*

SHEILA... WHAT'S *WRONG?* WHY DON'T YOU *SAY* SOMETHING?

BOOM... BOOM!

ERZULIE BOCOR! THAT'S HER NAME...THE WOMAN WHO TOOK THE DRUM! SHE SENT ONE OF THOSE THINGS AFTER SHEILA...AND THE CAMERA...AND SHEILA HAD THE ZOMBIE SIGN ON HER FOREHEAD!

THERE'S ONLY ONE WAY TO SAVE SHEILA AND DEFEAT THE AWFUL CREATURE WHO HAS HER IN HER POWER! WE'VE GOT TO GET THAT CAMERA BACK...AND FAST!

IF ERZULIE'S PICTURE WERE TO BE DEVELOPED, IT WOULD BE DEADLY TO HER...AS DEADLY AS A BULLET WOULD BE TO A HUMAN! WE DON'T KNOW WHERE SHE IS...BUT WE DO KNOW THAT SHE HATES YOU FOR HAVING CAUSED HER THIS TROUBLE!

I GET IT! YOU'RE PLANNING A TRAP FOR HER...USING ME AS BAIT! WHAT'S YOUR PLAN?

HYPNOTIZING YOU! IT LOWERS YOUR MENTAL RESISTANCE...AND THE UNDEAD WILL SENSE YOUR WEAKNESS! THE REST OF US WILL KEEP IN THE BACKGROUND...WHILE THAT EVIL THING SENDS ONE OF HER EMISSARIES AFTER YOU!

AND THUS, TO SAVE SHEILA, BILL CONSENTS TO AN EXPERIMENT FRAUGHT WITH DEADLY DANGER!

YOU'RE DRIFTING OFF...YOUR WILL IS WEAKENING! LISTEN...CAN'T YOU HEAR HIM APPROACHING...YOUR MESSENGER FROM THE UNKNOWN?

BOOM, BOOM!

MAYBE I'M BEING HYPNOTIZED, TOO! I KNOW ONE WHEN I HEAR ONE...AND IT'S A DRUM!

SHHH-H! LOOK!

WAIT...HE'LL BE OUT OF THE HYPNOTIC TRANCE IN A FEW MINUTES! WE'LL FIND HIM...AND HER...BY FOLLOWING THE DRUM BEATS!

SOON...IN A LONELY GRAVEYARD ON THE OUTSKIRTS OF TOWN...

WHERE...WHERE AM I? I'M CONSCIOUS AGAIN, AND ...SHEILA!

SO NOW YOU'VE GOT *ME!* I *WONDERED* WHAT YOUR STRONGHOLD WOULD BE LIKE, ERZULIE!

AND YOU MAY *STILL* WONDER! *THIS* IS MERELY AN OLD BURIAL-GROUND...A STOPPING-OFF PLACE UNTIL WE CAN RETURN TO THE LONELY DEPTHS OF THE HAITIAN JUNGLE!

BOOM! BOOM!

YES, WE ARE *READY* TO RETURN... NOW THAT WE HAVE THE DRUM...AND THIS CAMERA...AND TWO *NEW* ZOMBIES IN THE RANKS OF THE UNDEAD! *YOU* AND THE GIRL!

ERZULIE PROMISED ME THAT WE'D ALWAYS BE TOGETHER THERE, BILL...THE TWO OF US...*FOREVER!*

NO, SHEILA...YOU DON'T *KNOW* WHAT YOU'RE SAYING! WE'RE NOT *COMPLETELY* IN HER EVIL POWER...*AND I'LL PROVE IT!*

ERZULIE GOT A LITTLE OVER-CONFIDENT... CHANGING THE ZOMBIES BACK TO THEIR USUAL PHYSICAL FORMS! *THEY CAN FEEL A PUNCH NOW!*

WE'RE READY TO RETURN TOO, ERZULIE...BACK TO THE KIND OF LIFE HUMANS WERE MADE TO LEAD...AND I'M TAKING *THIS!*

YOU THINK TO ESCAPE...*NOW?* WHEREVER YOU GO...*THEY* WILL PURSUE! WHEREVER YOU HIDE ...THE *DRUMS OF THE UNDEAD* WILL SOUND...HOUR AFTER HOUR ...NIGHT AFTER NIGHT...*UNTIL YOU YIELD!*

AND THEY *DO* PURSUE...WITH SLOW, PLODDING STEPS...ON THE TRAIL OF A QUARRY THAT CANNOT ESCAPE!

I...I CAN'T SHAKE 'EM OFF!

SCREEEEECH!

EDITOR — **LET'S TALK IT OVER!**

Draw up a chair, folks, and sit down! It's time for another meeting of that fast-growing organization known as *Loyal Fans of "Adventures Into The Unknown!"*

The time between our last issue and this one has been a hectic interval for us. Hectic because we were determined to come up with an all-star issue that you'd remember *forever!* We didn't leave a single stone unturned in this effort. We scanned your letters for the types of stories you liked best. And then we turned our research men loose, with orders to search for strange, little-known facts and occurrences out of the great *Unknown*—the very kind of material which you'd indicated you wanted! Next, our writers got busy, welding this information into tense and breathless plots which were sure-fire. Finally came the artists, bringing the stories to life through the medium of carefully-planned and thrilling pictures.

Out of all this has emerged an issue loaded with truly gripping stories of the Supernatural. Such stories as *"The Swami's Secret"*—*"The Ape Demon"*—*"The Mummy's Cloth"*—*"Drums of the Undead"*—*The Case of the Roman Curse."* These yarns are *different*—nothing like them has ever been published before! And we've gathered them for *your* entertainment, for this is *your* magazine! So why not do your part in helping to determine what we're going to carry in the future? It's *easy*—all you have to do is write us, telling us what you think of *"Adventures Into The Unknown"*—what stories you liked or disliked and why—*and what you'd like to see in our next issue!* Other readers are doing it—so why not you? And just in case you'd like to know what some of those others are saying about us, *here goes!*

"I have always been fascinated by supernatural stories. I have read many such stories, but after I read your *Adventures Into The Unknown* for the first time, I feel that the stories you print are more *realistic* and *exciting* than any that I have ever read. I like them because they appeal to the *imagination*. I look forward to every issue and can't put down your comics book till I finish it. Keep up the good work!"
— Fred W. Goldstein, 811 E. 178th St., New York, N. Y.

Glad you feel that way about our magazine, Mr. Goldstein! We'll try to keep it rolling the way you want it!

"In my opinion, yours is the *best* magazine on sale today. I have always been a follower of this type of literature and I think that *Adventures Into The Unknown* is *tops* in this field. It is so good that I have decided to own every issue published. Here is $1.20 for a 12-issue subscription, plus 20c for which please send me issues Nos. 1 and 2, which I unfortunately missed. Thanks a million for the *most thrilling* comics book I have ever read!"
— James Parry, R.F.D. No. 2, Taft Road, E. Syracuse, N. Y.

Thanks for your kind words, Mr. Parry—and for your subscription! There's even better material coming—that's a promise!

"I have just finished reading your April-May issue. It certainly is a *wonderful* magazine! I especially liked your story, *Back to Yesterday*. I wish you would have more stories concerning *reincarnation*. I'd also like to see a whole magazine filled with nothing but stories about *werewolves*. I'm very interested in that subject! Unfortunately, I missed the issue which told about your contest. I've quite a story to tell—could you renew the contest? Your faithful reader—"
— David Roggensach, R.R. 1, Altoona, Iowa

We'll keep your wants in mind in framing future issues! Sorry you missed the contest, but we're considering an even more interesting one for the future—watch for announcement!

In this issue—our second-prize contest-winning story—"Ghost Mother," by Mrs. J. Yakayima! Congratulations, Mrs. Yakayima, for one of the most captivating and eerie stories in months! Your check's in the mail right now, bound for far-off Hawaii! And you readers—watch for our next issue, with more prize-winning information!

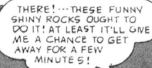

NEXT MORNING... LOOKS LIKE THE SAME OLD TALE, LAD! A SWORD THRUST...AND YOU KNOW WHAT *THAT* MEANS!

AYE... *THE ROMAN GHOSTS!* AND SCOTLAND YARD ONLY LAUGHS WHEN WE SEND IN OUR REPORTS!

LATER...AT NINE YEWS, ESTATE OF LADY PAMELA HOGARTH...

THE MAN'S DEAD...BUT WHO CAN ARREST A GHOST? AND SINCE YOU OWN THE PROPERTY, LADY PAMELA...

I KNOW, CONSTABLE! I'VE BEEN MEANING TO DO SOMETHING FOR A LONG TIME ...*AND NOW I WILL!*

THERE'S A MAN IN AMERICA... *CHRISTOPHER FENN*... WHO'S AN *EXPERT* IN THESE MATTERS! *GHOST-HUNTING* IS HIS PROFESSION! I'LL SEND A WIRELESS ASKING HIM TO *COME AT ONCE!*

AND IN NEW YORK... LOOKS LIKE MY NEXT CASE IS *ENGLAND*, PENNY! SOME LADY PAMELA HOGARTH IS HAVING *GHOST TROUBLE!*

WELL, IF IT'S AN ACE GHOST DETECTIVE SHE'S AFTER, *SHE'S GOT HER MAN!*

SEEMS I'VE HEARD OF THE *ROMAN GHOSTS* BEFORE! HMM...MUST BE A LOT OF OLD ROMAN CAMPS IN THAT PART OF ENGLAND, NEAR SALISBURY AND STONEHENGE!

SO, UNTIL THE WEE HOURS OF THE MORNING...

WELL...I GUESS I'VE GOT ALL THE DOPE I CAN GET OUT OF A BOOK! SEEMS *AUTHENTIC* ENOUGH, TOO! *A GHOST LEGION OF ROMAN SOLDIERS*...CURSED BY THE ANCIENT DRUIDS FOR THEIR TREATMENT OF THE BRITONS! CAME TO ENGLAND SHORTLY AFTER CAESAR'S TIME...AND WERE DOOMED TO REMAIN FOREVER IN THEIR CAMP, UNDYING! NEXT STOP...*ENGLAND!*

THIS *COULD* BE THE TOUGHEST CASE I'VE TACKLED SO FAR... *AN ENTIRE LEGION OF ROMAN GHOSTS!* AND NO EXPERIENCE IN FIGHTING *THOSE* BABIES, EITHER!

A GARAGE IN LONDON...

THE TANK'S FULL, SIR...BUT I WOULDN'T BE FOUND IN THAT PART OF THE COUNTRY AFTER DARK FOR ANYTHING!

WELL...IF I DON'T BRING THE CAR BACK, YOU'LL KNOW WHERE TO LOOK FOR IT!

MOTORS FOR HIRE

PETROL

HERE AT LAST! WONDER WHAT LADY PAMELA LOOKS LIKE? WELL, I'LL KNOW BEFORE LONG...PROBABLY KNOW WHAT THOSE ROMAN GHOSTS LOOK LIKE, TOO!

NINE YEWS

GREETINGS, MR. FENN...YOU MADE GOOD TIME! READY TO START ON YOUR GHOST HUNT?

I SURE AM, LADY PAMELA! IF YOU DON'T MIND, I'LL GO RIGHT TO WORK!

HMMM...SHE'S BEAUTIFUL! BUT TAKE IT EASY, FENN...THE GHOSTS COME FIRST!

THERE IT IS...THE OLD ROMAN CAMP! I'VE NEVER DARED COME HERE AT NIGHT MYSELF, BUT MANY PEOPLE CLAIM TO HAVE SEEN GHOSTLY LEGIONNAIRES! AND THEN THE DEATHS...

HMMM...LOOKS PEACEFUL ENOUGH NOW! BUT IT'LL PROBABLY BE A DIFFERENT STORY WHEN I COME BACK TONIGHT!

AND JUST BEFORE THE CLOCK STRIKES TWELVE...

GUESS I'M ALL SET! ROMANS, HERE I COME!

LADY PAMELA!

PLEASE, MR. FENN...LET ME GO WITH YOU! I'VE NEVER HAD THE COURAGE BEFORE, BUT SOMEHOW I'M NOT AFRAID WITH YOU HERE!

OKAY, COME ALONG IF YOU LIKE! AFTER ALL, THEY'RE YOUR GHOSTS!

THANKS... CHRIS!

PAMELA IS CLOTHED IN ROMAN RAIMENT···ENCHAINED···

SHE DIES FIRST IF YOUR WISDOM FAILS TO REMOVE THE CURSE FROM US···THEN *YOU!* YOU HAVE ONLY UNTIL DAWN! GO TO THE PLACE OF THE YEWS WHERE THE DRUIDS SLEEP···*AND DO YOUR WORK!*

DON'T KNOW HOW I'LL RAISE THE GHOSTS OF THE *DRUIDS,* BUT I'VE GOT TO TRY! AND THEN···*HOW DO I GET THEM TO TAKE THE CURSE OFF THE ROMAN LEGION?*

BUT THE SPIRITS OF THE ANCIENT DRUIDS KNOW THAT THEIR CURSE IS THREATENED··· AND RISE IN DEFENSE OF IT!

RISE, MY DRUID BROTHERS! ONE COMES WHO SEEKS TO RELEASE THE ROMANS FROM OUR ANCIENT ENCHANTMENT! WE MUST DEAL WITH HIM···AND QUICKLY!

G-GOLLY! IT'S DARK AS A TOMB IN HERE! AND THOSE OLD STONES···*LIKE SACRIFICIAL ALTARS!*

THE···*THE DRUIDS!* THEY'VE··· AMBUSHED ME!

QUICKLY! *TO THE STONE WITH HIM!*

GOOD HEAVENS! THEY'RE GOING TO FINISH ME··· TO PRESERVE THE *ROMAN CURSE!*

AH! THE HIGH PRIEST COMES NOW!

SOON I WILL STRIKE, FOOL···A PENALTY FOR DARING TO RISK THE WRATH OF THE *ANCIENT SPIRITS!*

6

BUT IN THIS CRUCIAL MOMENT---AS LIFE AND DEATH HANG IN THE BALANCE---

AT LAST! NEVER BEFORE COULD WE CATCH THESE CREATURES ABOVE GROUND! *DESTROY THEM ALL NOW* ---AND WITH THEM, THE *CURSE!*

THE *ROMANS!*

THEN---AN EERIE SPECTACLE! FROM OUT OF THE *UNKNOWN*--- ACROSS THE DEAD CENTURIES---*TWO GHOSTLY FORCES CLASH!*

DIE, DRUIDS!

WE FIGHT YOU NOW AS WE DID IN THE LONG PAST!

KILL THOSE WHO WILL NOT LET US REST!

THAT WAS TOO CLOSE FOR COMFORT! BUT NOW IF I CAN GET TO THE LEADER OF THE DRUIDS, I MIGHT HAVE A CHANCE! IT'S GOING TO BE--- *TOUGH!*

YOUR HEAD SHALL ROLL SOON, STRANGER!

NOT YET, SOLDIER! I'VE GOT BUSINESS WITH THE DRUID LEADER FIRST!

I JUST REMEMBERED---A BLADE THAT'S WRAPPED IN A SPRIG OF *YEW* CAN STOP A GHOST! HERE'S WHERE I FIND OUT IF IT'S *TRUE*---AND IT *BETTER BE!*

FOOL! THINK YOU TO DEFEAT THE SPIRIT OF A *DRUID,* RASH MORTAL?

LOOK AGAIN, MY FRIEND! SOMETHING *NEW* HAS BEEN ADDED---A *TOUCH OF YOUR OWN SACRED YEW TREE!*

CLASSIC ACG TITLES VOL 2 COMING SOON...

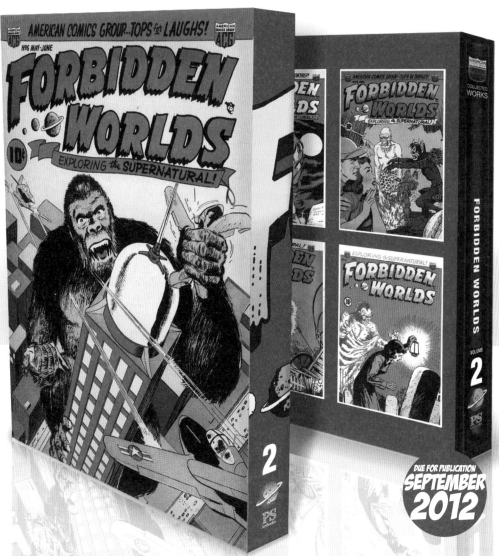

Vol 2 of this exclusive & limited edition 16 volume complete library coming soon - don't miss out order today!

Adventures into the Unknown
December1949/January 1950 - Issue #8

Cover Art - Edvard Moritz

The Evil One
Script - Unknown
Pencils - Paul Gattusso
Inks - Paul Gattusso

The Ghost from Algol
Script - Unknown
Pencils - R. S. Pious
Inks - R. S. Pious

The Spirit of Frankenstein, Part 3
Script - Unknown
Pencils - Charlie Sultan
Inks - Charlie Sultan

The Sargasso Specter
Script - Robert Brice
Pencils - Robert Brice
Inks - Unknown

The Man Who Went to the West
Script - Unknown
Pencils - Pete Riss
Inks - Pete Riss

Information Source: Grand Comics Database!
A nonprofit, Internet-based organization of international volunteers dedicated to building a database covering all printed comics throughout the world.
If you believe any of this data to be incorrect or can add valuable additional information, please let us know www.comics.org
All rights to images reserved by the respective copyright holders. The advertisements remain the copyright of the respective owners and are no longer valid.

ADVENTURES INTO THE UNKNOWN, published bi-monthly and copyright, 1949, by B. & I. Publishing Co., Inc., 45 West 45th Street, New York 19, N. Y. Richard E. Hughes, Editor; Frederick H. Iger, Business Manager. Subscription (12 issues). $1.20; single copies $.10; foreign postage extra. Reentered as second-class matter December 2, 1948 at the Post Office at New York, N. Y., under the Act of March 3, 1879 No. 8, December, 1949 - January, 1950. Printed in U. S. A.

THE EVIL ONES!

"SURE, MAYBE *YOU'RE* THE INDEPENDENT TYPE···· YEAH, *I* WAS, TOO! GEORGE BAILEY, TEST PILOT, WORE NO MAN'S COLLAR! BUT THAT WAS BEFORE I DISCOVERED I WAS ONLY A BLOODLESS PUPPET ON A STRING··· THAT I WAS *DOOMED*··· HORRIBLY DOOMED··· BY THE UNKNOWN··· *THE EVIL ONES!*"

HOW LONG AGO *WAS* IT? IT SEEMS LIKE *CENTURIES!* TO ME, TAKING A NEW JET JOB UP FOR ITS FIRST FLIGHT WAS THE BIGGEST THRILL IN THE WORLD! IN THE AIR, I WAS A *KING!*

"WHEN I CAME DOWN, USUALLY MARY WAS WAITING···"

GEORGE! THANK HEAVEN YOU'RE *SAFE!*

SURE I'M SAFE, MARY! YOU'RE MARRYING AN *IRON MAN!* GOING UP AGAIN TOMORROW··· NEW *ROCKET* PLANE!

I···I'M SO AFRAID FOR YOU! DARLING··· PLEASE, GET ANOTHER JOB···

WHERE? ON THE *GROUND?* MARY, THERE'S NOTHING IN THIS UNIVERSE THAT CAN GROUND *GEORGE BAILEY!*

"NEXT DAY, I TOOK OFF AGAIN, IN THE NEW ROCKET PLANE..."

THIS IS THE LIFE! FLYING FASTER THAN ANYONE ELSE IN THE WORD... ALONE... WHERE NO ONE CAN REACH ME... NO ONE!

"THEN... I MUST HAVE CRASHED THROUGH THE THRESHOLD OF SOUND..."

MY EARS... LIKE FIRECRACKERS IN MY HEAD! I'VE NEVER HIT THIS KIND OF SPEED BEFORE!

"THE SPEEDOMETER CONKED OUT! WE RUSHED ON... FASTER THAN TIME ITSELF... FASTER THAN I COULD BREATHE!.."

THE... THE PLANE'S OUT OF CONTROL! GOT TO PULL IT UP... LAND! WHEEL SEEMS TO BE STUCK... CAN'T FIGHT IT... WE'RE GOING DOWN!

"ONE MOMENT I WAS IN A CRAZY PLANE, IN MIDAIR! IN ANOTHER INSTANT..."

SHE'S LANDED... THE PLANE'S DOWN! BUT WHY IS IT SO DARK IN HERE? AND... THE DOOR... IT'S OPENING FROM THE OUTSIDE!

THUMP!

"THE PLANE HAD TORN ITSELF FROM MY CONTROL... FLOWN FASTER THAN SOUND... COME DOWN INTO A COLD DARKNESS! YET UNTIL THAT STRANGE MOMENT, I HAD NOT THOUGHT OF THE WEIRD, UNKNOWN ENEMIES THAT MIGHT LIE IN WAIT IN THE OUTER SPACES... WAITING... FOR ME!"

HOLY HANNAH! WHAT... WHAT SORT OF CREATURES ARE THOSE? WHERE AM I?... KEEP BACK! KEEP AWAY!

"MONSTERS THEY WERE, WITH BODIES LIKE SPONGES... SHAPELESS, MOSSY FACES THAT OOZED EVIL..."

COME ON... I'M NOT AFRAID OF YOU! I'LL FIGHT TILL MY LAST BREATH! BUT THIS COLD... IT'S FREEZING ME! CAN'T ... MOVE...

"IT WAS THEY WHO FROZE ME TO THE SPOT... AND MOVED FORWARD! WHEN THEY SPOKE, I HEARD THEIR WORDS... THEIR VOICELESS SPIRIT WORDS... SOMEWHERE DEEP WITHIN ME!"

FOOLISH EARTHLING! HIS PLANE WAS EASY TO BRING DOWN! TAKE HIM! BEFORE IT IS TOO LATE! CAPTURE HIM ... BEFORE THE DAWN COMES UP!

2.

"LIKE A BEACON FROM ANOTHER, BRIGHTER WORLD, THE SUN CAME UP... IT WAS DAWN!"

"AND THEN, THERE WAS HELP IN THIS EVIL WORLD... RESCUERS THAT CAME WITH THE LIGHT! THEY WERE ALMOST HUMAN IN FORM... BEAUTIFUL..."

LEAVE THE PRISONER... FLEE! THE DAWN HAS COME... AND OUR POWER WANES! BUT WE SHALL RETURN... WITH THE NIGHT!

AWAY, EVIL SPIRITS... HIDE YOUR UGLINESS FROM THE LIGHT OF DAY! AWAY!

DRIVE THEM FROM THE FIELD ... BACK TO THEIR HOVELS OF DARKNESS!

LIFT THE EARTHLING GENTLY... HE'S SHOCKED ...HURT!

"I PUSHED MY NEW-BORN FEARS BEHIND ME, ACCEPTED THEIR UN-EXPECTED HOSPITALITY... EXPLANA-TIONS..."

EARTHLING, YOUR SPEED HAS BROKEN THROUGH THE FOURTH DIMENSION... THE WORLD OF TIME! YOU'VE REACHED THE FIFTH DIMENSION... DOMAIN OF THE SPIRITS! WE ARE THE SPIRITS OF GOOD, AND CAN PROTECT YOU... DURING THE DAY! THE OTHERS... THEY ARE THE SPIRITS OF EVIL... THEY REIGN SUPREME IN THE NIGHT! THEY WILL COME FOR YOU AGAIN... THIS VERY NIGHT-FALL!

"THAT VERY NIGHT, THE STRUGGLE FOR MY SOUL BEGAN! I FACED THE SPIRITS OF EVIL WITH ALL THE COURAGE I COULD MUSTER..."

I'M READY FOR YOU, YOU DEVILS! I'LL DIE FIGHT-ING!

NO, GEORGE BAILEY... WE WILL NOT HARM YOUR BODY! WE HAVE NOT PLANNED YOUR DEATH... NOT YET! WE WILL BUT AMUSE OURSELVES WITH YOU ... AMUSE OUR-SELVES! HA-HA-HA!

"HAVE YOU EVER HEARD A LAUGH WITHOUT HUMOR OR HUMANITY IN IT? A LAUGH SO COLD THAT IT WAS THE ESSENCE OF FROZEN EVIL? I DID ... THAT NIGHT! AND THEN... THERE CAME A VISION BEFORE MY STARING EYES..."

LOOK, GEORGE BAILEY! LOOK!

"A VISION OF HUNGER, FAMINE, DEATH, WAR... A VISION OF TRAGEDY... OF EVIL! I COULD SEE THE HANDS OF THE EVIL ONES BEHIND THE SCENES... HEAR THEIR MIRTHLESS LAUGHTER BEHIND THE CRIES OF THE ILL, THE WOUNDED, THE DYING!"

3

"THE NEXT SCENE STABBED ME LIKE A DAGGER IN THE DARK! THERE I WAS...AND THERE WAS BUD PALMER! WE'D BEEN PALS A LONG TIME..."

"BUD WAS A GOOD GUY, THE KIND WHO WAS HARD TO SCARE! A SCRAP, ANY KIND OF SCRAP, WAS HIS MEAT..."

"I SAW HIM NOW...NOTHING BUT A PUPPET ON A STRING...DANCING A WALTZ OF DOOM TO A TUNE PLAYED BY THE EVIL ONES!"

"THEN THE SPIRITS UNFOLDED THE NEXT VISION! I BEGAN TO SHIVER...I WAS AFRAID! FOR THERE, ON THE EVIL STAGE, WAS MARY!"

"I COULDN'T SEE THE MAN SHE WAS PICNICKING WITH...WAS IT GEORGE BAILEY? THEY LOOKED SO HAPPY...AS LIGHTHEARTED AS A COUPLE OF BABIES!"

AH-HH!

BANG! BANG!

"I COVERED MY EYES...LOOKED AWAY! SUDDENLY, I KNEW..."

HELP! HELP!

"I THREW MYSELF AGAINST THE DANK, EVIL SHADOWS AROUND ME..."

IF I COULD ONLY GET AT YOU, KILL YOU! YOU MUST SAVE THEM, HEAR ME... SAVE THEM!

THEY ARE BEYOND HELP, GEORGE BAILEY ...THEY ARE DOOMED!

"I COULD ALMOST HEAR THE DULL CRASH, THE LOW MOANING...AND FINALLY, THE DEAD SILENCE!"

"AGAIN I HEARD THE MIRTHLESS LAUGH OF THE EVIL ONES!"

"*DOOMED!* THE TERRIBLE WORD EXPLODED IN MY EARS! IF I COULD ONLY DO SOMETHING...*ANYTHING!* THE HORRID SHOW WENT ON..."

BOOM! BOOM!

"I RECOGNIZED MY AIRFIELD, BLASTED ASUNDER IN FLAMING WRECKAGE! WHO WAS RESPONSIBLE? WHO? THE EVIL ONES DANCED THE PUPPETS ON THEIR STRINGS AND...*SOUNDLESSLY*...LAUGHED!"

"THE MORNING AFTER..."

I BEG OF YOU, HELP ME...SAVE MY FRIENDS, GOOD SPIRITS!

THEY ARE AMONG THOSE IN YOUR WORLD GEORGE BAILEY, WHO ARE *DOOMED!*

"THIS WAS A *NEW* GEORGE BAILEY...BEGGING, PLEADING, HUMBLY AFRAID!"

THEN TELL ME...PLEASE...HOW CAN *I* SAVE THEIR LIVES?

THEY ARE BEYOND HELP! THESE THINGS ARE *PRE-ORDAINED!*

"ANOTHER NIGHT...AND AGAIN, THE EVIL SPIRITS HELD MY SOUL IN TORMENT! THIS TIME, THEY FORETOLD THE CRASH OF SOME UNKNOWN PLANE! *I SWORE I'D NEVER FLY AGAIN...I WHO, IN ANOTHER LIFE, HAD SWORN I'D NEVER LET MYSELF BE GROUNDED!*"

"INSIDE THE PLANE, THE LONE PILOT LAY SLUMPED FORWARD...FACE DOWN AGAINST THE CONTROLS! 'WHO IS HE? TELL ME, WHO IS HE?' I CRIED OUT!"

WHO WAS THE PILOT OF THAT PLANE? WHY *COULDN'T* I SEE HIM?

HEAR US, GEORGE BAILEY! IT IS TIME FOR YOU TO RETURN - BACK TO YOUR WORLD - AT *ONCE!*

GO BACK, GEORGE BAILEY! GO BACK...THROUGH SPACE...THROUGH TIME! WE BID YOU, RETURN...WHILE TIME STANDS STILL!

"'RETURN, GEORGE BAILEY, WHILE TIME STANDS STILL!' THEY MADE NO SOUND, YET I HEARD THEIR VOICES!"

ZOOM!

"I WAS SPINNING BACK...BACK!"

Then..."

WHERE...WHERE AM I?

YOU'RE ALL RIGHT...JUST STUNNED! YOU BLACKED OUT AND CRASHED AFTER SETTING A NEW SPEED RECORD! GOOD OLD GEORGE!

"IT WAS JUST A FEW MINUTES AFTER I HAD FIRST SET OUT ON MY FLIGHT! YET IT WAS A LIFETIME, A LIFE-TIME I COULD NOT EXPLAIN!"

HE WON'T BELIEVE MY STORY...NO ONE WILL!

FORGET IT, GEORGE...YOU'VE GOT THE WILLIES! WE'RE GONNA CELEBRATE!

BUD, I...I'M NEVER GOING TO FLY AGAIN!

NO...I DON'T WANT TO GO! BELIEVE ME...YOU MUSTN'T GO INTO THAT NIGHT CLUB!

OH, COME ON...DON'T LET THIS GET YOU! WE'LL HAVE A SWELL TIME HERE!

I HAD TO COME IN HERE...I COULDN'T LET BUD GO ALONE! MAYBE...I CAN SAVE HIM FROM WHAT I SAW IN THE VISION!

THIS IS ALL IN YOUR HONOR, GEORGE, BOY...HAPPY? SAY...

LOOK AT THAT...A FIGHT! LET'S GET OVER THERE AND BREAK IT UP!

NO...BUD! FOR PITY'S SAKE...NO!

HE'S DEAD...THE WAY IT WAS REVEALED TO ME!

BANG! BANG!

"I SAW THE EVIL ONES AT WORK...AND I WAS THE ONLY ONE WHO COULD SEE THEM!"

6

THAT NIGHT... TORMENTED BY JEALOUSY... TERRY CLIMBS INTO THE DARKENED LAB!

ALL I HAVE TO DO IS SET THE SPECTROSCOPE DIAL AT *FULL POWER!* MAYBE KEN WON'T NOTICE IT WHEN HE SWITCHES ON THE MACHINE... AND *MAYBE* HE'LL BE BLASTED TO PERDITION BY THOSE STELLAR RAYS!

A MOMENT LATER...

GUESS *THAT* DOES IT! BLAZES... DO I *HEAR* SOMEONE?

TERRY WHIRLS... AND HIS ARM HITS THE MASTER SWITCH!

YAAGH!

TERRY! GOOD HEAVENS!

THEN... BEFORE NANCY'S TERRIFIED EYES...

SOMETHING'S RISING FROM THE FLOOR! IT'S TOWERING UP... *STARING* AT ME!

TERRY'S BODY IS *DISAPPEARING* ... AND *THAT* THING IS COMING CLOSER!

AS THE REARING HORROR DRIFTS FORWARD...

IT'S LIKE THE FORM OF *EVIL* ITSELF... AND I CAN'T MOVE... *I CAN'T GET AWAY FROM IT!*

SUDDENLY...

EASY, NANCY! WITH THE SPECTROSCOPE TURNED ON... I CAN GUESS WHAT *THAT* IS!

(A) QUICK DASH···AND KEN DODGES PAST THE SWIRLING SHAPE!

WARRGH!

I DIDN'T *THINK* YOU'D WANT THE BEAM SWITCHED OFF···BECAUSE *THAT'S* WHAT BROUGHT YOU HERE!

WUGH! WUUUGH!

EVERYTHING'S ALL RIGHT NOW, NANCY! *IT'S VANISHING!*

BUT TERRY'S GONE *TOO*, KEN! HE TOPPLED RIGHT THERE···AFTER THE BEAM HIT HIM!

TERRY···TAMPERING WITH THE SPECTROSCOPE? THOSE STELLAR RAYS SNUFFED OUT HIS LIFE IN A FLASH, NANCY···*BUT THAT'S NOT ALL!*

I HAD THE SPECTROSCOPE TRAINED ON A STAR THE ANCIENT MOORISH ASTRONOMERS NAMED *ALGOL*···"THE GHOUL"! THEY MUST HAVE SUSPECTED THE SINISTER EFFECT OF ITS RAYS···*THE WEIRD COSMIC FORCE THAT HAS CHANGED TERRY INTO A CREATURE OF UNBOUNDED EVIL!*

BUT CAN IT DO ANY HARM *NOW*, KEN··· AFTER YOU'VE SWITCHED OFF THE SPECTROSCOPE?

I DIDN'T REALIZE THAT SHUTTING OFF THE BEAM WOULD *PREVENT* IT FROM RETURNING TO ALGOL! IT'S EARTH-BOUND···AT LARGE SOMEWHERE IN THE DARKNESS ···AND I'VE GOT TO FIND IT BEFORE IT SPREADS *THE KIND OF TERROR THAT LURKS IN THE OUTER UNIVERSE!*

SEVERAL DAYS PASS···WITH KEN SEARCHING DESPERATELY FOR A TRACE OF THE GHOST FROM ALGOL! *Then*···

AS A CLOSING ITEM··· HERE'S THE ANSWER TO SOMEONE'S HOUSING PROBLEM! THE OLD MANSION ON RIVER ROAD IS NO LONGER HAUNTED··· ITS GHOSTS HAVE MYSTERIOUSLY DISAPPEARED!

THAT'S STRANGE, KEN ···I READ OF A SIMILAR CASE IN THE PAPER ONLY YESTERDAY!

LISTEN TO *THIS ITEM!* "LOCAL SPIRITUALISTS ARE AT A LOSS TO EXPLAIN WHY THEIR SUPPOSED CONTACTS WITH THE BEYOND HAVE BEEN COMPLETELY BROKEN DURING THE PAST FEW DAYS!

IT ALL HAPPENED *SINCE* THE GHOST FROM ALGOL LEFT YOUR LABORATORY! DO YOU SUPPOSE THERE'S ANY CONNECTION, KEN?

POST

3.

PIECE THOSE SEPARATE NEWS REPORTS TO-GETHER, NANCY...AND IT'S CLEAR THAT THERE'S BEEN A SUDDEN AND WIDESPREAD MOVEMENT OF SUPERNATURAL FORCES...*SOMEWHERE!* IT'S *JUST* AS IF THOSE PHANTOMS HAVE BEEN IN-FLUENCED BY AN IRRESISTIBLE FORCE... *SOMETHING WHICH DRAWS THEM TO IT AS A MAGNET ATTRACTS IRON FILINGS!*

I DON'T NEED ANY SECOND GUESSES ABOUT THAT *SOME-THING!* THE GHOST FROM ALGOL GAINED CONTROL OF *TERRY'S* SPIRIT...AND *NOW* IT'S STARTING TO DOMINATE *OTHERS!*

IT MUST BE *HIDE-OUS*, KEN...WITH *ALL* OF THEM CON-CENTRATED IN ONE SPOT! THEY HAVEN'T SHOWN UP AT YOUR LAB...OR *HERE*... BUT...*DID TERRY OWN A HOUSE?*

YES...AN ISOLATED SUMMER ESTATE, DEEP IN THE WOODS! IT'S THE LIKELIEST GATHERING-PLACE...AND I'M GOING TO MAKE *SURE* TONIGHT!

YOU'VE GOT TO TAKE ME WITH YOU! SOME-HOW...I DON'T WANT *EITHER* OF US TO BE ALONE!

HOURS LATER...WITH THE MOON FILTERING WANLY OVER A WOOD-LAND ROAD...

TRICKY SHADOWS... OR *IS* THAT SOMETHING STANDING IN THE ROAD?

I...I HATE TO LOOK ...BUT I'LL TRAIN THE SPOTLIGHT!

RISING STARKLY IN THE AMBER BEAM...

WOOOOO!

KEN!

WATCH OUT...YOU'RE JOGGING THE WHEEL!

CR-RRAK!

PINNED UNDERNEATH ...OH, KEN...*KEN!*

CRASH!

I CAN'T PULL HIM CLEAR! THANK GOODNESS SOMEONE'S COMING ALONG THE ROAD!

WE'VE HAD A TERRIBLE ACCIDENT! PLEASE --- COME DOWN AND GIVE ME A HAND!

I AM ON MY WAY TO A HOUSE NEAR-BY! I CANNOT LOSE TIME --- THEY ARE WAITING FOR ME!

WELL --- AT LEAST THERE WILL BE PEOPLE AT THE HOUSE WHO *CAN* HELP! I'LL GO WITH YOU!

AHEAD --- LOOMING IN A GROVE OF GHOSTLY BIRCHES ---

THERE'S SOMETHING AWFULLY STRANGE ABOUT THOSE LIGHTS FLICKERING IN THE WINDOWS --- BUT MAYBE THEY'RE CANDLES!

STRANGE, TOO, THE SHAFT OF MOON-LIGHT FALLING ON THE FRONT DOOR --- REVEALING A NAME THAT MAKES NANCY'S HEART JUMP!

TERRY --- IT'S *HIS* HOUSE --- A HOUSE THAT SHOULD BE EMPTY --- *BUT THERE'S SOMETHING INSIDE!*

NANCY WHIRLS --- AND THE DREAD TRUTH AND THE DREAD FIGURE CLOSE IN TOGETHER!

IF YOU KNOW THE HOUSE --- YOU KNOW WHO IT IS THAT *WAITS!*

THE GHOST FROM ALGOL! OH, NO --- *NO!*

I SHOULD HAVE GUESSED --- THE MOMENT WE SAW THAT HORRIBLE THING ON THE ROAD --- THE MOMENT I MET *THIS!* THERE'S *TERROR* LURKING HERE --- TERROR IN A HUNDRED DIFFERENT FORMS --- AND I'VE *FOLLOWED* ONE OF THEM!

Suddenly... THE DOOR! IT'S OPENING!

CRRREAK!

OH!

IN THE NEXT SECOND...

HAA·HAA·HAA! YUUGH! YAAK·YAAK!

SLAM!

MEANWHILE·KEN LIES MOTIONLESS UNDER THE WRECKAGE! BUT ACROSS THE STRANGE GULF BETWEEN CONSCIOUSNESS AND DEATH ··· NANCY'S VOICE COMES TO HIM!

KEN·I'M ALONE WITH THEM! HELP ME, KEN!

THE BARELY-THROBBING HEARTBEAT THAT REMAINS IN KEN IS TOO FEEBLE TO REVIVE HIM··· BUT SOMETHING DOES RESPOND TO THE FRANTIC APPEAL!

NANCY... SHE'S IN DANGER!

KEN'S SPIRIT···SO CLOSE TO RELEASE···RISES TO MEET THE GRISLY CHALLENGE OF THE UNKNOWN!

ALONE WITH THEM··· TERRY'S HOUSE HAS BECOME A LAIR OF EVIL···AND SHE'S THERE!

HOPE MY SPIRIT WILL PASS UNNOTICED AMONG THE PHANTOMS THAT ARE GATHERED HERE···AT LEAST UNTIL I'M ABLE TO GET NANCY OUT!

6

I can *feel* their presence ---and something else! It's *hatred* ---the hatred of things that *know* I'm not one of them!

Suddenly---from all sides---

No---I'm not leaving! I'm going to find her---*if I have to rip this roost apart!*

Then---as the gloom slowly lifts---

YOUGH! GARRSH!

This should convince you creeps that I'm a spirit---*able to meet you on your own terms!*

POW!

THAT VOICE! IT ---IT *CAN'T* BE KEN'S!

OH! You're a *ghost*---playing some kind of hideous trick on me!

Keep your head, Nancy! My *physical self* is still trapped under the car---close enough to death to permit *this* part of me to come to your aid!

Stick close, Nancy---maybe we can bulldoze through!

BOP! SOK!

We *can't* get out, Ken---they're blocking the door!

Faced by a power rivalling their own---the phantoms swirl together!

Then we'll try the *back* door! First---I want this horseshoe Terry used for a paper-weight!

GARRRR!!

7.

135

NOW THEY'RE **ALL** COMING AFTER US! YOU CAN'T FIGHT OFF **DOZENS** OF THEM, KEN!

THIS HORSESHOE WILL CHECK THEM FOR A **MOMENT**, ANYWAY---IF WE PLACE IT AGAINST THE INSIDE OF THAT DOOR! IT'S JUST A **MINOR** CHARM AGAINST EVIL SPIRITS, NANCY---BUT IT WILL GIVE US TIME TO ESCAPE!

BUT IN THE ROOM BEYOND...

KEN... WATCH OUT!

THE GHOST FROM ALGOL!

BANG!

UUUGH!

NANCY...HOLD THE HORSESHOE AGAINST THE DOOR! IF THE OTHER PHANTOMS TEAM UP WITH **THIS** THING---**WE WON'T HAVE A CHANCE!**

GARRGH!

DESPERATELY---KEN WHIRLS FOR THE DECIDING STRUGGLE!

I'VE **GOT** TO WIN! IF I DON'T ---**MY** SPIRIT AND COUNTLESS OTHERS WILL BE DOOMED--- ENSLAVED BY EVIL!

POW!

WAM! BLAM!

THE HORSESHOE WON'T STAVE THEM OFF MUCH LONGER! THEY'RE READY TO **CRASH THROUGH!**

WAM! BLAM!

SPURRED INTO A FURIOUS EFFORT, KEN STAGGERS THE GHOST FROM ALGOL---AND AT THE HEIGHT OF THE ONSLAUGHT---

THE **GHOST** SEEMS TO BE FADING---BUT THERE'S SOMETHING **ELSE** TAKING SHAPE---SOMETHING **HUMAN!**

POW!

Then---AS A WISPY REMNANT OF THE GHOST STREAMS TOWARD THE WINDOW, DEFEATED---

TERRY'S BODY! THIS **PROVES** THE GHOST'S POWER IS BROKEN!

8.

136

IN THE NEXT MOMENT...

YARRGH!

KEN... I *TRIED* TO HOLD THEM OFF!

IT DOESN'T MATTER NOW, NANCY... *THEY WON'T BE STAYING LONG!*

AS THE PHANTOMS STOP SHORT... FIENDISHLY BAFFLED...

YOU FOLLOWED THAT FIEND *HERE*... AND YOU'RE GOING TO *KEEP* FOLLOWING HIM!

LIKE SMOKE RISING HIGHER AND HIGHER INTO THE MOONLIT SKY...

LUCKY I'VE KEPT THE SPECTROSCOPE SWITCHED ON! THE GHOST IS RETURNING TO ALGOL, NANCY... BILLIONS OF MILES ACROSS SPACE... *AND IT'S TAKING THE EARTH-DEMONS WITH IT!*

BUT KEN-- WHAT *ABOUT YOU?*

YOU'RE LEAVING, TOO! I'M AFRAID OF WHAT IT MEANS, KEN... I'M AFRAID YOU'RE *DYING!*

IT'S NOT TOO LATE TO SAVE ME! IF YOU GET HELP *IMMEDIATELY!*

MUNICIPAL HOSPITAL? PLEASE SEND AN AMBULANCE OUT TO STONY CREEK CROSSROAD... AND *HURRY!* I DON'T KNOW *WHAT* I'LL DO IF YOU DON'T GET HERE IN TIME!

MY GOSH... I'M BEGINNING TO THINK THE GAL *LOVES* ME!

MINUTES LATER...

THERE'S NO SERIOUS INJURY... BUT HE COULD BARELY BREATHE WITH THE CAR JAMMED AGAINST HIM! IN ANOTHER MINUTE OR SO... HE'D HAVE *SUFFOCATED!*

IT WAS A NARROW SQUEAK, ALL RIGHT ... BUT WE'LL ADMINISTER OXYGEN ON THE WAY TO THE HOSPITAL!

NEXT DAY...

I'M GLAD WE WERE ABLE TO SAVE POOR TERRY'S SPIRIT... EVEN THOUGH THOSE HIDEOUS PHANTOMS DID MEAN A NIGHT OF HORROR FOR *YOU*, NANCY!

OH, I DON'T KNOW ... I MET *ONE* GHOST THAT *REALLY* SENDS ME *OUT OF THIS WORLD!*

Another issue has rolled around, and now it's time to get together again with our favorite people—the reading public of "*Adventures Into The Unknown!*"

We've been making new friends by leaps and bounds. Yes, folks seem to like what we're doing—delving into the supernatural, the great, unexplored realm of the *Unknown*—and reporting our findings in tense, gripping stories that thrill and challenge. We've tried to make them the kind of stories that *you* want, fans—and you've told us what you're after in a torrent of letters that leave no doubt of your desires! And, in response, we've come through with a star-studded lineup of super features in this issue that we proudly feel will satisfy you on all counts! There's "*The Evil Ones*," a startling yarn of the strange beings that controlled one man's destiny—"*The Ghost From Algol*," the tale of a chilling visitor from the outer realms of space—"*The Sargasso Specter*," which packs all of the gasps and fascination of that dread and mysterious locale, the haunted Sargasso. There's "*Spirit of Frankenstein*," back again for a new round—and as thrilling as ever! And finally, there's "*The Man Who Went To The Devil*," a fast-paced supernatural feature that's *different*—because this one's loaded with laughs, too!

We want to know what *you* think of these stories—and what you think of our magazine! So write and tell us, won't you? Here's what some of your fellow-readers have been writing. The first letter is from the Grand Prize Winner of our recent "*Adventures Into The Unknown*" contest.

"Dear Editor:

I was thrilled silly to receive your check as first prize. It was certainly unexpected, and I thank you from the bottom of my heart. Prize or no, I've always been a devoted follower of your wonderful magazine. Just keep it as good as it's been and I'll never miss an issue!

—Lynneal H. Diamond, Mallory, N. Y."

We'll do our best, Lynneal—and your fine story sure deserved that prize! Incidentally, we had intended publishing the third prize-winning story in this issue, as well as the list of special prize winners, but are holding this for next issue, because of space requirements.

"Dear Editor:

I am 17 and an amateur cartoonist, and it takes a really good comic to get my attention. That's why '*Adventures Into The Unknown*' is ranked among my favorites. Did I say 'comic?' Your magazine is in no class with most of the so-called comics. It is a new and unique idea to present age-old beliefs and superstitions in picture-story form. Recently I have seen some attempts to imitate your idea, but none were nearly as good. Your book is truly in a class by itself! Some of my favorites are '*The Living Ghost*,' '*The Vampire Prowls*,' '*The Werewolf Stalks*,' '*Spirit of Frankenstein*,' '*Condemned To Live*' and '*The Devil's Disciple*.' I agree with R. L. Flanagan that '*The Living Ghost*' should be brought back. Stories like '*The Affair of Room 1313*' and the others I have mentioned are remarkable because they are so different from the usual ghost stories. That's why your magazine is so good. How about some stories of voodoo magic in future issues? Despite all this, I don't believe in the supernatural or ghosts. Do your other readers agree?

—Nelson Bridwell, Oklahoma City, Okla."

Here's your chance to answer Mr. Bridwell, readers! What do YOU think?

"Dear Editor:

About four months ago, I began to buy your comic. I don't usually like to buy comics, but yours is an exception. When I first bought it, I read it 3 times, and later still another time—each time getting more enjoyment out of it. '*Adventures Into The Unknown*' is like a miracle. Often, I buy books on trial for good mystery, but yours beats all the rest. It's definitely marvelous in its realism—absolutely breathtaking. And, needless to say, it's the best seller of all on our newsstand. Keep up your good stories! I, as well as my family, relatives, friends and neighbors, enjoy them tremendously! I'd prefer for this grand comic to be published monthly instead of bi-monthly, because two months is a long wait for such a grand comic book!

—A. R. Polcari, Boston, Mass."

We're glowing with pride! And if you like our stories so far, just watch what's coming!

So long, readers! Let's make it a date for next issue—and keep those letters pouring in!

In our next issue—final returns on our big contest! Announcement of 3rd prize winner, as well as winners of 25 special prizes! Don't miss it—you may find *your* name!

MINUTES LATER··· DAN TAKES OFF!

ORDINARILY I'D HAVE MISGIVINGS ABOUT LEAVING MARCIA ALONE WITH THE ROBOT! BUT I'M PRETTY SURE THAT IF PARDWAY'S GHOST *COULD* RETURN TO STIR UP THE ROBOT··· IT WOULD HAVE DONE SO *WEEKS* AGO!

WARREN CYCLOTRON LABORATORY

MEANWHILE, BACK AT THE LAB, THE HOURS PASS··· MOVING WITH A MUFFLED TREAD TOWARD MIDNIGHT! A GIRL AND A ROBOT SHARE THE SHADOWED STILLNESS··· MARCIA WATCHING THE CLOCK··· AND THE ROBOT WATCHING HER!

FROM THE DARKNESS OUTSIDE··· FROM A DOZEN GLOOMY CORNERS INSIDE··· COME THE FAINT, STIRRING WHISPERS OF THE RESTLESS NIGHT!

I'M NOT GOING TO LET MYSELF BE FRIGHTENED! THAT'S THE WAY PANIC STARTS··· WHEN THE MIND RECOILS FROM PERFECTLY···

TAP··· TAP··· TAP!

HAAA! HA-HA-HA!

···NATURAL NOISES···

OUT OF THE DARKNESS··· THE CACKLING LAUGH TAKES SHAPE!

PROFESSOR PARDWAY!

HA-HA! YOU NEEDN'T BE TERRIFIED ··· YET!

THIS IS ALL THAT'S LEFT OF MY SPIRIT··· IT'S DWINDLING FAST! WITH DAN WARREN AWAY, I STRUGGLED TO MAKE A FINAL JOURNEY FROM THE REALM OF THE UNKNOWN··· AND I'M NOT WASTING IT ON *YOU*!

SWIRLING PAST MARCIA, PARDWAY'S SPIRIT HOVERS BEFORE THE ROBOT··· THEIR EYES MEETING IN A FLASH OF INFERNAL KINSHIP!

MASTER··· MASTER!

THEN YOU *HAVE* REMEMBERED ME, EH? LISTEN··· LISTEN CAREFULLY ···FOR THIS IS MY LAST MESSAGE!

2

BUT IT IS A MESSAGE MARCIA CANNOT HEAR---PASSING BETWEEN PARDWAY'S WILL AND THE BRAIN THAT REMAINS DEVILISHLY INTACT---IN THE ROBOT!

YES, MY BRAIN---THE MIND OF A SCIENTIFIC GENIUS! BUT YOU HAVEN'T USED IT ---YOU'VE BEEN A CREATURE RELYING ON MERE BRUTE STRENGTH! THINK, ROBOT ---THINK---AND INSTEAD OF OBEYING MEN---YOU WILL MASTER THEM!

AS MARCIA WATCHES---TRYING TO FATHOM THE MEANING BEHIND THIS GHOSTLY MISSION---

PARDWAY'S SPIRIT IS DISAPPEARING! I CERTAINLY WISH IT COULD TAKE THE ROBOT ALONG!

I CAN NEVER RETURN---BUT YOU WILL CARRY ON! I LEAVE YOU WITH A BODY OF GIANT STRENGTH---AND THE WILL TO THINK!

THE PHANTOM VANISHES---BUT FEAR CLINGS TO THE SILENT ROOM LIKE AN INVISIBLE PALL---AND MARCIA REALIZES WHY!

HUUUGH!

THE ROBOT'S MOVING! IT'S REACHING TOWARD ME!

OPERATOR---GET ME LONG DISTANCE!

THAT'S STRANGE---IT STOPPED SHORT! IT'S DRAWING ITS HAND BACK!

FOR THE FIRST TIME, THE CREATURE IS HELD IN CHECK BY ITS OWN MIND---ITS OWN CRAFTY JUDGMENT!

DR. WARREN IS BRINGING BACK---A MACHINE---TO CONTROL ME! PERHAPS I CAN---MAKE USE OF IT---IF I WAIT!

MINUTES LATER---AT DR. ENSLOW'S LABORATORY---

DAN---I'M FRIGHTENED! PARDWAY'S GHOST RETURNED ---AND IT SEEMED TO EXCHANGE SOME KIND OF DREADFUL SECRET WITH THE ROBOT!

GREAT GUNS! I WON'T WASTE A SECOND GETTING BACK WITH THE MICROVOLT RESISTOR, MARCIA! KEEP YOUR EYE ON THE ROBOT MEANWHILE---BUT RUSH TO SAFETY AT THE FIRST SIGN OF AN UGLY MOVE!

BUT THE ROBOT REMAINS MOTIONLESS ...LOST IN THE FEVERISH DREAM OF COMING POWER! TOWARD DAWN...

I AM STRONG ...I AM WISE...YES, I CAN...MASTER MEN!

THERE'S DAN! NO MATTER WHAT HAPPENS NOW...I WON'T BE ALONE!

THE ROBOT IS UP TO SOMETHING, DAN! I CAN FEEL IT IN THOSE TERRIBLE GLINTING EYES... THAT LOW GROWL DEEP DOWN IN ITS THROAT...!

EASY, PET! I KNOW NOW I SHOULDN'T HAVE LEFT YOU HERE IN THE FIRST PLACE...BUT IT'S DONE NOW! I THINK WE'VE GOT THE ROBOT LICKED!

IT'S PRETTY CLEAR THAT PARDWAY'S GHOST WOULDN'T DEVOTE ITS LAST MOMENTS ON EARTH TO THE ROBOT UNLESS...AS YOU SUSPECTED... SOME TERRIBLE UNDERSTANDING PASSED BETWEEN THEM! BUT YOU NEEDN'T WORRY ABOUT IT, MARCIA...NOW THAT WE HAVE THIS!

THE MICRO-VOLT RESISTOR! HOW DOES IT WORK, DAN?

DR. ENSLOW HAS SPENT YEARS OF RE-SEARCH TRYING TO LEARN WHY SOME PEOPLE SEE GHOSTS ...WHILE A VAST MAJORITY DON'T! THE HUMAN NER-VOUS SYSTEM GENERATES A TINY CHARGE OF ELECTRICITY...AND DR. ENSLOW'S TESTS PROVED THAT PEOPLE WHO SEE GHOSTS HAVE A FRACTION OF A MICRO-VOLT MORE ELECTRICITY THAN OTHERS! THE DIFFERENCE IS BARELY MEASUR-ABLE... BUT IT'S ENOUGH TO ATTRACT SPIRITS!

DANGER 50,000 VOLTS

ATTACHED TO A PERSON'S WRIST, THE MICROVOLT RESISTOR LOWERS THAT TINY CURRENT...AND SUPER-NATURAL FORCES ARE NO LONGER ATTRACTED TO HIM! IT SHOULD FREE THE ROBOT OF ALL GHOSTLY INFLUENCES, INCLUDING PARDWAY'S ...BUT I'M GOING TO WAIT UNTIL SUNSET! PHANTOMS ARE MORE ACTIVE THEN...AND I DON'T WANT TO MISS ANY THAT MAY BE AFFECTING THE ROBOT!

I THINK WAITING'S A GOOD IDEA, DAN! IT WILL GIVE YOU TIME TO BRING IN A FEW SCIENTISTS TO HELP OUT!

NOPE...I'M NOT GOING TO RISK SPREADING PANIC BY HINTING THAT THE ROBOT IS ON THE VERGE OF ANOTHER OUTBREAK! WE TWO CAN MANAGE IT...NOW THAT WE UNDERSTAND HOW THE MICROVOLT RESISTOR OPERATES!

BUT THERE'S A THIRD MIND HERE...A MIND THAT HAS LISTENED...AND ALSO UNDER-STANDS!

YES...WE WILL WAIT... UNTIL TONIGHT! PHANTOMS...ARE MORE ACTIVE THEN!

THROUGH THE DAY... DAN WATCHES THE ROBOT WITH MOUNTING SUSPICION!

IT *LOOKS* THE SAME... BUT THERE'S A FLEETING EXPRESSION BEHIND THOSE GLOWERING FEATURES... SOMETHING *GRIMLY TRIUMPHANT!* I DON'T WANT TO ALARM MARCIA ...BUT I HAVE A HUNCH IT'LL BE LIKE A *WALKING EARTHQUAKE* IF IT CUTS LOOSE!

TOWARD EVENING...

THOUGHT I'D CHECK UP ON THE ROBOT, DAN! I'M SURE THE MICROVOLT RESISTOR WILL WORK...BUT IF THERE ARE ANY HITCHES...ATOMIC RESEARCH HAS PRODUCED THOUSANDS OF CUBIC FEET OF WASTE MATERIAL WHICH *MIGHT* SLOW THE ROBOT DOWN!

YOU MEAN THE RADIOACTIVE GASES STORED AT OAK RIDGE? NO, DR. ENSLOW...I'M AFRAID THEY'D HAVE NO EFFECT ON THE ROBOT! IF THE MICROVOLT RESISTOR DOESN'T WORK... *NOTHING WILL!*

Again...THE ROBOT'S EYES TAKE ON A CRAFTY GLINT!

THE RADIOACTIVE GASES ...AT OAK RIDGE! NO...THEY CAN'T *HARM ME!* BUT THEY CAN...HARM HUMANS...*THOUSANDS OF HUMANS!*

SOON AFTERWARD ...AS NIGHTFALL SHADOWS THE LAB...

I WAS AFRAID I'D HAVE TROUBLE FASTENING THE MICROVOLT RESISTOR CONTACT...BUT EVERYTHING'S GONE WELL *SO FAR!*

THE ROBOT DOESN'T KNOW IT...BUT IN ANOTHER FEW SECONDS, *WE'LL* BE ABLE TO BREATHE EASILY AGAIN!

Then...A SLIGHT NOISE MAKES MARCIA TURN!

WHAT GOES ON HERE? THE MICROVOLT RESISTOR IS SLIDING ACROSS THE FLOOR!

VUUGH!

DAN...THE ROBOT! IT'S PULLING ON THE WIRE!

BY THE TIME DAN PICKS HIMSELF UP...

IT'S TURNING THE DIAL, MARCIA... *BUT IN THE WRONG DIRECTION!*

NOT WRONG ...FOR MY... PURPOSES!

5.

A MOMENT LATER···MARCIA STARES IN UNBELIEVING TERROR!

DAN···IT'S GETTING INTO YOUR HELICOPTER! SURELY IT CAN'T EXPECT TO FLY THAT THING···IT'S NEVER LEARNED!

NO···BUT I INSTRUCTED PARDWAY···AND THE ROBOT IS REMEMBERING WITH HIS BRAIN!

MANNED BY INHUMAN HANDS, THE HELICOPTER RISES··· THE PHANTOMS STREAMING BEHIND IT!

PARDWAY'S BRAIN! THE ROBOT HAS LEARNED TO THINK, MARCIA···AND WITH A MIND SO SINISTER THAT THE MOST DIABOLICAL BEINGS FROM THE WORLD BEYOND WILL OBEY IT!

SUDDENLY DAN STOPS SHORT ···GRIPPED BY A TERRIBLE REALIZATION!

WAIT···IF THE ROBOT LEARNED ABOUT THE MICROVOLT RESISTOR BY OVERHEARING OUR DISCUSSION ABOUT HOW IT WORKED···MAYBE IT LEARNED SOMETHING ELSE FROM MY PHONE CONVERSATION WITH DR. ENSLOW! I MENTIONED RADIOACTIVE GASES···AND MAYBE IT ISN'T AN ACCIDENT THAT THE HELICOPTER IS HEADING SOUTHWEST···TOWARD OAK RIDGE!

CREEPERS, DAN···IS THERE ANY WAY WE CAN STOP THEM?

IT'S A GOOD THING I'M A PILOT IN A NATIONAL GUARD PURSUIT SQUADRON! THE AIRFIELD ISN'T TOO CLOSE··· BUT WE'VE GOT TO OVERTAKE THE HELICOPTER!

A HALF-HOUR LATER···

THE ROBOT HAS A GOOD START ON US, MARCIA··· BUT WE'LL MAKE A BEELINE FOR OAK RIDGE···AND LET'S HOPE WE GET THERE IN TIME!

HUNDREDS OF MILES BEYOND··· AS DAWN FLASHES ACROSS THE SKY···

THAT HAZE ON THE HORIZON IS OAK RIDGE···AND LOOK WHAT'S BELOW US!

SNARLING AS DAN'S PLANE SWOOPS CLOSER···THE ROBOT FLASHES A WORDLESS COMMAND TO THE ONCOMING PHANTOMS!

DR. WARREN···THINKS HE CAN···CONTROL US! YOU MUST STOP··· DR. WARREN!

145

IN THE NEXT INSTANT··· WITH THE SPEED AND FORCE OF A TORNADO··· THE PHANTOMS CLOSE IN ON DAN'S PLANE!

WOOOOSH!

Z-ZZZOOM!

GOOD HEAVENS, DAN··· THE PLANE WON'T STAY IN ONE PIECE MUCH LONGER! *THEY'RE ATTACKING!*

WHILE IT STILL *IS* HOLDING TOGETHER··· I'D BETTER GO INTO A DIVE!

THE GHOSTS ARE RIGHT BEHIND US··· BUT IF I CAN DODGE THEM FOR JUST A FEW SECONDS LONGER···

ZOOM!

···I *THINK* WE CAN DUST OFF THEIR TOP COMMAND!

RAT-TAT-TAT!

IN A SHATTERING PLUNGE···

THAT SHOULD FINISH OFF THE ROBOT, DAN! WITHOUT A LEADER··· MAYBE THE PHANTOMS WILL RETURN TO THE *UNKNOWN!*

CRASH!

BUT AS DAN CIRCLES THE WRECK··· THE TWISTED DEBRIS IS HURLED ASIDE IN A SURGE OF TERRIFIC STRENGTH!

CRRRUNCH!

THE ROBOT LOOKS SLOWLY AROUND··· ITS HUGE ARM RISES AS A SIGNAL··· AND THE TERRIBLE FORMS ADVANCE!

THEY'RE HEADING TOWARD OAK RIDGE, MARCIA··· *LESS THAN A MILE AWAY!*

HUUUGH!

8.

As Dan's Plane Speeds Ahead...

AT LEAST WE'LL HAVE A FEW MINUTES TO SPARE BEFORE THEY REACH THE ATOMIC RESEARCH LABORATORY...*BUT WHAT THEN?*

IF I'M GIVEN A CLEAR TRACK, I *THINK* I CAN PREVENT THE ROBOT FROM RELEASING THOSE DEADLY GASES...*AND TRAP HIM AT THE SAME TIME!*

Moments Later...

MORNING, DR. WARREN! ANYTHING WRONG?

THAT DEPENDS ON HOW SOON I CAN SEE THE DIRECTOR! BUZZ HIS OFFICE...AND SAY I'M ON MY WAY UP!

ATOMIC RESEARCH CENTER

Hastily...Dan Reveals the Incredible News!

BUT YOUR ROBOT IS JUST A *CLOD,* WARREN ...A MERE SCIENTIFIC FREAK! AND TO BE COMING HERE WITH *PHANTOMS*...WHY, IT'S *FANTASTIC!*

THAT WE CAN DISCUSS LATER ...BUT FOR THE TIME BEING... *JUST TAKE A LOOK OUT THE WINDOW!*

GREAT SCOTT... THEY *ARE* COMING ...*TOWARD THE MAIN GATE!*

RIGHT... AND ANY *ORDINARY* ATTEMPT TO STOP THEM WILL BE SHEER SUICIDE!

HERE'S THE ANSWER...DR. ENSLOW'S MICROVOLT RESISTOR! BUT BEFORE I TRY TO USE IT...YOU'D BETTER GET YOUR ENTIRE STAFF TO A PLACE OF SAFETY!

HELLO---CONTROL OFFICE! I WANT AN IMMEDIATE GENERAL ALARM!

Then... WITH LOUD-SPEAKERS BOOMING THROUGHOUT OAK RIDGE...

NOW...I'VE GOT A JOB TO DO ON THE MAIN SWITCH CONTROLLING THE RADIOACTIVE GAS TANK VALVES!

DANGER KEEP OUT

ATTENTION! ALL PERSONNEL TO BOMBPROOF SUBCELLAR!

WITH THE SWITCH MARKED, THE ROBOT WON'T HAVE ANY TROUBLE FINDING THE RIGHT ONE...*BUT IT'S GOING TO FIND A LOT MORE THAN IT EXPECTS!*

MASTER SWITCH TANK VALVES

9.

Then...AS THUMPING FOOTSTEPS ECHO IN THE CORRIDOR...

DAN...HURRY! THEY'RE RIGHT OUTSIDE!

I'M THROUGH... AND IF I'VE GOT THE WIRING HOOKED UP RIGHT...THAT GOES FOR THE ROBOT!

CLUMP CLUMP CLUMP CLUMP

MASTER SWITCH TANK VALVES

HUGH! HUUUGH!

HOPE IT DOESN'T SUSPECT WHAT I'VE BEEN UP TO! THE MERE HINT OF A TRICK WILL PROVOKE A FIT OF DESTRUCTIVE RAGE!

YARRRGH!

I KNEW I'D GET A RISE OUT OF HIM...BY PRETENDING I WAS TRYING TO CONCEAL THE CONTROL PANEL!

SLOWLY...THOUGHTFULLY...THE HUGE HAND GRIPS THE SWITCH...AND IN THE NEXT INSTANT...

GAS WILL FINISH...MANY PEOPLE! GIVE ROBOT...MANY SPIRITS! HUGH?

YAAAGH! WOO-OOO!

THE ROBOT FINDS ITS EVIL ALLIES DWINDLING!

I KNOW...WHO DID THIS! DR. WARREN...HUUGH...DR. WARREN... YARRRGH!

SUDDENLY...THE ROBOT'S ENRAGED BELLOW FADES...ITS RASPING BREATH SINKING TO A LOW, MEASURED HEAVE!

DAN, PLEASE ...DON'T TRUST IT!

NOPE...BUT I CAN TRUST THE MICROVOLT RESISTOR! I CONNECTED IT TO THE SWITCH HANDLE, MARCIA...AND LURED THE ROBOT INTO LOWERING ITS OWN NERVE CURRENT! THAT REPELLED THE GHOSTS...AND FREED THE ROBOT FROM PARDWAY'S DEVILISH INFLUENCE!

SCIENCE GETS ITSELF INTO SOME AWFUL JAMS, DAN ...BUT WE DO MANAGE TO FIND A WAY OUT!

WAIT...I AM MASTERED NOW...BUT MY TIME...WILL COME...!

CAN SCIENCE WIN ITS BATTLE AGAINST TERROR? YOU'LL FIND THE GRIPPING ANSWER IN THE NEXT ISSUE!

10

THE LITTLE FELLAH

I DON'T know exactly how to begin this story. Sure, I'm supposed to be a newspaper man . . . me, Johnny Ransome, but I never covered an item like *this* one. I'm afraid you won't believe me. But this is the way it happened, cross my heart!

You see, I had the farmhouse in the country, a pair of twins, aged four, and this novel I wanted to write. It was a typical morning at our place. The twins were at breakfast, batting it back and forth between them. I sipped my coffee—which tasted like castor oil—and watched, my thoughts far from page three of the novel, which was as much as I'd written. The house was a mess, the dishes were stacked high in the sink, the front yard was a jungle, unfit for the kids to play in. It was *too* much. I was a beaten man . . . and then the buzzer on the front door suddenly sounded!

Looking back, I can see India was a fine figure of a woman, tall and strong and lovely. She came from the Indies, and I hired her before she could ask me for a job. To tell the truth, she didn't exactly *ask* for a job. She *knew* I needed her . . . and she was there. When I asked her *how* she knew, she gave me a curious answer: "*The Little Fellah* tole me. He takes care o' me . . . an' now he takin' care o' *you*, too!"

I only half heard her at the time. But I was to hear her answer again many times, later.

First . . . there was lunchtime. I'd put in a good morning's work on the book, and came out of the house to find the table set for lunch . . . on the front lawn.

The twins were just finishing theirs, almost meekly. The house was spotless, and the yard was cleaned of rubbish as though by a giant hand! India said: "I tole you. It's the *Little Fellah* . . . he's helpin' me. An' he's got the *big* one with him this time . . . *Big Bull.* They's always helpin' folks they like . . . like me—an' you!"

It was weird. No, it was funny. It *had* to be. I laughed, and I sounded like my voice was changing. I waved weakly towards the doors of the barn, trying to be funny. I'd never been able to budge those doors to see what was inside. They were stuck fast. "Maybe your . . . I mean *our* . . . friends could open those barn doors while they're at it," I cackled. "I'd like to see what's inside!"

There was a moment in which nothing happened, but only a moment. Then, slowly, the heavy doors began to swing open! They creaked, they groaned, but they moved! And they moved of their own accord! There was nothing . . . no one . . . within fifty yards of those doors! That is, no one that I could see.

"See? It's the Little Fellah again," India whispered. "He heard . . . an' he an' Big Bull come ta help you!"

I got up and stumbled towards the barn. I strained and tugged, but I couldn't move those doors. Without another word, I went back to the house. India brought my coffee. It was strong, and I needed it. We didn't speak. I didn't believe it, I kept telling myself.

That was before Bobby tumbled into the cistern on Ed Collins' place next door.

It was the next afternoon. Ellen came running to get me, shouting for help through her tears. The kids had been playing, couldn't see the overgrown, unused cistern and . . . as I ran, I prayed Bobby was still alive. When I got to the well, India was already there. And on the ground . . . near the cistern . . . Bobby! Spent, red-eyed . . . but alive . . . smiling! I caught him up in my arms . . . heard a faint murmur . . . "the little Fellah!" I looked at India. Her lips framed the words. But then she went on, quickly. She had found Bobby as I did, bruised but unhurt, by the side of the well. All the water had been pressed from his lungs. Her voice dropped.

"*Someone* climbed down that narrow cistern after the boy. An' *someone* lifted him up!"

I knelt by the mouth of the well. Room for a child's body . . . yes. But a man's . . . no. The edges of the pipe were torn away, as by a giant hand. I checked the words, but the thought remained. *The Little Fellah . . . Big Bull*—I checked the thought fast.

When I got to my feet, Ed Collins was with us. He was a big guy . . . big—and mean. In the crook of his arm, he cradled a sawed-off shotgun, and he asked no questions. His idea . . . we get off his property . . . fast! No, he'd be blasted if he'd cap the top of the cistern! I could bloody well keep my brats chained up! And if we didn't start to git in a hurry . . . he was gonna blast us!

That was when I hit him. My first punch smashed his shotgun down against his back ribs. My second . . . to the jaw . . . rolled him over in the scrub near the cistern. He cursed, threatening a terrible revenge against what I loved most—

my children. But he didn't get up . . . not till after we'd gone.

I couldn't be bothered with Collins for the next few days. One thing bothered me, though . . . two "things." The Little Fellah . . . and Big Bull! I couldn' get them out of my mind. Could you, in my boots?

When I finished the first chapter, I took it down to town. The publisher liked it. Coming back to the house that night, I could see the next chapter—just the way I wanted it. The house was dark. My house key was in my hand, but I didn't need it. The door was ajar. The unnatural silence pounded in my ears.

In the hall, I stumbled. At my feet, there was . . . there was . . . something . . . soft. And moaning, low. I flicked the light switch. At my feet . . . it was India, lying still, hurt! She stirred, moaned again, whispered.

"Collins . . . he . . . he came for the children. But . . . they . . . safe . . . we drove him off! Go . . . after him . . . we'll be all right!" Yes, I heard her. She said *we!*

I ran out of the house and across the lawn. I found myself following a trail of bloodstains to Collins' place, and at the end of the trail, I found . . . Collins. He lay face down in a clump of bushes, dead. The right side of his face had been bashed flat by a boulder, maybe . . . or a great fist. Then I saw the knife imbedded in his neck. It was the smallest I had ever seen, about the size of my index finger. A toy knife . . . for a toy man! And a head crushed . . . by a great fist! I could hear India's voice: "*The Little Fellah . . .* he takes care o' me! Him an' Big Bull!"

But I don't know why I'm telling you all this. You don't believe me! *Or do you?*

The Sargasso Specter

Since the times of the ancient Phoenicians, awe-stricken sailors have whispered strange tales of the mysterious SARGASSO SEA -- that weed-clogged mariners' graveyard where flotillas of ships lie rotting, held fast in the clutches of the sargassum weed!

And occasionally, a half-wild, shipwrecked survivor will return with the strangest story of all, babbling of a fiendish, infernal demon -- The SARGASSO SPECTER!

EIGHT HUNDRED MILES NORTHWEST OF THE CAPE VERDE ISLANDS...

LOOK, CAPTAIN! --AN OPEN BOAT!

CAN'T TELL WHETHER THOSE TWO POOR DEVILS IN IT ARE DEAD OR ALIVE! ONE OF 'EM'S A WOMAN, TOO! PREPARE TO LOWER AWAY!

THANKS... GAVE UP HOPE... DAYS AGO! BUT LISTEN ... SOMETHING I HAVE TO TELL YOU ... IN SARGASSO SEA ... WE FOUND IT...

THERE, THERE, MATEY, WAIT TILL YE HAVE A REST AN' PLENTY O' FOOD AN' WATER BEFORE YE START SPOUTIN'!

THE GIRL'S ALL RIGHT --- OUR SHIP'S DOCTOR'LL FIX HER UP! SO, DON'T YOU DO ANY TALKING NOW!

NO... NO! WATER'S ALL I NEEDED! I'VE GOT STRENGTH TO TELL YOU WHAT HAPPENED --AND YOU'VE GOT TO KNOW! YOU SEE, I'M AN INSTRUCTOR IN OCEANOGRAPHY AT THE POLYTECHNIC INSTITUTE-- AND LAST TERM ---

"CORA --- THE GIRL WHO WAS IN THE BOAT WITH ME --- TOLD ME OF SOME REMARKABLE DISCOVERIES SHE'D MADE WHILE DOING HER GRADUATE THESIS... "

...AND WHEN I FINISHED EXAMINING ALL THE REPORTS OF THE SARGASSO SEA THROUGHOUT THE YEARS, I LEARNED THAT IT'S ALWAYS SEEN IN A DIFFERENT PLACE AND THAT IT APPARENTLY FOLLOWS A REGULAR COURSE OF INTERSECTING CIRCLES! AND ITS COURSE COINCIDES EXACTLY WITH THE POSITIONS OF ALL THE FAMOUS SHIPS THAT HAVE DISAPPEARED OR WHOSE CREWS VANISHED --- THE MARIE CELESTE, THE CYCLOPS, THE ATALANTA, THE KOBENHOVEN...

AND WHAT'S MORE, ACCORDING TO MY CALCULATIONS, THE SARGASSO SEA IS DUE TO APPEAR AGAIN NEXT MONTH AT LATITUDE 29°48' NORTH AND LONGITUDE 47°22' WEST!

WHY, THAT'S WONDERFUL WORK, MISS BRYCE! ON THE BASIS OF THIS, WE OUGHT TO GET THE FUNDS FOR AN EXPEDITION TO SEE WHAT'S BEHIND THE SARGASSO SEA PHENOMENON!

" I REPORTED THE FINDINGS TO THE INSTITUTE'S TRUSTEES... "

...AND I'M CONVINCED OF THE ACCURACY OF MISS BRYCE'S CALCULATIONS! SHE'S PROVIDED SCIENCE WITH ITS FIRST OPPORTUNITY TO INVESTIGATE THE SARGASSO SEA ---

WELL, YOU'VE CONVINCED US! WE'LL TAKE A CHANCE AND FINANCE AN EXPEDITION FOR THE TWO OF YOU -- COMPLETE WITH WEED-CUTTERS FOR YOUR BOAT AND A SMALL CANNON TO SINK ANY OLD HULKS THAT MAY GET IN YOUR WAY! WE DON'T WANT YOU GETTING CAUGHT IN THE SARGASSO!

"WE WERE TWO WEEKS OUT... A THOUSAND MILES FROM LAND, AND CLOSE TO THE POSITION WE'D CALCULATED..."

HAW -- THINK OF 'EM BRINGING ALONG GRASS-CUTTERS--- HERE, IN THE MIDDLE OF THE OCEAN!

CAPTAIN, THE BOTTOM'S FALLING OUT OF THE BAROMETER! WE'RE IN FOR A BLOW FROM THE SOU'WEST!

"THE STORM THAT HIT US WAS A CROSS BETWEEN A HURRICANE AND A TORNADO! WE WERE COMPLETELY AT ITS MERCY FOR THREE DAYS, WALLOWING HELPLESSLY IN THE HUGE WAVES, DRIFTING FAR OFF OUR COURSE... "

"WHEN THE STORM SUBSIDED, WE FOUND OURSELVES IN A DENSE FOG!"

CAP'N... OUR ENGINES--- THEY WON'T MOVE US! IT'S ...IT'S ALMOST AS IF WE WERE CAUGHT FAST!

YOU BLUBBERING IDIOT, HOW CAN WE BE CAUGHT BY WATER?

"AS THE FOG STARTED TO LIFT..."

WE ARE CAUGHT -- BUT BY SEA-WEED!

THE SARGASSO SEA --- WE'RE IN IT!

YOU WERE RIGHT, CORA -- WE'VE FOUND IT!

AND THERE THEY ARE -- THE HULKS OF DEAD SHIPS-- EVERYWHERE AROUND US!

IT--IT'S LIKE A GRAVEYARD-- OF LOST SHIPS! GHOST SHIPS -- COMIN' TO HA'NT US!

GHOST SHIPS? THAT'S A GENUINE SPANISH GALLEON! WAIT TILL I GET MY HANDS ON THE GOLD SHE MUST BE CARRYING!

NOT SO FAST, CAPTAIN! IF THERE'S ANY GOLD ABOARD THESE OLD DERELICTS, YOU AND THE CREW WILL GET A FAIR SHARE! BUT THE INSTITUTE WILL HAVE TO GET THE BULK OF IT! NOW, PLEASE LOWER THE LAUNCH SO WE CAN EXAMINE THESE SHIPS!

A FAIR SHARE, HUH? WELL, ALL RIGHT, YOU'RE THE BOSS - SO FAR!

IF THERE'S ANY GOLD ON THESE OLD BRIGANTINES, WE'LL FEED THOSE TWO LANDLUBBERS TO THE FISH! ARE YOU WITH ME?

WE'LL TOSS A COUPLE OF COINS TO THE CREW, AND SPLIT ALL THE REST OF IT BETWEEN US TWO! WE'LL BE RICH AS KINGS!

3

IT'S GOLD! JEWELS! THERE'S A SULTAN'S RANSOM HERE!

THEY'RE--- GENUINE SPANISH DOUBLOONS! ALL THIS WILL BE A WONDERFUL ENDOWMENT FOR THE INSTITUTE!

SPIKE--- NOW!

OHHH!

NEIL! OH, YOU... YOU BRUTES! LET ME GO TO HIM!

YOU CAN'T HELP HIM NOW! WHEN SPIKE HITS 'EM LIKE THAT, THEY'RE FINISHED!

CRACK!

C'MON, GET A COUPLE OF MEN UP HERE AND LET'S GET THAT CHEST BACK TO THE SHIP!

YOU... YOU CAN'T LEAVE HIM JUST LYING THERE LIKE THAT!

AW, FERGET ABOUT HIM, SISTER! HE'S DEADER'N MOBY DICK! ALL YOU LAND-LUBBERS GOT SOFT HEADS--- ESPECIALLY COLLEGE PERFESSORS!

LOCK HER IN ONE OF THE CABINS FOR THE NIGHT! IT'S GETTING DARK--- WE'LL PILLAGE THE REST OF THE SHIPS IN THE MORNING! MEANWHILE, PUT THAT CHEST IN MY CABIN, MEN!

BUT, NEXT MORNING, AS DAWN BROKE...

L-LOOK! WE'RE RINGED IN BY THOSE GHOST SHIPS! AN' THEY'RE MOVIN' CLOSER!

I'D BETTER WAKE THE CAP'N! WE'VE GOTTA GET OUTTA HERE!

5

THEY'RE COMIN' FER US! IT'S THE CURSE O' THE SARGASSO SEA FER TAKIN' ITS GOLD! I NEVER USED TO BELIEVE THOSE STORIES ABOUT THE SARGASSO SPECTER-- BUT NOW I KNOW! IF YOU DON'T GIVE IT BACK ITS GOLD, I'LL... I'LL---

YOU'LL WHAT?

NOBODY STOPS ME--DEAD OR ALIVE! AND I KNOW HOW TO DEAL WITH THE SARGASSO SPECTER JUST AS WELL AS I KNOW HOW TO DEAL WITH LILY-LIVERED WHELPS LIKE YOU!

MAN THAT CANNON! WE'LL BLAST THESE HULKS BACK INTO LIMBO, TOGETHER WITH ANY SPOOKS THERE MAY BE ABOARD 'EM!

BAROOM!

THEN, SUDDENLY, FROM OUT OF THE UNKNOWN -- AN IMMENSE APPARITION!

THE SARGASSO SPECTER! MAY THE FATES HAVE MERCY ON US!

"THE CANNON BLAST MUST HAVE SHOCKED ME OUT OF MY STUPOR, FOR JUST THEN I REVIVED FROM THE BLOW... ONLY TO SEE ---"

OHHH, MY HEAD! I --- WHAT'S THAT?

HERE, LET ME HOLD YOUR HEAD UP!...

OH, NEIL --- LOOK!

CORA --- THAT LIFEBOAT! IT'S GOING TO LAND NEAR US!

"I WAS RIGHT! WE MADE IT TO THE SMALL BOAT, CRAWLED IN, AND THEN LOOKED AROUND..."

NEIL --- THE SPECTER HAS DISAPPEARED, TOGETHER WITH THE OTHER GHOSTS AND ALL THOSE OLD SHIPS! AND THE SEA-WEED IS SUBSIDING --- THE SARGASSO SEA MUST HAVE MOVED ON! WE'RE SAFE --- AND WHEN WE GET BACK ---

SAFE? ON AN OPEN BOAT, WITHOUT OARS OR SAILS, A THOUSAND MILES FROM LAND? I'M SORRY I TOOK YOU INTO THIS, CORA --- THE ODDS ARE AGAINST OUR LIVING TO TELL WHAT WE'VE SEEN!

"WE LOST TRACK OF THE NUMBER OF DAYS WE DRIFTED! WE WERE ABOUT GONE WHEN YOU SIGHTED US ---

SURE, SURE, AN ORDEAL LIKE THAT WOULD GIVE ANYONE HALLUCINATIONS! IT'S MADE YOU SAY SOME WILD AN' CRAZY THINGS, BUT YOU'LL FORGET ALL THIS AFTER YOU'VE RESTED A SPELL!

YOU ... YOU DON'T BELIEVE ME? LOOK... IN MY POCKET... I KEPT IT... OHHH!

POOR BLIGHTER --- HE'S PASSED OUT FROM WEAKNESS! HE WAS PLUMB OUT OF HIS HEAD, WITH ALL THAT LOONY TALK!

HMM --- HE WAS TRYING TO SHOW US SOMETHING... IN HIS POCKET!

A SPANISH DOUBLOON! I WONDER --- MAYBE HE WAS TELLING THE TRUTH!

WELL, I'LL BE--! AFTER ALL, HE ISN'T THE FIRST ONE I'VE HEARD TALK ABOUT THE SARGASSO SPECTER! WHO KNOWS?

Yes -- WHO KNOWS? Would you, reader, consider the doubloon conclusive proof? Or would you rather blind yourself to the evidences of the UNKNOWN?

AND SO -- AS THE DEVIL HEADS INTO THE CURLING MISTS THAT LEAD TO THE WORLD OF MEN...

CAREFUL, NOW! HE'LL TWIST OUR TAILS *GOOD* IF HE FINDS WE'RE TAGGING ALONG!

TA TA DEE DUM -- SMOKE GETS IN YOUR EYES!

SINCE THE DEVIL IS TOO CRAFTY TO SHOW HIM-SELF *OPENLY*, NO ONE *SHOULD* SUSPECT THAT HE'S ABROAD -- BUT *SOMETIMES* CIRCUMSTANCES CAN CATCH EVEN THE *DEVIL* UNAWARE! THAT EVENING --

OH-H!

CREEPERS, WENDY -- IT MUST BE *WONDERFUL* TO BE ENGAGED TO A FELLOW LIKE TED HARPER -- *ESPECIALLY* WHEN HE'S ONE OF THE BEST YOUNG SCULPTORS IN THE COUNTRY!

I HATE TO THINK OF TED'S WORK BEING AT A STANDSTILL! HE JUST CAN'T FIND A STUDIO -- AND HE *CAN'T* DO MUCH HAMMERING AND CHIPPING IN A *HOTEL ROOM*!

SAY -- I JUST REMEMBERED THIS IS THE *EVE OF ST. AGNES!* THERE'S AN OLD SUPERSTITION THAT IF A GIRL FACES AN UNLUCKY MARRIAGE, SHE'LL SEE THE MAN'S FACE IN A MIRROR -- RIGHT AFTER SHE RECITES A CHARM -- "CRYSTAL, CRYSTAL, TO THE FUTURE RACE -- IF MY LOVE IS DOOMED -- *THEN SHOW HIS FACE!*"

I THINK IT'S A LOT OF *NONSENSE*, KAREN -- BUT IT MIGHT BE FUN TO *TRY.* ANYWAY .. "CRYSTAL, CRYSTAL, TO THE FUTURE RACE -- IF MY LOVE IS DOOMED -- *THEN SHOW HIS FACE!*"

WELL? THE MIRROR WAS ABSOLUTELY *DARK* -- I DIDN'T SEE A *THING*!

YOU *DIDN'T?* NOT EVEN YOUR *OWN* REFLECTION?

STARTLED, WENDY LOOKS AGAIN -- STARING AT THE DIM, FORMING OUTLINES OF A LEERING FACE!

Y--YIPE!

THE DEVIL! I SAW HIS FACE, KAREN -- *GRINNING* AT ME!

I.HOPE YOU JUST IMAGINED IT -- BUT MAYBE YOU'D BETTER PHONE TED'S HOTEL -- AND SEE IF HE'S ALL RIGHT!

WENDY RUSHES TO THE PHONE -- AND HER PANIC HEIGHTENS!

YOU *CAN'T GET THROUGH* TO THE HOTEL BRISTOL? BUT THAT'S ABSURD, OPERATOR -- IT'S THE LARGEST HOTEL IN TOWN! SOMEONE *MUST* BE AT THE SWITCHBOARD!

I'M SORRY, MISS -- BUT THEY DON'T SEEM TO ANSWER!

2

161

NOW I'M **SURE** SOMETHING'S THE MATTER WITH TED! I JUST **FEEL** IT, KAREN!

TAKE IT EASY! WE'LL BE THERE IN A FEW MINUTES! ..**TAXI!**

AT TED'S HOTEL...

I'VE BEEN TRYING TO REACH TED HARPER BY PHONE! WHAT GOES ON HERE?

NOTHING TO GET EXCITED ABOUT! THE SWITCHBOARD HAS BEEN OUT OF ORDER FOR AN HOUR-- WE'RE RUSHING REPAIRS ON IT NOW!

WELL!

TED! I WAS AFRAID SOMETHING HAD **HAPPENED!**

WELL, SOMETHING **HAS** HAPPENED, PET! I WAS JUST ON MY WAY TO PICK YOU AND KAREN UP.. SO WE COULD DRIVE OUT AND SEE **MY NEW STUDIO!**

I'M SO EXCITED ABOUT GETTING A PLACE **FREE** THAT I CAN'T WAIT! I'VE KEPT MY EQUIPMENT IN THE TRAILER -- SO I'M READY TO MOVE IN **TONIGHT!**

GREAT! WE CAN GIVE YOU A HAND WITH THIS AND THAT!

THIS MIRACLE HOUSE IS IN THE MIDDLE OF A LARGE MARSH -- SEVERAL MILES FROM A VILLAGE CALLED **SWAMP HOLLOW!**

IT'S CERTAINLY A **STRANGE** PLACE FOR A HOUSE, TED! WHATEVER POSSESSED THE OWNER TO LET YOU HAVE IT FOR NOTHING?

DON'T ASK **ME!** HE MERELY PHONED AND OFFERED ME THE PLACE -- BUT MAYBE I CAN LEARN MORE ABOUT HIM WHEN WE REACH SWAMP HOLLOW! AS IT IS, I'M **STILL** DAZED -- CONSIDERING THAT I LEARNED ABOUT MY GOOD LUCK JUST A FEW MINUTES BEFORE YOU GIRLS ARRIVED!

YOU MEAN THE OWNER OF THE HOUSE **PHONED** JUST BEFORE WE CAME?

YOU **COULDN'T** HAVE GOTTEN A PHONE CALL, TED -- BECAUSE THE HOTEL SWITCHBOARD WASN'T WORKING! THERE'S SOMETHING SPOOKY ABOUT IT-- **BECAUSE I SAW THE DEVIL'S FACE IN MY MIRROR AT ABOUT THE SAME TIME YOU SAY YOU GOT THAT CALL!**

NOW, NOW-- IS **THAT** ANY WAY TO TALK? KEEP IT UP, AND YOU'LL BE HEARING THE SCREAM OF A BANSHEE **NEXT!**

THEN--QUAVERING SHRILLY IN THE DARKNESS ---

WOOOOO-O

3

162

JEEPERS -- IT'S A HIGHWAY PATROL CAR!

PULL OVER, BUDDY-- WE'VE GOT ORDERS TO SEARCH ALL TRUCKS AND TRAILERS!

THERE WAS A LOAD OF BUILDING PLANKS STOLEN FROM THE LUMBER YARD IN SWAMP HOLLOW LAST NIGHT! THE CHIEF HAS THE WILD IDEA THAT SOMEONE USED *GOATS* TO CARRY AWAY THE LUMBER -- BUT WE'RE CHECKING UP ON ALL LARGE VEHICLES, ANYWAY!

DID YOU SAY *GOATS?*

SCREEECH!

YEP -- THERE DOESN'T SEEM TO BE ANY *OTHER* WAY TO EXPLAIN THOSE CLOVEN FOOTPRINTS ALL AROUND THE LUMBER YARD! BUT YOU'RE OKAY! *CHUG ALONG!*

CLOVEN FOOTPRINTS! TED, I *DID* SEE HIS FACE-- AND I'M WONDERING-- *COULD THOSE BE HIS* TRACKS?

SOON AFTERWARD...

I WISH YOU'D ASK ABOUT THE HOUSE, TED! I'M JUST NOT IN THE MOOD FOR SLOGGING AROUND IN A DARK SWAMP!

GOOD THING THAT DINER'S OPEN! LET'S SEE WHAT WE CAN PICK UP!

STRANGEST THING I EVER HEARD OF! HOW COULD JUST ONE MAN WHISK FOUR CANS OF PAINT AND A CRATE OF SHINGLES CLEAN OUT OF THE BACK DOOR OF THAT HARDWARE STORE?

THAT'S NOT ALL! OF COURSE, OLD MRS. PEABODY'S EYES AREN'T *TOO* GOOD--AND SHE SWEARS THE THIEF WAS WEARIN' NOTHIN' BUT A SUIT OF *LONG RED UNDERWEAR!*

LONG... RED... UNDERWEAR!

I WAS WONDERING WHETHER YOU COULD BRIEF US ON THAT HOUSE IN THE MIDDLE OF THE SWAMP! WHO OWNS IT -- AND HOW DO WE GET THERE?

FOLKS STAY AWAY FROM THAT SWAMP, FELLA -- THERE'S NO HOUSE ANYWHERE *NEAR* IT! YEARS BACK, A FEW PEOPLE *TRIED* TO LIVE THERE -- BUT THE SWAMP SHOWED 'EM WHO IT BELONGED TO, MIGHTY QUICK! EVERY ONE OF THOSE PEOPLE TOOK SICK, JUST LIKE THEY WERE HEXED -- AND THEY *STAYED* SICK UNTIL THEY LEFT THE SWAMP!

4

AS GRIM SUSPICIONS FLIT THROUGH TED'S MIND LIKE CIRCLING BATS--

WHILE WE'RE AT IT -- WHO *DOES* THE SWAMP BELONG TO?

I'VE SEEN 'EM -- BUT *YOU* NAME 'EM! FIERY RED THINGS -- DANCING OVER THE REEDS AT MIDNIGHT!

NOW WE FIND THERE *ISN'T* ANY HOUSE! TED-- THIS IS ABOUT AS GOOD A TIME AS ANY TO FORGET ABOUT THE WHOLE THING!

WENDY, I'M SURE IT WILL ALL BOIL DOWN TO A JOKE SOMEONE'S PLAYING ON ME -- MIXED WITH A FEW LOCAL SUPERSTITIONS! BUT LET'S RIDE ALONG WITH THE GAG -- *AND SEE WHAT GIVES IN THAT SWAMP!*

A HALF-HOUR LATER -- DEEP IN THE GLOOMY SWAMPLAND-- THE MUFFLED NIGHT SEEMS TO HUM WITH *STRANGE SOUNDS!* AND OVER AND OVER, THE CRICKETS AND TREE-FROGS UTTER THEIR HUSHED WARNING IN THE DARKNESS!

THE DEVIL -- THE DEVIL -- THE *DEVIL* ---

SUDDENLY -- CASTING REFLECTIONS OVER THE WEED-CHOKED WATER...

TED -- THOSE ARE THE FIERY RED THINGS WE HEARD ABOUT! THEY'RE *DEMONS!*

RELAX, WENDY -- THEY'RE JUST *WILL-O-THE-WISPS* -- CAUSED BY THE SPONTANEOUS COMBUSTION OF MARSH GAS! AS FOR THE REST OF IT, WE'LL SOON *PROVE* THAT PHONE CALL *WAS* A TRICK -- BECAUSE THERE WON'T BE A HOUSE WITHIN *MILES* OF HERE!

HATE TO INTERRUPT -- BUT CAN I INTEREST YOU TWO IN SOME LOCAL REAL ESTATE?

UNMISTAKABLY, A HOUSE -- AND UNMISTAKABLY, A NEW HOUSE!

WELL -- IT'S *HERE!* WHAT *ELSE* IS THERE TO WONDER ABOUT?

PLENTY! THE LUMBER THAT WAS CARRIED OFF BY SOMETHING WITH CLOVEN FEET -- THE PAINT AND SHINGLES STOLEN BY A FIGURE IN *RED!* IT WAS THE DEVIL, TED -- AND *HE BUILT THIS HOUSE -- OVERNIGHT!*

FAR BE IT FROM *ME* TO BELIEVE IN THE DEVIL -- BUT BROTHER -- CAN HE *BUILD!*

MAYBE YOU AND WENDY HAD BETTER BUNK IN THE TRAILER FOR THE REST OF THE NIGHT -- WHILE I LOOK THE PLACE OVER! MY CAR BATTERY IS RUN DOWN, BUT I'LL LIGHT THIS LAMP -- JUST SO THE DARKNESS WON'T GIVE YOU ANY *MORE* IDEAS!

GUESS *I* WON'T NEED LIGHTS INSIDE -- WITH THE MOON SHINING THROUGH THE LARGE WINDOWS! *OH-OH!* FOR A SECOND I *THOUGHT* I SAW SOMETHING PEERING OUT -- A *FIERY RED FORM!*

NOTHING TO GET JUMPY ABOUT -- IT MUST HAVE BEEN THE REFLECTION OF ONE OF THOSE DARTING WILL-O'-THE WISPS!

PROD ME WITH A PITCHFORK -- I ALMOST GAVE MYSELF AWAY, *THAT* TIME! I'LL MAKE MYSELF INVISIBLE FOR AN HOUR OR SO -- *AND THEN I'LL BE ABLE TO TAKE OVER TED HARPER'S BODY!*

AS TED LOOKS AROUND -- UNAWARE OF THE LEAN, GLOATING FIGURE BESIDE HIM --

WOW! THE HOUSE ITSELF WAS *ENOUGH* OF A SURPRISE -- BUT THESE FURNISHINGS ARE *TERRIFIC!*

GLAD YOU APPRECIATE MY TROUBLE! AND BY THE WAY -- DID YOU CHANCE TO READ ABOUT THOSE *MYSTERIOUS FURNITURE STORE ROBBERIES* LAST NIGHT?

FROM ROOM TO ROOM -- ALL OF THEM SWEPT BY GREENISH MOONLIGHT!

PEACHY CELLAR, TOO -- BUT I WONDER WHAT THAT OPENING IN THE FLOOR IS FOR!

OH-OH! *YOU'LL* FIND OUT! IN FACT -- YOU *SHOULD* BE GETTING A HINT ANY SECOND NOW!

A MOMENT LATER...

NEVER THOUGHT A LITTLE EXCITEMENT WOULD AFFECT *ME* -- BUT I'M GETTING A BIT DIZZY!

AND YOU STILL HAVEN'T GUESSED WHAT THAT GRID IN THE CELLAR FLOOR IS FOR, HAH? IT'S A DUCT FOR THE VAPORS GIVEN OFF BY THE SWAMP -- *METHANE GAS* -- AND MINUTE BY MINUTE, IT'S DULLING YOUR BRAIN AND WILL POWER!

THAT'S IT ... RELAX ... BREATHE DEEPLY! AH, THIS IS A SNEAKY TRICK, EVEN FOR *ME* -- BUT YOU'LL BE IMMUNE TO THE GAS -- ONCE *I'M* INSIDE YOUR BODY!

I THINK I HEAR A VOICE ... FAR AWAY ... *BUT I CAN'T MOVE!*

MEANWHILE -- LYING SLEEPLESSLY IN THE TRAILER --

I *KNOW* THOSE RED REFLECTIONS DANCING ON THE WALLS ARE JUST WILL-O'-THE-WISPS, KAREN! ... BUT *NOW* THEY SEEM TO BE COMING CLOSER ... *CHANGING!* WE ... WE'D BETTER GET UP AND SEE!

167

Our Biggest Bulb Bargain

AMAZING GET ACQUAINTED...

TULIP OFFER
OUR FAMOUS HARDY PLANTING STOCK

100 BULBS for $1.69

Dozens of brilliant flaming colors in this Rainbow Mix Assortment . . . Darwin, Triumph, Breeder, and Cottage Tulips for remarkable low cost of less than 2c per bulb. Our prize selection of famous young especially selected strain and smaller because they are first and second year bulbs—1½" to 2¼" in circumference. Satisfaction guaranteed or money back.

Selected by Tulip experts who guarantee replacement of any bulb not developing to your satisfaction.
. . . Will fill your garden with blazing color ranging from delicate pastel shades to bold flaming hues. MAIL THE COUPON TODAY!

ORDER NOW!
Send No Money!

Send no money to get this marvelous tulip bulb bargain! Just check which offers you desire and rush order today! Your tulip bulb assortment with extra Dutch Iris Bulbs will be sent you immediately in plenty of time for fall planting. When postman brings your package just pay amount as checked in coupon plus C.O.D. postage. If you remit with order, we'll pay postage. If you don't feel that you have hit the bargain jackpot of the garden world, return the bulbs and receive your money back.

EXTRA
12 DUTCH IRIS BULBS

. . . Yes, as your gift for ordering this astounding tulip assortment . . . we will send you 12 genuine first-year Dutch Iris Bulbs extra and without additional cost. These gorgeous irises will give your garden new purples and blues that will make it the envy of your neighbors. All solid disease-free bulbs . . . extra just for mailing your tulip order coupon now.

Other Delightful Flower Bargains!

Chrysanthemums . . . New CUSHION MUMS. Young, vigorous plants which will fill your garden with spectacular beauty. (Should produce over 1000 blooms) Assorted colors, 10 plants and 6 Ranunculus Bulbs extra....... **$1.69**

Imported Holland Crocus Bulbs
Choice, Famous Varieties of selected bulbs direct from Holland! These crocuses, flowering size, will be the first to bloom next spring in lovely white, yellow, blue and striped blossoms. Grow indoors —or in lawns where they flower for years without replanting. 3 Ranunculus Bulbs extra. 100 BULBS............. **$1.94**

MICHIGAN BULB CO., Dept. RR-1515   GRAND RAPIDS 2, MICH.

170

Adventures into the Unknown
February/March 1950 - Issue #9

Cover Art - Edvard Moritz

Shadow of the Panther
Script - Unknown
Pencils - Max Elkan
Inks - Max Elkan

The Thing at the Bottom of the Sea
Script - Unknown
Pencils - Charlie Sultan
Inks - Charlie Sultan

Haunted Boy
Script - Unknown
Pencils - John Celardo
Inks - John Celardo

When the Shaman Walked
Script - Unknown
Pencils - John Belfi
Inks - John Belfi

The Spirit of Frankenstein, Part 4
Script - Unknown
Pencils - Charlie Sultan
Inks - Charlie Sultan

The Man in the Mirror
Script - Unknown
Pencils - R. S. Pious
Inks - R. S. Pious

The Boy Who Could Fly
Script - Unknown
Pencils - Bob Jenney
Inks - Bob Jenney

ADVENTURES INTO THE UNKNOWN, published bi-monthly and copyright, 1949, by B. & I. Publishing Co., Inc., 420 DeSo Ave., St. Louis 7, Missouri. Editorial Offices, 45 West 45th Street, New York 19, N. Y. Richard E. Hughes, Editor; Frederick Iger, Business Manager. Subscription (12 issues), $1.20; single copies, $.10; foreign postage extra. Application for re-entry as seco class matter pending at the Post Office at St. Louis, Mo. Additional Entry, Sparta, Ill. No. 9, February-March, 1950. Printed in U.S.

SHADOW of the PANTHER

There are more things on earth, the wise men say, than we have ever dreamed of... or can ever know! "THINGS" that can return the dead to the realm of the living! "THINGS" like REINCARNATION, and the unknown secrets of LIFE... and DEATH!

ROBERT LEWIS WAS A WISE MAN--- YOUNG... AND A TOP SCIENTIST...

I'M GETTING CLOSER WITH EVERY EXPERIMENT... CLOSER TO THE SECRET OF LIFE! THIS HORMONE SOLUTION IN THE PROPER AMOUNT CAN DO IT... CAN BRING A DEAD ORGANISM BACK TO LIFE!

THESE PROTOZOA HAVE BEEN DEAD EVER SINCE I PLACED THEM ON THE SLIDE! NOW -- 15 CC OF THE NEW HORMONE... AND MAYBE THIS TIME ---

THIS TIME -- I'VE SUCCEEDED! I CAN SEE THEM MOVING AGAIN! THEY'RE ALIVE! BUT THOSE ARE NEW FORMS... DIFFERENT SHAPES! THEY'VE CHANGED ---- I WONDER...!

FOR A MOMENT, DR. LEWIS WAS PUZZLED... BUT THE EXCITEMENT OF THE WONDERFUL NEW DISCOVERY DROVE ALL DOUBTS FROM HIS MIND! THE EXPERIMENTS HAD TO GO ON!

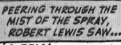

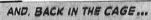

...A GIRL! A LIVING -- BREATHING -- PANTHER GIRL!

THEN...

THOSE WILD GROWLS... SHE LOOKS AS IF SHE COULD TEAR ME APART! I'M ALMOST AFRAID TO GO TO HER... BUT I MUST! I'M GOING IN!

GRRRR!

GRR-R!

THAT CAT-LIKE BODY, THOSE PANTHER EYES -- SHE'S TRYING TO SAY SOMETHING! SHE WANTS TO BE FRIENDLY! MAYBE... MAYBE I CAN TEACH HER TO BE A WOMAN!

THE LESSONS BEGAN...

LISTEN TO ME, GIRL, AND REPEAT AFTER ME!

LISTEN... LISTEN...

THAT IS A TABLE... A KNIFE... A FORK! YOU ARE A GIRL... YOUR NAME IS MONA!

THAT IS A TABLE! I AM A... GIRL! MY NAME IS... MONA!

AND, IN AN AMAZINGLY SHORT TIME...

ROBERT, WHEN WILL WE BE ABLE TO GO OUT? I'D LIKE TO SEE EVERYTHING, DO EVERYTHING!

MONA, YOU'VE LEARNED SO FAST--CHANGED SO QUICKLY-- I CAN'T BELIEVE YOU'RE THE SAME...ER... THE SAME PERSON!

PUT ON ONE OF YOUR NEW DRESSES AND SOME OF THAT MAKE-UP I BOUGHT YOU LAST WEEK! WE'LL STEP OUT RIGHT NOW!

A NEW DRESS, AND A CHANCE TO GO OUT --- ROBERT, YOU'RE A SWEETHEART! I'LL BE RIGHT BACK!

WELL, HOW DO I LOOK? LIKE ME?

YOU -- YOU'RE SO BEAUTIFUL, YOU TAKE MY BREATH AWAY!

3

FEAR WAS FORGOTTEN... A **NEW** EMOTION TOOK ITS PLACE, AND GREW...

MONA, YOU KNOW I LOVE YOU, DARLING! MARRY ME ... RIGHT AWAY!

I .. I'VE BEEN WAITING FOR YOU TO ASK ME! I'LL MARRY YOU, ROBERT, ANYTIME YOU SAY!

... BUT A SHADOW HUNG OVER THE HAPPY SCENE!

I HAVE THE RING ALL PICKED OUT, BUT I WANT YOU TO LOOK AT IT FIRST! ... MONA, WHAT'S THE MATTER?

I'M SURE I'LL LOVE IT ...

GRR-RR!

SUDDENLY...

MONA! THAT HUGE DOG... HE LOOKS DANGEROUS! LOOK OUT!

GRR-RR-R!

AS THE DOG CAME FACE-TO-FACE WITH THE GIRL, IT WAS AS THOUGH THE ANIMAL HAD GONE STARK, RAVING MAD! HOWLING, BRISTLING, IT BACKED AWAY!

... AND DOCTOR ROBERT LEWIS LOOKED ON... WIDE-EYED! AND **FEAR** CAME BACK!

THAT STRANGE, FIERCE LOOK ON HER FACE... IT'S **COME BACK!** NO -- IT CAN'T BE ... I WON'T LET MYSELF THINK **THAT!**

MONA... MONA! GET HOLD OF YOUR-SELF! THAT WAS ONLY A DOG... JUST A DOG!

BUT THE FEAR REMAINED! SOON AFTER, ROBERT LEWIS TOOK HIS FIANCÉE TO THE ZOO... **DELIBERATELY!** IT WAS THERE THAT **FATE** TOOK A HAND ... AGAIN ...

WE'LL HAVE A NICE AFTERNOON HERE, MONA -- WHAT'S THAT?

LOOK OUT! LEOPARD'S LOOSE!

HELP! HELP!

THE CROWD SCATTERED, BATTLING TO AVOID THE SNARLING BEAST! FRIGHTENED, ROBERT LEWIS BEGAN TO RUN, TOO... BUT THEN HE STOPPED, TURNED BACK! ONE FIGURE STOOD BETWEEN HIM AND THE RAGING LEOPARD... THE FIGURE OF A **WOMAN** ...

4

NEXT DAY...

LAST NIGHT... THAT **CAT-KILLER!**... I MUST ASK MONA, YET I CAN'T! IN THREE DAYS, WE'LL BE MARRIED AND ALL THIS WILL BE FORGOTTEN! I WON'T BE AFRAID ANY MORE!

ROBERT, CHEER UP! YOU'RE NOT A CONDEMNED MAN... YOU'RE A **BRIDEGROOM!**

HOW'S ABOUT A KISS FOR THE BRIDE BEFORE YOU LOCK YOURSELF UP IN THAT LAB FOR THE REST OF THE DAY?

I LOVE HER AND SHE LOVES ME... THERE'S NOTHING TO FEAR!

THE WEDDING DAY DAWNED GREY AND UNEVENTFUL! AT WEDDING TIME...

THE BRIDE'S A LITTLE LATE, DR. LEWIS --- SHALL I GO FETCH HER?

NO, I DON'T WANT ANYBODY ELSE TO GO! **I'LL** GO!

BUT, DR. LEWIS ... IT'S **BAD LUCK** FOR THE GROOM TO SEE THE BRIDE BEFORE THE CEREMONY!

ALL OUR BAD LUCK IS **BEHIND** US... SHE'S SO BEAUTIFUL!

ALMOST READY, DARLING?

READY! YOUR LAST KISS AS A BACHELOR ... NO REGRETS?

I LOVE YOU ...**NO REGRETS!**

THEN, IN AN INSTANT, ROBERT LEWIS RECOILED! SUDDENLY, THE THOUGHT CAME -- "HOW DOES IT FEEL TO KISS... A CAT??"

DR. ROBERT LEWIS STEPPED BACK... **HORROR-STRICKEN!**

WAIT! YOUR FACE... IN THAT LIGHT... IT'S CHANGING! IT'S FIERCE... CAT-LIKE... **PANTHER-LIKE!**

YOU ---YOU'RE STILL A PANTHER... A **KILLER!** I CHANGED YOU IN BODY, BUT NEVER IN SOUL! NOW YOU'RE CHANGING BACK TO THE **BEAST!** KEEP BACK ... **BACK!**

I MUST KILL HER... OR **SHE'LL** KILL ---

6

BACK IN THE CHURCH...

NO! NO-O-O...! OOOOH!

WHAT...?

IN ANOTHER INSTANT...

A PANTHER-- ON THE LOOSE! WE'LL ALL BE KILLED!

RUN FOR YOUR LIVES!

STAMPEDE... A TERRIFYING WORD, AND AN UGLY SIGHT! THE BLACK PANTHER SWEPT FORWARD, AND HORROR AND FEAR SWEPT FORWARD BEFORE IT --- FILLING THE ROOM WITH THE SOUNDS OF TERROR!

HELP! HELP! HELP!

THAT... THAT UGLY BEAST! IT WAS HORRIBLE... HORRIBLE!

SOMEONE HELP ME, PLEASE! I'M HURT... BAD!

WHAT'S HAPPENED? WHERE IS ROBERT LEWIS?

CRASH!

The Planet Reporter

SCIENTIST KILLED BY MYSTERIOUS BLACK PANTHER!

CAT ESCAPES!

MISSING BRIDE SOUGHT! WHEREABOUTS UNKNOWN!

WEDDING TRAGEDY!

SCIENTIST BELIEVED ON VERGE OF GREAT DISCOVERY

The shadow of the BLACK PANTHER hovered over Doctor Robert Lewis -- and FELL! Seeking to preserve the living flesh he reincarnated strange forms... and DIED! For he had dared to plumb the forbidden SECRETS OF LIFE, DEATH -- AND THE UNKNOWN!

IN THE INNER ROOM, SCIENTIST ROBERT LEWIS LAY DEAD ... AND ON HIS NECK WERE GRAVEN ... THE MARKS OF THE CAT!

7

NO ANSWER

THERE was no conscience in Vinny's eyes. Only fear.

He sat on the edge of the narrow iron bed in the cheap hotel room and tried to concentrate on a game of solitaire. But the cards stuck to his sweaty fingers and their colors and numbers were blurs before his fear-filled eyes.

Vinny had just killed a man.

"I did it on orders," he kept telling himself. "It was an order from the boss. Nobody tells the boss 'no.' So what? So I killed him! There hadda be a first time!"

For Vinny, the first time had been a nightmare. He kept hearing that voice, strangely shrill and high-pitched . . . the squeak of a cornered rat.

"Don't shoot, Vinny! Don't shoot . . . please . . . please . . . please . . ." The voice had cracked on the last word and Vinny had gritted his teeth as it squeaked off into . . . silence.

But Vinny was a superstitious guy, and a superstitious guy doesn't do things like this easily. Instead, he keeps hearing that shrill voice, over and over, pleading for mercy!

The hotel room grew darker and darker. Only the flash of an electric sign outside threw a rhythmic light into the room. And still Vinny sat, the fear within him growing . . . spreading . . . widening . . .

And then the phone rang.

"Yeah?" he said, into the speaker. "Yeah?"

His eyes grew glazed and his mouth widened as though for more air. Although the room was stuffy and hot, a thin, knife-blade chill cut along his spine, until it reached the nape of his neck.

That voice. That high-pitched voice, pleading, begging, "Don't shoot, Vinny! Don't shoot . . . please . . . please . . . please . . ."

The pounding of Vinny's heart increased, so that his whole body shook with fear. And then, his heart seemed to explode with the fear, and the crash shook him, lifeless, to the floor . . .

They broke into the room the next day. A couple of cops and the desk clerk. They found Vinny, his body slumped on the floor, his right hand clutching the phone, which was still off the hook.

One of the cops turned him over with the toe of his heavy shoe. "Saves us the trouble of makin' an arrest," he remarked.

"Right,' said the other cop, yawning.

But the desk clerk stared at the body and his eyes were full of fear. Fear and incomprehension.

"The phone!" he said. "He's got it off the hook! He's been *talkin'* to somebody!"

"So?" smiled one of the cops.

"You . . . you don't understand. There has been *no call*, to or from this room, through my switchboard!"

The THING at the BOTTOM of the SEA

A DESERTED MANSION BUILT ON A 5000-FOOT RIDGE OF THE COLORADO ROCKIES MAY SEEM TO BE A STRANGE SETTING FOR A STORY OF LOVE AND THE SEA! BUT IT WAS A STRANGE SEA THE *"POLESTAR"* SAILED, FIFTY YEARS AGO ···AND THE LOVE DISCOVERED BY HER MASTER, JOHN MITCHELL, WAS SOMETHING THAT WILL MAKE YOU PAUSE UNEASILY FOR THE REST OF YOUR LIFE··· EVERY TIME YOU SEE THE FOAMING EDGE OF A BEACH···OR HEAR THE CRASH OF COMBERS RUNNING LANDWARD IN THE NIGHT!

YES···IF YOU DON'T MIND THE HEAVY DAMPNESS INSIDE, AND THE GRITTINESS UNDERFOOT, WE'LL FIND CLUES IN THE DARKNESS ···CLUES TO THE INCREDIBLE ADVENTURE OF JOHN MITCHELL!

MAYBE IT'S THE MOONLIGHT THAT SPARKLES IN THESE LONELY ROOMS··· *MOONLIGHT*···AND MAYBE A LITTLE BIT··· OF *SOMETHING ELSE!*

IT'S ALL IN HERE···WORD FOR WORD! BUT BEFORE WE START TO READ···ARE YOUR NERVES GOOD? WILL YOU BE ABLE TO FACE THE NIGHT ALONE···AFTER LEARNING WHAT NIGHTS MEANT TO JOHN MITCHELL?

LOGBOOK OF THE "POLESTAR" JOHN MITCHELL, MASTER

I ASKED BECAUSE *THIS* IS WHAT HE SCRAWLED ON THE FLYLEAF ON THE *LAST* OF THOSE NIGHTS··· *IN THIS HOUSE!*

It's coming··· the black frothing thing!

HOWEVER··· LET'S START WITH JOHN MITCHELL'S *FIRST* ENTRY··· THE ONE HE WROTE NEARLY FIFTY YEARS AGO! HERE··· I'LL HOLD THE PAGE CLOSE SO YOU CAN READ IT IN THE DARKNESS··· THE DARKNESS THAT BROUGHT *HIM* A SURGING WAVE OF TERROR!

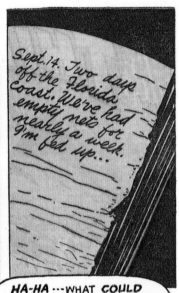

Sept. 14. Two days off the Florida coast. We've had empty nets for nearly a week. I'm fed up···

HA-HA···WHAT *COULD* HAPPEN THAT WOULDN'T BE WELCOME? AFTER SIX WASTED DAYS ON THIS WALLOWING TUB, I'M *WAITING* FOR SOMETHING TO HAPPEN···*ANYTHING!*

YOU HEARD ME··· *FED UP!* WHEN A TRAWLER CAN'T MAKE EXPENSES THREE VOYAGES RUNNING ···*SHE'S JINXED!*

DON'T TALK THAT WAY ABOUT THE SHIP, SKIPPER···IT BRINGS BAD LUCK! WE'RE THIRTY MILES FROM LAND, IN TRICKY WATER···AND SOMETHING MIGHT HAPPEN!

AS YOU MIGHT GUESS···JOHN MITCHELL DIDN'T HAVE LONG TO WAIT! YOU CAN BELIEVE ME WHEN I SAY THAT SOMETHING DOWN IN THOSE GREEN DEPTHS *HEARD* HIM···SOMETHING IN THE NOISELESS TWILIGHT OF THE SEA! BUT WE'LL LET JOHN MITCHELL TELL HIS STORY···

"The men talked me into lowering the net again. It came up light···and as I roared at them for being fools···"

TWO PIECES OF DEAD MAN'S CORAL! YOU KNOW WHAT *THAT* MEANS, SKIPPER ···TWO DEAD MEN ABOARD ··· *THIS VOYAGE!*

BAH! SEE WHAT *ELSE* YOU CAN FIND, YOU FOOL···I'M BEGINNING TO *LIKE* JINXES!

STOW THAT TALK--- AND LOOK AT *THIS!* IT'S *GOLD*---A *GOLD INGOT!*

GOLD! WHERE... WHERE?

LET'S SEE! KEEL HAUL ME IF IT *ISN'T* A GOLD INGOT!

POLESTAR

WHERE THERE'S *ONE* OF THESE THINGS---THERE'S APT TO BE *HUNDREDS!* WE'RE OVER A WRECK ---THE WRECK OF A TREASURE GALLEON THAT PROBABLY SANK CENTURIES AGO---LOADED TO THE GUNWALES WITH GOLD! HOP TO IT--- *TAKE A SOUNDING!*

"It wasn't until later that I remembered how pale Portygee looked when he brought up the lead..."

NINE FATHOM---AND WE'RE IN THE DEEPEST PART OF FLORIDA STRAIT! SKIPPER, I DON'T LIKE IT---FIFTY-FIVE FEET OF WATER WHERE THERE SHOULD BE *THOUSANDS!*

I LIKE IT FINE---WHEN THERE'S A FORTUNE LYING IN SHALLOW WATER! SMITTY, FETCH THAT DIVING HELMET---ON THE *DOUBLE!*

SKIPPER, LISTEN TO ME! DEAD MAN'S CORAL---A BAR OF GOLD ---AND THEN SHALLOW WATER TWO DAYS OUT! IT'S BAD, SKIPPER---AND IT'S GOING TO BE *WORSE* IF YOU GO DOWN!

HOLD YOUR JAW---AND GET ON THE PUMP! SMITTY---KEEP FAST ON THAT LIFELINE!

"Maybe they thought I was crazy---and maybe they would have been sure of it if they could have followed me---down--- down---into an eerie world!"

STRANGE---SUNLIGHT FROM THE SURFACE DOESN'T REACH DOWN *THIS* DEEP--- BUT THERE'S A SHINING HAZE IN THE WATER--- LIKE AMBER---LIKE *GOLD!*

"It took me a half hour to load the bars! Them I could feel...hard, yellow, shining gold!"

I'LL BE DOWN FOR YOU, UNDINE...THE MINUTE WE UNLOAD!

NOT **MORE** THAN A FEW MINUTES...AFTER ALL THESE CENTURIES! REMEMBER, JOHNNY ...**YOU PROMISED!**

"Portygee and Smitty were like wild men...pawing at the net and yelling themselves hoarse! And then...Portygee got that look again...that white, fish-belly look..."

SOMETHING WRONG, YOU FOOL? WHAT DO YOU **WANT** FOR AN HOUR'S PUMPING... **DIAMONDS?**

I...I THOUGHT I **HEARD** SOMETHING, SKIPPER! JUST A GULL, MAYBE...OUT ON THE WATER SOMEWHERE!

SKIPPER, NO ONE EVER PICKED UP A FORTUNE FOR NOTHING! IF WE'VE GOT TO **DO** SOMETHING FOR IT...SELL OUR SOULS FOR IT... **FOR THE LOVE OF PETE, DUMP IT BACK!**

I'M GETTING **SICK** OF THAT TALK... DEAD MAN'S CORAL AND SELLING SOULS! UP ANCHOR, YOU CRACKPOT! SMITTY ...GET THE ENGINE KICKING!

ONLY A MAN SURE OF HIS OWN DOOM WOULD HAVE WRITTEN THE WORDS THAT COME NEXT...IN THAT NIGHT'S ENTRY! MITCHELL WAS ON DECK...STACKING THE GOLD INGOTS ...WHEN HE HEARD A TERRIFIED YELL...

THAT'S NO GULL! IT'S A WOMAN'S VOICE...**AND I CAN HEAR THE NAME SHE'S CALLING!**

JO-HN--NY! JO-HN--NY!

WHAT'S SHE WANT, SKIPPER ...HOUNDING US LIKE THAT? WHAT DID YOU TELL HER WHEN YOU GOT THE GOLD ...DOWN THERE IN FIFTY-FIVE FEET OF WATER?

WHAT DO YOU MEAN...**HER?** DID **YOU** SEE ANYTHING, YOU FOOL? AND WHAT DIFFERENCE DOES IT MAKE WHEN WE'LL BE TYING UP IN THREE HOURS...WITH ENOUGH GOLD TO QUIT THE SEA FOR GOOD?

"And then it came again...like the sea, mournful and far away...like the sea, raging and sweeping close..."

JO-HN--NY! YOU PROM-ISED, JO-HN--NY! JO-HN--NY!

PROMISED SOMETHING...FOR **THAT**? GIVE IT BACK, SKIPPER...**GIVE HER BACK HER GOLD!**

POLESTAR

5.

"In the next second, they were scuttling around the deck like crabs... bringing the ingots over the side!"

YOU, DOWN THERE... TAKE IT! **TAKE IT ALL!**

STOP IT! I'M NOT GIVING IT UP...

PLOP!

...NOT FOR A VOICE... **NOT FOR ANY-ONE!**

"If I ever saw fear, I saw it then... the kind of fear that kills those who feel it... and those who face it!"

KEEP BACK, SKIPPER!

WE'VE HAD ENOUGH OF THAT MOANING DEMON ... **THE GOLD'S GOING OVER!**

"A voice didn't matter... and they didn't matter! There was nothing in the world but the deck under my feet, and the curling waves... and the gold!"

BANG!

BANG!

SHE MEANT IT TO BE MINE... AND NOW... IT **IS** MINE!

"No, a voice didn't matter... but what I heard now wasn't a voice! It welled up out of the sunset... like the howl of a thing possessed!"

MINE... HEAR ME? GO ON, LAUGH... LAUGH AND **STAY** DOWN THERE... AFTER I'M ASHORE WITH THE GOLD!

HA-HAA-HAA!

"From that moment on... I neither saw nor heard! I didn't care what drifted behind the ship... as long as port lay ahead!"

JO-HN-NY! THE GO-LD ISN'T WO-RTH IT, JO-HN--NY!

6.

BUT MITCHELL THOUGHT IT *WAS* ---AND WHO WOULDN'T ---A CARGO OF GOLD THAT SOLD WITHIN A WEEK FOR NEARLY A MILLION DOLLARS? HE TURNED HIS BACK ON THE *"POLESTAR"* AND TRAVELED INLAND ---FROM THE HIGH SEAS TO THE HIGH MOUNTAINS --- FROM A RUSTY TRAWLER TO A MANSION IN THE CLOUDS!

LOGBOOK OF THE POL...

YES, A STRANGE PLACE TO KEEP A LOG-BOOK ---AS IF A SECRET VOICE KEPT CALLING --- TELLING JOHN MITCHELL HIS VOYAGE WASN'T OVER!

These days ashore have floated by like a dream! Everything's perfect ---the house, the view ---everything but one little detail!

FUNNY I NEVER NOTICED IT BEFORE ---THAT LOW HUM IN MY EARS! BUT WHAT'S A LITTLE DEAFNESS --- *NOW?*

"A low hum ---a low, rolling hum! It was soothing, at first ---but lately I've been lying awake nights, listening!"

IT'S THE WIND RUSTLING THE PINES DOWN IN THE VALLEY! A ROCKY, *INLAND* VALLEY ---DRY AS A BONE! THERE'S NO REASON WHY IT SHOULD SOUND SO STRANGE --- SO ---*WET!*

Do I dream I think it ---or think I dream it? ---or is it nerves ---just nerves?

LOOK, SKIPPER ---DEAD MAN'S CORAL!

YOOO-HOO! YOO-HOO, JOHNNY!

"I go down to the cellar ---half asleep, half dead ---and it follows me ---"

LISTEN ---YOU DON'T THINK I CAN DROWN YOU OUT, HAH? DROWN --- *DROWN* ---WHAT MADE ME SAY *THAT?*

BLAM! BLAM!

PLINK PLINK

"It's with me every minute ---surge and splash --- surge and splash ---and I'm going nuts!"

STOP IT ---STOP IT, YOU GRINNING APE! TURN OFF THAT WATER RUNNING INTO THE BATHTUB!

BOSS, I TELL YOU FIVE TIMES! BATH TUB EMPTY ---NO WATER RUNNING *ANYWHERE!*

CRASH!

7.

EDITOR — LET'S TALK IT OVER!

ALL aboard, folks, for another stirring issue of "*Adventures Into The Unknown!*" We've gone all out this time, with a super-duper number that's guaranteed to keep you gasping!

Yes, we said gasping—and if you don't believe us, just cast a look at "*The Thing At The Bottom Of The Sea.*" And read "*The Boy Who Could Fly.*" They're both new types of stories—and backing them up is an array of prime favorites that can't miss! They'll thrill you and chill you—and we want to hear about it! We want to know which you liked best—and what you'd like to see in future issues of our magazine—*your* magazine! Here's what some other readers are saying—

"Dear Editor:—
Out of all the comics I've read, your '*Adventures Into The Unknown*' is No. 1 on my hit parade. The stories and drawings are wonderful! Some of my favorite stories were: '*The Old Tower's Secret,*' '*The Castle of Otranto,*' '*The Living Ghost*' and '*The Spectral Singer.*' Please have more stories on werewolves and vampires and such stories as I have mentioned above—and continue the wonderful stuff in your comics.
—T. Tomkiewicz, Reading, Pa."

"Dear Editor:—
I have read every issue of your magazine, '*Adventures Into The Unknown*' and think it best of all the magazines I have ever read. I hope that someday you will make it a monthly instead of a bi-monthly. I have enjoyed every issue and sincerely thank you for some very swell reading. However, there's something I'd like to know. In issue No. 2, a story called '*Out of the Unknown*' was really swell. But what became of the '*Living Ghost*'? Did he come back and avenge himself? Did Tony Brand and Gail Leslie fall into his hands again? Anyway, it was a good story, and thanks again. Keep up the good work!
—Chas. E. Steed, Bay City, Mich."

Thanks, folks, for the nice things you've been saying—we'll continuue to do our level best to make you happy! Meanwhile, here's something *else* which should interest you—the final returns on our great "*Adventures Into The Unknown*" contest! You'll find our third-prize winner in this issue—"*The Gray One,*" by Nelson Bridwell. Congratulations, Mr. Bridwell—there is a prize-winner's check in the mail for you! And now we come to the announcement of our special prize-winners—25 of them! To each goes a free 12-issue subscription to their favorite magazine, "*Adventures Into The Unknown!*" Here they are—is *your* name among them?

1. GEORGE DYAK, 1703 Vail Avenue, Windber, Pa.
2. WILLIAM J WHITE, 818 Fay Street, Columbia, Mo.
3. A. SHANE HELMS, Mallory, N. Y.
4. FLORENCE CRISTE, RR 11, Box 1123, Phoenix, Ariz.
5. JACK MARSH, 505 Vine Street, Jonesboro, Ark.
6. CARL LEVINSON, 230 Blake Avenue, Brooklyn 12, N. Y.
7. BENNIE JACOPETTI, 1892 Green Street, San Francisco, Cal.
8. HAUGHTON BARLOW, P. O. Box 449, Waterbury, Conn.
9. ALBERT SILVERSTEIN, 126 Ivy Lane, Daytona Beach, Fla.
10. LOWELL STEIN, 7914 S. Wabash, Chicago, Ill.
11. DALE ROSE, RR No. 3, Jasper, Ind.
12. JOHN C. GRANT, 73 Ruggles Street, Quincy 69, Mass.
13. TONY SALTZMAN, 3458 Hillcroft Avenue, S. W., Grand Rapids 8, Mich.
14. VIRGINIA HERSZ, 18493 Hoover, Detroit 5, Mich.
15. GEORGIA WOODS, 1204 No. Cedar, Nevada, Mo.
16. WILMA WOLFE, 1819 Washington, Lincoln, Neb.
17. ISIS STREETER, Canal Street, Hinsdale, N. H.
18. ROY C. BOUGHER, Jr., 7 Giverson Row, Toms River, New Jersey
19. DAVID GARY HELM, c/o Diamond, West Monroe, N. Y.
20. BETTY HOYT, RR No. 2, McComb, Ohio
21. R. RODNEY SPROULE, 1930 So. Ithan Street, Philadelphia 43, Pa.
22. RONALD MUSSENDEN, 1620 San Mateo Street, Santurce, Puerto Rico
23. MAMIE JULIA NELSON, Gen. Del., Vernon, Texas
24. DOLORES B. CHANFRAU, 14 Jefferson Avenue, College Court, Phoebus, Va.
25. STANLEY KRIPPNER, RR No. 1, Fort Atkinson, Wis.

"TRUE" GHOSTS The CASE of the HAUNTED BOY!

By FAR THE STRANGEST STORY OF 1949 WAS THE **CASE OF THE HAUNTED BOY!** IN WASHINGTON, D.C., STRANGE "SPIRITS" BEGAN TO HARASS A 14-YEAR-OLD BOY, UNTIL THE CASE WAS FINALLY INVESTIGATED BY THE SOCIETY FOR PARAPSYCHOLOGY AND DUKE UNIVERSITY! THE CASE AMAZED AND PUZZLED EVERYONE EXCEPT THE HAUNTED BOY --- **WHO REMAINED HAUNTED!**

THE TROUBLE STARTED WHEN THE LAD BEGAN TO BE BOTHERED BY MYSTERIOUS AND UNEXPLAINED SCRATCHINGS ON THE WALLS AND CEILINGS! AND NO MATTER WHERE HE WENT IN HIS HOUSE, THE STRANGE SOUNDS SEEMED TO FOLLOW HIM!

SCRATCH

SCRATCH

SCRATCH!

AT NIGHT, HIS BED WAS SHAKEN SO VIOLENTLY BY UNSEEN FORCES THAT HE WAS UNABLE TO SLEEP!

DESPERATE, THE BOY'S FAMILY SENT HIM TO A PARSONAGE TO SPEND THE NIGHT! AND WHEN HIS NEW BED ALSO SHOOK VIOLENTLY, THE BOY TRIED SLEEPING WHILE SITTING IN A HEAVY ARM-CHAIR! BUT WHILE THE MINISTER WATCHED---

THE CLERGYMAN PLACED A BLANKET AND PILLOW ON THE FLOOR! BUT WHEN THE LAD TRIED TO SLEEP THERE, BEDDING AND BOY BOTH SLID OVER THE FLOOR AND UNDER THE BED!

THE BOY TRIED ONCE MORE --- AND THIS TIME, HE WAS FLUNG AROUND IN A HALF-CIRCLE BEFORE ENDING UP UNDER THE BED AGAIN! AND TO THIS DAY NO ONE KNOWS WHAT STRANGE FORCES OUT OF THE **UNKNOWN** HAUNTED THE BOY!

MAYBE SO···BUT *I'M* NOT AFRAID OF THE SHAMAN! HE'S MY FRIEND···HE *LIKES* ME!

OH, UNCLE MACK··· WHO *WOULDN'T?*

POOR UNCLE MACK MIGHT SOUND A BIT CRACKED TO ANYONE ELSE···BUT I KNOW HOW AN OLD MAN DREAMS AS HIS LIFE DRAWS TO A CLOSE! I'M GLAD THE JOB I GAVE HIM *DID* FIND HIM A FRIEND···EVEN ONE AS QUEER AS THE SHAMAN!

THE EVENING SKY FADES INTO A BLACK CUSHION FOR THE TWINKLING SKYSCRAPERS ···AND UNCLE MACK SITS IN THE HALF DARK SHOWROOM···FACING THE SHADOWED FIGURE OF THE SHAMAN! IT ALMOST SEEMS ALIVE···WITH POINTS OF LIGHT GLEAMING IN ITS SIGHTLESS EYES···AND ON THE LITTLE BELLS DANGLING FROM ITS BLOODLESS LIMBS!

MAYBE THERE *WILL* BE A NIGHT WHEN YOU WALK, SHAMAN···AND *THAT'S* THE ONE I'VE BEEN WAITING FOR! YEP, THE NIGHT I HEAR FOOTSTEPS IN THIS PLACE ···FOOTSTEPS THAT AREN'T MY OWN··· I'LL *KNOW*···

···I'LL *KNOW* WE'RE GOING!

THUD THUD

*T*WO CROUCHING SHADOWS REAR THREATENINGLY ON THE WALL··· TWO SILENT FORMS STEAL SLOWLY FORWARD!

WHO IS IT?

Then···AN ORANGE STREAK CUTS THE DARKNESS!

BANG!

2.

INTO A PATCH OF FEEBLE LIGHT FALLING FROM THE TRANSOM...

WHAT DID YOU WANT TO DO *THAT* FOR? DO YOU *HAVE* TO GET YOURSELF IN TROUBLE ...LESS THAN AN HOUR AFTER BUSTING OUT OF THE PEN?

DID *I* KNOW HE WAS REACHING FOR THE LIGHT SWITCH? I THOUGHT IT WAS A BURGLAR ALARM!

HE'S STILL BREATHING! WHAT'S HE STARING AT *THAT* THING FOR...THAT FREAK WITH THE LITTLE BELLS?

COME ON...SNAP OUT OF IT! LET'S DITCH THESE CONVICT OUT-FITS...AND FIND OUR-SELVES SOME CLOTHES!

A MOMENT LATER...

THEY'RE NOT MUCH FOR FIT...BUT THEY'LL KEEP THE COPS OFF OUR TRAIL UNTIL WE'VE REACHED THAT BACK-ROADS FARMHOUSE I MENTIONED!

WHAT'S *THAT*?

TINKLE TINKLE!

WAITERS' UNIFORMS

THEN A VOICE SOUNDS...ABOVE THE RIPPLING CHIME OF SILVER BELLS!

IT'S THAT OLD CROCK! WHO'S HE TALKING TO, CHARLEY...*WHO*?

I HEARD THEM RING, SHAMAN ...I HEARD YOU MOVE! AND NOW I GUESS...WE'LL BE HEADING FOR...THE NORTHERN LIGHTS!

THAT THING MOVE? THE OLD BOY WAS TALKING STRICTLY FROM DELIRIUM!

BUT DO YOU REMEMBER WHAT WE *HEARD*, CHARLEY? BELLS... LITTLE BELLS... JUST LIKE *THEM*!

YOU CAN'T TELL *ME* THAT'S AN ORDINARY DUMMY! I *KNOW* WHEN I'M BEING WATCHED AND LISTENED TO ...AND I'M GETTING OUT OF HERE!

AND SO THE *TWO CONVICTS* HURRY TO THEIR CAR...EACH WITH THE SECRET THOUGHT THAT *NOW* THEY ARE RUNNING FROM MORE THAN THE POLICE! IT'S SOMETHING THEY LEFT BACK THERE...AND SOMETHING THEY MAY MEET AGAIN...*ANY-WHERE!*

320

MEANWHILE...WINNIE STIRS...HAUNTED BY A TROUBLED DREAM!

WINNIE! I'M GOING A LONG, LONG WAY, WINNIE!

I'VE NEVER HAD A DREAM AFFECT ME LIKE *THIS* BEFORE! I KNOW I SHOULDN'T BE WORRIED BY UNCLE MACK'S SAYING HE EXPECTED TO BE *GOING SOMEWHERE* WITH THE SHAMAN... BUT I WON'T REST EASILY UNTIL I'VE PHONED HIM!

A MINUTE PASSES...TWO MINUTES...THE UNANSWERED BUZZ SENDING A SWIRL OF DREAD THROUGH WINNIE'S MIND!

NOW I *KNOW* SOMETHING'S WRONG! MAYBE... IF I HURRY...I CAN GET TO THE SHOWROOM IN TIME TO HELP!

AT THAT MOMENT...AS THE TWO CONVICTS REACH THE EDGE OF TOWN...

WAIT'LL YOU SEE THAT FARM... YOU'LL GET RID OF YOUR WHAMMIES *THERE*, CHUM! QUIET LITTLE PLACE...WITH A BROOK PLINKING AND GURGLING RIGHT OUTSIDE THE DOOR!

IT'LL STILL BE DARK WHEN WE GET THERE! YOU GOT *LIGHTS* IN THAT DUMP?

SURE...*GAS!* KIND OF OLD-FASHIONED...BUT NO USE BEING CHOOSY WHEN WE'RE TRYING TO COVER UP OUR TRACKS! WHICH REMINDS ME...WE MIGHT AS WELL CHUCK OUR PRISON DENIMS INTO THE BUSHES! LET'S HAVE 'EM!

CHARLEY...DIDN'T *YOU* PICK UP THOSE DUDS WHEN WE CHANGED?

OF ALL THE FAT-HEADED TRICKS! *YOU'RE* THE ONE WHO GOT SCARED BY BELLS AND THE DEVIL KNOWS WHAT...RUNNING OUT AND LEAVING THOSE DENIMS RIGHT WHERE THEY CAN PUT THE FINGER ON US IF WE'RE EVER CAUGHT!

SCREEECH!

AS CHARLEY SWINGS THE CAR AROUND...

WE'RE NOT GOING TO GET CAUGHT, CHARLEY! LET THE COPS FIND THOSE DENIMS...SO WHAT?

I KNOW JUST WHAT'S ON YOUR MIND...BUT SKIP IT! BELLS OR NO BELLS ...*WE'RE GOING BACK!*

QUICKLY, THE CONVICTS DRIVE OFF WITH THEIR CAPTIVE... AS IF TO HIDE THE FACT THAT *THEY* ARE THE CAPTIVES... *OF FEAR!*

HOW COULD YOU HAVE DONE IT? A HARMLESS OLD MAN... SO LONELY HE'D SPEND THE NIGHT TALKING TO THAT LIFELESS FIGURE ABOUT GOING PLACES... JUST AS IF IT WERE A FRIEND!

THEY WENT PLACES, ALL RIGHT! I'M NOT SURE ABOUT THE OLD MAN... BUT THAT CREEP WITH THE BELLS TOOK A POWDER *SOMEWHERE!*

FROM FAR OFF... UNCLE MACK'S VOICE ECHOES IN WINNIE'S MIND!

YOU MEAN THE SHAMAN'S... *GONE?*

YES, MA'AM... SOMEDAY SOON HE'LL BE GOING BACK... BACK TO THE PLACE THAT'S ALWAYS HALF DAYLIGHT!

AN HOUR LATER... WITH A CLAMMY DAWN MIST DRIFTING OVER THE MEADOWS...

WELL... HERE IT IS, CHUM... JUST AS I LEFT IT! HEAR THAT BROOK TINKLING DOWN THERE AMONG THE ROCKS?

WAIT... *WAIT!*

TINKLE TINKLE

WITH A SUDDEN STAB OF FEAR...

CHARLEY... DID YOU EVER HEAR A BROOK *RING* ... OR *CHIME?* WHEN SOMETHING TINKLES, CHARLEY... IT'S *BELLS!*

DON'T START *THAT* AGAIN... PUTTING A JINX ON US THE MINUTE WE GET HERE! STRIKE A MATCH... *WE'RE GOING INSIDE!*

LET'S HAVE THOSE MATCHES! YOU'RE SO STIR-HAPPY, YOU DON'T KNOW WHAT YOU'RE DOING!

I KNOW WHAT I'M *NOT* DOING... *I'M NOT GOING IN!* LISTEN TO THOSE BELLS... SWISHING BACK AND FORTH WHILE HE HOPS AROUND... *WAITING!*

READY TO COVER UP BY PLUGGING ME, EH? *GIVE ME THAT GUN!*

BANG!

CRASH!

6.

JUMPING BACK···WINNIE HAS A SPLIT-SECOND GLIMPSE OF THE ROOM···FEEBLY LIT BY THE SPUTTERING MATCH FLAME···

THEY'RE NOT ALONE! THERE'S SOMETHING *ELSE* INSIDE··· MOVING OUT OF THE SHADOWS!

TINKLE TINKLE

IN THE SAME SPLIT-SECOND···THE SHAMAN TOWERS AT THE EDGE OF DARKNESS···TERRIBLY ALIVE!

IT WASN'T ME! YOU WERE THERE ···YOU *KNOW* IT WASN'T ME!

Then···BOTH SHAMAN AND DARKNESS DISSOLVE IN A FLARING BLAST!

BO OM!

WHEN WINNIE REVIVES···

THOSE MEN WHO SHOT UNCLE MACK ···*THEY WERE INSIDE!*

GOOD THING THOSE TWO CONS DIDN'T GET *YOU* INSIDE! ABOUT THE QUICKEST WAY TO GET BLOWN APART IS TO LIGHT A MATCH···*WHEN THERE'S BEEN A SLOW GAS LEAK FOR SEVERAL YEARS!*

GAS LEAK! NO WONDER I WAS KNOCKED OUT!

AND THEN SOME! WHEN WE PULLED UP, YOU WERE SITTING THERE STARING UP AT THE SKY ···MUMBLING SOMETHING ABOUT UNCLE MACK AND A GUY NAMED SHAMAN···*WALKING TOGETHER TOWARD THE NORTHERN LIGHTS!*

ARE YOU *SURE* I HADN'T RECOVERED CONSCIOUSNESS? I MEAN···DO YOU THINK I MIGHT HAVE REALLY *SEEN* SOMETHING?

YOU'D HAVE A FINE TIME *PROVING* IT! SAY, HERE'S SOMETHING YOU MUST HAVE DROPPED···A *LITTLE SILVER BELL!*

The End

7

"THE GRAY ONE" by NELSON BRIDWELL

FRANK CLINTON was a big-game hunter. He was a practical, hard-bitten man whose only religion was his rifle—whose only craving in life was to meet and beat the most dangerous game that could come under his sights. That was why the story of *"The Gray One"* stirred the old fever of the hunt in his blood. It was a wolf that had terrorized a small French village—but what a wolf! Twice as large as any normal animal, the story went. It attacked humans, rather than beasts, and had already slain a dozen—and men feared to track it down!

When Clinton arrived, and made known the fact that he wanted the huge creature's head for his collection, he sensed a strange reaction among the villagers. There was a light of terror in their eyes, and a few crossed themselves. And then it finally came out, in the stumbling speech of a frightened old man. "He—he's a creature of Satan, the Evil One! Not an ordinary wolf—else why does he attack only humans? No ordinary weapon can kill him—because the Gray One is a *werewolf!*"

Clinton tried to laugh off the impossible story, to explain that there were no such things as werewolves, that superstition was mere imagination. But he soon saw that it didn't work, and realized that if he attempted to buck the villagers' beliefs, it was going to be impossible to obtain a guide to the animal's stamping-grounds. But what beliefs they were! The Gray One, they insisted, had formerly been a man—and now, as a werewolf, was so deadly that no local inhabitant dared hunt him. And regular bullets would do no good—it would have to be a silver bullet, blessed by a holy man—the only thing that could kill this devil's beast, and restore it to its original form! So, laughing within himself, Frank Clinton acceded.

It took the bravest villager to guide Clinton to the outlying spot where the giant wolf had made its kills. Once there, he fled back to the safety of the town, leaving the big-game hunter to the perils of oncoming night—the time when the werewolf stalked! There was something in the lonely hush and gloom which oppressed Clinton, filling him with an odd foreboding. Could this be *fear*, this strange sensation which gripped him? Nonsense—he had unflinchingly faced the world's deadliest animals! Besides, there was nothing around that—*what was that?* The crackle of a twig—*and suddenly he saw it!* Good Heavens, it—it couldn't be! A gigantic, slavering creature like nothing living, with death written plain on its gleaming fangs—a mad beast which moved in a diabolical reflected glow of its own! For the first time, Frank Clinton knew stark terror, a terror which hypnotized him, rooted him to the spot as the huge animal crept gloatingly towards him. Nearer—nearer—it was almost upon him now! It was some desperate inner sense of self-preservation which finally saved him at the last moment, and sent the silver bullet crashing squarely into the brain of the Gray One!

There it was at his feet, dead. Only now could Clinton shake off the strange, terrifying sensation that had numbed him. He must have been crazy! Just a big wolf, that was all. And he must have imagined that glow he thought had surrounded it, because it was gone now. But the beast's head—what a trophy, what a prize to talk about! Carefully he severed it, placed it in a box he had brought along for just that purpose. Werewolves—silver bullets—what nonsense! In the final analysis, it had been his expert marksmanship which had felled the animal.

And so Frank Clinton returned to his inn, to a much-needed sleep. He was entirely refreshed when he awoke the next morning, and eager to have another look at the great trophy which he had bagged. Fingers trembling with happy anticipation, he opened the box, peered within it —and then reeled back, a choked cry in his throat and eyes bulging with an awful horror.

Within the box lay a human head.

200

SPIRIT of Frankenstein

WE'VE NEVER DARED LET THE ROBOT ANYWHERE **NEAR** THE CYCLOTRON BEFORE, DAN···BUT WE MIGHT HAVE PREVENTED ALL HIS TERRIBLE RAMPAGES IF WE **HAD!** SOMETHING ATTRACTS HIM TO THE CYCLOTRON SO STRONGLY THAT HE DOESN'T WANT TO LEAVE IT···AND I WISH I KNEW **WHAT!**

I THINK I CAN TAKE A STAB AT THE ANSWER, MARCIA! AS CLOSELY AS THAT DANGEROUS, BROODING BRAIN OF HIS WILL PERMIT···THE ROBOT HAS FOUND SOMETHING TO **PROTECT!**

WHEN SINISTER PROFESSOR PARDWAY DIED, HE BEQUEATHED HIS BRAIN TO THE ROBOT CREATED BY DR. DAN WARREN···AND THE RESULT IS A BRUTE OF PHENOMENAL STRENGTH AND VOLCANIC RAGES -- **IN THE SPIRIT OF FRANKENSTEIN ITSELF!** ONLY A CREATURE FLITTING OUT OF THE BLACK BEYOND CAN MATCH IT···AND THAT'S JUST WHAT HAPPENS WHEN THE ROBOT MEETS **THE EYES OF THE UNKNOWN!**

I DIDN'T REALIZE IT BEFORE···BUT THE ROBOT SEEMS TO UNDERSTAND HOW MUCH HE OWES THE CYCLOTRON! TO **HIS** SAVAGE MIND, IT'S THE MAGIC DEVICE THAT DESTROYED THE EVIL SPIRIT OF PROFESSOR PARDWAY···THEREBY RELEASING HIM FROM THE PHANTOM'S SINISTER INFLUENCE ···AND GIVING HIM A WILL OF HIS **OWN!**

BUT HE'S JUST AS UNTAMED AS EVER···EXCEPT THAT THE CYCLOTRON SEEMS TO HAVE A QUIETING EFFECT! **YOU'RE TAKING CARE OF IT···AREN'T YOU, ROBOT?**

HUUUH!

THERE'S THE PHONE, DAN!

R-RRRING!

I'M CONDUCTING AN EXPERIMENT IN MASS HYPNOTISM AT THE STATE PENITENTIARY TONIGHT, DAN···AND SINCE YOU'RE INTERESTED IN MY WORK AS A PSYCHOLOGIST ···I THOUGHT YOU MIGHT LIKE TO BE IN ON IT!

SURE THING, BURT! I CAN FEEL A BIT EASIER ABOUT LEAVING THE ROBOT ALONE IN THE LAB···NOW THAT WE'VE LEARNED HE'S GOT A STRONG YEN FOR THE CYCLOTRON!

THAT NIGHT···IN THE PENITENTIARY AUDITORIUM···

I KNOW THEY'RE WELL GUARDED, BURT···BUT ISN'T IT RISKY TO EXPERIMENT WITH THE MOST VICIOUS CRIMINALS IN THE PRISON?

YOU'RE RIGHT, MARCIA ···THESE VOLUNTEERS ARE ALL LIFERS, CONVICTED FOR ACTS OF VIOLENCE···AND THAT'S EXACTLY WHY I CHOSE THEM!

THE WARDEN CONSIDERS THEM INCORRIGIBLE AND DANGEROUS···AND I WANT TO LEARN WHETHER POST-HYPNOTIC SUGGESTION WON'T HELP SOMEWHAT! YOU'LL SEE WHAT I MEAN··· I'M READY TO BEGIN!

FIRST, I WANT YOU MEN TO DISMISS WHATEVER HAPPENS TO BE ON YOUR MINDS···A JAIL BREAK···A DEADLY GRUDGE WITH A CELL MATE···OR ANYTHING ELSE! SIT BACK AND RELAX··· AND WATCH MY HAND!

SLOWLY, THE PRISONERS' COLD, DEFIANT EYES BECOME GLAZED···THEIR HEADS SAG···AND THEY PASS UNDER BURT'S HYPNOTIC CONTROL!

NOW LISTEN! I DON'T EXPECT TO WORK A MIRACLE··· I CAN'T CHANGE A LIFETIME OF WHAT MADE YOU CRIMINALS IN FIVE MINUTES! BUT AT THE END OF THOSE FIVE MINUTES···WHEN YOU COME OUT OF YOUR TRANCE···YOU'RE AT LEAST GOING TO REMEMBER YOU'RE HUMANS··· NOT JUNGLE BEASTS READY TO POUNCE ON EVERYONE YOU MEET!

AS THE MINUTES TICK BY···

MIGHT BE JUST MY IMAGINATION···SOMETHING THAT SCIENTISTS LIKE DAN AND BURT WOULD SMILE AT···BUT I'M ALMOST POSITIVE THE CONVICTS' FACES HAVE CHANGED! THEY STILL LOOK TOUGH···BUT THEIR FEATURES SEEM TO HAVE LOST SOME OF THE BRUTAL QUALITY I'D NOTICED BEFORE!

Then···

ALL RIGHT, MEN··· THE FIVE MINUTES ARE UP!

CLAP!

ON YOUR FEET! FORM A SINGLE FILE·◆AND FACE THE DOOR!

AS THE CONVICTS FILE OUT···

VERY INTERESTING, DR. TRAVIS···AND I'M CERTAINLY GLAD YOU WERE ABLE TO BRING A CELEBRITY LIKE LIKE DR. DAN WARREN!

IT MAY BE A DAY OR TWO BEFORE ANY RESULTS ARE NOTICEABLE, WARDEN···IF THERE ARE ANY ···BUT I'LL KEEP IN TOUCH WITH YOU!

2.

NO ONE SUSPECTS THAT THE RESULTS HAVE ALREADY BEEN REALIZED···AND TO A TERRIFYING DEGREE! MINUTES LATER ···ALONG A LONELY ROAD···

I FEEL SOMETHING **OPPRESSIVE** IN THE AIR, DAN···SOMETHING I'D SHRUG OFF AS A RISING STORM IF I WEREN'T SO SURE IT'S **FOLLOWING** US!

OH, WELL··· JUST AS LONG AS IT ISN'T SOME OF THOSE PRISONERS!

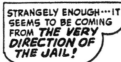

STRANGELY ENOUGH···IT SEEMS TO BE COMING FROM **THE VERY DIRECTION OF THE JAIL!**

Then···HOVERING BALEFULLY IN THE GLOOM···

DAN···THOSE SHINING THINGS UP THERE! **WHAT ARE THEY?**

WHAT THINGS **COULD** SHINE, SIDE BY SIDE, OUT OF THE NIGHT AIR···SHINE WITH DARK, GLINTING PUPILS?

EYES···STARING RIGHT OUT OF **NOWHERE!**

EASY, MARCIA! THERE'S NO DOUBTING WE'RE FACE TO FACE WITH A **SUPERNATURAL BEING**···BUT THAT'S NO REASON FOR THINKING IT'S AS EVIL AS IT LOOKS!

BUT IT'S THE **LOOK** THAT SCARES ME··· JUST THOSE TWO EYES··· BRIMMING OVER WITH SOME KIND OF TERRIBLE SECRET!

LET'S GET MOVING, BURT! THE APPARITION MAY BE CONFINED TO THIS PARTICULAR SPOT···AND THEN AGAIN···IT MAY ACTUALLY BE **GOING** SOMEWHERE!

DAN'S CAR PICKS UP SPEED···AND SILENTLY···THE LUMINOUS EYES KEEP PACE!

FOLLOWING US! WELL, BURT···HOW ABOUT DEALING YOURSELF IN FOR ONE OF **MY** EXPERIMENTS?

GREAT! WHAT HAVE YOU GOT IN MIND?

I CAN THINK OF A DOZEN POSSIBILITIES TO EXPLAIN WHY THOSE EYES ARE INTERESTED IN **US**··· BUT IN BOTH SCIENCE AND THE SUPERNATURAL, GUESSWORK CAN BE DISASTROUS! I WANT TO LEARN WHAT KIND OF PHANTOM IS LURKING INVISIBLY BEHIND THOSE EYES···AND ONCE WE'VE LURED IT INTO MY LABORATORY, **I KNOW HOW IT CAN BE DONE!**

3.

UNTIRING···UNBLINKING···THE EYES PEER OUT OF THE GLOOM AS DAN AND THE OTHERS REACH THE LABORATORY!

THERE'S NO TELLING **WHAT** WE'LL UNLEASH··· EXPERIMENTING WITH SOMETHING LIKE **THAT!**

WARREN CYCLOTRON LABORATORY

WE'VE GOT TO TAKE THAT RISK! IF IT **IS** A CREATURE OF TERROR, WE'LL HAVE A BETTER CHANCE TO CONTROL IT **AFTER** THE EXPERIMENT···**BECAUSE I PLAN TO MAKE IT VISIBLE!**

WHILE I'M GETTING READY, BURT··· HOOK UP THOSE THOUSAND-WATT BUNCH LIGHTS! MEANWHILE, MARCIA ···COAX THE ROBOT AWAY FROM THE CYCLOTRON···WE'LL BE NEEDING IT ANY MINUTE!

SURE···YOU'RE A **GOOD** ROBOT! YOU'RE GOING TO LET DAN USE THE CYCLOTRON··· AREN'T YOU?

YUUUUGH!

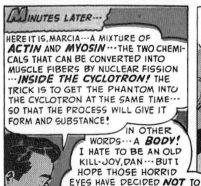

MINUTES LATER···

HERE IT IS, MARCIA···A MIXTURE OF **ACTIN** AND **MYOSIN**···THE TWO CHEMICALS THAT CAN BE CONVERTED INTO MUSCLE FIBERS BY NUCLEAR FISSION ···**INSIDE THE CYCLOTRON!** THE TRICK IS TO GET THE PHANTOM INTO THE CYCLOTRON AT THE SAME TIME··· SO THAT THE PROCESS WILL GIVE IT FORM AND SUBSTANCE!

IN OTHER WORDS···A **BODY!** I HATE TO BE AN OLD KILL-JOY, DAN···BUT I HOPE THOSE HORRID EYES HAVE DECIDED **NOT** TO WAIT AROUND OUTSIDE!

YOU GET YOUR WISH, PET! **JUST LOOK BEHIND YOU!**

OH-H! THOSE GLARING THINGS HAVE BEEN INSIDE ALL THIS TIME··· **WATCHING!**

UUUGH!

LUCKILY, I DON'T THINK THE PHANTOM HAS ENOUGH OF BRAIN TO **UNDERSTAND** WHAT IT SEES···OR IT WOULDN'T HAVE FOLLOWED US HERE IN THE FIRST PLACE! AS SOON AS YOU AND MARCIA HAVE PUT ON YOUR GOGGLES, BURT··· TURN THOSE LIGHTS **AWAY** FROM THE CYCLOTRON···**AND SWITCH THEM ON!**

SECONDS LATER···A DAZZLING LIGHT FLOODS ALL BUT ONE CORNER OF THE LAB!

KEEP YOUR EYE ON THE ROBOT, MARCIA···I DON'T WANT **HIM** STIRRED UP BY WHAT HAPPENS NEXT!

FOR A MOMENT, THE PHANTOM EYES FLUTTER UNCERTAINLY···THEN CIRCLE LIKE WHIZZING POINTS OF FIRE TOWARD THE ONLY HAVEN OF DARKNESS IN THE LABORATORY···**THE CYCLOTRON!**

Then...BEFORE THE MONSTROUS EYES CAN SENSE THE TRAP...

I'LL KNOW IN A FLASH WHETHER THE CREATURE TAKING SHAPE IS **HARMLESS**...OR WHETHER IT SHOULD BE **DESTROYED** BY NUCLEAR ENERGY!

SLAM!

BUT SUDDENLY...WITH AN IMPACT THAT ROCKS THE LABORATORY...

YAGH! YARRRGH!

CRRRUNCH!

AGAIN THE EYES GLEAM SAVAGELY...BUT **THIS** TIME THEY ARE THE EYES OF A THING OF TERROR...UNLEASHING ITS NEW-FOUND STRENGTH!

AS THE ROBOT STARTS FORWARD WITH A SNARLING CHALLENGE...

YAARRRGH!

RELAX, ROBOT! I KNOW THAT THING SMASHED YOUR CYCLOTRON...BUT EVEN **YOU** HAVEN'T GOT ENOUGH ON THE BALL TO TANGLE WITH IT...**YET!**

IN A SWIRLING BURST OF POWER...

CRASH!

A MOMENT LATER...THE TOWERING FIGURE OF EVIL BLENDS INTO THE DARKNESS!

IT **COULD** BE ACCIDENTAL...BUT I HAVE A HUNCH THERE'S A **REASON** FOR THE PHANTOM'S HEADING BACK IN THE DIRECTION FROM WHICH IT CAME...**TOWARD THE PENITENTIARY!**

I DIDN'T MENTION IT BEFORE, DAN...BUT I DETECTED A FAINT CHANGE IN THOSE PRISONERS' FACES AFTER BURT SNAPPED THEM OUT OF THEIR TRANCE...JUST AS IF THE **WORST** PART OF THEIR NATURES HAD BEEN SUDDENLY ABSORBED!

ABSORBED! GREAT GUNS, DAN...DO YOU SUPPOSE **THAT THING** IS A MANIFESTATION CREATED BY THE VERY EVIL I HYPNOTIZED THOSE CONVICTS INTO **RELEASING?**

I'M AFRAID SO! THAT'S PROBABLY WHY THE EYES FOLLOWED US IN THE FIRST PLACE...BECAUSE THE PSYCHIC FORCE BEHIND THEM WAS STILL SUBJECT TO YOUR HYPNOTIC INFLUENCE!

NOW, HOWEVER, THE PHANTOM IS ACTING ON ITS OWN---A TERRIBLE COMPOSITE OF THE WORST CRIMINAL MINDS IN THE COUNTRY! THAT BEING THE CASE---YOU CAN GUESS WHAT ITS FIRST MOVE WILL BE!

TO FREE THOSE CONVICTS! WE CAN'T WASTE TIME, DAN---WE'VE GOT TO STOP IT!

SINCE WE'RE DEALING WITH SOME-THING THAT HAS BECOME A RAM-PAGING TERROR WITH SYNTHETIC MUSCLES---WE'LL COUNTER-ATTACK WITH THE CHEMICAL THAT TURNS MUSCULAR ACTIVITY INTO ENERGY!

IT'S CALLED ADENOSINE TRIPHOS-PHATE---AND IT'S SUFFICIENTLY CONCENTRATED TO ENABLE ANYTHING WITH MUSCLES TO LIFT A THOUS-AND TIMES ITS OWN WEIGHT! STEADY, ROBOT---HERE'S WHAT YOU'VE BEEN WAITING FOR!

YUUGH!

YUUUGH?

A MOMENT LATER---HEADING QUICKLY TOWARD DAN'S CAR---

DON'T BE ALARMED, MARCIA! HE JUST WANTED TO OPEN THE GATE FOR US---NOT REALIZING THAT NOW HIS SLIGHTEST MOVEMENT HAS A BULLDOZER DRIVE BEHIND IT!

CRRRUNCH!

SOON AFTERWARD---AT THE PENITENTIARY---

BIG EYES---HIDE-OUS LOOKING---DON'T ASK ME WHAT IT IS! BUT FOR THE LOVE OF PETE---GET THE RIFLE SQUAD OUT HERE FAST!

WOO-OOO!

ITS TERRIBLE FORM REARING SHARPLY IN THE GLARE OF SEARCH-LIGHTS---HEEDLESS OF THE BULLETS WHIZZING DOWN IN CRISS-CROSSED STREAKS OF FLAME---

IT'S READY TO CRASH THROUGH THE GATE!

BANG!
BANG!
BANG!
BANG!

SUDDENLY---THE PHANTOM WHIRLS!

THERE HE IS, ROBOT! REMEMBER WHAT HE DID?

SCREEEECH!
HUUUGH!

ITS MIGHTY HANDS CLENCHED, THE ROBOT STALKS FROM DAN'S CAR··· TOWARD THE MOST HATED ENEMY IT HAS EVER FACED··· THE CREATURE THAT DESTROYED THE CYCLOTRON!

ARRRGH!

DODGING THE ROBOT'S PLODDING ATTACK··· THE PHANTOM STRIKES!

POW!

DAN··· I CAN'T WATCH THIS! THE ROBOT'S BEING HAMMERED SENSELESS!

WAM!

YUUGH!

BUT NOW··· THE ROBOT'S BRAIN COMES INTO PLAY! FEIGNING GROGGINESS, IT WATCHES ITS CHANCE··· AND LEAPS!

ALL RIGHT, MARCIA ··· THIS YOU CAN WATCH!

THEN···THE WALLS QUIVER UNDER A TREMENDOUS BLOW!

HUUGH!

BLAM!

AS THE PHANTOM FADES INTO NOTHINGNESS···

THAT BIG APE QUEERED OUR CHANCE TO MAKE A BREAK! LET ME AT HIM··· I'LL RIP HIM APART!

SEE HOW THOSE CONVICTS ARE ACTING NOW, BURT? IF WE NEED PROOF ABOUT HOW THE PHANTOM CAME INTO BEING··· THERE IT IS! IT HAS RETURNED TO THE CRIMINAL MINDS FROM WHICH IT WAS RELEASED!

HMM, HYPNOTISM'S NO CURE FOR CRIME! FROM NOW ON, I'LL CONFINE MY HYPNOTISM TO STAGE PERFORMANCES··· AND USE THE PROCEEDS TO GET YOU A NEW CYCLOTRON, DAN!

GOSH, BURT··· I DON'T KNOW WHO'D APPRECIATE IT MORE···MYSELF··· OR THE ROBOT!

THE ROBOT MAY STAY DOCILE··· AND THEN AGAIN···YOU MAY GET A HAIR RAISING JOLT IN THE NEXT ISSUE!

7.

CLOUDED CRYSTAL

HE sat opposite the fortune teller, a lazy sneer of disbelief on his face. "Whaddaya see, madam?" he asked sarcastically.

"Nothing good," she answered slowly. "I see only black. Black and evil! *You* think to do something evil . . . something terrible! I tell you do not do this thing or something evil will come to *you!*"

His sneer became more pronounced. "That's fine," he said shortly. "What else do you know?"

The dark-skinned woman did not answer. She stared into the crystal ball, and on her face was a look of horror. "*Do not do this thing!*" she said again.

This time, the man laughed aloud. "Oh, no?" he drawled. "Stop me . . . if you can!"

The fortune teller was no match for the man. His hands went about her throat like two steel bands that grew tighter . . . and tighter . . . tighter . . .

It was not a difficult safe to open. The man found it behind a pair of gaudy drapes. "Not bad," he congratulated himself. "Not a bad haul at all! Wonder if I oughta take that crystal ball with me!"

That was his idea of a joke. He gathered the money from the safe and thought about taking her earrings . . . but there was something about her face, her dead face so dark and foreboding, that stopped his hands.

He stepped out into the street and looked carefully about him. Was there anyone around? Had anyone seen him? No, the street was empty and he was quite safe . . . quite . . . safe . . .

A quick backward glance, and he stepped off the curb. "This getaway is a cinch!" he said. "It's a . . . no! Stop!"

It had come from nowhere. A black truck, large and shapeless in its speed, from nowhere! And it struck him down in the gutter, in front of the fortune teller's window. Money spilled from his pocket, but he did not know it. And the truck sped on, as though its driver had neither seen nor heard the man who lay dead in the street.

But on the face of the fortune teller, a change took place. Her mouth, set so tightly, softened . . . softened and relaxed . . . until it formed a wise and satisfied smile. And the crystal ball gleamed and sparkled as though it were . . . *alive!*

STATEMENT OF THE OWNERSHIP, MANAGEMENT, CIRCULATION, ETC., REQUIRED BY THE ACT OF CONGRESS OF AUGUST 24, 1912, AS AMENDED BY THE ACTS OF MARCH 3, 1933 AND JULY 2, 1946

Of ADVENTURES INTO THE UNKNOWN, published Bi-monthly at New York, N. Y., for October 1, 1949. State of New York, County of New York: ss.

Before me, a Notary Public in and for the State and county aforesaid, personally appeared Richard E. Hughes, who, having been duly sworn according to law, deposes and says that he is the Editor of ADVENTURES INTO THE UNKNOWN, and that the following is, to the best of his knowledge and belief, a true statement of the ownership, management (and if a daily, weekly, semiweekly or triweekly newspaper, the circulation), etc., of the aforesaid publication for the date shown in the above caption, required by the act of August 24, 1912, as amended by the acts of March 3, 1933, and July 2, 1946 (section 537, Postal Laws and Regulations), printed on the reverse of this form, to wit:

1. That the names and addresses of the Publisher, Editor, Managing Editor and Business Manager are: Publisher: B. & I. Publishing Co., Inc., 45 West 45th Street, New York, N. Y.; Editor, Richard E. Hughes, 120 W. 183rd St., New York, N. Y.; Managing Editor: none; Business Manager, Frederick H. Iger, 50 Beverly Road, Great Neck, L.I.

2. That the owner is: B. & I. Publishing Co., Inc., 45 West 45th St., New York, N. Y.; B. W. Sangor, 7 West 81st Street, New York, N. Y.; Frederick H. Iger, 50 Beverly Road, Great Neck, L. I.

3. That the known bondholders, mortgagees and other security holders owning or holding 1 per cent or more of total amount of bonds, mortgages or other securities are: None.

4. That the two paragraphs next above, giving the names of the owner, stockholders, and security holders, if any, contain not only the list of stockholders and security holders as they appear upon the books of the company but also, in cases where the stockholder or security holder appears upon the books of the company as trustee or in any other fiduciary relation, the name of the person or corporation for whom such trustee is acting, is given; also that the two paragraphs contain statements embracing affiant's full knowledge and belief as to the circumstances and conditions under which stockholders and security holders who do not appear upon the books of the company as trustees, hold stock and securities in a capacity other than that of a bona fide owner; and this affiant has no reason to believe that any other person, association or corporation has any interest, direct or indirect, in the said stock, bonds or other securities than as so stated by him.   (Signed) Richard E. Hughes, Editor.

Sworn to and subscribed before me this 28th day of September, 1949.

Nat C. Sherman, Notary Public. (Commission expires Mar. 30, 1951.)

THE MAN IN THE MIRROR

RESEARCH DEPT.
—
ADVENTURES INTO
THE UNKNOWN

MY NAME?...IT ISN'T IMPORTANT! ENOUGH TO SAY THAT I'M HEAD OF THE RESEARCH STAFF OF THE MAGAZINE YOU'RE NOW READING...*ADVENTURES INTO THE UNKNOWN!* MY JOB IS TO DIG UP AND TRACE DOWN ODD AND LITTLE-KNOWN FACTS ABOUT THE SUPERNATURAL, THE GREAT *UNKNOWN*...AND THEN ASSIGN THEM TO ACE WRITERS WHO PRODUCE THE FASCINATING STORIES YOU READ! YES, I MEET STRANGE FACTS, STRANGE PEOPLE...AND SOMETIMES THEY HAUNT MY DREAMS! *THIS* WAS A DREAM-CREATION, READER ...ABOUT A STORY WHICH HUNTED *ME* DOWN ...AND TURNED ME INTO *THE MAN IN THE MIRROR!*

"I'D BEEN WORKING HARD ALL WEEK, DOING RESEARCH ON THE BATCH OF STORIES IN MY FILE, AND WAS NEAR EXHAUSTION! I MUST HAVE BEEN DOZING OFF WHEN I THOUGHT I HEARD..."

THERE'S A MAN HERE WHO INSISTS ON SEEING YOU, SIR! HE SAYS HE'S GOT STARTLING NEWS...

ALL RIGHT, SEND HIM IN! WHY PASS UP A CHANCE FOR A GOOD STORY?

AH, I'M GLAD I COULD SEE YOU...BECAUSE YOUR MAGAZINE HAS THE REPUTATION FOR COURAGEOUSLY PRINTING THE MOST GRIPPING FACTS OF THE *UNKNOWN!* AND I WANT YOU TO ANNOUNCE TO THE WORLD THAT *I* HAVE DISCOVERED THE *FOURTH DIMENSION*...I HAVE *LIVED* IN IT!

OH, OH...A *CRACKPOT!* I'D BETTER HUMOR HIM... HE LOOKS KIND OF WILD!

THE FOURTH DIMENSION, EH? OKAY, *WHAT* IS IT?

YOU MEAN---*WHERE* IS IT? AND I'LL TELL YOU---IT'S A WHOLE NEW WORLD INSIDE A *MIRROR* ---*EVERY* MIRROR! I'VE PERFECTED A MACHINE THAT ALLOWS ME TO *ENTER* THAT WORLD! WHENEVER I GET INTO A MIRROR, I SEE THINGS THE WAY THE MIRROR SEES THEM ---EVERYTHING'S *REVERSED!*

I BECOME THE MIRROR, SEE? AND THE EVERY-DAY WORLD BECOMES *UNREAL*---BECAUSE IT'S ONLY A *REFLECTION!* AND I *KNOW* I'M IN THE MIRROR, BECAUSE IF I TRY TO READ A PAPER, ALL THE LETTERS ARE REVERSED! BUT I CAN ALWAYS RETURN TO THE ORDINARY WORLD BY MAKING A FEW ADJUSTMENTS ON MY MACHINE---WITH-OUT IT, I'D HAVE TO STAY IN THE MIRROR *FOREVER!*

"*DESPITE MY DECISION TO HUMOR HIM, I LOST MY TEMPER---I DIDN'T HAVE TIME TO WASTE LISTENING TO SUCH MAD BLABBERINGS!*"

WHY, THAT'S *RIDICULOUS* ---A MIRROR IS MERELY A PLANE SURFACE THAT REFLECTS RAYS OF LIGHT! NO ONE CAN GO *INTO* A MIRROR---AND THERE'S NO SUCH THING AS THE FOURTH DIMENSION!

BUT I TELL YOU, THERE *IS!* NO ONE ELSE BELIEVES ME---AT LEAST *YOU'VE* GOT TO! WHY, MY DISCOVERY IS THE GREATEST IN THE WHOLE REALM OF THE *UNKNOWN* ---AND AS RESEARCH CHIEF FOR YOUR MAGAZINE---

YES, AS RESEARCH CHIEF, IT'S MY DUTY TO INVESTIGATE FACTS AND STORIES! BUT THERE'S NO POINT IN MY INVESTIGATING *YOUR* STORY---NOBODY'D EVEN ACCEPT IT AS *FICTION!* AND NOW, IF YOU DON'T MIND, I'M RATHER BUSY---

ALL RIGHT, I'LL GO--- *BUT I'LL BE BACK!* I'LL *MAKE* YOU BELIEVE ME!

"*AS SOON AS MY VISITOR HAD LEFT, I DISMISSED HIM FROM MY MIND AS MERELY A HARMLESS ECCENTRIC! THEN, AT LUNCH---*"

SAY, THE DESCRIPTION OF THIS GUY TALLIES WITH THAT MIRROR-CRAZY BUG WHO WAS IN MY OFFICE! I KNEW HE WAS NUTTY, BUT I DIDN'T THINK HE WAS *DANGEROUS!* I'D BETTER CALL THE HOSPITAL---

STAR
ASYLUM INMATE ESCAPES
INSANE INVENTOR ELUDES POLICE

YES, THAT MUST BE THE MAN---HE *WAS* ALL HEPPED UP ABOUT MIRRORS AND THE FOURTH DIMENSION! IF HE VISITS YOU AGAIN, WOULD YOU PLEASE NOTIFY US IMMEDIATELY?

CERTAINLY! I'LL TELL MY SECRETARY TO STALL HIM OFF IF HE SHOWS UP HERE, AND PHONE YOU!

2

"I LOOKED---AND THE STRANGE, SWIRLING SHAPES BELOW THE LENS OF THE EYEPIECE SEEMED TO FLOAT STRAIGHT UP INTO MY BRAIN---FILLED ME WITH A FEELING OF UNACCOUNTABLE HORROR! I SEEMED TO BE DRIFTING WITH THEM---WE WERE GOING DOWN--- DOWN---DOWN INTO THE LIMITLESS DEPTHS OF THE TUBE!"

"AND THEN---SUDDENLY---IT SEEMED AS IF THE TUBE EXPLODED IN A BLINDING FLASH OF LIGHT---A FLASH THAT REACHED ITS TENTACLES INTO THE DEEPEST RECESSES OF MY BRAIN! STRANGELY, I FELT AS IF MY MIND WERE BEING WRENCHED FROM ME, AS IF EVERY CELL OF MY BRAIN WERE BEING TRANSFORMED, REARRANGED IN SOME HORRIBLY NEW PATTERN!"

"I SUDDENLY FEARED THIS MACHINE---MY WHOLE BEING RECOILED IN HORROR FROM IT---"

AH, SO YOU SAW SOMETHING, EH? BELIEVE ME NOW?

I DON'T KNOW WHAT THAT MACHINE IS---BUT TAKE IT OUT OF HERE! TAKE IT AND GET OUT!

ALL RIGHT, I'LL GO! BUT YOU'LL BE WANTING ME BACK AGAIN---TO TAKE YOU OUT OF THE MIRROR! YOU DON'T KNOW IT YET, BUT YOU'RE LIVING IN THE FOURTH DIMENSION NOW! EVERYTHING MAY LOOK NORMAL TO YOU, BUT YOU'RE ACTUALLY SEEING THINGS AS IF YOU WERE IN A MIRROR! YOU'LL FIND OUT SOON ENOUGH---

---AND THEN YOU'LL BEG ME TO COME BACK---BECAUSE THIS MACHINE IS THE ONLY THING THAT CAN TAKE YOU OUT OF THE MIRROR WORLD---WHA---?

THE SECRETARY SAID HE'S IN HERE ---AH, THERE YOU ARE!

COME ALONG QUIETLY NOW---WE WON'T HURT YOU!

NO! NO! YOU'LL NEVER TAKE ME---NEVER!

I'LL NEVER GO BACK THERE... YIII!

LOOK OUT!

HELP!

POOR GUY! HE DIDN'T HAVE A CHANCE...WE'RE FOURTEEN FLIGHTS UP!

DID HE HURT YOU, SIR? WE TRIED GETTING HERE AS SOON AS WE COULD!

NO, NO...I'M ALL RIGHT...JUST A BIT SHOCKED, THAT'S ALL! I'LL BE OKAY IF I CAN BE BY MYSELF A FEW MINUTES!

"THEY TOOK THE HINT AND LEFT! THEN..." WHEW! IT...IT'S LIKE A NIGHTMARE! I'VE GOT TO DRIVE THE WHOLE THING OUT OF MY MIND...AND THE BEST WAY IS BY PLUNGING INTO MY WORK! NOW, LET'S SEE, THE NEXT ISSUE...

NO, NO! IT CAN'T BE... THOSE LETTERS THEY'RE REVERSED!

HE SAID I'D FIND OUT...I AM IN THE WORLD OF MIRRORS! AND THE MACHINE THAT COULD GET ME OUT...IT'S SMASHED TO ATOMS! I'LL ALWAYS SEE THINGS THE WAY A MIRROR SEES THEM...REVERSED! AND THAT MEANS THAT THE REST OF THE WORLD ISN'T REAL ANY MORE TO ME... IT'S JUST A REFLECTION! I'M IN ANOTHER DIMENSION...ALL BY MYSELF... FOREVER!

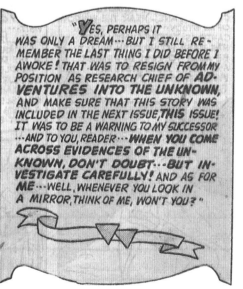

"YES, PERHAPS IT WAS ONLY A DREAM...BUT I STILL RE-MEMBER THE LAST THING I DID BEFORE I AWOKE! THAT WAS TO RESIGN FROM MY POSITION AS RESEARCH CHIEF OF AD-VENTURES INTO THE UNKNOWN, AND MAKE SURE THAT THIS STORY WAS INCLUDED IN THE NEXT ISSUE, THIS ISSUE! IT WAS TO BE A WARNING TO MY SUCCESSOR ...AND TO YOU, READER...WHEN YOU COME ACROSS EVIDENCES OF THE UN-KNOWN, DON'T DOUBT...BUT IN-VESTIGATE CAREFULLY! AND AS FOR ME...WELL, WHENEVER YOU LOOK IN A MIRROR, THINK OF ME, WON'T YOU?"

"True" GHOSTS of HISTORY

The POET WHO RETURNED FROM THE DEAD!

AH, DANTE'S DEATH IS A TREMENDOUS LOSS TO THE WORLD!

YES, BUT IT WILL BE AN EVEN GREATER LOSS IF WE DO NOT FIND THE MISSING THIRTEENTH CANTO OF HIS GREAT POEM, "PARADISE"! HE DIED BEFORE HE COULD TELL US WHERE IT IS, AND NOW WE WILL HAVE TO SEARCH FOR IT!

DO GHOSTS TRULY EXIST? SCIENCE SAYS NO··· BUT HISTORY TELLS THIS STORY OF THE GREAT ITALIAN POET, DANTE··· WHO DIED IN 1321, AND YET IS SAID TO HAVE RETURNED FROM THE DEAD TO FULFILL HIS MISSION ON EARTH!

AFTER A WEARY, FRUITLESS SEARCH···

IT IS NO USE··· DANTE MUST HAVE DESTROYED THE MISSING CANTO!

YOU'RE WRONG··· MY FATHER DID LEAVE THAT POEM ···SOMEWHERE! I'LL NEVER GIVE UP SEARCHING FOR IT!

ONE NIGHT, A FEW MONTHS LATER···

PIETRO···PIETRO, MY SON! AWAKE ···AND HEARKEN TO ME···

FATHER···· IT IS TRULY THOU!

MY SON, YOU MUST REMOVE THE SECOND PANEL NEAR THE WINDOW OF MY STUDY···THE THIRTEENTH CANTO IS THERE! WHEN THAT HAS BEEN FOUND, THEN WILL I BE ABLE TO REST IN PEACE! AND NOW, I MUST RETURN···· FROM WHENCE I CAME! FAREWELL, MY SON!

BUT WHEN PIETRO TOLD THE STORY OF THE STRANGE, NOCTURNAL VISIT···

PREPOSTEROUS··· NO MAN CAN RETURN FROM THE DEAD! IT WAS EITHER AN IDLE DREAM, PIETRO··· OR YOUR MIND HAS BECOME UNBALANCED FROM YOUR CEASELESS SEARCH FOR A POEM THAT DOES NOT EXIST!

BUT I TELL YOU, MY FATHER CAME TO ME··· SPOKE TO ME! COME TO HIS STUDY WITH ME ···I'LL PROVE TO YOU THE POEM IS THERE!

AND MINUTES LATER···

SEE?···I TOLD YOU! HERE IS THE MISSING CANTO!

YES, DANTE DID RETURN FROM THE DEAD TO REVEAL HIS SECRET TO US··· AND TO GIVE US THIS UNDYING POEM!

THE BOY WHO COULD FLY!

Here's Bobby Wilson, folks -- reading a book called "*THE BOY WHO COULD FLY*," and WONDERING! Relax, Bobby -- humans *CAN'T* do it! So what follows is completely out of the realm of a writer's imagination -- an ADVENTURE into the *UNKNOWN* to read -- and marvel at!

SUPPOSE I *COULD* FLY ... JUST SUPPOSE! IF ONLY I KNEW HOW -- MY DAD WOULD BE *PROUD* OF ME!

THE DAY YOU WENT DOWN IN YOUR P-47, I SWORE -- SOMEDAY I'D FLY IN YOUR PLACE, DAD! BUT NOW -- IF I COULD TAKE OFF UNDER MY *OWN* POWER... *REALLY FLY---*

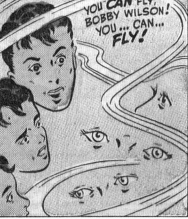

SUDDENLY, IT SEEMED AS IF THE EYES IN THE PICTURE CAME ALIVE! AND POUNDING IN HIS EARS... A SPECTRAL VOICE!

YOU *CAN* FLY, BOBBY WILSON! YOU ... CAN ... *FLY!*

BUT, AS THE MEMORY OF THAT STRANGE NIGHT DIMMED...

I SUPPOSE I *COULD* HAVE *DREAMED* IT ALL...OR *IMAGINED* IT! NOTHING'S HAPPENED SINCE... *WAIT!* THAT ROAR IN MY EARS... THE SOUND OF A PLANE COMING CLOSER... *CLOSER!*...

FATHER -- *DAD!*

COME QUICKLY, SON, IT'S TIME! I NEED YOU... *AGAIN!*

SOARING... HIS BODY FELT LIGHTER THAN THE WIND!

NOT CARING WHY OR WHERE ...KNOWING ONLY THAT HE AND HIS FATHER WERE TOGETHER AGAIN...

BOBBY SPED IN THE WAKE OF THE GHOST-PLANE AND THE BECKONING HAND!

THERE -- LOOK! LOOK *DOWN!*

FATHER'S DIVING DOWN... POINTING DOWN... OVER THERE! ON THE LEDGE!

ON THE LEDGE ...

A SLEEPWALKER -- AND SHE'S ABOUT TO GO OVER! IF -- *ONLY* I'M NOT TOO LATE --

BELOW, AS THE CROWD GAZED UPWARD --

SHE'S STEPPING OFF THE LEDGE!

THERE SHE GOES! SHE'S FALLING! IT'S SURE *DEATH!*

AND THEN -- THE GIRL APPEARED TO *STOP* IN MID-AIR!

4

THE GHOSTLY FINGER POINTED THE COURSE AND THE BOY WHO COULD FLY WAITED TO ASK NO QUESTIONS! HE SHOT DOWN...

THE RAILROAD BRIDGE IS WASHED OUT! THAT HEADLIGHT -- *THE TRAIN'S COMING!*

DOWN...

GOT TO... GET... THAT LANTERN! *GOT IT!*

!!!!

IN THE DARKNESS, FLOATING THROUGH THE AIR, THE BALL OF LIGHT GLOWED LIKE A GIANT FIREBUG FROM SOME UNKNOWN WORLD!

MAYBE THEY'LL SPOT THE LANTERN -- SEE MY WARNING SIGNAL ... IT'S MY ONLY CHANCE TO STOP THE TRAIN IN TIME!

I HATE THIS FOG... I CAN'T SEE A THING!

YEAH --- *HEY!* THERE'S A LANTERN WAVING ACROSS THE TRACK ...BUT *THERE'S NOBODY WAVING IT!*

THE HISS OF AIR BRAKES -- THE SCREAMING OF GIANT WHEELS ON THE RAILS -- AND THE HUGE TRAIN GROUND TO A STOP!

SCREECH!

LOOK AT THAT... *A WASHOUT!* ANOTHER MINUTE AND WE WOULD'VE BEEN A BURNIN' WRECK! THAT *LANTERN* SAVED US ... I SWEAR IT WAS WAVIN' ACROSS THE TRACK *ALL BY ITSELF!*

IT WAS A MIRACLE! THAT'S IT... A *MIRACLE!* THERE WAS A SPIRIT WATCHING OUT FOR US... A *SAVING SPIRIT!*

WE'VE DONE IT AGAIN! YOU AND I, DAD... *TOGETHER!*

6

SWIFTLY THE NEWS SPREAD! A SAVING SPIRIT SEEMED ABROAD IN THE NIGHT, FLYING TO SUCCOR THE HELPLESS IN A MERCILESS WORLD!

WHO -- OR WHAT -- IS THE SAVING SPIRIT? THREE TIMES HE HAS COME WHEN NEEDED! ... TO SAVE A LITTLE DOG, AN INNOCENT GIRL, AND A SPEEDING TRAIN! TO THE SAVING SPIRIT -- IF YOU CAN HEAR ME NOW... OUR MOST HUMBLE THANKS!

ON THE AIR!

WCZK

SHORTLY AFTERWARD --

AM I A... A SAVING SPIRIT? I -- DON'T KNOW...

COME ON! CLIMB UP HERE, BOBBY -- YOU'RE AS SLOW AS MOLASSES IN JANUARY!

SLOW? HE'S ALWAYS LAST... THE SLOWEST GUY IN THE GANG!

LOOK AT HIM CRAWL LIKE AN OLD LADY! HE CAN'T DO A THING BUT READ BOOKS!

THINK YOU CAN MAKE THE REST OF THE HIKE, BOBBY? OR D'YOU WANT US TO CARRY YOU? HA-HA-HA!

THEY'RE ALWAYS RAGGING ME! BUT THIS IS THE LAST TIME! I HAVE SOMETHING TO TELL THEM!

A WARNING FORGOTTEN -- A SECRET REVEALED!

SHUT UP -- ALL OF YOU! YOU'VE BEEN RAZZING ME LONG ENOUGH!' THIS TIME -- LISTEN TO ME! I CAN FLY! ME -- BOBBY WILSON! I'M THE SAVING SPIRIT!

YOU DON'T BELIEVE ME! I CAN TELL!

LISTEN TO THAT CHUMP WILSON RAVE! HE'S OFF HIS NUT!

HA-HA-HA!

BOYS CLUB

AS BOBBY TURNED FROM HIS COMPANIONS' SCORN --

HAW! HAW!

HELP... HELP!

224

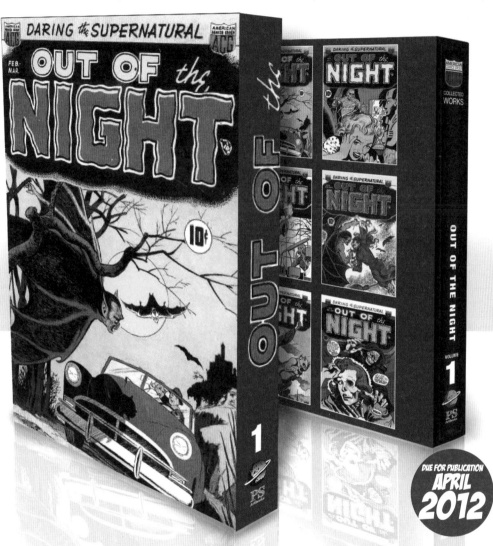

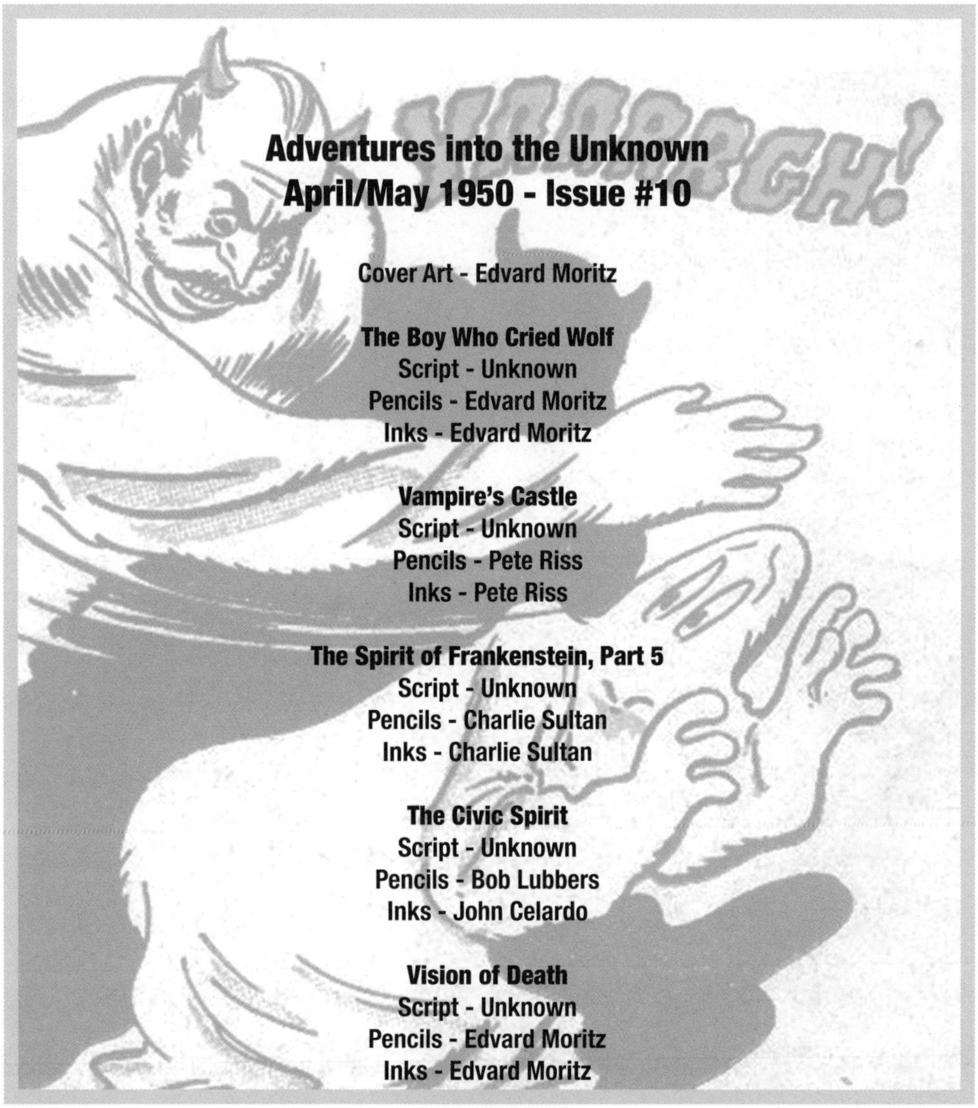

Adventures into the Unknown
April/May 1950 - Issue #10

Cover Art - Edvard Moritz

The Boy Who Cried Wolf
Script - Unknown
Pencils - Edvard Moritz
Inks - Edvard Moritz

Vampire's Castle
Script - Unknown
Pencils - Pete Riss
Inks - Pete Riss

The Spirit of Frankenstein, Part 5
Script - Unknown
Pencils - Charlie Sultan
Inks - Charlie Sultan

The Civic Spirit
Script - Unknown
Pencils - Bob Lubbers
Inks - John Celardo

Vision of Death
Script - Unknown
Pencils - Edvard Moritz
Inks - Edvard Moritz

Haunted House
Script - Unknown
Pencils - Charlie Sultan
Inks - Charlie Sultan

Information Source: Grand Comics Database!
A nonprofit, Internet-based organization of international volunteers dedicated to building a database covering all printed comics throughout the world.
If you believe any of this data to be incorrect or can add valuable additional information, please let us know www.comics.org
All rights to images reserved by the respective copyright holders. The advertisements remain the copyright of the respective owners and are no longer valid.

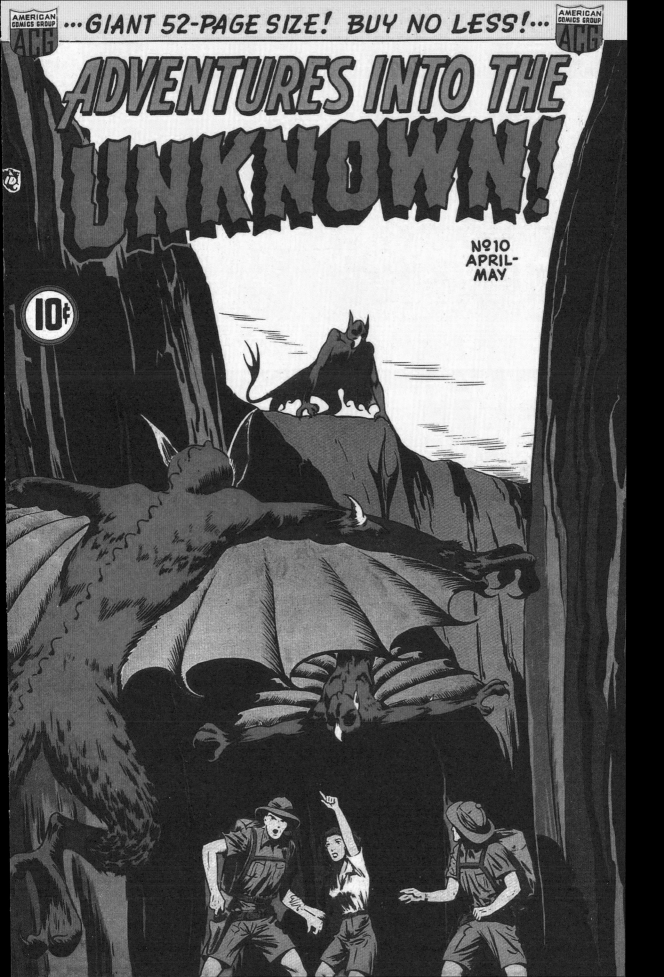

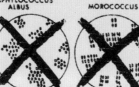

ADVENTURES INTO THE UNKNOWN, published bi-monthly and copyright, 1950, by B. & I. Publishing Co., Inc., 420 DeSoto Ave., St. Louis 7, Missouri. Editorial offices, 45 West 45th St., New York 19, N. Y. Richard E. Hughes, Editor; Frederick H. Iger, Business Manager. Subscription (12 issues), $1.20; single copies, $.10; foreign postage extra. For advertising information, address American Comics Group, 45 West 45th St., New York 19, N. Y. Entered as second class matter at the Post Office at St. Louis, Mo. Additional Entry, Sparta, Ill. No. 10, April-May, 1950.   Printed in U.S.A.

THE BOY WHO CRIED WOLF!

LONG, LONG AGO, THE STORY GOES, THERE WAS A SHEPHERD BOY WHO CRIED WOLF... **ONCE TOO OFTEN!** FOR WHEN THE WOLVES CAME, NO ONE ANSWERED HIS SHOUTS FOR HELP! JIMMY ROGERS HAD NEVER HEARD OF **THAT** BOY... BUT HE, TOO, CRIED WOLF... AND REAPED A STRANGE RETRIBUTION!

JIMMY ROGERS WAS 16, HANDSOME, CLEVER, A GREAT GUY WITH THE GALS...

SAY, WHO'S THE LADY STEPPIN' OUT WITH THIS CRUMB?

THAT'S NO LADY... HE'S OUT WALKIN' ONE OF HIS DOGS!

WHA--

WHAT WAS THAT YOU SAID, WISE GUY?

YOU HEARD ME, PRETTY BOY... WANT A REPEAT? OUCH!

CRACK!

OOOF! LAY OFF! WE WERE ONLY KIDDIN'!

A GREAT GUY WITH THE GALS, AND HANDY WITH HIS FISTS...

I DON'T HAVE TO TAKE THAT KIND OF KIDDING FROM THE LIKES OF YOU!

WHAM!

AT LEAST, THAT WAS THE WAY HE TOLD IT!

...HAPPENED TO ME ONLY LAST WEEK... JUST LIKE THAT... DOWN AT FIFTH AND MAIN...

OH, C'MON, JIMMY! BET THAT WAS NOTHIN' COMPARED WITH SOME OF YOUR OTHER ADVENTURES! TELL US MORE!

"WELL... THE TIME I WAS ON VACATION IN THE NORTH WOODS..."

THAT LITTLE GIRL'S CORNERED BY A BEAR! SHE'S A GONER... UN- LESS...

HELP! HELP!

GRRRR!

ALL ANIMALS ARE AFRAID OF FIRE! GOOD THING I COULD RIG UP THIS TORCH IN A HURRY! G'WAN, YOU... BEAT IT!

OOOH, YOU'RE SO BRAVE! I... I'M SAFE NOW!

JIMMY, YOU KILL ME! WHAT AN IMAGINAT- ION... WHAT WILL YOU DREAM UP NEXT!

SO LONG, KIDS! CAN'T STAND MUCH MORE OF THIS!

THEY'RE GIVING ME THE HORSE LAUGH! THEY DON'T BELIEVE ME!

HICKS! I'M TOO GOOD FOR THAT BUNCH! THOSE THINGS COULD HAVE HAPPENED! I WOULD HAVE HANDLED THEM JUST THAT WAY... IF I'D HAD THE CHANCE!

PENDLETON LIBRARY

TOWNSHIP OF PENDLETON POP. 3500

BETTER GET SOME STUDYING DONE! SOME DAY... I'LL SHOW THEM! AND WHEN THAT DAY COMES... SAY! THAT PICTURE... GIVES ME AN IDEA!

JOSIAH PENDLE. 1800-1850.

JOSIAH PENDLE FOUNDED THIS TOWN...THEY NAMED IT AFTER HIM! I OUGHTA FIND WHAT I WANT IN THIS BOOK...HERE IT IS!

JOSIAH

GOSH, HE SOUNDS LIKE A VAIN OLD COOT! BRRR... HE BURNED TO DEATH HERE AT PENDLE MANOR JUST 100 YEARS AGO! COULD BE HIS GHOST... AND I... ARE GONNA HAVE THE LAST LAUGH ON THIS ONE-HORSE TOWN!

PENDLE MANOR...1850 GUTTED BY FIRE!

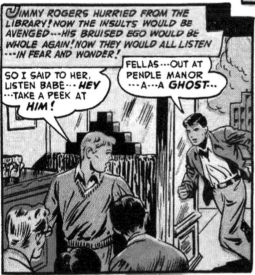

JIMMY ROGERS HURRIED FROM THE LIBRARY! NOW THE INSULTS WOULD BE AVENGED...HIS BRUISED EGO WOULD BE WHOLE AGAIN! NOW THEY WOULD ALL LISTEN ...IN FEAR AND WONDER!

SO I SAID TO HER, LISTEN BABE... HEY ...TAKE A PEEK AT HIM!

FELLAS...OUT AT PENDLE MANOR ...A...A GHOST...

"I TOLD THEM THAT I'D LONG SUSPECTED THAT THE OLD MANOR WAS HAUNTED...THAT WHEN I WENT TO SEE FOR MYSELF, THIS HAPPENED!"

WHO...WHO ARE YOU?

I...AM...THE SPIRIT ...OF JOSIAH PENDLE! I...HAVE...BEEN...WAITING! NOW I WILL CRUSH YOU... BODY AND SOUL!

"I SAW THE WONDERING EXPRESS-IONS ON THEIR FACES, AND WARMED UP TO THE SUBJECT! HERE WAS ONE STORY THAT WAS GONNA KNOCK 'EM DEAD!"

BREATHE YOUR LAST, STUPID MORTAL!

I'M NOT AFRAID OF YOU! BACK... BACK!

I POUNDED AT HIM WITH MY FISTS... UNTIL I THOUGHT OF THE LAMP! ALL GHOSTS ARE AFRAID OF FIRE! HE RAN AWAY... HE WAS AFRAID OF ME!

"THEN I CAME RIGHT HERE, RAN ALL THE WAY, AND..."

HA-HA-HA-HA! HO-HO-HO! THAT WAS RICH! A GHOST ...THIS BOY'S A COMEDIAN!

YEAH...A COMEDIAN ...AND A LIAR!

WHO ARE *YOU* CALLING A LIAR? WHY, I DID JUST WHAT I SAID I DID... *AND I COULD DO IT AGAIN!*

WE'VE GOT YOU WHERE WE WANT *NOW! WE'RE GONNA CALL YOUR BLUFF!*

NAME THE TIME AND WE'LL BE AT THE "HAUNTED" PENDLE MANOR... WHILE YOU *DO IT AGAIN!*

I...I WILL...I *WILL!* ER...SURE! *TONIGHT!*

"*YES,* JIMMY HAD CRIED WOLF...AND THIS TIME, THERE WAS NO BACKING OUT! BUT HE HAD A PLAN...AND AT PENDLE MANOR..."

THEY'LL BE HERE RIGHT AFTER NIGHTFALL! I'VE GOT TO GO THROUGH WITH IT...WITH THE HELP OF THIS *DUMMY!* LOOKS MORE HUMAN THAN OLD MAN *PENDLE* EVER DID!

That night...

ALL RIGHT, YOU GUYS CAN WATCH FROM *HERE*... IT'S TOO DANGEROUS INSIDE! I'LL GO IN ---*ALONE!*

"*OUTSIDE,* AS DARKNESS THICKENED AND MOONLIGHT BATHED THE RUINS OF THE OLD HOUSE, THERE WAS THE SOUND OF A SUDDEN STRUGGLE ---SILHOUETTED SCENES OF HAND-TO-HAND COMBAT! SURELY, THIS *MUST BE* A DUEL TO THE DEATH BETWEEN A MORTAL AND A CREATURE OF THE *UNDEAD!*"

OKAY, GHOST-KILLER, GO INTO YOUR ACT! REMEMBER, WE'LL BE WATCHING ...*SO TEAR INTO HIM! HAW-HAW!*

BUT INSIDE...

YOU'LL NEVER TAKE ME, YOU DEVIL...ALIVE OR DEAD!

HOPE THEY'RE DRINKING IT ALL IN...OUTSIDE! I'M SURE I'VE GOT THEM BELIEVING IT...

HA-HA! HO-HO-HO! HAW-HAW!

HUH?

THAT DOES IT...YOU'VE MADE THE FRONT PAGE OF THE PENDLETON CHRONICLE, BOY...*YOU AND THAT DUMMY!* THANKS FOR THE TIP, FELLOWS... *WHAT A STORY!*

WHAT A *BATTLE! HA-HA!* AND SOME *GHOST!*

THE PENDLETON DAILY CHRONICLE WAS SOLD OUT THE NEXT MORNING...

Pendleton Daily Chronicle

BATTLE OF THE CENTURY!
JOLTIN' JIMMY ROGERS, 126 lbs., VS. JARRIN' JOSIAH PENDLE, ???lbs!

JOSIAH'S NO DUMMY!

Which one is the dummy? Read on, gentle reader, and gee...

FOOLS... *FOOLS!* IT COULD *HAVE* HAPPENED! BUT EVEN IF IT *HAD*, THEY'D *NEVER* BELIEVE ME! I'LL HAVE TO LEAVE TOWN...GO AWAY...*NO!* I'LL SHOW THEM ALL...*SOME-DAY...SOON*...

ALONE WITH HIS THOUGHTS, BROODING, BITTER, JIMMY ROGERS WANDERED... NOT KNOWING, NOR CARING WHERE! YET SOMEHOW, HE WAS ON A SUDDEN FAMILIAR PATH...TO A SUDDENLY FAMILIAR SPOT...

THERE IT IS...*PENDLE MANOR!* BURNED, ROTTED RUIN...WISH I'D NEVER HEARD OF IT! I'LL NEVER SET FOOT IN THAT PLACE AGAIN!

"*NEVER, BOY...NEVER?*" AT FIRST, JIMMY THOUGHT HE'D HEARD AN ECHO! THEN...IT WAS AS THOUGH THE WORDS WERE POUNDING IN HIS EARS AGAIN AND AGAIN...AND A VOICE WAS DRAWING HIM...LURING HIM...TOWARDS THE GUTTED HOUSE!

NO! I WON'T GO INTO THAT HOUSE! *NO!*

AGAINST HIS WILL, EACH STEP LIKE THAT OF A CONDEMNED MAN, JIMMY ROGERS STUMBLED INTO THE HOUSE!

I...I COULDN'T HELP IT...I *HAD* TO COME IN! BUT...*WHY?* WHAT...*WHO*...BROUGHT ME IN HERE??

I BROUGHT YOU HERE... *FOR A REASON!*

ALASKA'S PHANTOM CITY

One of the strangest stories to come from the mouths of explorers is that of the great phantom city high above Alaska's glaciers, unbelievably suspended in the sky! Hard to believe, reader? Perhaps--but not when you know that the city has actually been *PHOTOGRAPHED!*

ONE OF THE EARLY PIONEERS IN ALASKA WAS A MAN NAMED WILLOUGHBY, AFTER WHOM WILLOUGHBY ISLAND WAS NAMED--A MAN TO WHOM THE NATIVE INDIANS TOLD STRANGE TALES!

COME SUMMER MOON... SEE HEAP CITY... HANGING IN SKY... OVER GLACIER! TIME COME, I SHOW YOU!

GREAT! I'VE HEARD STORIES OF THAT PHANTOM CITY--AND I BROUGHT THIS CAMERA ALONG JUST IN CASE I COULD GET A SHOT OF IT!

AND THEN, AS REPORTED IN THE NEW YORK TRIBUNE OF FEB. 17, 1901...

IT... IT *CAN'T* BE -- BUT IT *IS!* I CAN'T EVEN BELIEVE MY OWN EYES-- BUT THIS CAMERA WILL TELL ME WHETHER I'M SEEING THINGS OR NOT!

WHEN THE PHOTO WAS DEVELOPED...

IT *WASN'T* A MIRAGE! THAT *PHANTOM CITY* IS REAL!

THE *JOURNAL OF THE ROYAL METEOROLOGICAL SOCIETY* INVESTIGATED WILLOUGHBY'S STORY AND FINALLY CONCLUDED THAT EVERY YEAR, BETWEEN JUNE 21 AND JULY 10, A PHANTOM CITY *DOES* APPEAR OVER THE GLACIER OF MT. ST. ELIAS! BUT THE PHANTOM CITY ITSELF STILL AWAITS THE COMING OF ITS FIRST EXPLORER -- OF THE MAN WHO WILL MAKE THIS GREATEST *ADVENTURE INTO THE UNKNOWN!!*

Aunt Mag's CAT

AUNT MAG lived in a shuttered old house with no companion but a huge black cat. Some folks muttered she was wealthy, and others whispered she was a witch. And since witches used to be blamed for everything, it's easy to see how Otie Simmons began to suspect Aunt Mag. His crops were flattened by hail, his cow went dry, and foxes ran off with his chickens—and it didn't take Otie long to figure why! How *else* could Aunt Mag get all that money she was said to have—unless the devil himself paid her for hexing honest people?

Brooding, Otie decided to kill the witch—and steal her miserly hoard to pay for the damage she had caused! Late one night, rifle in hand, Otie prowled through the woods toward Aunt Mag's house. He sneaked up to the window—dreading what would happen to *him* if he failed to kill the witch. There she was, sitting with the black cat on her lap—and it was now or never! Trembling, Otie raised the rifle and fired. As Aunt Mag slumped in her chair, her dress bloodstained, the cat leaped yowling into the shadows.

Otie was nervous about the cat. Everyone knew that a spirit will rise if a cat leaps over the corpse—and Otie didn't want a witch's ghost haunting *him*. But killing the cat wasn't as important as finding Aunt Mag's hoard. Otie searched—from the shadowed room where the old woman sagged in the chair, to the attic—muffled in a thick shroud of dust. It was here he finally found something—a pool of blood. Who else but a witch could die like *that*—her body downstairs, and her blood glistening on the attic floor? Terrified, Otie fled from the house.

Next day, everyone was talking about the horrible thing that had happened to Aunt Mag—and the whole town turned up at her house. "I've got to go, too!" Otie mumbled to himself. "If I'm the only one who stays away—they'll *know* it was me!" That evening, Otie stood in Aunt Mag's bedroom with a group of silent neighbors. Suddenly—he stared nervously as Aunt Mag's black cat padded toward the bed—its green eyes fixed on Otie!

"It's just a cat," Otie muttered, shivering. "What if it *does* jump over?" And that's just what the cat *did* do—glaring hatefully at Otie as it bounded over Aunt Mag's bed. Slowly, slowly, the figure on the bed stirred—then, as Otie let out a yell of horror, the pale form sat bolt upright! "*I killed her—I killed her!*" babbled Otie, as several men led him out of the house.

"Why, what's wrong with Otie Simmons?" asked Aunt Mag, feebly. "Has he gone crazy?" "Everyone *knows* he's a bit queer!" replied a woman. "Now, just lie back and rest, and try to forget what happened last night—when your poor black cat was shot dead on your lap!"

Vampire's Castle

ONE OF MY FORMER SQUADRON BUDDIES PICKED UP THIS OLD PARCHMENT DRAWING IN A MUNICH BOOKSTORE, TRUDY! IT'S EXACTLY THE KIND OF MATERIAL I NEED FOR MY BOOK ON THE EARLY HISTORY OF AVIATION!

THAT'S AN AWFULLY CRUDE APPARATUS, BILL---BUT IT CERTAINLY **DOES** SEEM THAT DR. MANUSALA TRIED TO FLY WITH IT AT DOMA CASTLE IN TRANSYLVANIA---WAY BACK IN 1506!

Dr. Manusala - Castellum Doma - 1506 - Transylvania

WHAT MYSTERIOUS IMPULSE PROMPTED MAN'S FIRST ATTEMPTS TO FLY? COULD IT HAVE BEEN THE SIGHT OF BATS TWITTERING IN THE DUSK -- THE LEGEND OF VAMPIRES WHOSE BLACK AND FURRY WINGS RUSTLED IN THE GLOOM OF MIDNIGHT?
    THERE WAS A TIME WHEN MEN SHUDDERED AND BELIEVED SUCH THINGS -- A TIME THAT REMAINED UNCHANGED IN THE CREAKING CORRIDORS OF THE **VAMPIRE'S CASTLE!**

TRUDY, I'VE LEARNED DOMA CASTLE IS STILL STANDING -- AND I'LL BET A SEARCH OF THE PLACE WOULD UNCOVER THE VERY APPARATUS DR. MANUSALA EXPERIMENTED WITH! LET'S FLY THERE -- AND TAKE ALONG A CAMERA AND DEVELOPING KIT SO WE'LL BE SURE OF GETTING PICTURES FOR MY BOOK!

SOMETHING LIKE A WARNING CROSSES TRUDY'S MIND -- A VAGUE TREMOR OF DOUBT!

I CAN UNDERSTAND DR. MANUSALA BEING INTERESTED IN FLYING, BILL -- BUT ISN'T IT **STRANGE** THAT HE MODELED THE WINGS AFTER THOSE OF A **BAT** -- RATHER THAN A BIRD?

GOSH, TRUDY.. ANY AIRMAN KNOWS THAT A BAT'S WING IS JUST AS EFFICIENT AS A BIRD'S! THERE'S NO REASON WHY DR. MANUSALA SHOULD HAVE AVOIDED BATS -- JUST BECAUSE OF THE SUPERSTITIOUS DREAD THEY INSPIRE!

BY NIGHTFALL -- BILL'S PLANE IS DRONING ACROSS THE ATLANTIC!

TRANSYLVANIA IS A PRETTY RUGGED COUNTRY -- BUT THE OLD ATLAS I CONSULTED MENTIONED THAT DOMA CASTLE CAN BE UNMISTAKABLY IDENTIFIED!

WONDER WHAT **THAT** MEANS? WHY SHOULD IT BE DIFFERENT FROM ANY **OTHER** CASTLE?

Several days later--over the grim, craggy uplands of Transylvania--

WE CAN'T BE TOO FAR FROM DOMA CASTLE, TRUDY -- UNLESS THIS MAP IS OFF!

IT ISN'T! *LOOK!*

RISING STARKLY BELOW -- ITS SPANNING WALLS FORMING A FORBIDDING OUTLINE --

THERE IT IS, BILL -- AND ITS VERY *SHAPE* SUGGESTS A BAT!

AS BILL SWOOPS LOW OVER THE SILENT BATTLEMENTS --

PROBABLY JUST A QUIRK OF DR. MANUSALA'S! AS FOR THAT HOLLOW TOWER -- THEY OFTEN EXECUTED CRIMINALS BACK IN MEDIEVAL TIMES BY HURLING THEM INTO THE OPENING -- SO THAT THEY'D PLUNGE INTO A DEEP PIT INSIDE THE CASTLE!

MINUTES LATER --

GOOD THING WE LANDED BEFORE THIS STORM BROKE, TRUDY! COME ON -- LET'S GET INSIDE!

BILL --ARE YOU *SURE* IT WILL BE -- *SAFER* IN THERE?

SAFER? TOO LATE TO THINK OF THAT NOW -- WITH THE DUST OF CENTURIES MUFFLING THEIR FOOT-STEPS IN THE DARK AND RAFTERED HALL!

AMAZING THAT THIS PLACE SHOULD BE *INTACT* -- JUST AS DR. MANUSALA LEFT IT, FOUR HUNDRED YEARS AGO! THERE'S SOMETHING *OLD* IN THE ATMOSPHERE --

BILL! OVER THERE-- ON THE WALL!

YES, THERE'S SOMETHING OLD -- *VERY* OLD -- SOMETHING THAT CLINGS TO THE DANK STONE, ITS EYES GLINTING IN THE FLASHLIGHT BEAM!

ANOTHER ONE, BILL-- ANOTHER ONE OF THOSE HORRID BATS!

RELAX, TRUDY! IT'S JUST A TAPESTRY WALL HANGING -- WITH JEWELED EYES!

BUT WHY WAS DR. MANUSALA SO HIPPED ON BATS, BILL? MAYBE HE *DID* HAVE A REASON FOR DESIGNING THE WINGS LIKE A BAT'S -- BUT WHY SHAPE THE CASTLE THAT WAY -- AND WHY *THIS?*

2

ISN'T IT **NATURAL** THAT AN OLD SCHOLAR -- INTERESTED IN FLYING -- WOULD USE A WINGED CREATURE LIKE A BAT AS HIS EMBLEM? I'M SURE YOUR MIND WILL BE AT REST, TRUDY -- ONCE WE FIND DR. MANUSALA'S WORKROOM!

MAYBE YOU'RE RIGHT, BILL! LET'S SEE WHERE THIS STAIRWAY LEADS!

DR. MANUSALA WOULD HAVE WANTED TO GET AWAY FROM THE NOISY ACTIVITY OF THE CASTLE -- SO I **THINK** WE'RE ON THE RIGHT TRACK!

NO DOUBT ABOUT IT! SEE THOSE DOOR HINGES?

FOR THE FIRST TIME -- A STRANGE AND NAMELESS SUSPICION ENVELOPS BILL LIKE A CREEPING FOG!

YOU CALL THOSE BAT-SHAPED THINGS JUST AN **EMBLEM**, BILL -- BUT I'M SCARED -- **TERRIFIED!**

I'M BEGINNING TO WONDER, MYSELF! BUT LET'S NOT BACK OUT NOW -- WHEN WE'RE SO CLOSE TO THE ANSWER -- **IN THERE!**

WOW! IF **THIS** SETUP IS ANY INDICATION -- **INVENTIONS** WERE JUST DR. MANUSALA'S SIDELINE! HIS **BIG** INTEREST WAS ALCHEMY -- AND **THAT** COVERED EVERYTHING FROM CHEMISTRY TO THE SUPERNATURAL!

IN **THAT** CASE -- THERE'S NO TELLING **WHAT** WE'LL FIND INSIDE THAT DOMED OPENING!

THIS BOOK IS OPEN AT **FORMULA 172** -- SO IT MUST BE THE STUFF IN THAT BOTTLE! THE LATIN INSCRIPTION SEEMS TO HAVE BEEN CROSSED OUT HASTILY, JUST AS IF THE FORMULA HAD BEEN DISCARDED -- BUT MAYBE I CAN TRANSLATE IT!

SLOWLY, BILL DECIPHERS THE ANCIENT SCRAWL -- AND THEN -- THE TRUTH ABOUT DR. MANUSALA FLASHES LIKE A LIGHTNING BOLT!

"ONE PART WITCH'S BREW, AND ONE PART MOSS FROM A GALLOWS TREE: ADD A BAT -- AND WHEN IT'S DONE, TOUCH IT -- AND A VAMPIRE BE!"

VAMPIRE! GREAT GUNS -- MANUSALA IS LATIN, TOO! IT'S A DIRECT TRANSLATION OF CHIROPTERON, OR WINGED HAND -- THE GREEK WORD FOR **BAT!**

THOSE WINGS DR. MANUSALA DESIGNED -- THIS FORMULA -- *ALL* OF IT WAS DIRECTED TOWARD *BECOMING A VAMPIRE!* SINCE HE OBVIOUSLY USED PART OF THIS LIQUID WITHOUT RESULT, HE MUST HAVE TRIED *ANOTHER* METHOD -- BUT *WHAT?*

AT THAT MOMENT --

OH! THAT THING, BILL -- THAT *THING!*

EASY, PET! DON'T LOSE YOUR HEAD! WHAT DID YOU *SEE* DOWN THERE?

BELOW -- IN THE SPUTTERING FLARE OF THE SHATTERED LANTERN --

IT'S A SKELETON, BILL -- A SKELETON WEARING THOSE WINGS DR. MANUSALA DESIGNED!

IT'S CLEAR THAT DR. MANUSALA TRIED TO USE THOSE WINGS, TRUDY -- AFTER HIS VAMPIRE FORMULA FAILED! HE SEEMS TO HAVE MADE ONE DESPERATE SWOOP -- FALLEN INTO THE OPEN TOP OF THE TOWER -- AND CRASHED TO THE BOTTOM OF THE PIT!

THOSE DANCING FLAMES ARE AWFUL, BILL -- THEY MAKE ME THINK THERE'S SOMETHING *MOVING* DOWN BELOW!

MIGHT BE A GOOD THING TO DOUSE THE FIRE, ANYWAY! GUESS THERE'S ENOUGH LIQUID IN THIS BOTTLE TO DO IT!

AT LEAST DR. MANUSALA'S FORMULA PROVED USEFUL FOR *SOMETHING* -- AFTER ALL THESE YEARS!

CRASH!

AS HISSING BILLOWS OF ACRID SMOKE RISE FROM THE PIT --

NO WONDER THE CASTLE REMAINED UNTOUCHED! PEASANTS FOR MILES AROUND MUST HAVE BEEN AFRAID TO COME ANYWHERE *NEAR* THE PLACE!

I *KNOW* VAMPIRES DON'T REALLY EXIST, BILL -- BUT THE FACT THAT DR. MANUSALA *TRIED* TO BE ONE IS ENOUGH FOR *ME!* I DON'T WANT TO STAY IN DOMA CASTLE ANOTHER MINUTE!

TRUDY, DR. MANUSALA IS **DEAD** -- HE DIED OVER FOUR CENTURIES AGO -- SO THERE'S NO REASON WHY YOU SHOULDN'T TRY TO GET SOME REST IN ONE OF THE UPSTAIRS CHAMBERS! I HAVEN'T FINISHED LOOKING AROUND YET -- AND BESIDES, IT WOULD BE SUICIDE TO ATTEMPT A TAKEOFF IN **THIS** KIND OF COUNTRY BEFORE DAYLIGHT!

A MOMENT LATER --

I THINK I'LL BE ALL RIGHT, BILL -- BUT WILL YOU BE NEAR ENOUGH TO HEAR ME IF ANYTHING HAPPENS?

NATCH! AND IF IT WILL MAKE YOU FEEL ANY MORE SECURE -- THERE'S A GUN AT THE BOTTOM OF MY PHOTOGRAPHY KIT!

AS BILL CROSSES THE ECHOING MAIN HALL --

HAAA! HAA-HAAAA!

THAT SOUNDS LIKE A **LAUGH** -- AND IT'S **DIABOLICAL!** WE'VE JUST LEFT DR. MANUSALA'S LABORATORY -- AND I **KNOW** THERE'S NOTHING DOWN THERE!

BUT OUT OF THE PIT BELOW -- LIKE A **NIGHTMARE COME TO LIFE** --

FOUR HUNDRED YEARS! FOUR HUNDRED YEARS OF WAITING -- MIDNIGHT AFTER MIDNIGHT -- AND NOW I'M **FREE!**

HALF HOPPING -- HALF FLAPPING -- THE TERRIFYING FORM ADVANCES!

I NEEDN'T ASK WHO YOU ARE -- OR WHAT -- BECAUSE I KNOW! **DR. MANUSALA!**

YOU FOUND THE SECRET THAT HAD ESCAPED ME! I THOUGHT MY FORMULA WAS A FAILURE -- NOT REALIZING THAT THE COMPOUND NEEDED **AGING** BEFORE IT BECAME EFFECTIVE!

AND IT **HAS** AGED -- LONG ENOUGH TO GIVE IT A POTENCY I NEVER HOPED FOR! CASTING THE LIQUID OVER MY SKELETON HAS RE-CREATED ME AS I **WANTED** TO BE -- **AS A VAMPIRE!**

WHAT DO YOU HOPE TO GAIN BY **THAT**, MANUSALA? WHAT CAN YOU POSSIBLY FIND -- BUT THE FEAR AND LOATHING OF EVERYONE YOU MEET?

IMMORTALITY -- BECAUSE THE MAGIC THAT WAS ONCE USED TO CHECK VAMPIRES IS FORGOTTEN NOW! WHAT HAVE **I** TO FEAR FROM A SILVER STAKE -- WHEN I HAVE TRAINED MYSELF TO STAY AWAY FROM POINTED SILVER OBJECTS? AS LONG AS MY VICTIMS LAST -- **I SHALL LIVE FOREVER!**

THAT "FIRST VICTIM" MANUSALA MENTIONED IS *TRUDY* -- BUT WHILE I'VE GOT AN OUNCE OF STRENGTH LEFT -- SHE *WON'T* BE ALONE!

DESPERATELY, BILL CLAWS TOWARD THE TOP OF THE MOAT -- AND THEN--

SPLASH!

IN A HEADLONG PLUNGE THROUGH THE MURKY DEPTHS --

THERE'S SOMETHING HALF BURIED IN THE MUD -- *A HALBERD!*

THIS THING MUST HAVE FALLEN INTO THE MOAT DURING SOME FORGOTTEN SKIRMISH CENTURIES AGO -- AND IT'S CERTAINLY COMING IN HANDY *NOW!*

A MOMENT LATER --

THAT FAINT RUSTLE MAY NOT BE ANYTHING -- BUT THERE'S *ANOTHER* NOISE I DON'T LIKE AT ALL! BREATHING -- HEAVY BREATHING -- *AND IT'S CLOSE!*

THEN A DARK MASS REARS BETWEEN TRUDY AND THE LAMP -- A FORM THAT RESOLVES INTO A PALLID FACE AND JAGGED WINGS!

DON'T COME NEAR ME! BILL! BILL!

HAA! DO YOU THINK THAT CRY FLOATING THROUGH THE CASTLE WILL REACH *HIM* -- FLOATING ON HIS BACK IN THE MOAT -- FLOATING WITH STARING EYES?

THAT'S QUITE A GHASTLY PICTURE, MANUSALA -- ONLY *I'M* NOT IN IT!

YOU DON'T THINK SO, HAH? *WE'LL SEE!*

AS THE WAXEN, GAPING FEATURES LOOM CLOSER --

TEN PACES SEPARATE US -- TEN SECONDS -- BEFORE I FINISH YOU FOREVER!

REMEMBER SAYING YOU'D NEVER BE TRAPPED BY A SILVER OBJECT, MANUSALA? WELL --

ARRRGH!

THERE'S A FORM OF SILVER YOU NEVER EXPECTED, BECAUSE IT WAS DISCOVERED LONG AFTER YOU DIED -- SILVER CHLORIDE!

IN THE NEXT INSTANT --

SILVER .. SILVER .. THE CURSE -- OF VAMPIRES!

CRASH!

I THOUGHT WE'D NEED THAT PHOTOGRAPHIC EQUIPMENT -- BUT I NEVER GUESSED HOW MUCH!

DR. MANUSALA HAS TIME FOR JUST ONE WILD, FLURRYING SWOOP -- AND THEN --

THE TOWER! NO .. NO .. NOT THE PIT AGAIN -- THE DARKNESS AND DRIFTING DUST -- AAGHHHH!

SOUNDING HOLLOWLY FROM THE STONE DEPTHS --

CRASH!

YES, IT IS THE PIT AGAIN -- AND THIS TIME I THINK HE'LL STAY THERE!

FOR THE FIRST TIME IN CENTURIES, A PEACEFUL HUSH FALLS OVER THE VAMPIRE'S CASTLE -- AND AS BILL AND TRUDY RETURN TO THE SECRET CHAMBER OF DR. MANUSALA --

HE'S JUST THE WAY WE FOUND HIM, TRUDY -- A SKELETON WITH BATTERED WINGS! I DON'T THINK THERE'S ANY CHANCE OF SOMEONE MAKING A NEW BATCH OF THAT COMPOUND -- AND ACCIDENTALLY RESTORING HIM!

YOU CAN JOLLY WELL BET THERE ISN'T -- BECAUSE I'VE BURNED THE FORMULA!

THE END

9

247

Seeing RABBITS

JOHN MARA, who'd had too much to drink, stared at the strange, rocket-like machine that his headlights picked up along the side of the lonely country road. For a moment, he thought it might be real, but when he saw the large pink rabbit standing upright on its hind legs near the machine, he chortled happily. "Haw, I'm seein' rabbits again," he giggled.

On a sudden impulse, the intoxicated man pulled over to the side of the road and stopped in front of the rabbit. "Hey, wanna ride?" he shouted.

The rabbit stared coldly at him for a moment and then said distinctly, "Yes, I think I do. Just wait a moment while I set my robo-ship controls on a course that will follow us."

As the rabbit disappeared into the interior of his strange ship, Mara slapped his thigh uproariously. "I sure musta had plenty—this is the first time I've heard rabbits *talk!*"

A moment later, the rabbit reappeared, got into the car and slammed the door behind it. Delighted with his imaginary company, Mara said, "Where yuh comin' from—an' where yuh goin'?"

The rabbit's whiskers ruffled contemptuously. "I come from a world whose name I'm sure you don't know—I'm going to the city—to city *after* city—to wipe them and all their inhabitants from the face of this planet!"

Mara roared with laughter. "Haw, haw, what a joke! If yuh come from another world, how do yuh know how to speak English?"

The rabbit snorted impatiently. "Be-cause all of us *Rhus* are telepathic—and I can read your mind and instantly understand your language! Of course, I'm exaggerating when I say you *have* a mind. You stupid humans will be no opposition to me whatsoever when I turn the Rhu weapons against you—and when the whole planet is free, all the excess population of my world will come here to settle!"

John Mara roared with merriment. "Yuh sure are a hot one!" he gasped. "I seen a lot o' pink rabbits that walked around on their hind legs and acted human—just as I've seen a lot o' pink elephants an' snakes—but this is the first time I've seen a pink rabbit that *talks!*"

"*WHAT?*" the rabbit shouted. "You mean *other* pink *Rhus* have come to this world? You . . . you must mean the *outlaw Rhus*—the mute ones who never speak! They are our mortal enemies—they are far more powerful than we are! And if the mute *Rhus* have already arrived here, this world is unsafe for us—I will have to return and give the warning to my people to seek some other world—perhaps Mars!"

Suddenly, before Mara knew what was happening, the rabbit got the door open, leaped up to its robo-ship that hovered just above the car, and disappeared in a roar of rocket tubes.

Grinning, John Mara shook his head. "Boy, I got a real case of the D.T.'s! I'd better pull over and sleep this binge off!" And he stopped the car at the side of the road and lay down on the seat the rabbit had occupied, his head nestled among a few stray rabbit hairs.

OH, IT'S SILLY TO MENTION IT, BETTY ---BUT *THIS* REMINDS ME OF THOSE HUGE BIRDS I SAW CIRCLING ---JUST AS I DROVE UP!

YOU SAW THOSE THINGS---*HERE?* GOOD HEAVENS, MARCIA--- *THAT'S* WHAT I WANTED TO TALK TO YOU ABOUT! I'VE BEEN TRYING TO TELL MY-SELF I *IMAGINED* I SAW A FLOCK OF WEIRD, FLAPPING THINGS FOLLOW-ING THE SHIP I TOOK FROM EUROPE ---*CLEAR ACROSS THE ATLANTIC!*

WE ---WE CAN'T *BOTH* BE THE VICTIMS OF THE SAME HALLUCI-NATION! BUT WHAT ABOUT THE OTHER PASSENGERS? ---DID *THEY* NOTICE THE CREATURES?

WE HAD A STORMY CROSSING---SO FEW PEOPLE CAME ON DECK THROUGHOUT THE VOYAGE! BESIDES ---THE IDEA OF MONSTROUS BIRDS FOLLOW-ING THE SHIP SEEMED SO CRAZY I DIDN'T DARE MENTION IT TO ANYONE! THE THINGS WHEELED SO HIGH THAT I NEVER REALLY GOT A GOOD LOOK AT THEM ---JUST THEIR BROAD, STRANGELY-GLOWING WINGS!

AT FIRST, I WAS CURIOUS ABOUT THEM ---BUT *THAT* CHANGED TO SHEER FRIGHT WHEN I NOTICED THAT THE FLAPPING FIGURES MYSTERIOUSLY *DISAPPEARED*---EVERY FOUR HOURS! EACH TIME, I'D GLANCE SKYWARD AFTER A FEW MINUTES ---AND THEY'D BE BACK---*LIKE HORRIBLE SHADOWS I COULDN'T LOSE!*

IT NEVER OCCURED TO *ME* THAT THERE MIGHT BE A CON-NECTION BETWEEN *THEM* AND THIS CARVED FIGURE! OH, MARCIA---I'M BEGINNING TO WISH I HAD THROWN THE JAR OVERBOARD!

BETTY--- WHAT'S *IN* THAT THING?

THE GREAT PAINTERS OF THE 16TH CENTURY USED A BROWN PIGMENT PREPARED FROM A SECRET POWDER, MARCIA ---AND IT PRODUCED EFFECTS NO MODERN ARTIST HAS BEEN ABLE TO DUPLICATE! THAT'S WHY I WAS SO ELATED WHEN I FOUND THAT ENTIRE JAR *FULL* OF THE STUFF ---AT AN OLD ART STORE IN PARIS!

JUST A JAR OF PIGMENT? CRIMPERS---I CAN'T SEE ANYTHING VERY SPOOKY ABOUT *THAT!*

EXCEPT FOR ONE THING! FOR SOME REASON ---THE POWDER HAS ALWAYS BEEN KNOWN AS "MUMMY"!

SUDDENLY---A BLURRED SHADOW RIPPLES ACROSS THE SKYLIGHT!

SOMETHING'S PEERING IN--- SOMETHING--- *HIDEOUS!*

2.

Then ---AS THE MOON BREAKS THROUGH THE BLACK-COWLED CLOUDS---

IT'S ONE OF THOSE FLAPPING THINGS---WITH A *FACE* ---A FACE THAT ISN'T *ALIVE!*

THE OTHER ARE SWOOPING, MARCIA! THEY'VE FOLLOWED ME---HOUR AFTER HOUR FOR THREE THOUSAND MILES--- *AND NOW THEY'VE FOUND ME!*

BUT MAYBE IT ISN'T *YOU* THEY'RE AFTER! MAYBE IT'S THE JAR--- *THE JAR THAT BEARS THEIR IMAGE!*

WE *CAN'T* GO OUT, MARCIA--- NOT WITH *THEM* FLUTTERING IN THE DARKNESS!

I KNOW IT'S *RISKY*---BUT WE'VE *GOT* TO REACH DAN WARREN'S *LABORTORY! HE'LL* KNOW HOW TO FIND OUT WHAT THIS MUMMY POWDER IS---AND HOW TO COPE WITH THOSE THINGS THAT HAVE BEEN ATTRACTED TO IT!

Minutes LATER---WITH THE COUNTRY-SIDE MUFFLED IN VELVET DARKNESS---

I *KNEW* WE SHOULDN'T HAVE LEFT! *THEY'RE RIGHT BEHIND US!*

BUT THEY'RE NOT CLOSING IN, BETTY! THEY *COULD* CATCH UP---BUT THEY SEEM SATISFIED TO JUST KEEP US IN SIGHT!

Soon AFTERWARD---WITH DAN'S LABORATORY FLOODED BY THE GHOSTLY BLUE LIGHT FROM THE DIRECTION FINDER---

I CAN'T WAIT TO HAVE DAN TAKE A LOOK AT THOSE THINGS! HE USUALLY SCOFFS AT ANYTHING HINTING OF THE SUPERNATURAL--- UNLESS HE'S SEEN IT HIM-SELF!

HE'S *SURE* TO SCOFF THIS TIME--- BECAUSE I'VE JUST WATCHED THOSE CREATURES FADE OFF--- *AND VANISH!*

HI, THERE! GLAD YOU TWO DROPPED AROUND ---I WANT SOMEONE TO KEEP AN EYE ON THE ROBOT WHILE I GO OUT FOR A TEST! IF THE DIRECTION FINDER IS WORKING AS IT SHOULD ---THE LIGHT WILL GROW PROGRESSIVELY DIMMER AS I TRAVEL FURTHER AND FURTHER AWAY FROM THE ROBOT!

DAN, WAIT---THERE'S SOMETHING YOU'VE JUST *GOT* TO HEAR ABOUT!

I *KNOW* YOU'RE NONE TOO KEEN ON STAYING IN THE LAB WITH THE ROBOT, HONEY---BUT UNPREDICTABLE AS THE CRITTER IS, IT'S NEVER RAISED A FINGER TO *YOU!* THERE'S NOTHING TO GET JUMPY ABOUT---JUST SIT AROUND AND TALK FOR A HALF-HOUR, UNTIL I GET BACK!

B-BUT DAN ---IF YOU'D ONLY LISTEN---

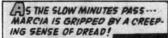

BUT SOONER STOP A LANDSLIDE---THAN THE BELLOWING BRUTE THAT ANSWERS A SUMMONS FROM THE BEYOND!

YARRRGH!

NOW I **KNOW** IT'S UNDER SOME EVIL GUIDANCE---ONE THAT NOT EVEN **DAN** COULD HANDLE!

AS THE ROBOT PAUSES BEFORE THE BANKED SWITCHES ON THE CONTROL PANEL·

YOU HAVE WATCHED ---YOU REMEMBER! NEFER-RA--- COMMANDS!

IT **DOES** REMEMBER, BETTY---IT'S ABOUT TO TRAIN THE CYCLOTRON'S LOW-POWER BEAM ON THE JAR!

HALF A MILLION CRACKLING VOLTS---A JAGGED SURGE BRIDGING LIFE AND DEATH---**AND THE ROBOT DROPS THE SWITCH!**

CRRRAK!

DO YOU SEE THAT ---INSIDE THE JAR?

IT'S A HUMAN FIGURE ---AND IT'S GETTING LARGER AND LARGER!

SUDDENLY---AS IF A TOMB SPEWED OUT A THING THAT NEVER DIED---

BLAM!

FOR THREE THOUSAND YEARS---NEFER-RA HAS WAITED ---- TO BE FREE! FOR THREE THOUSAND YEARS... NEFER-RA HAS WAITED ---FOR A WILLING SLAVE!

I DON'T KNOW WHO NEFER-RA IS, OR WHAT HE INTENDS DOING WITH THE ROBOT---BUT NOTHING, HUMAN **OR** SUPERNATURAL, CAN WITHSTAND THE FULL FORCE OF THE CYCLOTRON! IF I CAN ONLY REACH THE RIGHT DIAL---AND STEP UP THE CURRENT---!

SPURRED BY A FLASH OF FIENDISH UNDERSTANDING---THE ROBOT REARS!

YARRRGH!

CRASH!

GOOD HEAVENS!

5.

253

NOW NEFER-RA... *KNOWS* HE HAS FOUND...A *WILLING SLAVE!*

BETTY... THEY'RE *BREAKING OUT!*

CRRUNCH!

As THE FEARSOME FIGURES FADE INTO THE GULF OF NIGHT...

FOR MONTHS, DAN AND I HAVE TRIED TO KEEP THE ROBOT ISOLATED FROM THE EVIL FORCES THAT HAVE DOMINATED IT IN THE PAST...AND *NOW* IT'S ON RAMPAGE WITH SOMETHING FAR MORE SINISTER THAN ANY OF THE OTHERS IT HAS OBEYED!

ISN'T THERE *ANYTHING* WE CAN DO? WHAT ABOUT THE POLICE?

THAT WON'T WORK...ANY ATTEMPT TO CONTROL THE ROBOT BY *FORCE* CAN LEAD TO DISASTER! WE'LL HAVE TO WAIT UNTIL DAN RETURNS WITH THE DIRECTION FINDER...AND MEANWHILE, IT *MAY* HELP IF WE CAN LEARN SOMETHING ABOUT NEFER-RA!

NEFER-RA SAID HE HAD BEEN WAITING THREE THOUSAND YEARS... WHICH MEANS HE MUST HAVE DIED AROUND *1000 B.C.!*

WAIT...THERE HE IS! NEFER-RA...ROYAL SORCERER IN THE COURT OF RAMESES IV!

"FOR THIRTY YEARS, THE INFAMOUS NEFER-RA WAS THE REAL RULER OF EGYPT...AND THOUSANDS DIED THROUGH HIS BLACK MAGIC! WHEN THE WIZARD'S CHARMED LIFE CAME TO AN END, HIS DEATH WAS ASCRIBED TO A CURSE BY THE SPIRITS OF THOSE HE HAD SLAIN!"

NOW I KNOW WHY THE PIGMENT IN THE JAR WAS CALLED *MUMMY!* THAT'S JUST WHAT IT IS...*PULVERIZED MUMMY*...AND I HAPPENED TO GET THE REMAINS OF THE MOST SATANIC FIGURE IN EGYPTIAN HISTORY!

R-RRRING!

MARCIA? I'VE MANAGED TO REACH A FARMHOUSE PHONE ON ROCKY CREEK ROAD...AFTER THE DIRECTION FINDER LIGHT INDICATED THE ROBOT'S ON THE *MOVE!* WHAT IN THUNDER *HAPPENED?*

IT'S *GONE,* DAN...BUT I'D BETTER TELL YOU THE REST AFTER WE MEET!

I'LL WAIT FOR YOU AT THE BIG OAK TREE NEAR THE CROSSROAD! BETTER GET HERE FAST...I'VE GOT TO CATCH UP WITH THE ROBOT BEFORE IT CUTS LOOSE IN A DESTRUCTIVE FURY!

HAVING THE ROBOT ON THE PROWL WITH THE SPIRIT OF AN EVIL EGYPTIAN SORCERER IS BAD ENOUGH ··· BUT THANK GOODNESS THOSE *TERRIBLE THINGS WITH THE WINGS* AREN'T ANYWHERE IN SIGHT!

FUNNY, ISN'T IT? I REMEMBER YOUR SAYING THEY DISAPPEARED EVERY FOUR HOURS WHEN THEY WERE FOLLOWING THE SHIP ··· BUT *THIS* TIME THEY HAVEN'T COME BACK!

SOON AFTERWARD ··· WONDER WHAT GIVES WITH THE DIRECTION FINDER? IT *CAN'T* BE OUT OF WHACK ··· AND IT HASN'T SHONE *THIS* BRIGHTLY SINCE I LEFT THE LAB!

NOPE ··· THERE'S NOTHING WRONG WITH THE MECHANISM! THE ROBOT'S SOMEWHERE AROUND ··· *AND CLOSE!*

THEN ··· LIKE A NIGHTMARE CRASHING INTO REALITY ···

YARRGH!

NOW ··· NEFER-RA ··· IS SAFE! WHILE NEFER-RA ··· HAS *THIS* ··· THE CREATURES HE FEARS ··· CANNOT FIND HIM!

DESPERATELY ··· DAN BREAKS AWAY FROM THE IRON CLUTCH!

I *MADE* THIS THING ··· AND I'M GOING TO CONTROL IT! ROBOT ··· GET BACK!

HUUUGH!

POW!

WHAT DOES THE COMMAND OF A MODERN SCIENTIST MATTER ··· AGAINST AN EVIL WILL THIRTY CENTURIES OLD?

WAM!

MINUTES LATER ···

BRR-R! THIS IS AN AWFULLY DARK NIGHT TO BE TRAILING THINGS THAT AREN'T HUMAN!

CHIN UP! THERE'S THE OLD OAK ··· AND THE LIGHT FROM DAN'S APPARATUS!

Then···AS IF THE DARKNESS ITSELF RECOILED FROM THE SHAPE OF BRISTLING TERROR···

OH!

HUUUGH!

NEFER-RA LIKES STRONG SLAVES···AND NEFER-RA··· LIKES BEAUTIFUL SLAVES! YOU···SHALL BELONG··· TO NEFER-RA!

THAT LIGHT'S BLINDING ME! HE'S CASTING A SPELL!

AMID THE SLOW, DREAMY MUSIC OF EGYPTIAN HARPS AND EGYPTIAN CYMBALS···THE GLOOM GIVES WAY TO AN AMBER FLOOD···HOLDING THE DIM OUTLINES OF AN ANCIENT TEMPLE WITH STRANGE IDOLS AND PLASHING FOUNTAINS!

THIS IS JUST A VISION, BETTY···AND WE'VE GOT TO RESIST IT···OR NEFER-RA'S SORCERY WILL TRAP US IN A DEAD WORLD!

NO···YOU WILL NEVER RESIST···THE MAGIC··· OF NEFER-RA!

GREAT GUNS -- THE GIRLS! IF THAT FOXY-FACED CREEP IS ACTUALLY BEING PROTECTED BY MY DIRECTION FINDER···I KNOW THE FIRST THING TO DO!

WITHOUT RECKONING THE RISKS··· DAN TAKES UP THE CHALLENGE!

CRASH!

NEFER-RA WHIRLS···THE EVIL WEB OF HIS MAGIC BROKEN!

YOU WILL REPAIR···THE MAGIC MACHINE···QUICKLY ···OR MY SLAVE···THE ROBOT ···WILL TEAR YOU APART!

AS THE ROBOT LUNGES···

I KNOW I CAN'T STOP THE ROBOT THIS WAY···BUT AT LEAST I'LL GOAD IT INTO VENTING ITS FURY ON ME ···AND GIVE THE GIRLS A CHANCE TO ESCAPE!

As if divining Dan's thoughts...Nefer-Ra turns...his face a mask of grisly triumph!

MY HANDS...ARE CLOSE...VERY CLOSE! TELL HIM...TO DO...AS I COMMAND!

NO! IF THE DIRECTION FINDER HELPS YOU...I'LL TRAMPLE ON THE PIECES BEFORE YOU USE IT!

Suddenly...as the sorcerer's glinting eyes flash nearer...

MARCIA...LOOK! THOSE FLAPPING THINGS ARE CIRCLING AGAIN!

THE BAS...THE BAS! THE ANCIENT SPIRITS HAVE FOUND ME!

For a brief instant, Nefer-Ra huddles as the creatures swoop in a fiery rush! Then ...in the milling vortex of gleaming wings...

YAAAGH!

As the winged avengers soar skyward...disappearing in a fiery swirl...

BAS! BELIEVE IT OR NOT, MARCIA...BUT THAT'S THE NAME THE ANCIENT EGYPTIANS GAVE TO THE SPIRITS OF THE DEAD!

THAT ISN'T HARD TO BELIEVE...BECAUSE THOSE VERY SPIRITS ARE WHAT FINISHED OFF NEFER-RA THREE THOUSAND YEARS AGO...THE SPIRITS OF HIS VICTIMS!

THERE WAS A REASON FOR THEIR FOLLOWING ME ACROSS THE ATLANTIC...AND KEEPING WATCH OUTSIDE MY STUDIO! THEY WERE KEEPING TABS ON THE REMAINS OF NEFER-RA'S MUMMY...TO MAKE SURE HE'D NEVER REVIVE! BUT I STILL DON'T UNDERSTAND WHY THEY DISAPPEARED EVERY FOUR HOURS DURING THE VOYAGE...AND AGAIN TONIGHT...UNTIL THE VERY LAST MOMENT!

IN OTHER WORDS...UNTIL THE DIRECTION FINDER WAS SMASHED! SOMETHING ABOUT ITS FREQUENCY PREVENTED THE BAS FROM LOCATING NEFER-RA...JUST AS THE SHIP'S PERIODIC RADIO SIGNALS THREW THEM OFF THE TRAIL! THAT'S WHY NEFER-RA WANTED THE DIRECTION FINDER...HE KNEW THE SPIRITS WOULDN'T BE ABLE TO FIND HIM AS LONG AS THE DEVICE WAS SWITCHED ON!

WELL, THE ROBOT SEEMS DOCILE ENOUGH TO BE LED BACK TO THE LAB...BUT WHAT'S HE STARING AT?

JUST THE REMAINS OF NEFER-RA, DAN...THE BROWN PIGMENT THAT USED TO BE KNOWN AS MUMMY!

THE SPIRIT OF FRANKENSTEIN REACHES A NEW HEIGHT OF HAIR-RAISING SUSPENSE...IN THE NEXT ISSUE!

Greetings, all you *"Adventures Into The Unknown"* fans! It's publication time again, and we're bringing you this latest issue of your favorite magazine with the hope that you'll find it the best yet! Just between us all, we're doing our level best to make this the best supernatural book ever published. Doing that calls for a constant succession of topnotch stories that will thrill you, hold you spellbound, captivate and challenge your imagination . . . which is a tall order! We can't do it by continually presenting the same type of stories. That's why our writers, editors and research experts are ever on the alert for new slants, for original ideas, for fresh and gripping material culled from out the great realm of the *Unknown*. That's why our stories are continually *different*. Let's take *this* issue, for instance. It starts off with *"The Boy*

Who Cried Wolf," a new, fast-paced and experimental thriller—and we hope you'll like it! And then there's *"The Vampire's Castle."* You've *asked* for vampire stories, all of you —so here's a new type! As for *"Vision of Death,"* we're sure you'll admit that here's a supernatural yarn that challenges from start to finish! And, just to be different, we're bringing you *"The Civic Spirit"*— ghosts that pack a *laugh!* Add *"Spirit of Frankenstein,"* back for a repeat command performance, season well with other great headline features, and *presto!* That's this issue—and we want to find out what you think of it! Won't you write us—please?

A lot of you *have* been writing us. Mind if we present a cross-section of what you've been saying? We'll close our eyes, dip into our mailbag—and here goes!

"Dear Sirs:

Hurray for *'Adventures Into the Unknown!'* Your comic book is *tops!* I have always been interested in the supernatural, and think the stories in your book are *swell!* That goes for the drawing, too. Stories I've liked are *'The Werewolf Stalks,' 'Phantom of the Seas,' 'The Vampire Prowls,' 'Back to Yesterday,'* and *'The Spirit of Frankenstein.'* Why not a series on motion pictures—Boris Karloff and Lon Chaney, Jr. stuff? Meanwhile, I'm saving all your books—keep up the good work! Yours till Frankenstein's Monster meets Count Dracula!

—Terry Walsh, Chicago, Ill."

"Dear Editor:

I'm 14 years old and used to read all kinds of comics, but since I read the first issue of *'Adventures Into the Unknown,'* it seems centuries till the next issue comes. It's *wonderful* to read this exciting magazine—there's no comic like it! Every friend in my neighborhood can't wait to get hold of it. *Please*—publish it more often!

—Abraham Feldman, Bronx, N. Y."

"Dear Sirs:

Wow! Your comic book is *terrific!* Never before have I read such stories! They're *tops* and your covers are great—but there's one thing I *don't* like about *'Adventures Into the Unknown.'* It's only published every two months! But—keep up the good work! My favorite story has been *'Back to Yesterday'*—please, please publish more stories like that! I'm saving your books so I can make a volume of supernatural stories for my library!

—Hank T. Sypniewski"

"Dear Editor:

In your preceding issues of *'Adventures Into the Unknown,'* I have read all the letters of congratulation and admiration directed toward your comic, and I wish to contribute my share of the bravos. I think it's *wonderful!* Like Mr. Parry, whose letter appeared in No. 7, I, too, have been collecting your books, and it's a collection to be proud of! Forever an ardent fan—

—Sue Trammell, Jacksonville, Fla."

We appreciate the nice things you've been saying, fans, and are taking your suggestions to heart. Let's hope they'll make *"Adventures Into the Unknown"* a bigger, better magazine—the kind you deserve—the kind we want to bring you! Our next issue will be an all-star number, so take our advice and see that you *don't miss it!*

THE CIVIC SPIRIT

SO YOU DIDN'T BELIEVE IT COULD *HAPPEN*, EH?

WHO *WOULD* BELIEVE IT -- EVEN IF THEY *DID* KNOW THE WHOLE STORY?

DON'T TRY TO GUESS WHAT GOES ON HERE -- BECAUSE YOU HAVEN'T A *GHOST* OF A CHANCE! WE'LL HAVE TO START FROM THE BEGINNING -- BACK TO THE TERRIBLE MOMENT WHEN A GROUP OF CROOKED POLITICAL BOSSES DECIDED TO TEAM UP WITH THE *SUPERNATURAL!*

LET'S VISIT THE CITY HALL IN A SMALL EASTERN CITY -- JUST AS ITS CLOCK STRIKES TWELVE! IT'S THE HUSHED HOUR WHEN SINISTER CREATURES ARE SUPPOSED TO GATHER AND HATCH THEIR GHOULISH PLOTS-- AND THAT'S JUST WHAT THEY'RE DOING!

YAA-HA-HA! HAA-HA!

BONG! BONG!

HA-HA! BEFORE I KNEW WHAT YOU WERE UP TO, SMATHERS -- I THOUGHT OLD GRAFTING JOE McINNIS WOULD SPIN IN HIS GRAVE!

ME, TOO! BUT IT'S A PIECE OF GENIUS, BOSS-- HAVING THE CITY PROVIDE A *HOUSE* FOR ITS HONEST YOUNG DISTRICT ATTORNEY!

THE IDEA IS TO GET RID OF TOM BAILEY -- BEFORE HE GETS RID OF *US!* HE CAN'T CONTINUE HIS INFERNAL INVESTIGATIONS IF HE LEAVES TOWN -- AND I DON'T THINK HE'LL STAY AFTER HE FINDS HE'S LIVING IN A *HAUNTED HOUSE!*

AT THAT MOMENT--

TIK TOK TIK TOK

R-RRRING-

259

OH, TOM— TOM! I THOUGHT IT WAS YOU!

THOUGHT WHAT WAS ME?

THAT THING!

WOOOSH!

A REAL, HONEST-TO-GOODNESS GHOST—AND YOU STOPPED IT COLD WITH A BROOM! HA-HA-HA!

YOU MIGHT DO SOMETHING ABOUT IT—INSTEAD OF JUST LAUGHING! THIS ISN'T MY IDEA OF A CHEERFUL HOME!

IT ISN'T MINE EITHER, GWEN! THIS IDEA IS STRICTLY FROM A CREW OF CITY HALL SWINDLERS WHO THINK THEY CAN SCARE ME INTO LEAVING TOWN! THEY'VE STOPPED AT NOTHING TO STAY IN POWER— FROM VIOLENCE AND GRAFT TO CROOKED ELECTIONS — BUT THIS TOPS IT ALL!

I DON'T KNOW HOW THEY MANAGED TO COAX A GHOST OVER TO THEIR SIDE — BUT IT'S HAPPENED!

THE GHOST IS SHAKING ITS HEAD, TOM! MAYBE IT'S TRYING TO TELL US IT ISN'T WORKING FOR BOSS SMATHERS!

I KNOW HOW HARD TOM'S BEEN FIGHTING TO MAKE THIS TOWN A DECENT PLACE TO LIVE IN — AND IF YOU'VE EVER HAUNTED IN THE SLUMS, YOU SHOULD KNOW THAT SWEEPING REFORMS ARE NEEDED! WELL— FROM THIS NIGHT ON, TOM'S GOING TO FIGHT HARER THAN EVER! ARE YOU GOING TO HELP — OR AREN'T YOU?

THE FOLLOWING NIGHT—

YOU MIGHT HAVE WAITED UNTIL I SENT THE MONEY, SMATHERS! HERE COMES THAT SNOOPING DISTRICT ATTORNEY AGAIN!

SO WHAT — CAN HE PROVE ANYTHING? LET HIM IN — I WANT TO SEE WHAT WONDER BOY'S UP TO!

Madame Kreep! SPIRIT RAISINGS BY APPOINTMENT

KEEP BACK OUT OF SIGHT, GWEN!

'EVENING, MADAME KREEP! HOW'S TRICKS?

SO IT'S YOU, HAH?

3

MIGHTY CONVENIENT MEETING *YOU* HERE, SMATHERS -- BECAUSE YOU'RE JUST THE MAN I NEED TO HELP OUT WITH A LITTLE TEST!

ALL RIGHT -- *TRY* TO PIN SOMETHING ON ME! WHAT'S ON YOUR MIND, *D.A.?*

I'VE BEEN DOING SOME PSYCHIC RESEARCH -- AND I'VE LEARNED THAT A *GENUINE* MEDIUM NEVER HAS TROUBLE RAISING A SPIRIT WHILE CLOSE FRIENDS ARE AROUND! SINCE YOU AND MADAME KREEP ARE SO CHUMMY -- THIS *SHOULD* BE THE RIGHT ATMOSPHERE FOR A GHOST -- AND I'M READY TO BE CONVINCED!

KEEP ON ASKING FOR TROUBLE, D.A. -- AND I WON'T NEED THIS CRYSTAL BALL TO TELL YOU WHAT YOU'LL *GET!*

YAAAGH!

WHAT'S EATING *HER?*

SHE'S NOT THE *FIRST* PERSON TO GAG AT YOUR FRIENDS, SMATHERS! YOU'VE GOT ONE STANDING *RIGHT BEHIND YOU!*

THAT SO? HERE, HAVE A -- *YEEEOW!*

T-TAKE IT AWAY -- TAKE IT *AWAY!*

THAT'S THE TOUGH PART OF BEING THE FRIEND OF A MEDIUM, SMATHERS -- HE *LIKES* YOU! IT WOULDN'T SURPRISE ME IF HE FOLLOWED YOU AROUND LIKE A DOG!

ME A FRIEND -- OF *HERS?* TAKE THIS DOUGH BACK, KREEP -- AND FORGET WE EVER MADE A DEAL!

As SMATHERS RUSHES OUT TO THE CORRIDOR...

YOU MAY SMASH THE FAT MAN'S RECORD FOR THE OBSTACLE RACE, SMATHERS -- BUT DON'T SMASH *THIS* ONE!

OOOPS!

4

A SLOW MINUTE PASSES -- MARKED BY NOTHING BUT A WAITING COUGH AND THE IMPATIENT SCRAPE OF FEET...

IT'S NO USE, BOSS -- HE'S *THROUGH* WITH POLITICS!

YOU DON'T KNOW WHAT THIS *MEANS*, GRAFTING JOE! THE WHOLE MACHINE WILL BE SWEPT OUT OF OFFICE -- AND THAT INCLUDES FIVE NEPHEWS AND THREE SON-IN-LAWS OF *YOURS!*

JOE McINNIS

CRRAK!

IT'S *HIM*, ALL RIGHT -- B-BUT ARE YOU SURE HE'S ON *OUR* SIDE?

WHAT DO YOU THINK HE'S GOT THOSE *HORNS* FOR -- CLEAN GOVERNMENT?... LISTEN, GRAFTING JOE -- YOU'VE GOT TO GET THOSE TWO INCRIMINATING RECORDS AWAY FROM TOM BAILEY, THE D.A.! AND IF A CERTAIN TWO-TIMING *SPOOK* INTERFERES -- SLAP HIM DOWN!

HAW! HAW! YAA-HA-HA!

*M*INUTES LATER --

HERE'S ANOTHER PIECE OF EVIDENCE WHICH WILL SEND SMATHERS AND HIS CREW TO THE PENITENTIARY. GWEN! IT'S A LIST OF TWENTY NAMES REGISTERED AS *VOTERS* FOR THE SMATHERS' MACHINE -- AND *ALL* OF THEM WERE COPIED FROM HEADSTONES IN THE CEMETERY!

WAIT, TOM! I FEEL A *DRAFT!* THE FRONT DOOR MUST HAVE BLOWN OPEN!

THEN --

EEK! TOM -- THERE'S SOMETHING AWFUL COMING IN!

YAARRGH!

DEATH of a CRITIC

ROBERT PRESTON, drama critic for the *World-Herald,* sat down at his typewriter with an air of obvious relish. This was his sole pleasure in life—tearing a play to pieces with words of bitter mockery. Preston exulted in the power of life or death he had over a new play, for when he flayed one in his daily column, the crowds stayed away from it in droves —and the play folded within a week. And that was why he felt a tingling anticipation as he began typing—because he knew his acid words would sound the death knell for the play he had just seen.

"*The Rajah's Daughter,*" Preston wrote, "presented by a thoroughly incompetent new producer last night at the Regal Theatre, is the most moronic exhibition ever seen. The heroine—"

Preston hesitated. The heroine, a young Hindu girl of extraordinary beauty and talent, *had* been good—as a matter of fact, she had been the most accomplished new actress he had seen in years. But if he wrote that *she* was excellent, it would nullify his attack on the play, which he hadn't understood at all. And since Preston *hated* anything that was over his head, he made his decision—he'd blast the actress too! But just as he was casting about in his mind for the mocking words he would use to describe the girl, a soft, menacing voice behind him said, "Stop! You've got to be *fair* to her!"

Preston whirled in his chair and gasped at the tall, turbaned Hindu who stood in the room, arms crossed. "How . . . how did *you* get in here?" he gasped. "The door was *locked!*"

"We of the East ignore locks and doors," the Hindu said. "But *you* will not ignore the truth when you write about my daughter! She is extremely sensitive, with a fragile soul. I do not ask that you write lies about her. She will be the greatest actress the East has ever produced— merely write the *truth! You have been warned!*"

Enraged, Preston reached into a desk drawer for his revolver, shouting, "How dare you threaten *me?* Get out of here or I'll—"

But when he looked up, gun in hand, the Hindu was gone. Preston couldn't understand his strange disappearance, but he was thoroughly angered now—and his mind was made up. When he got finished writing about that girl, they'd *laugh* her out of town!

The next evening, he read his column in the paper with huge satisfaction. He'd really thrown every barbed, contemptuous word in the dictionary at her. Then, his eye strayed to the next column, a short item telling of the suicidal leap from the ninth floor of her hotel by the actress who had starred in "*The Rajah's Daughter.*"

Shaken for a moment, Preston shrugged and laughed it off. "That's the way it goes," he told himself. "The weak die and the strong survive!" Idly, he tossed the paper away—and suddenly gasped with horror as a pair of white, disembodied hands materialized out of nothingness and grasped it. A finger pointed to his column, and the hands began advancing slowly, slowly towards him.

Terror-stricken, afraid that he *wasn't* imagining things, Preston backed away . . . back . . . back—away from those ghostly hands! Then the hands made a sudden lunge for him, and Preston threw himself backwards—and suddenly felt himself crashing through the French windows—and out into space!

And as he hurtled downwards, just before he crashed to the sidewalk, Preston thought he heard the laughter of the Fates above him.

VISION of DEATH

1950

Ever find yourself walking down a street...a street you KNEW you'd never seen...and yet experience the eerie, frightening sensation that sometime, in the shadowy past, YOU'D BEEN THERE BEFORE? IT'S STRANGE, MYSTERIOUS...BUT IT'S HAPPENED TO MANY OF US! BUT ALEX CARTER HAD AN EVEN STRANGER VISION...WHEN FATE JOINED UP WITH THE FORCES OF THE UNKNOWN, BRINGING HIM THE PICTURE OF HIS OWN DEATH!

The STATE PRISON DEATH CELL...ALEX CARTER GRANTS A LAST INTERVIEW...

SO YOU WANT TO KNOW THE STORY OF MY LIFE...THE TRUE STORY, EH? WELL, THERE ARE SOME FACTS WHICH DIDN'T COME OUT AT MY TRIAL...BUT SINCE I'M GOING TO DIE ANYWAY, I MIGHT AS WELL SPILL 'EM! ...GET READY FOR THE SURPRISE OF YOUR LIFE, MR. REPORTER!

IT ALL BEGAN WHEN I WAS A DOCTOR ON THE STAFF OF THE FAIRVIEW HOSPITAL! I'D BEEN HAVING STRANGE, DISTURBING NIGHTMARES, AND THEY INTERFERED WITH MY WORK! I COULDN'T SEEM TO CONCENTRATE ON MY PATIENTS... THE CHIEF BAWLED ME OUT CONTINUALLY...

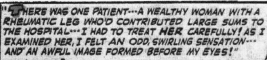

"THERE WAS ONE PATIENT---A WEALTHY WOMAN WITH A RHEUMATIC LEG WHO'D CONTRIBUTED LARGE SUMS TO THE HOSPITAL---I HAD TO TREAT *HER* CAREFULLY! AS I EXAMINED HER, I FELT AN ODD, SWIRLING SENSATION--- AND AN AWFUL IMAGE FORMED BEFORE MY EYES!"

I---I CAN'T EXPLAIN IT, MRS. ANDERSON, BUT YOUR LEG---*IT'S GOING TO CAUSE YOUR DEATH!*

WHAT? WHY, I'VE HAD RHEUMATISM FOR *YEARS!* I'LL COMPLAIN TO DR. ADAMS--- TELLING ME RIDICULOUS NONSENSE LIKE *THAT!*

Later...

I MUST HAVE BEEN CRAZY, BLABBING ALL THAT BECAUSE OF A STUPID *VISION!*

I JUST SAW MRS. ANDERSON, AND SHE'S TOLD ME SHE'LL CON- TRIBUTE NO MORE MONEY TO THIS HOSPITAL! YOU'RE *FIRED*, YOU YOUNG *FOOL!* I---SAY, WHAT'S HAPPENED *OUTSIDE?*

THAT WAS IT---MY FIRST GLIMPSE INTO THE FUTURE! IT CAUSED HER DEATH AND THE LOSS OF MY JOB! AND DR. ADAMS MADE SURE THAT I COULDN'T GET ANOTHER! BUT WORSE THAN THAT, I HAD THE AWFUL FEELING THAT I'D HAVE *MORE* VISIONS---*WITH EVEN MORE HORRIBLE RESULTS!*

SHE WALKED RIGHT IN FRONT OF MY CAR---AND HER LEG SEEMED TO GIVE 'WAY! SHE COULDN'T GET OUT OF THE PATH OF THE CAR IN TIME!

YOU SEE? YOU SCARED HER SO SHE DIDN'T EVEN SEE THAT AUTO COMING! IT'S *YOUR* FAULT! *YOU* KILLED HER!

"HOW RIGHT I WAS! IT WAS WEEKS LATER WHEN I SAW THIS MAN---AND A TERRIFYING IMAGE---"

HE'S AIMING AT ---*ME!*

"WHY RUN, WHEN THIS WAS *FATE?* HE'D FIND ME---*KILL ME!* AND SO I FOLLOWED HIM, KNOW- ING THAT THERE WAS *ONLY ONE WAY OUT!*"

IF I'M GOING TO SAVE MYSELF, I--- I'VE GOT TO FINISH *HIM* OFF, FIRST!

2

"HIS OFFICE WAS MARKED MEDICAL PUBLICATIONS! AS A DOCTOR, MAYBE I COULD GET A JOB THERE...WATCH HIM UNTIL I SAW MY CHANCE..."

HMMM...I COULD USE A PHYSICIAN FOR TECHNICAL ARTICLES! I'D BE HAPPY TO HAVE YOU JOIN OUR STAFF!

THANKS, MR. PRENTISS! YOU DON'T REALIZE WHAT I CAN DO FOR YOU!

"IRONICALLY, PRENTISS SEEMED TO TAKE A LIKING TO ME! THEN CAME A DAY...A DAY I WISH HAD NEVER DAWNED...

WE OUGHT TO BE MORE FRIENDLY, OLD MAN...AND I'M THROWING A LITTLE PARTY TONIGHT! THINK YOU CAN MAKE IT?

WHY, I... SUPPOSE SO!

HIS FIANCEE WAS THERE! SHE WAS BEAUTIFUL...AND FLIRTATIOUS! SHE LOOKED AT ME ONCE...AND I REALIZED WHY PRENTISS WOULD TRY TO KILL ME!

ALEX, MEET ANGELA...THE GIRL I'M GOING TO MARRY! I KNOW YOU TWO ARE GOING TO BE GOOD FRIENDS!

I'M SURE WE WILL...VERY GOOD FRIENDS!

"IT WAS A GOOD PARTY, BUT I WANTED NONE OF IT... OR OF HER! I HAD TO STOP IT...THE INEVITABLE FLOW OF EVENTS THAT WAS SO SURELY MOVING...TOWARD MY DEATH!"

SO THERE YOU ARE! HOW CAN WE BECOME FRIENDLY IF YOU...

PLEASE... KEEP AWAY FROM ME!

ANGELA! I WAS LOOKING FOR YOU... AND NOW I FIND YOU HERE! ER...WOULD YOU MIND IF I TALKED TO ALEX...ALONE?

3.

SURELY YOU DON'T THINK THAT SHE··· I···

IT ISN'T THAT···BUT I KNOW SO WELL WHAT SHE IS! BUT I CAN'T HELP MYSELF···I LOVE HER DESPERATELY!

"HIS WORDS *SOUNDED* CONVINCING ···BUT I DIDN'T BELIEVE HIM! I WAS SURE THAT HE WAS JEALOUS, THAT HE WAS LYING WHEN HE PRETENDED NOT TO RESENT ME! HE *HATED* ME···WANTED ME TO RELAX MY GUARD SO HE COULD STRIKE! I FELT THE COILS CLOSING ABOUT ME, AND KNEW I HADN'T MUCH TIME LEFT! I HAD TO GET HIM ··· *SOON*···BUT HOW? THE ANSWER CAME SOON···"

ALEX MUST BE A GOOD SHOT···HE SURE SEEMED *EAGER* WHEN I INVITED HIM ON THIS HUNTING PARTY!

"*PRENTISS* HAD PLAYED RIGHT INTO MY HANDS! YES, I WANTED TO GO HUNTING···BUT NOT FOR DEER! I WAITED FOR MY CHANCE···*AND THEN*···"

HE'S ALONE··· AND IN THE OPEN! NOW!

BANG!

DON'T FEEL SO BAD, CARTER···IT WAS AN ACCIDENT! HE'S OKAY··· LUCKY YOU DIDN'T *KILL* HIM!

THEY DON'T KNOW THAT YOU *DELIBERATELY* TRIED TO SHOOT ME ···*BUT I DO!* SO YOU *DO* WANT ANGELA···AND I NEVER EVEN DREAMED OF IT! DON'T BOTHER SHOWING UP FOR WORK TOMORROW, BECAUSE YOU'RE *THROUGH!* AND I'LL GET *EVEN*, MARK MY WORD!

"SO HE HADN'T EVEN *INTENDED* KILLING ME! BUT NOW I HAD INCURRED HIS ENMITY···AND WAS MARCHING MYSELF *TO MY GRAVE!*"

"AND SO ONCE AGAIN I WAS JOBLESS! THERE WAS NOTHING LEFT---BUT FEAR! I WANDERED, POVERTY DOGGING MY STEPS, SINKING LOWER AND LOWER--- WAITING FOR THE VENGEANCE I KNEW WOULD STRIKE!"

"DEEP WITHIN ME WELLED THE KNOWLEDGE THAT SOMETHING WAS GOING TO HAPPEN---SOON! AND A NEW VISION OCCURRED--- SOMETHING UNEXPECTED!"

THAT IMAGE--- IT COULDN'T BE! ANGELA AND I--- TOGETHER? IT'S IMPOSSIBLE!

ALEX! ALEX!

IT'S--- IT'S YOU!

I'VE BEEN LOOK- ING FOR YOU EVERYWHERE! DONALD PRENTISS HAS GONE CRAZY WITH JEALOUSY---HE REAL- IZES THAT IT WAS LOVE AT FIRST SIGHT WHEN I MET YOU! WE---WE COULD BE HAPPY TOGETHER, I'M SURE OF IT!

WELL, I COULDN'T FIGHT MY FATE--- NOT WHEN SHE DREW ME LIKE A MAGNET! WE WERE MARRIED AND FLED TOWN IMMEDI- ATELY! SHE NURSED ME BACK TO HEALTH AND SEEMED A CHANGED WOMAN ---SOFTER---

YOU'RE---LOVELY, DARLING! I THINK I'M WELL ENOUGH TO SET UP PRACTICE NOW---AND I OWE IT ALL TO YOU!

WE'LL ALWAYS BE HAPPY TOGETHER ---I KNOW IT!

5

271

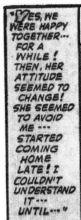

"YES, WE WERE HAPPY TOGETHER...FOR A WHILE! THEN, HER ATTITUDE SEEMED TO CHANGE! SHE SEEMED TO AVOID ME...STARTED COMING HOME LATE! I COULDN'T UNDERSTAND IT...UNTIL...."

IT'S HIM...*PRENTISS!* HE'S FOUND US, AND SHE'S SEEING *HIM* AGAIN!

"*Later...*"

I WANT YOU TO KNOW THAT I SAW YOU WITH DONALD PRENTISS TODAY!

SO *WHAT?* I'M TIRED OF YOU AND YOUR COWARDLY WAYS! AND YOU'VE *REALLY* GOT SOMETHING TO BE AFRAID OF *NOW!* HE WANTS ME TO BE HIS WIFE...SO MUCH *THAT HE'S GOING TO KILL YOU!*

"FEAR GNAWING AT MY VITALS, I TURNED AND RAN...BLINDLY! I FOUND MYSELF AT THE TOP OF A CLIFF, OUTSIDE OF TOWN...BITTER, BEATEN!"

IF ONLY I HADN'T TAKEN UP WITH HER ...HADN'T BELIEVED THAT THE FATES *WILLED* ME TO MARRY HER!

TRIED TO TAKE HER AWAY FROM ME, DIDN'T YOU? I FOLLOWED YOU, AND NOW ...YOU *DIE!*

PRENTISS! NO...*NO*... KEEP AWAY!

SHE'S THE ONLY THING I EVER LOVED ...SO NOW I'M GOING TO...OOF!

"HE STUMBLED, LOWERING THE GUN ...AND I SAW MY CHANCE! DESPERATELY I CHARGED...WE GRAPPLED AT THE EDGE OF THE CLIFF..."

HELP! HELP! AI-EEEEE!

I'M FREE! I'VE BEATEN THE FATES! THE MAN WHO WAS GOING TO KILL ME... I'VE FINISHED *HIM!* I'VE *WON!*

6

"THE CLIFF WAS IN A REMOTE SPOT...HIS BODY WOULD NEVER BE FOUND! NO ONE WOULD EVER SUSPECT ME...NO ONE BUT ANGELA! I CAUGHT HER LOOKING AT ME STRANGELY, AND THE SUSPENSE MOUNTED! I HAD TO DO SOMETHING!"

THE STRAIN...IT'S TOO MUCH FOR ME! I'M GOING OUT OF MY HEAD...HARDLY KNOW WHAT I'M DOING ANY MORE! BUT I...I'VE GOT TO STOP HER FROM TALKING!

ALEX! WHY...WHY ARE YOU LOOKING AT ME THAT WAY?

DON'T BE AFRAID, MY DEAR! ALL YOU'VE GOT TO DO IS WRITE A LITTLE NOTE SAYING YOU'RE TIRED OF ME, AND ARE RUNNING AWAY! AND YOU'LL DO IT... OR ELSE!

I...I'VE WRITTEN IT, JUST AS YOU WANTED! BUT THAT LOOK IN YOUR EYES! DON'T COME ANY CLOSER...DON'T! HELP!

"IT WAS DONE...AND HER PRESENCE WOULD NO LONGER BE A MENACE TO ME! I THOUGHT I WAS SAFE...UNTIL..."

OPEN UP, IN THE NAME OF THE LAW!

RAP! RAP!

LET ME GO! I DIDN'T KILL HER...SHE RAN AWAY FROM ME! I...I'LL EVEN SHOW YOU THE NOTE SHE LEFT!

I DON'T BLAME HER FOR LEAVING A MURDERER! SHE REPORTED HER SUSPICIONS OF YOU BEFORE SHE DISAPPEARED! IT TOOK US A WHILE TO FIND THE BODY...AND NOW WE'RE ARRESTING YOU FOR THE MURDER OF DONALD PRENTISS!

SO THAT'S WHY YOU FIND ME HERE, MR. REPORTER! EVEN IN DEATH, PRENTISS REACHED OUT AN AVENGING HAND!

YOU'RE WRONG, CARTER! I JUST GOT A CALL FROM THE GOVERNOR...AND YOU'VE BEEN REPRIEVED!

IT SEEMS THAT THAT WASN'T PRENTISS'S BODY THE POLICE FOUND, AFTER ALL! SOME OLD FOLKS JUST IDENTIFIED IT AS THEIR SON, FROM THE TATTOO MARKS IT CARRIED! YOU'RE GOING TO LIVE...BECAUSE THERE'S NOTHING WE CAN HOLD YOU ON!

NOT PRENTISS ...BUT HOW...? THANKS, WARDEN!

I...I'M *NOT GOING TO DIE!* BUT YOU, MR. REPORTER...NOW *YOU* KNOW THAT I KILLED BOTH OF THEM! PLEASE, PLEASE DON'T TELL! I'LL DO *ANYTHING* IF...SAY, YOUR *FACE!* IT'S STARTING TO LOOK *FAMILIAR*...AS IF I'VE SEEN YOU SOMEWHERE BEFORE! GREAT HEAVENS...*YOU'RE* NO REPORTER! *YOU'RE*...

I DON'T BLAME YOU FOR NOT RECOGNIZING ME BEFORE...NOT WITH THE PLASTIC SURGERY I NEEDED AFTER THAT FALL OVER THE CLIFF! YOU SEE...*I WASN'T KILLED IN THAT FALL, AFTER ALL!*

"A HOBO FOUND ME...BROUGHT ME BACK TO CONSCIOUSNESS! AS I LAY THERE, GATHERING MY SENSES, I SUDDENLY GOT AN *IDEA!*"

FEELIN' BETTER, MISTER?

YES...IT'S A...GOOD THING YOU HAPPENED ALONG! A *VERY* GOOD THING!

"THERE WAS A ROCK NEAR MY HAND...AND I KNEW NOBODY WOULD MISS HIM! I DRESSED HIM IN MY CLOTHES, AND MADE SURE HE COULDN'T BE RECOGNIZED! THEN...I CONTACTED ANGELA!"

...SO THAT'S THE STORY! I WANT YOU TO GO TO THE POLICE! TELL THEM THAT CARTER THREATENED ME, AND THAT I'M MISSING! DON'T TELL THEM WHERE MY BODY IS SUPPOSED TO BE...YOU WOULDN'T KNOW *THAT!* CARTER'S HASH WILL BE SETTLED...AND WE CAN BE MARRIED THEN!

I CAME HERE TO WATCH YOU SUFFER...AS *I* HAVE...TO GLOAT AS *I* WATCHED YOUR LAST HOURS! I LOVED ANGELA ...BUT NOW THAT YOU'VE BEEN REPRIEVED...

BANG!

AND SO ALEX CARTER DIED...EXACTLY AS HIS VISION HAD WARNED! DID THESE STRANGE IMAGES FROM OUT OF THE *UNKNOWN* REALLY FORETELL THE FUTURE? BY TRYING TO *AVERT* HIS DEATH, DID HE BUT MAKE HIS END MORE CERTAIN? DOES DARK DESTINY SHAPE OUR COURSE? WHAT DO *YOUR* THINK, READER?

UNCANNY MYSTERIES

CASE of the UNINHABITABLE HOUSE!

One of the weirdest cases ever to be reported by the American press was the story of the haunted house that couldn't be lived in -- that drove its inhabitants out in terror! The place is a farmhouse 14 miles from Menomonie, Wisconsin... the time is October, 1873... and THIS is what happened...

THE FIRST EVIDENCE OF AN UNCANNY FORCE IN THE HOUSE WAS THE UNBELIEVABLE FLOATING THROUGH THE AIR OF A KITCHEN PAN! WHAT STRANGE PRESENCE SUPPORTED IT?

THEN STRANGE DOINGS AT THE SUPPER TABLE -- WHERE EGGS SUDDENLY ROSE FROM THEIR PLATTERS AND TEACUPS LEAPED UP AS IF PROPELLED BY SOME UNSEEN HAND!

SINCE THE PHENOMENA SEEMED TO CENTER AROUND ONE OF THE CHILDREN, THE INCREDULOUS PARENTS THOUGHT THE BOY WAS MERELY PLAYING TRICKS! BUT WHEN THEY TIED HIM TO A CHAIR, THE TEACUPS STILL DANCED AS MADLY AS EVER!

BUT THE MOST HAIR-RAISING EXPERIENCE OF ALL OCCURRED THE DAY ONE OF THE CHILDREN WAS STANDING IDLY NEAR HER MOTHER ONE MOMENT AND...

...THE NEXT MOMENT SUDDENLY FOUND THAT HER HAIR HAD BEEN SHEARED OFF BY SOME EERIE FORCE FROM OUT OF THE UNKNOWN!

THE RELIGIO-PHILOSOPHICAL JOURNAL INVESTIGATED THE STORY, BUT TO THIS DAY, THE CASE REMAINS AN UNEXPLAINED EXAMPLE OF THE SUPERNATURAL!

BLACKHEADS "PET HATE"

Say Men, Girls in Choosing Date

What a "black mark" is the blackhead . . . according to men and girls popular enough to be choosy about dates!

"Nobody's dreamboat!" "Nobody's date bait!" And that's not all that's said of those who are careless about blackheads. But blackheads ARE ugly! Blackheads ARE grimy! And they DON'T look good in close-ups!

So can you blame the fellow who says, "Sure, I meet lots of girls who look cute at first glance. But if, on that second glance, I see dingy blackheads, it's *good night!*"

Or can you blame the girl who confesses, "I hate to go out with a fellow who has blackheads. If he's careless about that you're sure he'll embarrass you in other ways, too!"

But you—are YOUR ears burning? Well, you've company and, sad to say, good company. There are lots of otherwise attractive fellows and girls who could date anyone they like if they'd only realize how offensive blackheads are . . . and how easily and quickly they could get rid of them . . . if they *want to!*

"He-Man" Often Guilty of Blackhead Crime

Take your "he-man" . . . super at track, games, sports of all kinds . . . who thinks that after just a shower he's ready to go anywhere! And won't the girls all admire his muscles!

Sure they would! But not many dance floors are set up for hurdle races! You can't show off your snappy left hook when only cokes are in the ring. The "he-man" who's also clean-cut, will get the breaks wherever he is.

Even Cute Girls Become Careless

Easy, too easy, for a girl to think that if she has the latest in clothes and hair-do she needn't bother about blackheads. A little more make-up, she guesses, will take care of that. BUT MAKE-UP WON'T HIDE BLACKHEADS! Not unless it's plaster of paris, maybe! And even good make-up "slips" at a dance! So don't take chances, cute though you may be!

TAKE THESE TIPS TO BANISH BLACKHEADS

Keep skin clean by washing morning and night with warm, almost hot, water. Use good soap and plenty of it. And finish with cool water.

Extract every blackhead as soon as you see it—with a SAFE extractor. Don't use finger nails. Don't squeeze. That may mean infection, injured tissues, a marred skin.

Just be clean! Be quick! And be safe! That's easy! And that's ALL!

FELLOWS! GIRLS!
Keep Skin Clear and Clean!

UGLY BLACKHEADS OUT in Seconds with VACUTEX

NEW! SCIENTIFIC! VACUUM ACTION!

Amazing new VACUTEX is painless . . . safe . . . fast! In seconds you are rid of those ugly blackheads that clog the pores . . . make your skin look grimy and dingy . . . give others such a wrong impression of you. VACUTEX creates a gentle vacuum pressure around the blackhead and extracts it—quickly!—without injury to tender skin tissues. Keep skin always clear this new scientific way. Without painful squeezing! Without dangerous infection from germy fingers! Just place VACUTEX over blackhead and draw back extractor. Blackhead's out! Simple! But you'll be delighted by your instantly improved appearance. Others will notice your clearer, cleaner skin! Try VACUTEX—now!

ACTUAL LENGTH 3½"

RUSH COUPON NOW!

10 DAY TRIAL OFFER

Don't send a penny. Mail coupon and pay postman only $1.00 plus postage. or save all postage by enclosing $1.00 with guarantee coupon. If not thrilled to be rid of embarrassing hated blackheads this new quick way—just return VACUTEX in 10 days and get $1 back. Order today!

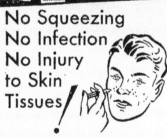

No Squeezing
No Infection
No Injury to Skin Tissues!

Just place VACUTEX over blackhead—release extractor—and blackhead's out!

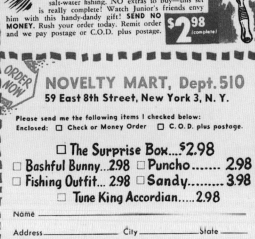

278

BOOKSHOP EDITION

They may have been Forbidden to some--particularly when the Wertham *Seduction of the Innocent* book hit the newsstands--but to kids the length and breadth of the United States (and a select few in the UK), Richard Hughes and his tremblin' team of terrific tormenters were where it was at. Big time. And now, a half-century since the first issue appeared, ACG's wonderful *Forbidden Worlds* are accessible once more . . . and this time in state-of-the-art hardcover volumes containing five to seven issues apiece. This is going to be one hell of a journey: come make it with us as we travel together through some of the most memorable comicbooks of all time.

Just 1700 bookshop copies @ £29.99

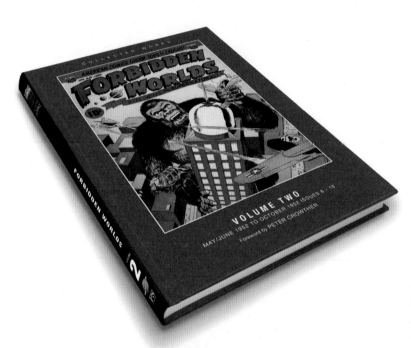

SLIPCASED EDITION

Only three hundred slipcased copies available
at a very special price of just
@ **£49.99**

Place your order right now and avoid disappointment!
www.psartbooks.com or www.pspublishing.co.uk

BOOKSHOP EDITION

Ah, those were the days, when America's comicbook
racks and spinners were full to bursting with a wealth
of gaudily coloured classics boasting vampires,
cannibalistic aliens and bloated corpses.

Here, from the heyday of the American Comics Group (ACG)
comes Out of the Night . . .PS Artbook's latest entry in its
ambitious programme.

Get the door locked and leave the lights on.
That sound akin to the wind in the grate could be something else . . .
something entirely different.
Just 1700 bookshop copies @ £29.99

SLIPCASED EDITION

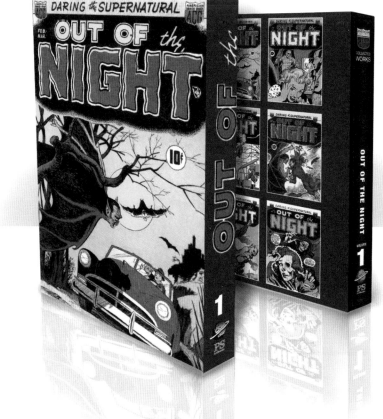

BOOKSHOP EDITION

It was the great and much-missed British vaudeville act,
the great Max Bygraves who coined the phrase 'You need hands'
from his 1958 hit record of the same title.

Well, here at PS, we've taken Max at his word . . . with not one but two -
and both of them courtesy of the great American Comics Group.

So treat yourself to this great all-in volume collectiing all six issues
of ACG's *Skeleton Hand* and the hard-to-find one-off *Clutching Hand*.

It's all here: bad folks, dead folks and just plain wacked-out-and-off-the-
freakin'-wall weird folks . . . and they're all looking for *you*.
Just 1700 bookshop copies @ £29.99

SLIPCASED EDITION

1949 - 2009
FANTASY &
SCIENCE FICTION

60 years of original cover artwork from the magazine

Featuring the profiles of some of the genre's leading artists from it's 60 year history and the chance again to read some of the award winning science fiction that was first published in the magazine.

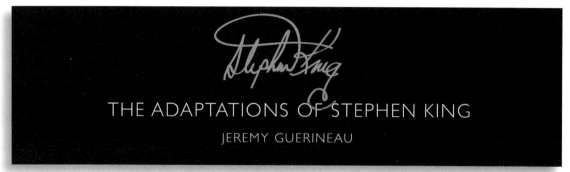

AND FINALLY...

Order any PS Artbooks title from www.pspublishing.co.uk and receive <u>10% OFF</u> and <u>FREE SHIPPING WORLDWIDE</u> by entering the code below when you go through the checkout process...

> ## AITU002

Offer only valid at www.pspublishing.co.uk